www.**totallyrandombooks**.co.uk

Also by Lauren Kate:

THE BETRAYAL OF NATALIE HARGROVE

The FALLEN series:

FALLEN
TORMENT
PASSION
RAPTURE
FALLEN IN LOVE

LAUREN KATE

DOUBLEDAY

TEARDROP
A DOUBLEDAY BOOK
HARDBACK: 978 0 857 53226 8
TRADE PAPERBACK: 978 0 857 53227 5

Published in Great Britain by Doubleday,
an imprint of Random House Children's Publishers UK
A Random House Group Company

This edition published 2013

1 3 5 7 9 10 8 6 4 2

Text copyright © Lauren Kate, 2013
Jacket art copyright © Colin Anderson, 2013

The right of Lauren Kate to be identified as the author of this work has been asserted in
accordance with the Copyright, Designs and Patents Act 1988.

The Random House Group Limited supports the Forest Stewardship Council® (FSC®),
the leading international forest-certification organisation. Our books carrying the FSC label are
printed on FSC®-certified paper. FSC is the only forest-certification scheme supported by the
leading environmental organisations, including Greenpeace. Our paper procurement policy can
be found at www.randomhouse.co.uk/environment

MIX
Paper from
responsible sources
FSC® C016897
FSC
www.fsc.org

Set in 11.5-point Simoncini Garamond

RANDOM HOUSE CHILDREN'S PUBLISHERS UK
61–63 Uxbridge Road, London W5 5SA

www.**randomhousechildrens**.co.uk
www.**totallyrandombooks**.co.uk
www.**randomhouse**.co.uk

Addresses for companies within The Random House Group Limited
can be found at: www.randomhouse.co.uk/offices.htm

THE RANDOM HOUSE GROUP Limited Reg. No. 954009

A CIP catalogue record for this book is available from the British Library.

Printed and bound in Great Britain by Clays Ltd, St Ives plc

For Matilda

It is such a secret place, the land of tears.

—Antoine de Saint-Exupéry,

The Little Prince

Teardrop

PROLOGUE

∞

PREHISTORY

So this was it:

Dusky amber sunset. Humidity tugging on lazy sky. Lone car hauling up the Seven Mile Bridge, toward the airport in Miami, toward a flight that wouldn't be caught. Rogue wave rising in the water east of the Keys, churning into a monster that would baffle oceanographers on the evening news. Traffic stopped at the mouth of the bridge by construction-suited men staging a temporary roadblock.

And him: the boy in the stolen fishing boat a hundred yards west of the bridge. His anchor was down. His gaze hung on the last car allowed to cross. He had been there for an hour, would wait only moments more to watch—no, to *oversee* the coming tragedy, to make sure that this time everything went right.

The men posing as construction workers called them-selves the Seedbearers. The boy in the boat was a Seedbearer, too, the youngest in the family line. The car on the bridge was a champagne-colored 1988 Chrysler K-car with two hundred thousand on the odometer and a duct-taped rearview mirror. The driver was an archaeologist, a redhead, a mother. The passenger was her daughter, a seventeen-year-old from New Iberia, Louisiana, and the focus of the Seedbearers' plans. Girl and mother would be dead in minutes . . . if the boy didn't mess anything up.

His name was Ander. He was sweating.

He was in love with the girl in the car. So here, now, in the soft heat of a late Florida spring, with blue herons chasing white egrets through a black opal sky, and the stillness of the water all around him, Ander had a choice: fulfill his obliga-tions to his family, or—

No.

The choice was simpler than that:

Save the world, or save the girl.

The car passed the first mile marker out of seven on the long bridge to the city of Marathon in the central Florida Keys. The Seedbearers' wave was aimed at mile four, just past the midpoint of the bridge. Anything from a slight dip in temperature to the velocity of the wind to the texture of the seafloor could alter the wave's dynamic. The Seedbearers had to be ready to adapt. They could do this: craft a wave out of

2

the ocean using antediluvian breath, then drop the beast on a precise location, like a needle on a turntable, letting hellish music loose. They could even get away with it. No one could prosecute a crime he didn't know had been committed.

Wave crafting was an element of the Seedbearers' cultivated power, the Zephyr. It wasn't dominance over water, but rather an ability to manipulate the wind, whose currents were a mighty force upon the ocean. Ander had been raised to revere the Zephyr as divinity, though its origins were murky: it had been born in a time and place about which the elder Seedbearers no longer spoke.

For months they had spoken only of their certainty that the right wind under the right water would be powerful enough to kill the right girl.

The speed limit was thirty-five. The Chrysler was going sixty. Ander wiped sweat from his brow.

Pale blue light shone within the car. Standing in his boat, Ander couldn't see their faces. He could see just two crowns of hair, dark orbs against the headrests. He imagined the girl on her phone, texting a friend about her vacation with her mother, making plans to see the neighbor with the splash of freckles across her cheeks, or that boy she spent time with, the one Ander could not stand.

The whole week, he'd watched her reading on the beach from the same faded paperback, *The Old Man and the Sea.* He'd watched her turn the pages with the slow aggression of the terrifically bored. She was going to be a senior that fall. He knew she'd signed up for three honors classes; he'd once stood an aisle over at a grocery store and listened through the cereal as she talked about it with her father. He knew how much she dreaded calculus.

Ander didn't go to school. He studied the girl. The Seed-bearers made him do it, stalk her. By now, he was an expert.

She loved pecans and clear nights when she could see the stars. She had horrible posture at the dinner table, but when she ran, she seemed to fly. She plucked her eyebrows with bejeweled tweezers; she dressed up in her mother's old Cleopatra costume every year for Halloween. She doused all her food with Tabasco, ran a mile in under six minutes, played her grandfather's Gibson guitar with no skill but plenty of soul. She painted polka dots on her fingernails and her bed-room walls. She dreamed of leaving the bayou for a big city like Dallas or Memphis, playing songs at open mikes in dark-ened clubs. She loved her mother with a fierce, unbreakable passion that Ander envied and struggled to understand. She wore tank tops in winter, sweatshirts to the beach, feared heights yet adored roller coasters, and planned on never get-ting married. She didn't cry. When she laughed, she closed her eyes.

He knew *everything* about her. He would ace any exam on her complexities. He had been watching her since the leap day she was born. All of the Seedbearers had. He had been

4

watching her since before he or she could speak. They had never spoken.

She was his life.

He had to kill her.

The girl and her mother had their windows rolled down. The Seedbearers wouldn't like that. He was certain one of his uncles had been charged with jamming their windows while mother and daughter played gin rummy at a blue-awninged café.

But Ander had once seen the girl's mother shove a stick in the voltage regulator of a car with a dead battery and start it up again. He'd seen the girl change a tire at the side of the road in hundred-degree weather and barely break a sweat. They could do things, these women. *More reason to kill her,* his uncles would say, shepherding him always toward defending his Seedbearer line. But nothing Ander saw in the girl frightened him; everything deepened his fascination.

Tan forearms dangled out both car windows as they passed mile marker two. Like mother, like daughter—wrists twisting in time to something on the radio that Ander wished he could hear.

He wondered how the salt would smell on her skin. The idea of being close enough to breathe her in gripped him in a wave of dizzy pleasure that crested into nausea.

One thing was certain: he would never have her.

He sank to his knees on the bench. The boat rocked under

his weight, shattering the reflection of the rising moon. Then it rocked again, harder, signaling a disturbance somewhere in the water.

The wave was building.

All he had to do was watch. His family had made that very clear. The wave would strike; the car would flow with it over the bridge like a blossom spilling over a fountain's rim. They would be swept to the depths of the sea. That was all.

When his family had schemed in their shabby Key West vacation rental with the "garden view" of a weedy alley, no one had spoken of subsequent waves that would wash mother and daughter into nonexistence. No one mentioned how slowly a corpse decomposed in cold water. But Ander had been having nightmares all week about the girl's body's afterlife.

His family said that after the wave it would be over and Ander could begin a normal life. Wasn't that what he said he wanted?

He simply had to ensure that the car stayed under the sea long enough for the girl to die. If by some chance—here the uncles began to bicker—mother and daughter somehow freed themselves and rose to the surface, then Ander would have to—

No, his aunt Chora said loudly enough to silence the roomful of men. She was the closest thing Ander had to a mother. He loved her, but he did not like her. It wouldn't happen, she said. The wave Chora would produce would be strong enough. Ander would not have to drown the girl with his hands. The Seedbearers weren't murderers. They were stewards of humanity, preventers of apocalypse. They were generating *an act of God*.

But it *was* murder. At this moment the girl was alive. She had friends and a family who loved her. She had a life before her, possibilities fanning out like oak branches into infinite sky. She had a way of making everything around her seem spectacular.

Whether she might someday do what the Seedbearers feared she would do was not something Ander liked thinking about. Doubt consumed him. As the wave rolled closer, he considered letting it take him, too.

If he wanted to die, he would have to get out of the boat. He would have to let go of the handles at the end of the chain welded to his anchor. No matter how strong the wave was, Ander's chain would not break; his anchor would not be wrested from the sea floor. They were made of orichalcum, an ancient metal considered mythological by modern archae-ologists. The anchor on its chain was one of five relics made of the substance that the Seedbearers preserved. The girl's mother—a rare scientist who believed in things she could not prove existed—would have traded her entire career to un-cover just one.

Anchor, spear and atlatl, lachrymatory vial, and the small carved chest that glowed unnatural green—these were what remained of his lineage, of the world no one spoke of, of the past the Seedbearers made it their sole mission to repress.

The girl knew nothing of the Seedbearers. But did she know where she had come from? Could she trace her line backward as swiftly as he could trace his, to the world lost in the flood, to the secret to which both he and she were inextricably linked?

It was time. The car approached the marker for mile four. Ander watched the wave emerge against the darkening sky until its white crest could no longer be mistaken for cloud. He watched it rise in slow motion, twenty feet, thirty feet, a wall of water moving toward them, black as night.

Its roar almost drowned out the scream that came from the car. The cry didn't sound like hers, more like her mother's. Ander shuddered. The sound signaled that they had seen the wave at last. Brake lights flashed. Then the engine gunned. Too late.

Aunt Chora was as good as her word; she'd built her wave perfectly. It carried the whiff of citronella—Chora's touch to mask the burnt-metal odor that accompanied Zephyr sorcery. Compact in width, the wave was taller than a three-story building, with a concentrated vortex in its deep belly and a foaming lip that would dash the bridge in half but leave the land on either side intact. It would do its work cleanly and, more importantly, quickly. There would hardly be time for the tourists stopped at the mouth of the bridge to pull out their phones and hit record.

When the wave broke, its barrel stretched across the bridge, then doubled back to crash into the highway divider ten feet ahead of the car, precisely as planned. The bridge groaned. The road buckled. The car swirled into the whirl-pool center. Its undercarriage flooded. It was picked up by the wave and rode the crest, then shot off the bridge on a slide made of roiling sea.

Ander watched the Chrysler somersault into the face of the wave. As it teetered down, he was appalled by a view through the windshield. There she was: dirty-blond hair splayed out and up. Soft profile, like a shadow cast by candlelight. Arms reaching for her mother, whose head knocked the steering wheel. Her scream cut Ander like glass.

If this hadn't happened, everything might have been different. But it did:

For the first time in his life, she *looked* at him.

His hands slipped from the handles of the orichalcum anchor. His feet lifted off the floor of the fishing boat. By the time the car splashed into the water, Ander was swimming toward her open window, fighting the wave, drawing on every ounce of ancient strength that flowed through his blood.

It was war, Ander versus the wave. It bashed into him, thrusting him against the shoal bottom of the Gulf, pummeling his ribs, turning his body into bruise. He gritted his teeth and swam through pain, through coral reef that slashed his skin, through shards of glass and splintered fender, through thick curtains of algae and weeds. His head shot above the surface and he gasped for air. He saw the twisted silhouette of the car—then it vanished beneath a world of foam. He nearly wept at the thought of not getting there in time.

Everything quieted. The wave retreated, gathering flotsam, dragging the car up with it. Leaving Ander behind.

He had one chance. The windows were above the level of the water. As soon as the wave returned, the car would be crushed in its trough. Ander could not explain how his body rose from the water, skidded across air. He leapt into the wave and reached out.

Her body was as rigid as a vow. Her dark eyes were open, churning blue. Blood trickled down her neck as she turned to him. What did she see? What *was* he?

The question and her gaze paralyzed Ander. In that bewildered moment, the wave curled around them, and a crucial chance was lost: he would have time to save only one of them. He knew how cruel it was. But, selfishly, he could not let her go.

Just before the wave exploded over them, Ander grabbed her hand.

Eureka.

1

EUREKA

In the stillness of the small beige waiting room, Eureka's bad ear rang. She massaged it—a habit since the accident, which had left her half deaf. It didn't help. Across the room, a doorknob turned. Then a woman with a gauzy white blouse, olive-green skirt, and very fine, upswept blond hair appeared in the lamplit space.

"Eureka?" Her low voice competed with the burbling of a fish tank that featured a neon plastic scuba diver buried to his knees in sand but showed no sign of containing fish.

Eureka looked around the vacant lobby, wishing to invoke some other, invisible Eureka to take her place for the hour.

"I'm Dr. Landry. Please come in."

Since Dad's remarriage four years ago, Eureka had

survived an armada of therapists. A life ruled by three adults who couldn't agree on anything proved far messier than one ruled by just two. Dad had doubted the first analyst, an old-school Freudian, almost as much as Mom had hated the second, a heavy-lidded psychiatrist who doled out numbness in pills. Then Rhoda, Dad's new wife, came onto the scene, game to try the school counselor, and the acupuncturist, and the anger manager. But Eureka had put her foot down at the patronizing family therapist, in whose office Dad had never felt less like family. She'd actually half liked the last shrink, who'd touted a faraway Swiss boarding school—until her mother caught wind of it and threatened to take Dad to court.

Eureka noted her new therapist's taupe leather slip-ons. She'd sat on the couch across from many similar pairs of shoes. Female doctors did this little trick: they slipped off their flats at the beginning of a session, slid their feet back into them to signal the end. They all must have read the same dull article about the Shoe Method being gentler on the pa-tient than simply saying time was up.

The office was purposefully calming: a long maroon leather couch against the shuttered window, two upholstered chairs opposite a coffee table with a bowl of those coffee gold-wrapped candies, a rug stitched with different-colored footprints. A plug-in air freshener made everything smell like cinnamon, which Eureka did not mind. Landry sat in one of the chairs. Eureka tossed her bag on the floor with a loud thump—honors textbooks were bricks—then slid down low on the couch.

"Nice place," she said. "You should get one of those swinging pendulums with the silver balls. My last doctor had one. Maybe a water cooler with the hot and cold taps."

"If you'd like some water, there's a pitcher by the sink. I'd be happy to—"

"Never mind." Eureka had already let slip more words than she'd intended to speak the whole hour. She was nervous. She took a breath and reerected her walls. She reminded herself she was a Stoic.

One of Landry's feet freed itself from its taupe flat, then used its stockinged toe to loosen the other shoe's heel, revealing maroon toenails. With both feet tucked under her thighs, Landry propped her chin in her palm. "What brings you here today?"

When Eureka was trapped in a bad situation, her mind fled to wild destinations she didn't try to avoid. She imagined a motorcade cruising through a ticker-tape parade in the center of New Iberia, stylishly escorting her to therapy.

But Landry looked sensible, interested in the reality from which Eureka yearned to escape. Eureka's red Jeep had brought her here. The seventeen-mile stretch of road between this office and her high school had brought her here—and every second ticked toward another minute during which she wasn't back at school warming up for that afternoon's cross-country meet. Bad luck had brought her here.

Or was it the letter from Acadia Vermilion Hospital, stating that because of her recently attempted suicide, therapy was not optional but mandatory?

Suicide. The word sounded more violent than the attempt had been. The night before she was supposed to start her senior year, Eureka had simply opened the window and let the gauzy white curtains billow toward her as she lay down in her bed. She'd tried to think of one bright thing about her future, but her mind had only rolled backward, toward lost moments of joy that could never be again. She couldn't live in the past, so she decided she couldn't live. She turned up her iPod. She swallowed the remainder of the oxycodone pills Dad had in the medicine cabinet for the pain from the fused disc in his spine.

Eight, maybe nine pills; she didn't count them as they tumbled down her throat. She thought of her mother. She thought of Mary, mother of God, who she'd been raised to believe prayed for everyone at the hour of death. Eureka knew the Catholic teachings about suicide, but she believed in Mary, whose mercy was vast, who might understand that Eureka had lost so much there was nothing to do but surrender.

She woke up in a cold ER, strapped to a gurney and gagging on the tube of a stomach pump. She heard Dad

14

and Rhoda fighting in the hallway while a nurse forced her to drink awful liquid charcoal to bind to the poisons they couldn't purge from her system.

Because she didn't know the language that would have gotten her out sooner—"I want to live," "I won't try that again"—Eureka spent two weeks in the psychiatric ward. She would never forget the absurdity of jumping rope next to the huge schizophrenic woman during calisthenics, of eating oatmeal with the college kid who hadn't slit his wrists deep enough, who spat in the orderlies' faces when they tried to give him pills. Somehow, sixteen days later, Eureka was trudging into morning Mass before first period at Evangeline Catholic High, where Belle Pogue, a sophomore from Opelousas, stopped her at the chapel door with "You must feel blessed to be alive."

Eureka had glared into Belle's pale eyes, causing the girl to gasp, make the sign of the cross, and scuttle to the farthest pew. In the six weeks she'd been back at Evangeline, Eureka had stopped counting how many friends she'd lost.

Dr. Landry cleared her throat.

Eureka stared up at the drop-panel ceiling. "You know why I'm here."

"I'd love to hear you put it into words."

"My father's wife."

"You're having problems with your stepmother?"

"Rhoda makes the appointments. That's why I'm here."

Eureka's therapy had become one of Dad's wife's causes. First it was to deal with the divorce, then to grieve her mother's death, now to unpack the suicide attempt. Without Diana, there was no one to intercede on Eureka's behalf, to make a call and fire a quack. Eureka imagined herself still stuck in sessions with Dr. Landry at the age of eighty-five, no less screwed up than she was today.

"I know losing your mother has been hard," Landry said. "How are you feeling?"

Eureka fixed on the word *losing,* as if she and Diana had been separated in a crowd and they'd soon reunite, clasp hands, saunter toward the nearest dockside restaurant for fried clams, and carry on as if they'd never been apart.

That morning, across the breakfast table, Rhoda had sent Eureka a text: *Dr. Landry. 3 p.m.* There was a hyperlink to send the appointment to her phone's calendar. When Eureka clicked on the office address, a pin on the map marked the Main Street location in New Iberia.

"New Iberia?" Her voice cracked.

Rhoda swallowed some vile-looking green juice. "Thought you'd like that."

New Iberia was the town where Eureka had been born, had grown up. It was the place she still called home, where she'd lived with her parents for the unshattered portion of her life, until they split and her mom moved away and Dad's confident stride began to resemble a shuffle, like that of the blue claw crabs at Victor's, where he used to be the chef.

That was right around Katrina, and Rita came close behind. Eureka's old house was still there—she'd heard another family lived in it now—but after the hurricanes, Dad hadn't wanted to put in the time or emotion to repair it. So they'd moved to Lafayette, fifteen miles and thirty light-years from home. Dad got a job as a line cook at Prejean's, which was bigger and far less romantic than Victor's. Eureka changed schools, which sucked. Before Eureka knew that Dad was even over her mom, the two of them were moving into a big house on Shady Circle. It belonged to a bossy lady named Rhoda. She was pregnant. Eureka's new bedroom was down the hall from a nursery-in-progress.

So, no, Rhoda, Eureka did not like that this new therapist lived way out in New Iberia. How was she supposed to drive all the way to the appointment and make it back in time for her meet?

The meet was important, not only because Evangeline was racing their rival, Manor High. Today was the day Eureka had promised Coach she'd make her decision about whether to stay on the team.

Before Diana died, Eureka had been named senior captain. After the accident, when she was physically strong enough, friends had begged her to run a few summer scrimmages. But the one run she'd gone to had made her want to scream. Underclassmen held out cups of water drenched in pity. Coach chalked up Eureka's slow speed to the casts binding her wrists. It was a lie. Her heart wasn't in the race

17

anymore. It wasn't with the team. Her heart was in the ocean with Diana.

After the pills, Coach had brought balloons, which looked absurd in the sterile psych-ward room. Eureka hadn't even been allowed to keep them after visiting hours ended.

"I quit," Eureka told her. She was embarrassed to be seen with her wrists and ankles bound to her bed. "Tell Cat she can have my locker."

Coach's sad smile suggested that after a suicide attempt, a girl's decisions weighed less, like bodies on the moon. "I ran my way through two divorces and a sister's battle with cancer," Coach said. "I'm not saying this just because you're the fastest kid on my team. I'm saying this because maybe running is the therapy you need. When you're feeling better, come see me. We'll talk about that locker."

Eureka didn't know why she'd agreed. Maybe she didn't want to let another person down. She'd promised to try to be back in shape by the race against Manor today, to give it one more shot. She used to love to run. She used to love the team. But that was all before.

"Eureka," Dr. Landry prompted. "Can you tell me something you remember about the day of the accident?"

Eureka studied the blank canvas of the ceiling, as if it might paint her a clue. She remembered so little about the accident there was no point opening her mouth. A mirror hung on the far wall of the office. Eureka rose and stood before it.

"What do you see?" Landry asked.

Traces of the girl she'd been before: same small, open-car-door ears she tucked her hair behind, same dark blue eyes like Dad's, same eyebrows that ran wild if she didn't tame them daily—it was all still there. And yet, just before this appointment, two women Diana's age had passed her in the parking lot, whispering, "Her own mother wouldn't recognize her."

It was an expression, like a lot of things New Iberia said about Eureka: *She could argue with the wall in China and win. Couldn't carry a tune in a bucket covered in glue. Runs faster than a stomped-on pissant at the Olympics.* The trouble with expressions was how easily they rolled off the tongue. Those women weren't thinking about the reality of Diana, who would know her daughter anywhere, anytime, no matter the circumstances.

Thirteen years of Catholic school had told Eureka that Diana was looking down from Heaven and recognizing her now. She wouldn't mind the ripped Joshua Tree T-shirt under her daughter's school cardigan, the chewed nails, or the hole in the left big toe of her houndstooth canvas shoes. But she might be pissed about the hair.

In the four months since the accident, Eureka's hair had gone from virgin dirty-blond to siren red (her mother's natural shade) to peroxide white (her beauty-salon-owning aunt Maureen's idea) to raven black (which finally seemed to fit) and was now growing out in an interesting ombré shag. Eureka tried to smile at her reflection, but her face looked strange, like the comedy mask that had hung on her drama class wall last year.

"Tell me about your most recent positive memory," Landry said.

Eureka sank back onto the couch. It must have been that day. It must have been the Jelly Roll Morton CD on the stereo and her mother's awful pitch harmonizing with her awful pitch as they drove with the windows down along a bridge they'd never cross. She remembered laughing at a funny lyric as they approached the middle of the bridge. She remembered seeing the rusted white sign whizz by—MILE MARKER FOUR.

Then: Oblivion. A gaping black hole until she awoke in a Miami hospital with a lacerated scalp, a burst left eardrum that would never fully heal, a twisted ankle, two severely broken wrists, a thousand bruises—

And no mother.

Dad had been sitting at the edge of her bed. He cried when she came to, which made his eyes even bluer. Rhoda handed him tissues. Eureka's four-year-old half siblings, William and Claire, clasped small, soft fingers around the parts of her hands not enclosed in casts. She'd smelled the twins even before she opened her eyes, before she knew anyone was there or that she was alive. They smelled like they always did: Ivory soap and starry nights.

Rhoda's voice was steady when she leaned over the bed and promoted her red glasses to the top of her head. "You've been in an accident. You're going to be fine."

They told her about the rogue wave that rose like a myth out of the ocean and swept her mother's Chrysler from the bridge. They told her about scientists searching the water for a meteor that might have caused the wave. They told her about the construction workers, asked whether Eureka knew how or why their car was the only one allowed to cross the bridge. Rhoda mentioned suing the county, but Dad had motioned *Let it go.* They asked Eureka about her miraculous survival. They waited for her to fill in the blanks about how she'd ended up on the shore alone.

When she couldn't, they told her about her mother.

She didn't listen, didn't really hear any of it. She was grateful that the tinnitus in her ear drowned out most sounds. Sometimes she still liked that the accident had left her half-deaf. She'd stared at William's soft face, then at Claire's, thinking it would help. But they looked afraid of her, and that hurt more than her broken bones. So she stared past them all, relaxed her gaze on the off-white wall, and left it there for the next nine days. She always told the nurses that her pain level was seven out of ten on their chart, ensuring she'd get more morphine.

"You might be feeling like the world is a very unfair place," Landry tried.

Was Eureka still in this room with this patronizing woman paid to misunderstand her? *That* was unfair. She pictured Landry's broken-in taupe shoes rising magically from the carpet, hovering in the air and spinning like minute and hour hands on a clock until time was up and Eureka could speed back to her meet.

"Cries for help like yours often result from feeling misunderstood."

"Cry for help" was shrink-speak for "suicide attempt." It wasn't a cry for help. Before Diana died, Eureka thought the world was an incredibly exciting place. Her mother was an adventure. She noticed things on an average walk most people would pass by a thousand times. She laughed louder and more often than anyone Eureka ever knew—and there were times that had embarrassed Eureka, but these days she found she missed her mother's laughter above everything else.

Together they had been to Egypt, Turkey, and India, on a boat tour through the Galápagos Islands, all as part of Diana's archaeological work. Once, when Eureka went to visit her mother on a dig in northern Greece, they missed the last bus out of Trikala and thought they were stuck for the night—until fourteen-year-old Eureka hailed an olive oil truck and they hitchhiked back to Athens. She remembered her mother's arm around her as they sat in the back of the truck among the pungent, leaky vats of olive oil, her low voice murmuring: "You could find your way out of a foxhole in Siberia, girl.

You're one hell of a traveling companion." It was Eureka's favorite compliment. She thought of it often when she was in a situation she needed to get out of.

"I'm trying to connect with you, Eureka," Dr. Landry said. "People closest to you are trying to connect with you. I asked your stepmother and your father to jot down some words to describe the change in you." She reached for a marbled notebook on the end table next to her chair. "Would you like to hear them?"

"Sure." Eureka shrugged. "Pin the tail on the donkey."

"Your stepmother—"

"Rhoda."

"Rhoda called you 'chilly.' She said the rest of the family engages in 'eggshell walking' around you, that you're 'reclusive and impatient' with your half siblings."

Eureka flinched. "I am not . . ." Reclusive—who cared? But impatient with the twins? Was that true? Or was it another one of Rhoda's tricks?

"What about Dad? Let me guess—'distant,' 'morose'?"

Landry turned a notebook page. "Your father describes you as, yes, 'distant,' 'stoic,' 'a tough nut to crack.'"

"Being stoic isn't a bad thing." Since she'd learned about Greek Stoicism, Eureka had aspired to keep her emotions in check. She liked the idea of freedom gained through taking control of her feelings, holding them so that only she could see them, like a hand of cards. In a universe without Rhodas

23

and Dr. Landrys, Dad's calling her "stoic" might have been a compliment. He was stoic, too.

But that tough-nut phrase bothered her. "What kind of suicidal nut *wants* to be cracked?" she muttered.

Landry lowered the book. "Are you having further thoughts of suicide?"

"I was referring to the nuts," Eureka said, exasperated. "I was putting myself in *opposition* to a nut who . . . Never mind." But it was too late. She'd let the s-word slip, which was like saying "bomb" on a plane. Warning lights would be flashing inside Landry.

Of course Eureka still thought about suicide. And yeah, she'd pondered other methods, knowing mostly that she couldn't try drowning—not after Diana. She'd once seen a show about how the lungs fill with blood before drowning victims die. Sometimes she talked about suicide with her friend Brooks, who was the only person she could trust not to judge her, not to report back to Dad or worse. He'd sat on muted conference call when she'd called this hotline a few times. He made her promise she would talk to him whenever she thought about it, so they talked a lot.

But she was still here, wasn't she? The urge to leave this world wasn't as crippling as it had been when Eureka swallowed those pills. Lethargy and apathy had replaced her drive to die.

"Did Dad happen to mention I've always been that way?" she asked.

Landry set her notebook on the table. "Always?"

Now Eureka looked away. Maybe not always. Of course not always. Things had been sunny for a while. But when she was ten, her parents split up. You didn't just find the sun after that.

"Any chance you could dash out a Xanax prescription?" Eureka's left eardrum was ringing again. "Otherwise this seems to be a waste of time."

"You don't need drugs. You need to open up, not bury this tragedy. Your stepmother says you won't talk to her or your father. You've shown no interest in conversing with me. What about your friends at school?"

"Cat," Eureka said automatically. "And Brooks." She talked to them. If either of them had been sitting in Landry's seat, Eureka might even have been laughing right now.

"Good." Dr. Landry meant: *Finally.* "How would they describe you since the accident?"

"Cat's captain of the cross-country team," Eureka said, thinking of the wildly mixed emotions on her friend's face when Eureka said she was quitting, leaving the captain position open. "She'd say I've gotten slow."

Cat would be on the field with the team right now. She was great at running them through their drills, but she wasn't brilliant at pep talks—and the team needed pep to face Manor. Eureka glanced at her watch. If she dashed back as soon as this was over, she might make it to school in time. That was what she wanted, right?

When she looked up, Landry's brow was furrowed. "That would be a pretty harsh thing to say to a girl who's grieving the loss of a mother, don't you think?"

Eureka shrugged. If Landry had a sense of humor, if she knew Cat, she would get it. Her friend was joking, most of the time. It was fine. They'd known each other forever.

"What about . . . Brooke?"

"Brooks," Eureka said. She'd known him forever, too. He was a better listener than any of the shrinks Rhoda and Dad wasted their money on.

"Is Brooks a he?" The notebook returned and Landry scribbled something. "Are the two of you *just friends?*"

"Why does that matter?" Eureka snapped. Once upon an accident she and Brooks had dated—fifth grade. But they were kids. And she was a wreck about her parents splitting up and—

"Divorce often provokes behavior in children that makes it difficult for them to pursue their own romantic relationships."

"We were *ten*. It didn't work out because I wanted to go swimming when he wanted to ride bikes. How did we even start talking about this?"

"You tell me. Perhaps you can talk to Brooks about your loss. He seems to be someone you could care deeply about, if you would give yourself permission to feel."

Eureka rolled her eyes. "Put your shoes back on, Doc."

She grabbed her bag and rose from the couch. "I've gotta run."

Run from this session. Run back to school. Run through the woods until she was so tired she didn't ache. Maybe even run back to the team she used to love. Coach had been right about one thing: when Eureka was low, running helped.

"I'll see you next Tuesday?" Landry called. But by then the therapist was talking to a closing door.

2

OBJECTS IN MOTION

Jogging through the potholed parking lot, Eureka pressed her key chain remote to unlock Magda, her car, and slid into the driver's seat. Yellow warblers harmonized in a beech tree overhead; Eureka knew their song by heart. The day was warm and windy, but parking under the tree's long arms had kept Magda's interior cool.

Magda was a red Jeep Cherokee, a hand-me-down from Rhoda. It was too new and too red to suit Eureka. With the windows rolled up, you couldn't hear anything outside, and this made Eureka imagine she was driving a tomb. Cat had insisted they name the car Magda, so at least the Jeep would be good for a laugh. It wasn't nearly as cool as Dad's powder-blue Lincoln Continental, in which Eureka had learned to drive, but at least it had a killer stereo.

She plugged in her phone and cranked up the online school radio station KBEU. They played the best songs by the best local and indie bands every weekday after school. Last year, Eureka had DJ'd for the station; she'd had a show called *Bored on the Bayou* on Tuesday afternoons. They'd held the slot for her this year, but she hadn't wanted it anymore. The girl who'd spun old zydeco jams and recent mash-ups was someone she could barely remember, let alone try to be again.

Rolling down all four windows and the sunroof, Eureka peeled out of the lot to the tune of "It's Not Fair" by the Faith Healers, a band formed by some kids from school. She had all the lyrics memorized. The loopy bass line propelled her legs faster through her sprints and had been the reason she dug up her grandfather's old guitar. She'd taught herself a few chords but hadn't touched the guitar since the spring. She couldn't imagine the music she'd make now that Diana was dead. The guitar sat gathering dust in the corner of her bedroom under the small painting of Saint Catherine of Siena, which Eureka had lifted from her grandmother Sugar's house after she died. No one knew where Sugar got the icon. For as long as Eureka could remember, the painting of the patron saint of protection from fire had hung over her grandmother's mantel.

Her fingers rapped on the steering wheel. Landry didn't know what she was talking about. Eureka *felt* things, things like . . . annoyed that she'd just wasted another hour in another drab therapy room.

There were other things: Cold fear whenever she drove

over even the shortest bridge. Debilitating sadness when she lay sleepless in bed. A heaviness in her bones whose source she had to trace anew each morning when her phone's alarm sounded. Shame that she'd survived and Diana hadn't. Fury that something so absurd had taken her mother away.

Futility at seeking vengeance on a wave.

Inevitably, when she allowed herself to follow her sad mind's wanderings, Eureka ended up at futility. Futility annoyed her. So she veered away, focused on things she could control—like getting back to campus and the decision awaiting her.

Even Cat didn't know Eureka might show up today. The 12K used to be Eureka's best event. Her teammates moaned about it, but to Eureka, sinking into the hypnotic zone of a long run was rejuvenating. A sliver of Eureka wanted to race the Manor kids, and a sliver was more of her than had wanted to do anything other than sleep for months.

She would never give Landry the satisfaction, but Eureka *did* feel utterly misunderstood. People didn't know what to do with a dead mother, much less her living, suicidal daughter. Their robotic back pats and shoulder squeezes made Eureka squirrelly. She couldn't fathom the insensitivity required to say to someone, "God must have missed your mother in Heaven" or "This might make you a better person."

This clique of girls at school who'd never acknowledged her before drove by her mailbox after Diana died to drop off a cross-stitched friendship bracelet with little crosses on it. At first, when Eureka ran into them in town bare-wristed, she'd avoided their eyes. But after she'd tried to kill herself, that wasn't a problem anymore. The girls looked away first. Pity had its limits.

Even Cat had only recently stopped tearing up when she saw Eureka. She'd blow her nose and laugh and say, "I don't even *like* my mom, and I'd lose it if I lost her."

Eureka *had* lost it. But because she didn't fall apart and cry, didn't lunge into the arms of anyone who tried to hug her or cover herself with handmade bracelets, did people think she wasn't grieving?

She grieved every day, all the time, with every atom of her body.

You could find your way out of a foxhole in Siberia, girl. Diana's voice found her as she passed Hebert's whitewashed Bait Shack and turned left onto the gravel road lined by tall stalks of sugarcane. The land on either side of this three-mile stretch of road between New Iberia and Lafayette was some of the prettiest in three parishes: huge live oak trees carving out blue sky, high fields dotted with wild periwinkles in the spring, a lone flat-roofed trailer on stilts about a quarter of a mile back from the road. Diana used to love this part of the drive to Lafayette. She called it "the last gasp of country before civilization."

Eureka hadn't been on this road since before Diana died.

She'd turned here so casually, not thinking it would hurt, but suddenly she couldn't breathe. Every day some new pain found her, stabbed her, as if grief were the foxhole she would see no way out of until she died.

She almost stopped the car to get out and run. When she was running, she didn't think. Her mind cleared, oak trees' arms embraced her with their fuzzy Spanish moss, and she was just feet pounding, legs burning, heart beating, arms pumping, blending into trails until she became something far away.

She thought of the meet. Maybe she could channel desperation into something useful. If she could just make it back to school in time . . .

The week before, the last of the heavy casts she'd had to wear on her shattered wrists (the right one had been broken so severely it had to be reset three times) had finally been sawed off. She'd hated wearing the thing and couldn't wait to see it shredded. But last week, when the orthopedist tossed the cast in the trash and pronounced her healed, it sounded like a joke.

As Eureka pulled up to a four-way stop sign on the empty road, bay branches bent in an arc over the sunroof. She pushed the green sleeve of her school cardigan up. She turned her right wrist over a few times, studying her forearm. The skin was as pale as the petal of a magnolia. Her right arm's circumference seemed to have shrunk to half the size of her left. It looked freakish. It made Eureka ashamed. Then she became ashamed of her shame. She was alive; her mother wasn't—

Tires screeched behind her. A hard *bump* split her lips open in a yelp of shock as Magda lurched forward. Eureka's foot ground against the brake. The airbag bloomed like a jelly-fish. The force of the rough fabric stung her cheeks and nose. Her head snapped against the headrest. She gasped, the wind knocked out of her, as every muscle in her body clenched. The din of crunching metal made the music on the stereo sound eerily new. Eureka listened to it for a moment, hearing the lyric "always not fair" before she realized she'd been hit.

Her eyes shot open and she jerked at the door handle, for-getting she had her seat belt on. When she lifted her foot off the brake, the car rolled forward until she jerked it into park. She turned Magda off. Her hands flailed under the deflating airbag. She was desperate to free herself.

A shadow fell across her body, giving her the strangest sense of déjà vu. Someone was outside the car, looking in.

She looked up—

"You," she whispered involuntarily.

She had never seen the boy before. His skin was as pale as her uncasted arm, but his eyes were turquoise, like the ocean in Miami, and this made her think of Diana. She sensed sad-ness in their depths, like shadows in the sea. His hair was blond, not too short, a little wavy at the top. She could tell there were plenty of muscles under his white button-down. Straight nose, square jaw, full lips—the kid looked like Paul Newman from Diana's favorite movie, *Hud,* except he was so pale.

"You could help me!" she heard herself shout at the stranger. He was the hottest guy she'd ever yelled at. He might have been the hottest guy she'd ever seen. Her exclamation made him jump, then reach around the open door just as her fingers finally found the seat belt. She tumbled gracelessly out of the car and landed in the middle of the dusty road on her hands and knees. She groaned. Her nose and cheeks stung from the airbag burn. Her right wrist throbbed.

The boy crouched down to help her. His eyes were startlingly blue.

"Never mind." She stood up and dusted off her skirt. She rolled her neck, which hurt, though it was nothing compared to the shape she'd been in after the other accident. She looked at the white truck that had hit her. She looked at the boy.

"What is wrong with you?" she shouted. "Stop sign!"

"Sorry." His voice was soft and mellow. She wasn't sure he sounded sorry.

"Did you even try to stop?"

"I didn't see—"

"Didn't see the large red car directly in front of you?" She spun around to examine Magda. When she saw the damage, she cursed so the whole parish could hear.

The rear end looked like a zydeco accordion, caved in up

to the backseat, where her license plate was now wedged. The back window was shattered; shards hung from its perimeter like ugly icicles. The back tires were twisted sideways.

She took a breath, remembering that the car was Rhoda's status symbol anyway, not something she'd loved. Magda was screwed, no question about it. But what did Eureka do now?

Thirty minutes until the meet. Still ten miles from school. If she didn't show up, Coach would think Eureka was blowing her off.

"I need your insurance information," she called, finally remembering the line Dad had drilled into her months before she got her license.

"Insurance?" The boy shook his head and shrugged.

She kicked a tire on his truck. It was old, probably from the early eighties, and she might have thought it was cool if it hadn't just crushed her car. Its hood had sprung open, but the truck wasn't even scratched.

"Unbelievable." She glared at the guy. "Your car's not wrecked at all."

"Whaddya expect? It's a Chevy," the boy said in an affected bayou accent, quoting a truly annoying commercial for the truck that had aired throughout Eureka's childhood. It was another thing people said that meant nothing.

He forced a laugh, studied her face. Eureka knew she turned red when she was angry. Brooks called it the Bayou Blaze.

"What do I expect?" She approached the boy. "I expect

to be able to get in a car without having my life threatened. I expect the people on the road around me to have some rudimentary sense of traffic laws. I expect the dude who rear-ends me not to act so smug."

She had brought the storm too close, she realized. By now their bodies were inches apart and she had to tilt her neck back, which hurt, to look him in those blue eyes. He was a half a foot taller than Eureka, and she was a tall five eight.

"But I guess I expected too much. Your dumb ass doesn't even have insurance."

They were still standing really close for no reason other than Eureka had thought the boy would retreat. He didn't. His breath tickled her forehead. He tilted his head to the side, watching her closely, studying her harder than she studied for tests. He blinked a few times, and then, very slowly, he smiled.

As the smile deepened across his face, something fluttered inside Eureka. Against her will, she yearned to smile back. It made no sense. He was smiling at her like they were old friends, the way she and Brooks might snicker if one of them hit the other's car. But Eureka and this kid were total strangers. And yet, by the time his broad smile slid into a soft, intimate chuckle, the edges of Eureka's lips had twitched upward, too.

"What are you smiling at?" She meant to scold him, but it came out like a laugh, which astonished her, then made her mad. She turned away. "Forget it. Don't talk. My stepmonster is going to *kill* me."

"It wasn't your fault." The boy beamed like he'd just won the Nobel Prize for Rednecks. "You didn't ask for this."

"Nobody does," she muttered.

"You were stopped at a stop sign. I hit you. Your monster will understand."

"You've obviously never had the pleasure of Rhoda."

"Tell her I'll take care of your car."

She ignored him, walking back to the Jeep to grab her backpack and pry her phone out of its holster on the dashboard. She'd call Dad first. She pressed speed dial number two. Speed dial one still called Diana's cell. Eureka couldn't bear to change it.

No surprise, Dad's phone rang and rang. After his long lunch shift was over, but before he got to leave the restaurant, he had to prep about three million pounds of boiled seafood, so his hands were probably coated with shrimp antennae.

"I promise you," the boy was saying in the background, "it's going to be okay. I'll make it up to you. Look, my name is—"

"Shhh." She held up a hand, spinning away from him to stand at the edge of the sugarcane field. "You lost me at 'It's a Chevy.'"

"I'm sorry." He followed her, his shoes crunching on the thick stalks of cane near the road. "Let me explain—"

Eureka scrolled through her contacts to pull up Rhoda's

number. She rarely called Dad's wife, but now she didn't have a choice. The phone rang six times before it went to Rhoda's endless voice mail greeting. "The one time I actually *want* her to pick up!"

She dialed Dad again, and again. She tried Rhoda twice more before stuffing her phone in her pocket. She watched the sun sinking into the treetops. Her teammates would be dressed out for the race by now. Coach would be eyeing the parking lot for Eureka's car. Her right wrist still throbbed. She clenched her eyes in pain as she clutched it to her chest. She was stranded. She began to shake.

Find your way out of a foxhole, girl.

Diana's voice sounded so close it made Eureka light-headed. Goose bumps rose on her arms and something burned at the back of her throat. When she opened her eyes, the boy was standing right in front of her. He gazed at her with guileless concern, the way she watched the twins when one of them was really sick.

"Don't," the boy said.

"Don't what?" Her voice quavered just as unannounced tears gathered in the corners of her eyes. They were so foreign, clouding her perfect vision.

The sky rumbled, reverberating inside Eureka the way the biggest thunderstorms did. Dark clouds rolled across the trees, sealing the sky with a green-gray storm. Eureka braced for a downpour.

A single tear spilled from the corner of her left eye and was about to trickle down her cheek. But before it did—

The boy raised his index finger, reached toward her, and *caught* the tear on his fingertip. Very slowly, as if he held something precious, he carried the salty drop away from her, toward his own face. He pressed it into the corner of his right eye. Then he blinked and it was gone.

"There, now," he whispered. "No more tears."

3

EVACUATION

Eureka touched the corners of her eyes with her thumb and forefinger. She blinked and remembered the last time she had cried—

It was the night before Hurricane Rita devastated New Iberia. On a warm, damp evening in late September, a few weeks after Katrina, the hurricane hit their town . . . and the frail levees in Eureka's parents' marriage finally flooded, too.

Eureka was nine. She'd spent an uneasy summer in the care of one parent at a time. If Diana took her fishing, she would disappear into the bedroom as soon as they got home, leaving Dad to scale and fry the fish. If Dad got movie tickets, Diana found other plans and someone else to take her seat.

Earlier summers of the three of them sailing around

Cypremort Point, with Dad tucking State Fair cotton candy into Eureka's and Diana's mouths, seemed like a dream Eureka could barely remember. That summer, the only thing her parents did together was fight.

The big one had been brewing for months. Her parents always argued in the kitchen. Something about Dad's calmness there as he stirred and simmered complex reductions seemed to ignite Diana. The hotter things got between them, the more of Dad's kitchenware she broke. She'd mangled his meat grinder and bent the pasta rollers. By the time Hurricane Rita hit town, there were only three whole plates left in the cupboard.

The rain grew heavy around nightfall, but it wasn't heavy enough to drown out the fighting downstairs. This one had started when a friend of Diana's had offered them a ride in the van she was driving toward Houston. Diana wanted to evacuate; Dad wanted to ride out the storm. They'd had the same kind of fight fifty times, under hurricane and cloudless skies. Eureka alternated between burrowing her face in a pillow and pressing her ear against the wall to hear what her parents were saying.

She heard her mother's voice: "You think the worst of everyone!"

And Dad: "At least *I* think at all!"

Then came the sound of glass shattering against the tile floor of the kitchen. A sharp, briny odor carried upstairs and

Eureka knew Diana had broken the jars of okra Dad was pickling on the windowsill. She heard curse words, then more crashing. Wind wailed outside the house. Hail rattled the windows.

"I won't just sit here!" Diana cried. "I won't wait to drown!"

"Look outside," Dad said. "You can't go now. It would be worse to leave."

"Not for me. Not for Eureka."

Dad was quiet. Eureka could picture him eyeing his wife, who would be boiling in a way he'd never let his sauces boil. He always told Eureka the only heat to use when you loved a sauce was the softest simmer. But Diana was never one to be tempered.

"Just say it!" she shouted.

"You'd want to go even if there was no hurricane," he said. "You run. It's who you are. But you can't disappear. You have a daughter—"

"I'll take Eureka."

"You have me." Dad's voice shook.

Diana didn't respond. The lights flickered off, then on, then off for good.

Just outside Eureka's bedroom door, there was a landing that looked down on the kitchen. She crept from her room and gripped the railing. She watched her parents light candles and shout about whose fault it was they didn't have more. When Diana placed a candlestick on the mantel, Eureka noticed the floral suitcase, packed, at the foot of the stairs.

Diana had made up her mind to evacuate before this fight had even started.

If her father stayed and her mother left, what would happen to Eureka? No one had told her to pack.

She hated when her mother went away for a weeklong archaeological dig. This seemed different, bathed in a sickly glow of forever. She sank to her knees and leaned her forehead against the banister. A tear slid down her cheek. Alone at the top of the stairs, Eureka let out a painful sob.

An explosion of breaking glass sounded above her. She ducked and covered her head. Peeking through her fingers, she saw that the wind had pushed the elbow of a large branch from the oak tree in the backyard through the second-story window. Glass rained on her hair. Water streamed through the gash in the pane. The back of Eureka's cotton nightgown was soaked.

"Eureka!" Dad shouted, running up the stairs. But before he could reach her, there was an odd creaking from the hallway below. As her father spun to locate it, Eureka watched the door to the water heater closet burst from its hinges.

A vast swell of water gushed from inside the small closet. The wooden door spun onto its side like a raft riding a wave. It took Eureka a moment to realize that the water tank had split down its center, that its contents were making a giant bathtub out of the hallway. Pipes hissed streams across the walls, twisting like garter snakes as they spewed. Water drenched the carpet, sloshed against the bottom step in the stairwell. The force of the spill tipped over kitchen chairs. One of them tripped Diana, who'd been moving toward Eureka, too.

"It's only going to get worse," Diana shouted at her husband. She pushed away the chair and righted herself. When she looked at Eureka, a strange expression crossed her face.

Dad had made it halfway up the stairs. His gaze darted between his daughter and the gushing water tank, as if he didn't know what to attend to first. When the water thrust the busted closet door into the coffee table in the living room, the shattering of glass made Eureka jump. Dad shot Diana a hateful look that crossed the space between them like lightning.

"I told you we should have called a real plumber instead of your idiot brother!" He flung a hand up toward Eureka, whose wailing had deepened into a hoarse moan. "Comfort her."

But Diana had already pushed past her husband on the stairs. She swept Eureka into her arms, brushed the glass from her hair, and carried her back to her bedroom, away from the window and the invading tree. Diana's feet left soggy footprints on the carpet. Her face and clothes were drenched. She sat Eureka on the old four-poster bed and gripped her shoulders roughly. Wild intensity filled her eyes.

Eureka sniffed. "I'm scared."

Diana gazed at her daughter as if she didn't know who she was. Then her palm flicked backward and she slapped Eureka, hard.

Eureka froze mid-moan, too stunned to move or breathe. The whole house seemed to reverberate, echoing the slap. Diana leaned close. Her eyes bored into her daughter's. She said in the gravest tone Eureka had ever heard: "Never, ever cry again."

4

LIFT

Eureka's hand went to her cheek as she opened her eyes and came back to the scene with her wrecked car and the strange boy.

She never thought about that night. But now, on the hot, deserted road, she could feel the sting of her mother's palm against her skin. That was the only time Diana had ever hit her. It was the only time she'd ever frightened Eureka. They'd never spoken of it again, but Eureka had never shed another tear—until now.

It wasn't the same, she told herself. Those tears had been torrential, shed as her parents broke up. This sudden urge to cry over a banged-up Jeep had already retreated inside her, as if it had never surfaced.

Fast-moving clouds clotted the sky, teeming with nasty gray. Eureka glanced at the empty intersection, at the sea of tall blond sugarcane bordering the road and the open green glade beyond the crop; everything was still, waiting. She was shivery, unsteady, the way she got after she'd run a long trail on a hot day without water.

"What just happened?" She meant the sky, her tear, the accident—everything that had passed since she'd encountered him.

"Maybe some kind of eclipse," he said.

Eureka turned her head so that her right ear was closer to him, so she could hear him clearly. She hated the hearing aid she'd been fitted for after the accident. She never wore it, had stuffed its case somewhere in the back of her closet and told Rhoda it gave her a headache. She'd gotten used to turning her head subtly; most people didn't notice. But this boy seemed to. He shifted closer to her good ear.

"Seems like it's over now." His pale skin shone in the peculiar darkness. It was only four o'clock, but the sky was as dim as in the hour before sunrise.

She pointed to her eye, then to his eye, destiny of her tear. "Why did you . . . ?"

She didn't know how to ask this question; it was that bizarre. She stared at him, his nice dark jeans, the kind of pressed white shirt you didn't see on bayou boys. His brown oxford shoes were polished. He didn't look like he was from around here. Then again, people said that to Eureka all the time, and she was a born-and-bred New Iberian.

She studied his face, the shape of his nose, the way his pupils widened under her scrutiny. For a moment, his features seemed to go blurry, as though Eureka were seeing him underwater. It occurred to her that if she were asked to describe the boy tomorrow, she might not remember his face. She rubbed her eyes. Stupid tears.

When she looked at him again, his features were focused, sharp. Nice features. Nothing wrong with them. Still . . . the tear. She didn't do that. What had come over her?

"My name's Ander." He stuck out his hand politely, as though a moment ago he hadn't intimately wiped her eye, as though he hadn't just done the strangest, sexiest thing anyone had ever done.

"Eureka." She shook his hand. Was her palm sweating or was his?

"Where'd you get a name like that?"

People around here assumed Eureka was named for the tiny town in far north Louisiana. They probably thought her parents snuck up there one summer weekend in her dad's old Continental, stopped for the night when they got low on gas. She'd never told anyone but Brooks and Cat the real story. It was hard to convince people that things happened outside of what they knew.

The truth was, when Eureka's teenaged mother got

knocked up, she boogied out of Louisiana quick. She drove west in the middle of the night, outrageously violating all of her parents' strict rules, and ended up in a hippie co-op near Lake Shasta, California, which Dad still referred to as "the vortex."

But I came back, didn't I? Diana had laughed when she was young and still in love with Dad. *I always come back.*

On Eureka's eighth birthday, Diana took her out there. They'd spent a few days with her mother's old friends at the co-op, playing spades and drinking cloudy unfiltered apple cider. Then, when both of them got to feeling landlocked— which happened fast with Cajuns—they drove out to the coast and ate oysters that were briny and cold, with bits of ice clinging to their shells, just like the ones bayou kids were raised on. On their way home, Diana took the Oceanside highway to the city of Eureka, pointing out the roadside clinic where Eureka had been born, eight years earlier, on leap day.

But Eureka didn't talk about Diana with just anyone, because most people didn't grasp the complex miracle that was her mother, and struggling to defend Diana was painful. So Eureka kept it all inside, walled herself off from worlds and people like this boy. "Ander's not a name you hear every day."

His eyes dropped and they listened to a train heading west. "Family name."

"Who are your people?" She knew she sounded like all the other Cajuns who thought the sun rose and set on their bayou. Eureka didn't think that, never had, but there was something about this kid that made him seem like he'd appeared spontaneously next to the sugarcane. Part of Eureka found that exciting. Another part—the part that wanted her car repaired—was uneasy.

Car wheels on the gravel road behind them made Eureka turn her head. When she saw the rusty tow truck jerk to a stop behind her, she groaned. Through the bug-splattered windshield, she could barely see the driver, but all of New Iberia recognized Cory Statutory's truck.

Not everyone called him that—just females aged thirteen to fifty-five, almost all of whom had contended with his roving eyes or hands. When he wasn't towing cars or hitting on underage or married women, Cory Marais was in the swamp: fishing, crabbing, tossing beer cans, absorbing the marsh's reptilian putrescence into the crags of his sunburnt skin. He wasn't old but he looked ancient, which made his advances even creepier.

"Y'all need a tow?" He leaned an elbow out the window of his cloud-gray truck. A wad of chewing tobacco sat lodged in his cheek.

Eureka hadn't thought to call a tow truck—probably because Cory's was the only one in town. She didn't understand how he'd found them. They were on a side road hardly anybody drove on. "Are you clairvoyant or something?"

"Eureka Boudreaux and her five-dollar words." Cory

50

glanced at Ander, as if to bond over Eureka's strangeness. But when he looked more closely at the boy, Cory's eyes narrowed, his alliance shifted. "You from outta town?" he asked Ander. "This kid hit you, Reka?"

"It was an accident." Eureka found herself defending Ander. It bothered her when locals thought it was Cajuns versus the World.

"That's not what ol' Big Jean said. He's the one said you needed a tow."

Eureka nodded, her question answered. Big Jean was a sweet old widower who lived in the cabin about a quarter mile off this road. He used to have a hellish wife named Rita, but she'd died about a decade ago and Big Jean didn't get around too well on his own. When Hurricane Rita bulldozed the bayou, Big Jean's house was hit hard. Eureka had heard his hoarse voice say, twenty times, "The only thing meaner than the first Rita was the second Rita. One stayed in my house, the other tore it down."

The town helped him rebuild his cabin, and even though it was miles from shore, he insisted on propping the whole thing up on twenty-foot stilts, muttering, "Lesson learned, lesson learned."

Diana used to bring Big Jean sugar-free pies. Eureka would go with her, play his old Dixieland jazz 78s on his floor console hi-fi. They'd always liked each other.

The last time she'd seen him, his diabetes had been bad,

and she knew he didn't make it down those stairs often. He had a grown son who brought his groceries, but most of the time, Big Jean stayed perched on his porch, in his wheelchair, watching swamp birds through his binoculars. He must have seen the accident and called for the tow. She glanced up at his elevated cabin and saw his robed arm waving.

"Thanks, Big Jean!" she shouted.

Cory was out of his truck and hitching Magda up to his tow. He wore baggy, dark-wash Wranglers and an LSU basketball jersey. His arms were freckled and huge. She watched the way he connected the cables to her undercarriage. She resented his low whistle when he surveyed the damage to Magda's rear.

Cory did everything slowly except hook up his tows, and for once Eureka was grateful in his vicinity. She still held out hope she might make it to school in time for the meet. Twenty minutes left and she still hadn't decided whether to run the race or quit.

Wind rustled the sugarcane. It was nearly *fauchaison,* harvest time. She glanced at Ander, who was watching her with a focus that made her feel nude, and she wondered if he knew this country as well as she did, if he knew that in two weeks farmers would appear on tractors to sever cane stalks at their base, leaving them to grow for another three years into the mazes children ran through. She wondered whether Ander had run through these fields the way she and every bayou kid had. Had he spent the same hours Eureka had spent listening to the arid rustle of their golden stalks, thinking there was no lovelier sound in the world than sugarcane due for its reaping? Or was Ander just passing through?

Once her car was secured, Cory looked at Ander's truck. "Need anything, kid?"

"No, sir, thank you." Ander didn't have the Cajun accent, and his manners were too formal for the country. Eureka wondered if Cory had ever been called "sir" in his life.

"Right, then." Cory sounded offended, as if Ander in general was offensive. "Come on, Reka. You need a ride somewhere? Like to a beauty salon?" He cackled, pointing at her grown-out dye job.

"Shut up, Cory." "Beauty" sounded like "ugly" in his mouth.

"I'm teasing." He reached out to tug her hair, but Eureka flinched away. "That the way girls style it these days? Pretty . . . pretty *interesting*." He hooted, then jerked his thumb toward the passenger-side door of his truck. "Okay, sister, haul it in the cab. Us coon-asses gotta stick together."

Cory's language was disgusting. His truck was disgusting. One glance through the open window told Eureka she did not want a ride in that. There were dirty magazines everywhere, greasy bags of cracklins on the dash. A spearmint air freshener hung from the rearview mirror, leaning on a wooden icon of Saint Theresa. Cory's hands were black with axle grease. He needed the kind of power wash reserved for soot-stained medieval buildings.

"Eureka," Ander said. "I can give you a ride."

She found herself thinking of Rhoda, wondering what she'd say if she were sitting in her shoulder-padded business suit upon Eureka's shoulder. Neither option constituted what Dad's wife would call "a sound decision," but at least Cory was a known phenomenon. And Eureka's sharp reflexes could keep the creep's hands on the wheel.

Then there was Ander. . . .

Why was Eureka thinking about what Rhoda, instead of Diana, would advise? She didn't want to be anything like Rhoda. She wanted to be a lot like her mother, who never talked about safety or judgment. Diana talked about passion and dreams.

And she was gone.

And this was just a ride to school, not a life-changing decision.

Her phone was buzzing. It was Cat: *Wish us luck leaving Manor in the dust. Whole team misses you.*

The race was in eighteen minutes. Eureka intended to wish Cat luck in person, whether or not she ran herself. She gave Ander a quick nod—*Okay*—and walked over to his truck. "Take the car to Sweet Pea's, Cory," she called from the passenger door. "My dad and I will pick it up later."

"Suit yourself." Cory heaved himself into his truck, annoyed. He nodded toward Ander. "Watch out for that dude. He's got a face I'd like to forget."

"I'm sure you will," Ander muttered as he opened the driver's-side door.

The inside of his truck was immaculate. It must have been thirty years old, but the dashboard shone as if it had just been hand-polished. The radio was playing an old Bunk Johnson song. Eureka slid up on the soft leather bench and fastened her seat belt.

"I'm supposed to be back at school already," she said as Ander started up the truck. "Would you step on it? It's faster if you take the—"

"Side roads, I know." Ander turned left down a shady dirt road that Eureka thought of as her shortcut. She watched as he gunned the gas, driving with familiarity on this seldom-traveled, maize-lined road.

"I go to Evangeline High. It's on—"

"Woodvale and Hampton," Ander said. "I know."

She scratched her forehead, wondering suddenly if this kid went to her school, had sat behind her in English for three years in a row or something. But she knew every one of the two hundred and seventy-six people at her small Catholic high school. At least, she knew them all by sight. If someone like Ander went to Evangeline, she would more than know about him. Cat would be absolutely all over him, and so, according to the laws of best friendship, Eureka would have his birthday, his favorite weekend hangout, and his license plate number memorized.

So where did he go to school? Instead of being plastered with bumper stickers or mascot paraphernalia on the dashboard, like most public school kids' cars, Ander's truck looked bare. A simple square tag a few inches wide hung from the rearview mirror. It had a metallic silver background and featured a blue stick figure holding a spear pointed toward the ground. She leaned forward to examine it, noting that it bore the same image on both sides. It smelled like citronella.

"Air freshener," Ander said as Eureka breathed in a whiff. "They give them out free at the car wash."

She settled back in her seat. Ander didn't even have a bag. In fact, Eureka's overstuffed purple tote spoiled the tidiness of the truck.

"I've never seen a kid with such a spotless car. Don't you have homework?" she joked. "Books?"

"I can read books," Ander said curtly.

"Okay, you're literate. Sorry."

Ander frowned and turned up the music. He seemed aloof until she noticed his hand trembling as it moved the dial. He sensed her noticing it and clamped the hand back on the steering wheel, but she could tell: the accident had shaken him up, too.

"You like this kind of music?" she asked as a red-tailed hawk swept across the gray sky in front of them, looking for dinner.

"I like old things." His voice was quiet, uncertain, as he took another fast turn down a gravel road. Eureka glanced at her watch and noted with pleasure that she might actually make it on time. Her body wanted this run; it would help calm her before facing Dad and Rhoda, before she had to break the news about the crumpled heap called Magda. It would make Coach's month if Eureka raced today. Maybe she *could* go back—

Her body lurched forward as Ander slammed on the brakes. His arm shot across the cab of the truck to hold Eureka's body back, the way Diana's arm used to do, and it was startling: his hand on her.

The car squealed to an abrupt stop and Eureka saw why. Ander had hit the brakes to avoid running over one of the plentiful fox squirrels that threaded through Louisiana trees like sunshine. He seemed to realize his arm was still pinning her against the seat. His fingertips pressed into the skin below her shoulder.

He let his hand drop. He caught his breath.

Eureka's four-year-old twin siblings had once spent an entire summer trying to catch one of these squirrels in the backyard. Eureka knew how fast the animals were. They dodged cars twenty times a day. She'd never seen anyone slam on the brakes to avoid hitting one.

The animal seemed surprised, too. It froze, peering into the windshield for an instant, as if to offer thanks. Then it darted up the gray trunk of an oak tree and was gone.

"Say, your brakes work after all." Eureka couldn't stop herself. "Glad the squirrel escaped with tail intact."

Ander swallowed and hit the gas again. He stole long glances at her—unabashed, not like the guys at school, who were sneakier with their staring. He seemed to be searching for words.

"Eureka— I'm sorry."

"Take this left," she said.

He was already turning left down the narrow road. "No, really, I wish I could—"

"It's just a car." She cut him off. They were both on edge. She shouldn't have teased him about the squirrel. He was trying to be more cautious. "They'll fix it up at Sweet Pea's. Anyway, the car's no big deal to me." Ander hung on her words and she realized she sounded like a private school brat, which was not her style. "Believe me, I'm grateful to have my own wheels. It's just, you know, it's a car, that's all."

"No." Ander turned down the music as they entered town and passed Neptune's, the horrible café where Evangeline kids hung out after school. She saw some girls from her Latin class, drinking sodas from red paper cups and hanging over the railing, talking to some older guys with Ray-Bans and muscles. She turned away from them to focus on the road. They were two blocks from school. Soon she'd be out of this truck and sprinting toward the locker room, then the woods. She guessed that meant she'd made up her mind.

"Eureka."

Ander's voice reached her, interrupting her plans on how to change into her uniform as quickly as possible. She wouldn't change her socks, just yank her shorts on, toss off her shirt—

"I mean I'm sorry about everything."

Everything? They had stopped at the back entrance to the school. Outside, past the parking lot, the track was shabby and old. A ring of unlaned, uneven dirt surrounded a sad, brown, disused football field. The cross-country team warmed up here, but their meets took place in the woods beyond the track. Eureka couldn't imagine anything more boring than running around a track over and over again. Coach was always trying to get her to join the relay team in the spring track season, but what was the point of running in circles, never getting anywhere?

The rest of the team was already dressed out, doing stretches or warming up along the straights of the track. Coach was glaring at her clipboard, certainly wondering why she hadn't checked Eureka's name off the roll yet. Cat was yelling at two sophomores who'd drawn something in black Sharpie on the backs of their uniforms—something Cat and Eureka used to get yelled at for doing when they were sophomores themselves.

She unbuckled her seat belt. Ander was sorry, for everything? He meant hitting her car, of course. Nothing more than that. Because how could he know about Diana?

"I gotta go," she said. "I'm late for my—"

"Cross-country meet. I know."

"How did you know that? How do you *know* all these—"

Ander pointed to the Evangeline cross-country emblem stitched into the patch on the side of her bag.

"Oh."

"Also"—Ander turned off the engine—"I'm on the team at Manor."

He walked around the front of the truck and opened the passenger door. She slid out, dumbfounded. He handed over her bag.

"Thanks."

Ander smirked and jogged off toward the side of the field where the Manor High team was gathered. He looked back over his shoulder, a mischievous gleam in his eyes. "You're going down."

5

STORMED OUT

Cat Estes had a particular way of arching her left eyebrow and parking one hand on her hip, which Eureka knew meant *Dish*. Her best friend had a splash of big, dark freckles across her nose, a charming gap between her two front teeth, curves in all sorts of places Eureka didn't, and highlighted hair braided in thick pigtails.

Cat and Eureka lived in the same neighborhood near campus. Cat's father was a professor of African American studies at the university. Cat and her younger brother, Barney, were the only two black kids at Evangeline.

When Cat spotted Eureka—head ducked, sprinting away from Ander's truck in an attempt not to be noticed by Coach— she capped the tirade she'd been directing at the sophomore uniform-violators. Eureka heard her order the girls to do fifty push-ups on their knuckles before she swiveled past them.

"Part the seas, please!" Cat shouted as she plowed through a group of freshman boys staging a lightsaber battle with triangular paper cups. Cat was a sprinter; she caught Eureka's arm just before Eureka ducked into the locker room. She wasn't even out of breath.

"You're back on the team?"

"I told Coach I'd run today," Eureka said. "I don't want to make it a big deal."

"Sure." Cat nodded. "We have other things to talk about anyway." The left eyebrow rose to an astonishing height. The hand slid up the hip.

"You want to know about the guy in the truck," Eureka guessed, swinging open the heavy gray door and pulling her friend inside.

The locker room was empty, but the lingering presence of heat and hormones brought on by so many teenage girls was palpable. Half-open lockers spilled hair dryers, foundation-stained cosmetics cases, and blue sticks of deodorant onto the tan tiled floor. Various items of Evangeline's lenient dress code lay haphazardly on every surface. Eureka hadn't been in here yet this year, but she could easily picture how that skirt got flung across that locker door in the midst of a conversation about a horrible religion exam, or how those oxfords had been unlaced while someone whispered to a friend about a game of Spin the Bottle the Saturday before.

Eureka used to love locker-room gossip; it was as elemental to being on the team as running. Today she was relieved to change in an empty locker room, even if it meant she had to hustle. She dropped her bag and kicked off her shoes.

"Um, *yeah,* I want to know about the guy in the truck." Cat pulled Eureka's running shorts and polo shirt out of her bag helpfully. "And what happened to your face?" She gestured at the airbag scrapes on Eureka's cheekbone and nose. "You'd better get your story straight for Coach."

Eureka flipped her head upside down to gather her long hair into a ponytail. "I already told her I had a doctor's appointment and might be a little late—"

"A lotta late." Cat extended her bare legs across the bench and reached for her toes, settling into a deep stretch. "Forget that. What's the story with Monsieur Stud?"

"He's a moron," Eureka lied. Ander wasn't a moron. He was unusual, hard to read, but not a moron. "He hit me at a stop sign. I'm fine," she added quickly. "Just these scrapes." She ran a finger along her tender cheekbone. "But Magda's totaled. I had to get her towed."

"Ew, no." Cat scrunched up her face. "Cory Statutory?" She wasn't from New Iberia; she'd lived in the same nice house in Lafayette her whole life. But she'd spent enough time in Eureka's hometown to know the local cast of characters.

Eureka nodded. "He offered to give me a ride, but I wasn't going to—"

"No way." Cat understood the impossibility of riding

shotgun in Cory's truck. She shuddered, shaking her head so that her braids whopped her face. "At least Crash—can we call him Crash? Least he gave you a ride."

Eureka tugged her shirt over her head and tucked it into her shorts. She started lacing up her running shoes. "His name is Ander. And nothing happened."

"'Crash' sounds better." Cat squirted sunscreen into her palm and brushed it lightly across Eureka's face, careful of her scrapes.

"He goes to Manor, that's why he drove me here. I'll be racing against him in a few minutes, and I'll probably suck because I'm not warmed up."

"Ooh, it's sooo *race*-y." Suddenly Cat was in her own world, making big hand gestures. "I'm seeing the adrenaline high of the run transforming into burning passion at the finish line. I'm seeing *sweat*. I'm seeing *steam*. Love that 'goes the distance' "—

"Cat," Eureka said. "Enough. What is it with people trying to hook me up today?"

Cat followed Eureka toward the door. "I try to hook you up every day. What's the point of calendars without dates?"

For such a smart, tough girl—Cat had a blue belt in karate, spoke non-Cajun French with an enviable accent, got a scholarship the previous summer to a molecular biology camp at LSU—Eureka's best friend was also a horn-dog romantic. Most kids at Evangeline didn't know how smart she was because her boy-craziness tended to obscure it. She met guys on her way to the bathroom at the movies, didn't own a bra that wasn't full-on lace, and really was trying to fix up everyone she knew all the time. Once, in New Orleans, Cat had even tried to put two homeless people together in Jackson Square.

"Wait"—Cat stopped and tilted her head at Eureka— "who else was trying to set you up? That's my specialty."

Eureka pressed on the metal bar to open the door and stepped out into the humid late afternoon. Low, green-gray clouds still coated the sky. The air had the smell of aching to be a storm. To the west was an alluring pocket of clearness where Eureka could see the sun sneaking lower, turning the sliver of cloud-bare sky a deep shade of violet.

"My wonderful new shrink thinks I have the hots for Brooks," Eureka said.

At the far end of the field, Coach's whistle drew the rest of the team together under the rusted football upright. The visiting team from Manor was gathering in the other end zone. Eureka and Cat would have to pass them, which made Eureka nervous, though she didn't see Ander yet. The girls jogged toward their team, aiming to slide in unnoticed at the back of the huddle.

"You and Brooks?" Cat feigned amazement. "I'm shocked. I mean, I'm just—well, stunned is what I am."

"Cat." Eureka used her serious voice, which made Cat stop jogging. "My mom."

"I know." Cat enveloped Eureka and squeezed. She had skinny arms, but her hugs were mighty.

They'd paused at the bleachers, two long rows of rusty benches on either side of the track. Eureka could hear Coach talking about pacing, the regional meet next month, finding the right position at the starting arc. If Eureka were captain, she'd be talking the team through these topics. She knew prerace drill backward in her sleep, but she couldn't imagine standing up there anymore, saying anything with certainty.

"You're not ready to think about boys yet," Cat said into Eureka's ponytail. "Stupid Cat."

"Don't you start crying." Eureka squeezed Cat harder.

"Okay, okay." Cat sniffed and pulled away. "I know you hate it when I cry."

Eureka flinched. "I don't hate it when you—" She broke off. Her eye caught Ander's as he was coming out of the visitors' locker room on the other side of the track. His uniform didn't quite match the other kids'—his yellow collar looked bleached; his shorts were shorter than those worn by the rest of the team. The uniform seemed dated, like the ones in the fading photographs of cross-country teams of yesteryear that lined the walls of the gym. Maybe it was a hand-me-down from an older brother, but it looked like the kind of thing you picked up at the Salvation Army after some kid graduated and his mom cleaned out his closet so she'd have more room for shoes.

Ander watched Eureka, oblivious to all else around him: his team in the end zone, pregnant clouds pressing closer in the sky, how peculiar it was to stare like that. He didn't seem to realize it was unusual. Or maybe he didn't care.

Eureka did. She dropped her eyes, blushing. She started to jog again. She remembered the sensation of that tear gathering in the corner of her eye, the astonishing touch of his finger against the side of her nose. Why had she cried on the road that afternoon when she hadn't been tempted to cry at her own mother's funeral? She hadn't cried when they'd kept her locked up in that asylum for two weeks. She hadn't cried since . . . the night Diana had slapped her and moved out of the house.

"Uh-oh," Cat said.

"Don't stare back at him," Eureka muttered, certain Cat was referring to Ander.

"Him who?" Cat whispered. "I'm talking about Sorceress over there. Don't engage and she might not see us. Don't look, Eureka, don't—"

You can't not look when someone tells you not to, but one swift glance made Eureka regret it.

"Too late," Cat mumbled.

"Bou*dreaux*."

Eureka's last name seemed to shudder like a shock wave across the field.

Maya Cayce had a voice as deep as a teenage boy's—it

67

could fool you until you caught a glimpse of her face. Some never fully recovered from that first glimpse. Maya Cayce was extraordinary, with thick, dark hair that hung in loose waves all the way down to her waist. She was notorious for her fast clip down the hallways at school, her surprising, slender grace thanks to legs that stretched for decades. Her smooth, bright skin bore ten of the most intricately beautiful tattoos Eureka had ever seen—including a braid of three different feathers running down her forearm, a small cameo-style portrait of her mother on her shoulder, and a peacock inside a peacock feather underneath her collarbone—all of which she'd designed herself and had done at a place called Electric Ladyland in New Orleans. She was a senior, a roller-skater, a rumored Wiccan, a transcender of all cliques, a contralto in the choir, a state-champion equestrian, and she hated Eureka Boudreaux.

"Maya." Eureka nodded but didn't slow down.

In her peripheral vision, Eureka sensed Maya Cayce rising from the edge of the bleachers. She saw the black blur of the girl taking long strides to stop in front of her.

Eureka skidded to avoid a collision. "Yes?"

"Where is he?" Maya wore a micro-length, flowy black dress with extra-long, extra-flared bell sleeves, and no makeup, save for a coat of black mascara. She batted her eyes.

She was looking for Brooks. She was always looking for Brooks. How she could still be hung up on Eureka's oldest friend after they'd been out but twice last year was one of the galaxy's most inscrutable mysteries. Brooks was boy-next-door sweet. Maya Cayce was spellbinding. And yet, somehow, she was deranged for the boy.

"I haven't seen him," Eureka said. "Perhaps you've noticed that I'm on the cross-country team, which is about to begin a race?"

"We can maybe help you stalk him later." Cat tried to angle past Maya, who was over a foot taller than Cat in her six-inch platform wedges. "Oh, wait, no, I'm busy tonight. Signed up for this webinar. Sorry, Maya, you're on your own."

Maya raised her chin, seeming to weigh whether to take this as an insult. If you studied her small, lovely features individually, she actually looked far younger than seventeen.

"I prefer to work alone." Maya Cayce looked down her nose at Cat. Her perfume smelled like patchouli. "He mentioned he might stop by, and I thought Freak Show here"—she pointed at Eureka—"might have—"

"I haven't." Eureka remembered now that Brooks was the one person she'd confided in about her agreement with Coach. He hadn't told her he'd planned on coming to the meet, but it was a sweet gesture if he was. Sweet until you added Maya Cayce; then things soured.

As Eureka pushed past, something swatted the back of her head, just above her ponytail. Slowly she spun around to see Maya Cayce's palm retreat. Eureka's cheeks blazed. Her head stung, but her pride ached. "Is there something you want to say, Maya, maybe to my face?"

"Oh." Maya Cayce's husky voice softened, sweetened. "You had a mosquito on your scalp. You know they carry diseases, flock to standing water."

Cat snorted, grabbing Eureka's hand and pulling her down the field. She called over her shoulder: "You're malarious, Maya! Call us when you get a stand-up gig."

The sad thing was, Eureka and Maya used to be friends, before they'd started Evangeline, before Maya had entered puberty a dark-haired angel and exited an unapproachable Goth goddess. They used to be two seven-year-old girls taking theater at the university summer camp. They'd traded lunches every day—Eureka would swap Dad's elaborate turkey clubs for Maya's white bread PB&Js in a heartbeat. But she doubted Maya Cayce remembered that.

"Estes!" The shrill screech of Coach Spence—Eureka knew it well.

"Let's do it, Coach," Cat responded with zest.

"Loved your pep talk," Coach barked to Cat. "Next time try to be a little more *present* for it?" Before Coach could rail on any further, she spotted Eureka at Cat's side. Her grimace didn't soften, but her voice did. "Glad you're here, Boudreaux," she called past the other students' turning heads. "Just in time for a quick yearbook picture before the race."

Everyone's eyes were on Eureka. She was still flushed from

her interaction with Maya, and the weight of so many gazes made her claustrophobic. A few of her teammates whispered, like Eureka was bad luck. Kids who used to be her friends were scared of her now. Maybe they didn't *want* her back.

Eureka felt tricked. A yearbook picture hadn't been part of her deal with Coach. She saw the photographer, a man in his fifties with a short black ponytail, setting up a massive flash apparatus. She imagined huddling into one of the lines alongside these other kids, the bright light going off in her face. She imagined the photo being printed in three hundred yearbooks, imagined future generations flipping the pages. Before the accident, Eureka never thought twice about posing for the camera; her face contorted into smiles, smirks, and air kisses all over friends' Facebook and Instagram pages. But now?

The permanence this single photo would imply made Eureka feel like an imposter. It made her want to run away. She had to quit the team right now, before there was any documentation that she'd intended to run this year. She imagined the lie of her high school résumé—Latin Club, cross-country team, a list of honors classes. Survivor's guilt, the one extra-curricular activity Eureka *was* invested in, was nowhere in that file. She stiffened so it wouldn't be obvious she was shaking.

Cat's hand was on her shoulder. "What's wrong?"

"I can't be in this picture."

"What's the big deal?"

Eureka took a few steps backward. "I just can't."

"It's only a picture."

Eureka's and Cat's eyes lifted skyward as the sharpest crack of thunder shook the field. A wall of cloud burst open over the track. It began to pour.

"Just perfect!" Coach shouted at the sky. The photographer raced to cover his equipment with a thin wool blazer. The team around Eureka scattered like ants. Through the rain, Eureka met Coach's steely eyes. Slowly she shook her head. *I'm sorry*, it meant, *this time I really quit.*

Caught in the storm, some kids were laughing. Others shrieked. Within moments, Eureka was soaked. At first the rain was cold on her skin, but after she was drenched, her body warmed the way it did when she was swimming.

She could hardly see across the field. Sheets of rain looked like chain mail. The triple tweet of a whistle sounded from the huddle of the Manor kids. Coach Spence triple whistled back. It was official: the storm had won the meet.

"Everybody back inside!" Coach bellowed, but the team was already sprinting for the locker room.

Eureka sloshed through mud. She'd lost Cat. Halfway across the field, something shimmered in the corner of her eye. She turned to see a boy standing there alone, gazing up into the torrent.

It was Ander. She didn't understand how she could see

him clearly when the world around her had become Niagara Falls. Then she noticed something strange:

Ander wasn't wet. Rain cascaded around him, pummeling the mud at his feet. But his hair, his clothes, his hands, his face were as dry as they had been when he stood on the dirt road and reached out to catch her tear.

6

SHELTER

By the time Cat dropped Eureka at home, the rain had dwindled from deluge to downpour. Truck tires on the main road behind their neighborhood hissed against wet pavement. The begonias in Dad's flower bed were trampled. The air was dank and briny from the salt plug south of Lafayette where the Tabasco plant got its seasoning.

From her doorstep, Eureka waved to Cat, who responded with two toots on the horn. Dad's old Lincoln Continental was sitting in the driveway. Rhoda's cherry-red Mazda, mercifully, was not.

Eureka turned her key in the bronze lock and shoved the door, which always stuck when it stormed. It was easier to open from the inside, where you could rattle the handle a certain way. From the outside you had to push like a line-backer.

As soon as she was inside, she kicked off her soggy running shoes and socks, noticing that the rest of her family had had the same idea. Her half brother's and half sister's matching Velcro sneakers had been flung to all corners of the foyer. Their tiny socks were balled up like stamped-on roses. The untied laces of her dad's heavy black work boots had left short snakes of mud across the marble tile, slithering toward where he'd tossed them at the entrance to the den. Raincoats dripped from their wooden pegs along the wall. William's navy-blue one had a reversible camouflage lining; Claire's was pale violet with white appliqué flowers on the hood. Dad's draping black hand-me-down slicker came from his own dad's days in the Marines. Eureka added her heather-gray raincoat to the last peg in the row, dropped her track bag on Rhoda's antique entry bench. She sensed the glow of the TV in the den, its volume low.

The house smelled like popcorn—the twins' favorite after-school snack. But Eureka's chef dad didn't prepare anything plainly. His popcorn exploded with truffle oil and shaved Parmesan, or chopped pretzels and chewy flecks of caramel. Today's batch smelled like curry and toasted almonds. Dad communicated through food better than through words. Creating something majestic in the kitchen was his way of showing love.

She found him and the twins nestled in their usual spots on the enormous suede couch. Dad, stripped to dry clothes—gray boxers and white T-shirt—was asleep on the long end of the L-shaped couch. His hands were clasped over his chest and his bare feet were turned out, pointed up like shovels. A soft buzz purred from his nose.

The lights were off, and the storm outside made everything darker than usual, but a fading, crackling fire kept the room warm. An old *Price Is Right* played on the Game Show Network—certainly not one of the three half-hour programs endorsed by the parenting magazines Rhoda subscribed to—but none of them would tell.

Claire sat next to her dad, a triangle of stubby legs in the corner of the couch, knees splayed out from her orange jumper, fingers and lips golden from the curry. She looked like a piece of candy corn, a shock of white-blond hair piled on top of her head with a yellow barrette. She was four years old and an excellent sport about TV watching but nothing else. She had her mother's jaw, and clenched it the way Rhoda did when she finished making a point.

On the near side of the couch was William, his feet hovering a foot above the floor. His dark brown hair needed cutting. He kept blowing puffs of air out the side of his mouth to keep his hair out of his eyes. Other than that, he sat still, his hands folded in a neat cup on his lap. He was nine minutes older than Claire, careful and diplomatic, always occupying as little space as possible. There was a mangled stack of cards on the coffee table next to the bowl of popcorn, and Eureka knew that he'd been practicing a lineup of magic tricks he'd learned from a library book published in the fifties.

"Eureka!" he whisper-sang, sliding off the couch to run to her. She picked her brother up and twirled him around, holding the still-damp back of his head in her hand.

One might think Eureka would resent these kids for being the reason Dad was married to Rhoda. Back when the twins had been two beans inside Rhoda, Eureka *had* sworn she'd never have anything to do with them. They were born on the first day of spring when she was thirteen years old. Eureka had shocked her dad, Rhoda, and herself by falling in love the moment she'd held each infant's tiny hand.

"I'm thirsty," Claire called, without looking up from the TV.

Sure, they were annoying, but when Eureka was down the foxhole of her depression, the twins managed to remind her that she was good for something.

"I'll get you some milk." Eureka put William down and the two of them padded to the kitchen. She poured three cups of milk from Rhoda's organized refrigerator, where no Tupperware ventured unlabeled, and let in their soaking-wet Labradoodle, Squat, from the backyard. He shook out his fur, flinging muddy water and leaves across the kitchen walls.

Eureka looked at him. "I didn't see that."

Back in the den, she turned on the small wooden lamp over the fireplace and leaned against the arm of the couch. Her father looked young and handsome asleep, more like the dad she'd worshipped as a girl than the man she'd struggled to connect with in the five years since he'd married Rhoda.

She remembered the way Uncle Travis had pulled her aside, unprompted, at Dad's wedding. "You might not be not crazy about sharing your daddy with someone else," he'd said. "But a man needs taking care of, and Trenton's been alone a long time."

Eureka had been twelve. She hadn't understood what Travis meant. She was always with her dad, so how could he be alone? She wasn't even conscious of not wanting him to marry Rhoda that day. She was conscious of it now.

"Hey, Dad."

His dark blue eyes shot open and Eureka registered the fear in them when he startled, as if he'd been released from the same nightmare she'd been having for the past four months. But they didn't speak about those things.

"I think I fell asleep," he mumbled, sitting up and rubbing his eyes. He reached for the bowl of popcorn, handed it to her as if it were a greeting, as if it were a hug.

"I noticed," she said, tossing a handful into her mouth. Most days Dad worked ten-hour shifts at the restaurant, starting at six in the morning.

"You called earlier," he said. "Sorry I missed you. I tried you soon as I got off work." He blinked. "What happened to your face?"

"It's nothing. Just a scratch." Eureka avoided his eyes and crossed the den to dig her phone from her bag. She had two missed calls from Dad, one from Brooks, and five from Rhoda.

She was as tired as if she had run the race this afternoon. The last thing she wanted to do was relive today's accident for Dad. He'd always been protective, but since Diana's death, he'd crossed the line into overly.

To call Dad's attention to the fact that there were people out there who drove like Ander might cause him to permanently revoke her use of any car. She knew she had to broach the subject, but she had to handle it just right.

Dad followed her into the foyer. He stood a few feet away and shuffled William's deck of cards, leaning against one of the columns that held up the faux-frescoed ceiling neither one of them could stand.

His name was Trenton Michel Boudreaux the Third. He had a defining slimness that he'd passed on to all three of his kids. He was tall, with wiry, dark blond hair and a smile that could charm a copperhead. You'd have to be blind not to notice how women flirted with him. Maybe Dad was trying to be blind to it—he always closed his eyes when he laughed off their advances.

"Track meet rained out?"

Eureka nodded.

"I know you were looking forward to it. I'm sorry."

Eureka rolled her eyes, because ever since Dad had married Rhoda he knew basically nothing about her. "Looking forward to it" was not a phrase Eureka would use about anything anymore. He'd never understand why she had to quit the team.

"How was your"—Dad glanced over his shoulder at the twins, who were absorbed in Bob Barker's description of the obsolete motor boat his contestant might win—"your . . . appointment today?"

Eureka thought about the crap she'd sat through in Dr. Landry's office, including Dad's *tough nut to crack*. It was another betrayal; everything with Dad was, now. How could he have married that woman?

But Eureka also understood: Rhoda was the opposite of Diana. She was stable, grounded, not going anywhere. Diana had loved him but not needed him. Rhoda needed him so much maybe it became a kind of love. Dad seemed lighter with Rhoda than he had without her. Eureka wondered if he ever noticed it had cost him his daughter's trust.

"Tell me the truth," Dad said.

"Why? It's not like complaining to you will get me out of going. Not in this Rhodeo."

"Was it that bad?"

"Suddenly you care?" she snapped.

"Baby, of course I care." He reached out but she jerked away.

"Baby *them*." Eureka waved a hand toward the twins. "I can take care of myself."

He handed her the cards. It was a stress killer, and he knew she could make them sail like birds between her hands. The deck was flexible from years of use and warm from his shuffling. Without her realizing, cards began to whir through Eureka's fingers.

"Your face." Dad studied the abrasions on her cheekbones.

"It's nothing."

He touched her cheek.

She calmed the flying cards. "I got in an accident on the way back to school."

"Eureka." Dad's voice rose and he folded her into his arms. He didn't seem angry. "Are you all right?"

"I'm fine." He was squeezing too tight. "It wasn't my fault. This boy ran into me at a stop sign. That's why I called earlier, but I took care of it. Magda's at Sweet Pea's. It's okay."

"You got this guy's insurance?"

Until that moment, Eureka had been proud of herself for handling the car without Dad's lifting a finger to help. She swallowed. "Not exactly."

"Eureka."

"I tried. He didn't have any. He said he'd take care of it, though."

Watching Dad's face tense in disappointment, Eureka realized how stupid she'd been. She didn't even know how to get in touch with Ander, had no idea what his last name was or whether he'd given her his real first name. There was no way he was going to take care of her car.

Dad ground his teeth the way he did when he was trying to control his temper. "Who was this boy?"

"He said his name was Ander." She set the cards down on the entry bench and tried to retreat up the stairs. Her college applications were waiting on her desk. Even though Eureka had decided she wanted to take next year off, Rhoda insisted she apply to UL, where she could get financial aid as a faculty family member. Brooks had also filled out most of an online application to Tulane—his dream school—in Eureka's name. All Eureka had to do was sign the printed-out last page, which had been glaring at her for weeks. She couldn't face college. She could barely face her own reflection in the mirror.

Before she climbed the first step, Dad caught her arm. "Ander who?"

"He goes to Manor."

Dad seemed to blink a bad thought away. "What matters most is you're okay."

Eureka shrugged. He didn't get it. Today's accident hadn't made her any more or less okay than she'd been the day be-

82

fore. She hated that talking to him felt like lying. She used to tell him everything.

"Don't worry, Cuttlefish." The old nickname sounded forced coming from Dad's lips. Sugar had made it up when Eureka was a baby, but Dad hadn't called her that in a decade. No one called her Cuttlefish anymore, except for Brooks.

The doorbell chimed. A tall figure appeared through the frosted glass door.

"I'll call the insurance company," Dad said. "You answer the door."

Eureka sighed and unlocked the front door, rattling the knob to get it open. She glanced up at the tall boy on the porch.

"Hey, Cuttlefish."

Noah Brooks—known to everyone outside his family simply as Brooks—had been weaned of his most extreme bayou accent when he started ninth grade in Lafayette. But when he called Eureka by her nickname, it still came out sounding just the way Sugar used to say it: soft and rushed and breezy.

"Hey, Powder Keg," she responded automatically, using the boyhood nickname Brooks had earned for the tantrum he'd thrown at his third birthday party. Diana used to say that Eureka and Brooks had been friends since the womb. Brooks's parents lived next door to Diana's parents, and when Eureka's mom was young and newly pregnant, she'd spent a few evenings sitting on log ends on the veranda playing gin with Brooks's mom, Aileen, who was two months further along.

He had a narrow face, a year-round tan, and, recently, a hint of stubble on his chin. His deep brown eyes matched hair that brushed the limits of Evangeline's dress code. It fell down along his eyebrows when he lifted the hood of his yellow raincoat.

Eureka noticed a large bandage on Brooks's forehead, almost obscured by his bangs. "What happened?"

"Nothing much." He eyed the scratches on her face, his eyebrows arching at the coincidence. "You?"

"Same." She shrugged.

Kids at Evangeline thought Brooks was mysterious, which had made him the object of several girls' admiration over the past few years. Everyone who knew him liked him, but Brooks avoided the popular crowd, which deemed it uncool to do anything besides play football. He was friends with the guys on the debate team, but mostly he hung out with Eureka.

Brooks was selective with his sweetness, and Eureka had always been a prime recipient. Sometimes she saw him in the hallway, joking with a cloud of boys, and she almost didn't recognize him—until he spotted her and broke through to tell her everything about his day.

"Hey"—he held up her right hand lightly—"look who got her cast off."

In the foyer's chandelier light, Eureka was suddenly

ashamed of her skinny, weird arm. She looked like a hatchling. But Brooks didn't seem to see anything wrong with it. He didn't look at her differently after the accident—or after the psych ward. When she'd been locked up at Acadia Vermilion, Brooks came to visit every day, sneaking her pecan pralines tucked inside his jeans pocket. The only thing he ever said about what happened was that it was more fun to hang out with her outside a padded cell.

It was like he could see past Eureka's changing hair color, the makeup she now donned like armor, the perma-frown that kept most everyone else away. To Brooks, the cast was a good thing to be free of, no downside. He grinned. "Wanna arm-wrestle?"

She swatted him.

"Just kidding." He kicked off his tennis shoes next to hers and hung his raincoat on the same hook she'd used. "Come on, let's go watch the storm."

As soon as Brooks and Eureka walked into the den, the twins looked up from the TV and leapt from the couch. If there was one thing Claire loved more than television, it was Brooks.

"Evenin', Harrington-Boudreauxs." Brooks bowed at the kids, calling them by their ridiculous hyphenated name, which sounded like an overpriced restaurant.

"Brooks and I are going to go look for alligators by the water," Eureka said, using their code phrase. The twins were terrified of alligators and it was the easiest way to keep them from following. William's green eyes widened. Claire backed away, resting her elbows on the couch.

"You guys want to come?" Brooks played along. "The big ones crawl up on land when the weather's like this." He held his arms out as wide as they would go to suggest the phantom alligators' size. "They can travel, too. Thirty-five miles an hour."

Claire squealed, her face bright with envy.

William tugged Eureka's sleeve. "Promise you'll tell us if you see any?"

"Sure thing." Eureka tousled his hair and followed Brooks outside.

They passed the kitchen, where Dad was on the phone. He gave Brooks a measured glance, nodded, then turned his back to listen more closely to the insurance agent. Dad was chummy with Eureka's female friends, but boys—even Brooks, who'd been around forever—brought out his cautious side.

Out back, the night was quiet, steady rain hushing everything. Eureka and Brooks drifted to the white swinging bench, which was sheltered by the upstairs deck. It creaked under their weight. Brooks kicked lightly to start it swinging, and they watched raindrops die on the begonia border. Beyond the begonias was a small yard with a bare-bones swing set Dad had built last summer. Beyond the swing set, a wrought-iron gate opened onto the twisting brown bayou.

"Sorry I missed your meet today," Brooks said.

"You know who was sorrier? Maya Cayce." Eureka leaned her head against the worn pillow padding the bench. "She was looking for you. And hexing me simultaneously. Talented girl."

"Come on. She's not that bad."

"You know what the cross-country team calls her?" Eureka said.

"I'm not interested in names called by people afraid of anyone who looks different than they do." Brooks turned to study her. "Didn't think you would be, either."

Eureka huffed because he was right.

"She's jealous of you," Brooks added.

This had never occurred to Eureka. "Why would Maya Cayce be jealous of me?"

Brooks didn't answer. Mosquitoes swarmed the light fixture over their heads. The rain paused, then resumed in a rich breeze that misted Eureka's cheekbones. The wet fronds of the palm trees in the yard waved to greet the wind.

"So what was your time today?" Brooks asked. "Personal best, no doubt, now that you got that cast off." She could tell from the way he was watching her that he was waiting for confirmation that she'd rejoined the team.

"Zero point zero zero seconds."

"You really quit?" He sounded sad.

"Actually, the meet was rained out. Surely you noticed the torrential downpour? The one about fifty times wilder than this? But, yeah"—she kicked the porch to swing higher—"also I quit."

"Eureka."

"How did you miss that storm, anyway?"

Brooks shrugged. "I had debate practice, so I left school late. Then, when I was going down the stairs by the Arts wing, I got dizzy." He swallowed, seeming almost embarrassed to continue. "I don't know what happened, but I woke up at the bottom of the stairs. This freshman found me there."

"Did you hurt yourself?" Eureka asked. "Is that what happened to your forehead?"

Brooks pushed the hair back from his forehead to expose a two-inch square of gauze. When he peeled back the bandage, Eureka gasped.

She wasn't prepared to see a wound that size. It was deep, bright pink, almost a perfect circle about the size of a silver dollar. Rings of pus and blood inside gave it the appearance of an ancient redwood's stripped trunk.

"What did you do, dive into an anvil? You just fell down, out of the blue? That's scary." She reached to brush his long bangs back from his forehead and studied the wound. "You should see a doctor."

"Way ahead of you, Toots. Spent two hours in the ER,

thanks to the panicked kid who discovered me. They say I'm hypoglycemic or some crap like that."

"Is that serious?"

"Nah," Brooks leapt from the swing, pulling Eureka off the porch and into the rain. "Come on, let's go catch us an alligator."

Her wet hair was slung down her back and she yelped, laughing as she ran with Brooks off the porch, down the short flight of stairs to the grassy yard. The grass was high, tickling Eureka's feet. The sprinklers were going off in the rain.

The yard around them was punctuated by four huge heritage oak trees. Orange hallelujah ferns, shimmering with raindrops, laced their trunks. Eureka and Brooks were out of breath when they stopped at the wrought-iron gate and looked up at the sky. Where the clouds were clearing, the night was starry, and Eureka thought there wasn't anyone in the world who could make her laugh anymore except for Brooks. She imagined a glass dome lowering from the sky, sealing the yard like a snow globe, capturing the two of them in this moment forever, with the rain eternally falling down, and nothing else to deal with but the starlight and the mischief in Brooks's eyes.

The back door opened and Claire stuck out her towhead.

"Reka," she called. The porch light made her round cheeks glow. "Is the alligator there?"

Eureka and Brooks shared a smile in the darkness. "No, Claire. It's safe to come out."

With extreme caution, the girl tiptoed as far as the edge of the doormat. She leaned forward and cupped her hands over her mouth to project her voice. "There's someone at the door. A boy. He wants to see you."

7

REUNION

"You."

Eureka dripped on the doorway's marble tile, staring at the boy who'd hit her car. Ander had changed back into the pressed white shirt and dark jeans. He must have hung up that creaseless shirt in the locker room; no one did that on her team.

Standing on the trellised porch in the dusk, Ander looked like he'd come from another world, one where appearance wasn't subject to the weather. He seemed independent of the atmosphere around him. Eureka became self-conscious of her tangled hair, her bare, mud-splattered feet.

The way his hands were clasped behind his back accentuated the span of his chest and shoulders. His expression was inscrutable. He seemed to be holding his breath. It made Eureka nervous.

Maybe it was the turquoise of his eyes. Maybe it was the absurd commitment with which he'd averted that squirrel's doom. Maybe it was the way he looked at her, like he saw something she hadn't known she yearned to see in herself. In an instant, this boy had gotten to her. He made her feel extreme.

How had she gone from being furious at him to chuckling with him before she'd even known his name? That wasn't something Eureka did.

Ander's eyes warmed, finding hers. Her body tingled. The doorknob she gripped felt like it was heated from within.

"How did you know where I lived?"

He opened his mouth to reply, but then Eureka sensed Brooks behind her in the doorway. His chest brushed her shoulder blade as he rested his left hand against the doorframe. His body spanned hers. He was as wet as she was from the storm. He peered over Eureka's head at Ander.

"Who's this?"

The blood drained from Ander's face, making his already pale skin ghostly. Though his body hardly moved, his whole demeanor changed. His chin lifted slightly, sending his shoulders a centimeter back. His knees bent as if he were about to jump.

Something cold and poisonous had taken hold of him.

His glare at Brooks made Eureka wonder if she'd ever seen fury before that moment.

No one fought with Brooks. People fought with his redneck friends at Wade's Hole on weekends. They fought with his brother, Seth, who had the same sharp tongue that got Brooks into trouble, but none of the brains that got him off the hook. In the seventeen years Eureka had known Brooks, he had never once thrown or received a punch. He edged closer against her, straightening his shoulders as if all that were about to change.

Ander flicked a gaze above Brooks's eyes. Eureka glanced over her shoulder and saw that Brooks's open wound was visible. The hair that usually fell across his brow was wet and swept to the side. The bandage he'd peeled back must have come off when they were running through the rain.

"Is there a problem?" Brooks asked, laying a hand on Eureka's shoulder with more possession than he'd used since their one date to see *Charlie and the Chocolate Factory* at the New Iberia Playhouse in fifth grade.

Ander's face twitched. He released his hands from behind his back, and for a moment Eureka knew he was going to punch Brooks. Would she duck or try to block it?

Instead he held out her wallet. "You left this in my truck."

The wallet was a faded brown leather bifold that Diana had brought back from a trip to Machu Picchu. Eureka lost and found the wallet—and her keys and sunglasses and phone—with a regularity that bewildered Rhoda, so it wasn't a huge shock that she'd left it in Ander's truck.

"Thanks." She reached to take the wallet from him, and when their fingertips touched, Eureka shivered. There was an electricity between them she hoped Brooks couldn't see. She didn't know where it came from; she didn't want to turn it off.

"Your address was on your license, so I thought I'd come by and return it," he said. "Also, I wrote down my phone number and put it in there."

Behind her, Brooks coughed into his fist.

"For the car," Ander explained. "When you get an estimate, call me." He smiled so warmly that Eureka grinned back like a village idiot.

"Who is this guy, Eureka?" Brooks's voice was higher than normal. He seemed to be looking for a way to make fun of Ander. "What's he talking about?"

"He, uh, rear-ended me," Eureka mumbled, as mortified in front of Ander as if Brooks were Rhoda or Dad, not her oldest friend. She was getting claustrophobic with him standing over her like that.

"I gave her a lift back to school," Ander said to Brooks. "But I don't see what it has to do with you. Unless you'd rather she'd walked?"

Brooks was caught off guard. An exasperated laugh escaped his lips.

Then Ander lurched forward, his arm shooting over Eureka's head. He grabbed Brooks by the neck of his T-shirt. "How long have you been with her? *How long?*"

Eureka shrank between them, startled by the outburst. What was Ander talking about? She should do something to defuse the situation. But what? She didn't realize she was leaning instinctively backward against the safe familiarity of Brooks's chest until she felt his hand on her elbow.

He did not flinch when Ander came at him. He muttered, "Long enough to know that assholes aren't her type."

The three of them were practically stacked on top of each other. Eureka could feel both of them breathing. Brooks smelled like rain and Eureka's entire childhood; Ander smelled like an ocean she'd never seen. Both of them were too close. She needed air.

She looked up at the strange, pale boy. Their eyes connected. She shook her head at Ander slightly, asking why.

She heard the rustle of his fingers loosening from Brooks's shirt. Ander took a few stiff steps backward until he was at the edge of the porch. Eureka took her first breath in what seemed like an hour.

"I'm sorry," Ander said. "I didn't come here for a fight. I just wanted to give you back your things and to tell you how to reach me."

Eureka watched him turn and reenter the gray drizzle. When his truck door slammed, she closed her eyes and imagined herself inside it. She could almost feel the warm, soft leather underneath her, hear local legend Bunk Johnson's trumpet on the radio. She imagined the view through the windshield as Ander drove under Lafayette's canopy of oak trees toward wherever was home. She wanted to know what it looked like, what color the sheets on his bed were, whether his mom was cooking dinner. Even after the way he'd just acted toward Brooks, Eureka longed to be back in that truck.

"Exit psychopath," Brooks muttered.

She watched Ander's taillights disappear into the world beyond her street.

Brooks massaged her shoulders. "When can we hang out with him again?"

Eureka weighed the overstuffed wallet in her hands. She imagined Ander going through it, looking at her library card, her horrifying student ID picture, receipts from the gas station where she bought mountains of Mentos, movie stubs from embarrassing chick flicks Cat dragged her to see at the dollar theater, endless pennies in the change pouch, a few bucks if she was lucky, the quartet of black-and-white photo booth pictures of her and her mother taken at a street fair in New Orleans the year before Diana died.

"Eureka?" Brooks said.

"What?"

He blinked, surprised by the sharpness in her voice. "Are you okay?"

Eureka walked to the edge of the porch and leaned on the white wooden balustrade. She breathed in the high rosemary bush and ran a palm over its branches, scattering the raindrops that clung to them. Brooks closed the screen door behind him. He walked over to her and the two of them stared out at the wet road.

The rain had stopped. Evening was falling over Lafayette. A golden half-moon searched for its place in the sky.

Eureka's neighborhood ran along a single road—Shady Circle—which formed an oblong loop and shot off a few short cul-de-sacs along the way. Everybody recognized everybody else, everybody waved, but they weren't up in each other's business as much as the people in Brooks's neighborhood in New Iberia would be. Her house was on the west side of Shady Circle, backing up against a narrow slip of bayou. Her front yard faced another front yard across the street, and through her neighbors' kitchen window Eureka could see Mrs. LeBlanc, wearing lipstick and a tight floral apron, stirring something on the stovetop.

Mrs. LeBlanc taught a catechism class at St. Edmond's. She had a daughter a few years older than the twins, whom she dressed in chic outfits that matched her own. The LeBlancs were nothing like Eureka and Diana used to be—aside, maybe, from their clear adoration of each other—and yet, since the accident, Eureka found her mother-daughter neighbors fascinating. She'd stare out her bedroom window, watch them leaving for church. Their high blond ponytails shone in precisely the same way.

"Is something wrong?" Brooks nudged her knee with his.

Eureka pivoted to look him in the eye. "Why were you so hostile to him?"

"Me?" Brooks flattened a hand against his chest. "Are you serious? He—I—"

"You were standing over me like some possessive older brother. You could have introduced yourself."

"Are we in the same dimension? The guy grabbed me like he wanted to bash me up against the wall. For no reason!" He shook his head. "What's with you? Are you into him or something?"

"No." She knew she was blushing.

"Good, because he could be spending homecoming in solitary confinement."

"Okay, point taken." Eureka gave him a light shove.

Brooks feigned stumbling backward, as if she'd pushed him hard. "Speaking of violent criminals—" Then he came at her, grabbing her waist and lifting her off the ground. He hauled her over his shoulder the way he'd been doing since his fifth-grade growth spurt gave him a half a foot on the rest of their class. He spun Eureka on the porch until she yelped for him to stop.

"Come on." She was upside down and kicking. "He wasn't that bad."

Brooks slid her to the ground and stepped away. His smile disappeared. "You totally want that wing nut."

"I do not." She stuffed the wallet in the pocket of her cardigan. She was dying to look at the phone number. "You're right. I don't know what his problem was."

Brooks leaned his back against the balustrade, tapping the heel of one foot against the toes of the other. He brushed his wet hair from his eyes. His wound blazed orange, yellow, and red, like a fire. They were quiet until Eureka heard muffled music. Was that Maya Cayce's husky voice covering Hank Williams's "I'm So Lonesome I Could Cry"?

Brooks pulled his buzzing phone from his pocket. Eureka caught a glimpse of sultry eyes in the photo on the display. He silenced the call and glanced up at Eureka. "Don't give me that look. We're just friends."

"Do all your friends get to record their own ringtones?" She wished she could have filtered the sarcasm from her voice, but it got through.

"You think I'm lying? That I'm secretly dating her?"

"I have eyes, Brooks. If I were a guy, I'd be into her, too. You don't have to pretend she isn't blazingly attractive."

"Is there something slightly more direct you want to say?"

Yes, but she didn't know what.

"I've got homework" was what she did say, more coldly than she meant it.

"Yeah. Me too." He pushed hard on the front door to

open it, grabbed his raincoat and his shoes. He paused at the edge of the porch, like he was going to say something more, but then they saw Rhoda's red car speeding up the street.

"Think I'll skedaddle," he said.

"See ya." Eureka waved.

As Brooks skipped off the porch, he called over his shoulder: "For what it's worth, I would love a ringtone of you singing."

"You hate my voice," she called.

He shook his head. "Your voice is enchantingly off-key. There's not a thing about you I could ever hate."

When Rhoda turned into their driveway, wearing her big sunglasses even though the moon was out, Brooks flashed her an exaggerated grin and wave, then jogged toward his car— his grandmother's emerald-and-gold, early-nineties slope-back Cadillac, which everyone called the Duchess.

Eureka started up the steps, hoping to make it upstairs and behind the closed door of her room before Rhoda exited the car. But Dad's wife was too efficient. Eureka had barely closed the screen door when Rhoda's voice blasted through the night.

"Eureka? I need a hand."

Eureka turned slowly, hopscotching along the circular bricks lining the garden, then stopped a few feet from Rhoda's car. She heard Maya Cayce's ringtone—again. Somebody sure wasn't concerned about seeming overeager.

Eureka watched Brooks close the Duchess's door. She couldn't hear the song anymore, couldn't see whether he'd answered the phone.

Her eyes were still following his taillights when a plastic-cased stack of dry cleaning landed in her arms. It smelled like chemicals and those mints they had at the register at the Chinese buffet. Rhoda slid grocery bag handles up her own arms and slung her heavy laptop case over Eureka's shoulder.

"Were you trying to hide from me?" Rhoda raised an eyebrow.

"If you'd rather I bailed on my homework, I can hang out here all night."

"Mmm-hmm." Rhoda had on the Atlantic-salmon-colored skirt suit today, and black heels that managed to look both uncomfortable and unfashionable. Her dark hair was swept into a twist that always reminded Eureka of an Indian burn. She was really pretty, and sometimes Eureka could even see it—when Rhoda was sleeping, or in the trance of watching her children, the rare moments when her face relaxed. But most of the time, Rhoda just looked late for something. She wore this orangey lipstick, which had worn off while she was instructing tonight's business class at the university. Little tributaries of faded orange ran down the creases of her lips.

"I called you five times," Rhoda said, slamming the car door closed with her hip. "You didn't pick up."

"I had a meet."

Rhoda clicked the lock button on her remote. "It looks like you were just bumming around with Brooks. You know it's a school night. What happened with the therapist? I hope you didn't do anything to embarrass me."

Eureka glanced at Rhoda's lip tributaries, imagining they were tiny poisoned creeks running from a land that had been contaminated with something evil.

She could explain everything to Rhoda, remind her of the weather that afternoon, tell her that Brooks had only swung by for a few minutes, extol Dr. Landry's clichés—but she knew they were also going to have to discuss the car accident before long, and Eureka needed to store up her energy for that.

As Rhoda's heels clicked up the brick path to the porch, Eureka followed, mumbling, "Fine, thanks, and how was *your* day?"

At top of the porch stairs, Rhoda stopped. Eureka watched the back of her head turn to the right to examine the driveway she'd just pulled into. Then she turned and glared. "Eureka— where's my Jeep?"

Eureka pointed at her bad ear, stalling. "Sorry. What was that?" She couldn't tell the story again, not right now, not to Rhoda, not after a day like this. She was as empty and exhausted as if she'd had her stomach pumped again. She gave up.

"The Jeep, Eureka." Rhoda tapped the toe of her pump on the porch.

Eureka worried a dent into the grass with her bare toe. "Ask Dad. He's inside."

Even Rhoda's back scowled as she turned toward the door and wrenched it open. *"Trenton?"*

Alone at last in the humid night, Eureka reached inside her cardigan pocket, pulled out the wallet Ander had returned. She looked in the fold and saw a little square of lined notebook paper among her seven dollar bills. He had scrawled in careful black ink:

Ander. A local phone number. And the words *I'm sorry.*

8

LEGACY

Eureka chewed on her thumbnail, staring at her bobbing knees under the lacquered oak table in the fluorescent-lit boardroom. She'd been dreading this Thursday afternoon since Dad had been summoned to appear at the office of J. Paul Fontenot, Esquire, of Southeast Lafayette.

Diana had never mentioned having a will. Eureka wouldn't have imagined that her mother and lawyers breathed the same air. But here they were at Diana's lawyer's office, gathered to hear the thing read, sandwiched between Diana's other living relatives—Eureka's uncle Beau and her aunt Maureen. Eureka had not seen them since the funeral.

The funeral was not a funeral. Her family called it a memorial service, because they hadn't found Diana's body yet, but everyone in New Iberia called the hour at St. Peter's a funeral, either out of respect or ignorance. The boundary was hazy.

Eureka's face had been cut up then, her wrists in casts, her eardrum blaring from the accident. She didn't hear a word the priest said, nor did she move from her pew until everyone else had walked past the blown-up photograph of Diana, which was propped on the closed casket. They were going to bury the bodiless casket in the plot Sugar had paid for decades ago. What a waste.

Alone in the emerald-hued sanctuary, Eureka crept toward the photograph, studying the smile lines around Diana's green eyes as she leaned over a balcony in Greece. Eureka had taken the picture the summer before. Diana was laughing at the goat licking their laundry, which was hanging out to dry in the yard below.

He doesn't think it's done, Diana had said.

Eureka's cast-stunted fingers had suddenly gripped the edges of the frame. She'd wanted to want to weep, but she could feel nothing of Diana through the flat, glossy surface of the photograph. Her mother's soul had flown away. Her body was still in the ocean—bloated, blue, nibbled by fish, haunting Eureka every night.

Eureka stayed there, alone, her hot cheek against the glass, until Dad came in and wrested the frame from her hands. He filled them with his hands and walked her to the car.

"Are you hungry?" he'd asked, because food was how Dad made things okay. The question had nauseated Eureka.

There was no party, like there'd been after the funeral for Sugar, the only other person Eureka had been close to who'd died. When Sugar passed five years earlier, she got a proper New Orleans–style jazz funeral: somber first-line music on the way into the cemetery, then joyous second-line music played on the way to the Sazerac celebration of her life. Eureka remembered the way Diana had held court at Sugar's funeral, orchestrating toast after toast. She remembered thinking she couldn't imagine handling Diana's death with such panache, no matter how old she might be or how peaceful the circumstances.

As it turned out, that didn't matter. No one wanted to celebrate after Diana's memorial. Eureka spent the rest of the day alone in her room, staring at the ceiling, wondering when she'd find the energy to move again, having her first truly suicidal thought. It felt like weights pressing down on her, like she couldn't get enough air.

Three months later, here she was, at the reading of Diana's will, with no more energy. The boardroom was large and sunny. Thick-paned windows offered views of tasteless loft apartments. Eureka, Dad, Maureen, and Beau sat around one corner of the huge table. Twenty swivel seats sat empty on the other side of the room. No one else was expected but Diana's lawyer, who was "on a call" when they arrived, according to his secretary. She placed Styrofoam cups of weak coffee in front of the family.

"Oh, honey, your roots!" Aunt Maureen winced across the table from Eureka. She blew into her coffee cup, slurped a sip.

For a moment, Eureka thought Maureen had been referring to her familial roots, the only ones Eureka cared about that day. She supposed the two were connected; the roots damaged by Diana's death had caused the offensive, grown-out ones on her head.

Maureen was the oldest of the De Ligne children, eight years Diana's senior. The sisters had shared the same dewy skin and wiry red hair, dimples on their shoulders, green, grainy eyes behind their glasses. Diana had inherited a truck-load more class; Maureen had gotten Sugar's ample breasts and wore dangerously low-cut blouses to show her heirlooms off. Studying her aunt across the table, Eureka realized that the main difference between the sisters was that Eureka's mother had been beautiful. You could look at Maureen and see Diana gone wrong. She was a cruel parody.

Eureka's hair was damp from her shower after her run that afternoon. The team did a six-mile loop through the Evangeline woods on Thursdays, but Eureka did her own solitary loop through the university's leafy campus.

"I can't hardly bear to look at you." Maureen clicked her teeth, eyeing the damp ombré hair Eureka flicked to the right, making it harder for her aunt to see her face.

107

"Ditto," Eureka muttered.

"Baby, that's not *normal*." Maureen shook her head. "Please. Come by American Hairlines. I'll give you a real good do. On the house. We're family, aren't we?"

Eureka looked to Dad for help. He'd drained his coffee cup and was staring into it as if he could read its dregs like tea leaves. From his expression, it didn't look like the dregs had anything nice to predict. He hadn't heard a word Maureen had said, and Eureka envied him.

"Can it, Mo," Uncle Beau said to his older sister. "More important things going on than hair. We're here about Diana."

Eureka couldn't help imagining Diana's hair undulating softly underwater, like a mermaid's, like Ophelia's. She closed her eyes. She wanted to close her imagination, but she couldn't.

Beau was the middle child. He'd been dashing when he was younger—dark hair and broad smile, the spitting image of his father, who, when he'd married Sugar, had acquired the nickname Sugar Daddy.

Sugar Daddy had died before Eureka was old enough to remember him, but she used to love looking at the black-and-white photos of him on Sugar's mantel, imagining what his voice would sound like, what stories he would tell her if he were still alive.

Beau looked drained and skinny. His hair was thinning at the back. Like Diana, he didn't have a steady job. He traveled

108

a lot, hitchhiked most places, had once somehow met Eureka and Diana on an archaeological dig in Egypt. He'd inherited Sugar and Sugar Daddy's small farm outside New Iberia, next to Brooks's house. It was where Diana had stayed whenever she was in town between digs, so Eureka spent a lot of time there, too.

"How you getting on at school, Reka?" he asked.

"All right." She was pretty sure she'd failed her calculus quiz this morning, but she'd done okay on her Earth Science test.

"Still running?"

"I'm captain this year," she lied when Dad lifted his head. Now was not the time to divulge that she'd quit the team.

"Good for you. Your mama's a real fast runner, too." Beau's voice caught and he looked away, as if he were trying to decide whether to apologize for having used the present tense in describing his sister.

The door opened and the lawyer, Mr. Fontenot, strode in, squeezing past the buffet to stand before them at the head of the table. He was a slope-shouldered man in an olive suit. It seemed impossible to Eureka that her mother could ever have met, much less hired, this man. Had she picked him out at random from the phone book? He made no eye contact, just picked up a manila folder from the table and flipped through the pages.

"I did not know Diana well." His voice was soft and slow,

and there was a little whistle in his *t*s. "She contacted me two weeks before her death to file this copy of her last will and testament."

Two weeks before she died? Eureka realized that would have been the day before she and Diana flew to Florida. Was her mother working on her will while Eureka thought she was packing?

"There isn't much here," Fontenot said. "There was a safe-deposit box at the New Iberian Savings and Loan." He glanced up, thick eyebrows arched, and looked around the table. "I don't know if y'all were expecting more."

Slight shakes of heads and murmurs. No one had expected even a safe-deposit box.

"Away we go," Fontenot said. "To a Mr. Walter Beau De Ligne—"

"Present." Uncle Beau raised his hand like a schoolboy who'd been held back for forty years.

Fontenot looked at Uncle Beau, then ticked off a box on the form in his hand. "Your sister Diana bequeaths to you the contents of her bank account." He made a quick note. "Minus the monies used for funeral expenses, there is a sum total of six thousand, four hundred, and thirteen dollars. As well as this letter." He withdrew a small white envelope with Beau's name scrawled across it in Diana's hand.

Eureka nearly gasped at the sight of her mother's big-looped handwriting. She yearned to reach out and wrest the envelope from Beau's fingers, to hold something that her mother had touched so recently. Her uncle looked stunned. He tucked the envelope into the inside pocket of his gray leather jacket and looked down at his lap.

"To a Miss Maureen Toney, née De Ligne—"

"That's me, right here." Aunt Maureen straightened in her seat. "Maureen De Ligne. My ex-husband, he—" She swallowed, adjusted her bra. "Never mind."

"Indeed." Fontenot's nasal bayou accent made the word stretch on and on. "Diana wished for you to take possession of your mother's jewelry—"

"Costume stuff, mostly." Maureen's lips twitched as she reached to take the velour pouch of jewelry from Fontenot. Then she seemed to hear herself, how absurd she was. She patted the pouch as if it were a small pet. "Course, it has its sentimental value."

"Diana also bequeathed to you her car, though, unfortunately the vehicle is"—he glanced briefly at Eureka, then seemed to wish he hadn't—"irretrievable."

"Dodged a bullet there," Maureen said under her breath. "I'm a leaser anyway."

"As well, there is this letter written by Diana," Fontenot said.

Eureka watched as the lawyer produced an envelope identical to the one he'd given Beau. Maureen reached across the table and took the envelope. She stuffed it into the bottomless cavern of her purse, where she put things she was eager to lose.

Eureka hated this lawyer. She hated this meeting. She hated her stupid, whiney aunt. She gripped the rough fabric of the ugly chair beneath her. Her shoulder blade muscles tensed in a knot in the center of her back.

"Now. Miss Eureka Boudreaux."

"Yes!" She jumped, craning her body so her good ear was closer to Fontenot, who cast a pitying smile in her direction.

"Your father is here as your guardian."

"I am," Dad piped up hoarsely. And suddenly Eureka was glad that Rhoda was still at work, that the twins were being looked after by the neighbor Mrs. LeBlanc. For half an hour her father didn't have to pretend he wasn't mourning Diana. His face was pale, his fingers laced tightly together on his lap. Eureka had been so caught up in herself, she hadn't considered how her father might be taking Diana's death. She slipped her hand over Dad's and squeezed.

Fontenot cleared his throat. "Your mother bequeaths to you the following three items."

Eureka leaned forward in her seat. She wanted these three items: her mother's eyes, her mother's heart, her mother's arms wrapped tightly around her now. Her own heart beat faster and her stomach churned.

"This bag contains a locket." Fontenot withdrew a blue

leather jewelry bag from his briefcase and slid it carefully across the table to Eureka.

Her fingers tore at the silk cord that held the bag closed. She reached inside. She knew what the necklace looked like before she even pulled it out. Her mother wore the locket with the smooth, gold-flecked lapis lazuli face all the time. The pendant was a large triangle, each side about two inches long. The copper setting holding the lapis was verdigris with oxidation. The locket was so old and grimy the clasp didn't open, but the brilliant blue face was pretty enough that Eureka didn't mind. Its copper back was marked with six overlapping rings, some recessed and some embossed, which Eureka had always thought looked like the map of a distant galaxy.

She remembered suddenly that her mother hadn't worn it in Florida, and Eureka hadn't asked why. What would have prompted Diana to store the locket in the safe-deposit box before their trip? Eureka would never know. She closed her fingers around the locket, then slipped its long copper chain over her head. She held the locket against her heart.

"She also directed that you were to receive this book."

A thick hardback book came to rest on the table before Eureka. It was sheathed in what looked like a plastic bag but was thicker than any Ziploc she'd ever seen. She slid the book from its protective case. She'd never seen it before.

It was very old, bound in cracked green leather with ridges

on its spine. There was a raised circle in the center of the cover, but it was so worn that Eureka couldn't tell whether it had been part of the cover design or a watermark left by some historic glass.

The book didn't have a title, so Eureka assumed it was a journal until she opened the cover. The pages were printed in a language she didn't recognize. They were thin and yellowed, made not of paper but of a kind of parchment. The small, dense print they bore was so unfamiliar her eyes strained staring at it. It looked like a cross between hieroglyphics and something the twins might draw.

"I remember that book." Dad leaned forward. "Your mother loved it, and I never knew why. She used to keep it at her bedside, even though she couldn't read it."

"Where did it come from?" Eureka touched the rough-edged pages. Toward the back, a section was stuck together as tightly as if it had been welded. It reminded her of what happened to her biology book when she'd spilled a bottle of Coke on it. Eureka didn't risk ripping the pages by trying to pry them open.

"She picked it up at a swap meet in Paris," Dad said. "She didn't know anything else about it. Once, for her birthday, I paid one of her archaeologist friends fifty bucks to carbon-date it. The thing didn't even register on their scale."

"Probably a forgery," Maureen said. "Marcie Dodson— girl at the salon—went to New York City last summer. She bought a Goyard bag in Times Square and it wasn't even *real.*"

"One more thing for Eureka," Fontenot said. "Something your mother calls a 'thunderstone.'" He slid over a wooden chest the size of a small music box. It looked like it had once been painted with an intricate blue design, but the paint was faded and chipped. On top of the box was a cream-colored envelope with *Eureka* written in her mother's hand.

"You also have a letter."

Eureka jumped for the letter. But before she read it, she took a second look at the box. Opening the lid, she found a mass of gauze as white as a bleached bone coiled around something about the size of a baseball. She picked it up. Heavy.

A thunderstone? She had no idea what it was. Her mother had never mentioned it before. Maybe the letter would explain. As Eureka drew the letter from the envelope, she recognized her mother's special stationery.

The dark purple letters at the top read *Fluctuat nec mergitur.*

It was Latin. Eureka had it memorized from the Sorbonne T-shirt she slept in most nights. Diana had brought the shirt back for her from Paris. On it was the motto of the city, and her mother's motto, too. "Tossed by waves, she does not sink." Eureka's heart swelled at the cruel irony.

Maureen, who had ben trying on her inheritance, yanked

one of Sugar's clip-on earrings off her lobe. Then the lawyer said something, and Beau's soft voice rose to argue, and Dad pushed back his chair—but none of it mattered. Eureka wasn't in the boardroom with them anymore.

She was with Diana, in the world of the handwritten letter:

My precious Eureka,

   Smile!

   If you're reading this, I imagine that might be hard to do. But I hope you will—if not today, then soon. You have a beautiful smile, effortless and effervescent.

   As I write this, you are sleeping next to me in my old bedroom at Sugar's—whoops, Beau's—house. Today we drove to Cypremort Point and you swam like a seal in your polka-dot bikini. The sun was bright and we shared the same tan lines on our shoulders this evening, eating boiled seafood down on the dock. I let you have the extra cob of corn, like I always do.

   You look so peaceful and so young when you are sleeping, Eureka. It's hard to believe you're seventeen.

   You're growing up. I promise not to try and stop you.

   I don't know when you'll read this. Most of us are not graced with the knowledge of how our deaths will find us. But if this letter makes its way to you sooner rather than later, please . . . don't let my death determine the course of your life.

I have tried to raise you so that there would not be much to explain in a letter like this. I feel we know each other better than any two people could. Of course, there will still be things you have to discover on your own. Wisdom holds a candle to experience, but you've got to take the candle and walk alone.

Don't cry. Carry what you love about me with you; leave the pain behind.

Hold on to the thunderstone. It's puzzling but powerful.

Wear my locket when you yearn to have me near; perhaps it will help guide you.

And enjoy the book. I know you will.

With deep love and admiration—

Mom

9

NOWHERE BOY

Eureka gripped the letter tightly. She pushed back against the possibility of feeling what her mother's words nearly made her feel.

At the bottom of the page, Diana's signature was smudged. At the edge of her cursive *Mom* lay three tiny raised circles. Eureka ran her finger over them, as if they were a language she had to touch to understand.

She couldn't explain how she knew: they were Diana's tears.

But her mother didn't cry. If she did, Eureka had never seen it. What else had she never known about Diana?

She could remember their most recent trip to Cypremort Point so clearly: early May, flat-bottomed jon boats jostling against their slips, sun blazing low in the sky. Had Eureka really slept so soundly afterward that she hadn't heard her mother crying? Why would Diana have been crying? Why did she write this letter? Did she know she was going to die?

Of course not. The letter said so.

Eureka wanted to scream. But the urge passed, like a scary face in a haunted-house ride at a county fair.

"Eureka." Dad stood before her. They were in the parking lot outside Fontenot's office. The sky above him was a pale blue, with pale white bars of clouds. The air was so humid, her T-shirt felt wet.

Eureka had stayed inside the letter as long as she could, not looking up as she'd followed Dad out of the boardroom, into the elevator, through the lobby, out to the car.

"What?" She clutched the letter, fearing anything might take it away.

"Mrs. LeBlanc's watching the twins for another half hour." He glanced at his watch. "We could get a banana freeze. It's been a while."

Eureka was surprised to find that she did want a banana freeze from Jo's Snows around the corner from their church, St. John's. It had been their tradition before Rhoda and the twins and high school and the accident and meetings with lawyers about dead mothers' bewildering inheritances.

A banana freeze meant two spoons, the window booth in the corner. It meant Eureka on the edge of her seat, laughing over the same stories she'd heard Dad tell a hundred times about growing up in New Iberia, about being the only boy to enter the pecan pie bake-off, or how the first time he invited Diana to dinner, he'd been so nervous, his flambé set the kitchen on fire. For a moment, Eureka let her mind travel to that booth at Jo's Snows. She saw herself spooning the cold banana ice cream into her mouth—a little girl who still thought her father was her hero.

But Eureka didn't know how to talk to Dad anymore. Why tell him how crippled she felt? If Dad breathed one wrong word to Rhoda, Eureka would be back on suicide watch, not even allowed to close her door. Besides, he had enough on his mind.

"I can't," she said. "I have another ride."

Dad looked around the mostly empty parking lot, like she was kidding.

She wasn't. Cat was supposed to pick her up at four to study. The reading of the will had finished early. Now Dad was probably going to wait awkwardly with her until Cat showed.

As Eureka scanned the lot looking for Cat, her gaze fell on the white truck. It was parked facing the building, under a golden-leaved buttonwood tree. Someone was sitting in the driver's seat, staring straight ahead. Something silver gleamed through the windshield.

Eureka squinted, remembering the shiny square—that

unusual citronella air freshener—hanging from Ander's rear-view mirror. She didn't need to see it up close to know it was his truck. He saw her see him. He didn't look away.

Heat coursed through her body. Her T-shirt felt oppressive, her palms clammy. What was he doing here?

The gray Honda almost ran Eureka over. Cat hit the breaks with a harsh squawk and rolled down her window. "S'up, Mr. B?" she called from behind her heart-shaped sunglasses. "Ready, Reka?"

"How are you, Cat?" Dad patted the hood of Cat's car, which they called Mildew. "Glad to see she's still kicking."

"I fear she'll never break down," Cat moaned. "My grand-kids will drive this POS to my funeral."

"We're going to study at Neptune's," Eureka said to Dad, walking around to the passenger door.

Dad nodded. He looked lost on the other side of the car and it made Eureka sad.

"Rain check," he said. "Hey, Reka?"

"Yeah?"

"You have everything?"

She nodded, patting her backpack, which held the ancient book and the strange blue chest. She touched her heart, where the locket lay. She held up Diana's tearstained letter, like a wave. "I'll be home for dinner."

Before she got into Cat's car, Eureka glanced over her shoulder, to the spot under the buttonwood tree. Ander was gone. Eureka didn't know what was stranger: that he'd been there or that she wished he hadn't left.

"So how'd it go?" Cat turned down *All Things Considered.* She was the only teenager Eureka knew who listened to talk instead of music. How was she supposed to flirt with college boys—was Cat's defense—if she didn't know what was going on in the world? "Are you the heiress to a fortune, or at least a pied à terre I can crash at in the south of France?"

"Not exactly." Eureka opened up her backpack to show Cat her inheritance.

"Your mother's locket." Cat touched the chain around Eureka's neck. She was used to seeing it around Diana's neck. "Nice."

"There's more," Eureka said. "This old book and this rock in a box."

"Rock in a huh?"

"She wrote a letter, too."

Cat put the car in park in the middle of the lot. She leaned back in her seat, propping her knees on the steering wheel, and turned her chin toward Eureka. "Feel like sharing?"

So Eureka read the letter once more, this time aloud, trying to keep her soft voice steady, trying not to see the tearstains at the end.

"Amazing," Cat said when Eureka was finished. She quickly wiped her eyes, then pointed at the back of the page. "Something's written on the other side."

Eureka flipped the page over. She hadn't noticed the postscript.

P.S. About the thunderstone . . . Beneath the layer of gauze lies a worked-stone artifact shaped like a triangle. Some cultures call them elf-arrows; they are believed to ward off storms. Thunderstones are found among the remains of most ancient civilizations throughout the world. Remember the arrowheads we unearthed in India? Think of them as distant cousins. This particular thunderstone's origin is unknown, which makes her all the more dear to those who give themselves permission to imagine the possibilities. I did. Will you?

P.P.S. Don't unwrap the gauze until you need to. You'll know when the time comes.

P.P.P.S. Always know I love you.

"Well, that explains the rock," Cat said in a way that meant she was totally confused. "What's the story with the book?"

They studied the fragile pages filled with line after handwritten line of an indecipherable language.

"What is this, medieval Martian?" Cat squinted, turned the book upside down. "It's like my illiterate great-aunt Dessie finally wrote that romance novel she's been yapping about."

A rap on Eureka's window made both girls jump.

Uncle Beau stood outside with one hand stuffed in his jeans pocket. Eureka had thought he'd already left; he didn't like to linger in Lafayette. She glanced around for Aunt Maureen. Beau was alone. She rolled down the window.

Her uncle leaned in, elbows resting on the window frame. He pointed at the book.

"Your mom"—his voice was even quieter than normal—"she knew what that book said. She could read it."

"What?" Eureka took the book from Cat and flipped through its pages.

"Don't ask me how," Beau said. "Saw her going through it once, taking notes."

"Do you know where she learned—"

"Don't know anything more than that. But what your dad said about no one being able to read it—I wanted to set you straight. It's possible."

Eureka leaned forward to kiss her uncle's weathered cheek. "Thanks, Uncle Beau."

He nodded. "Gotta get home, let the dogs out. Y'all come by the farm anytime, okay?" He gave the girls a small salute as he walked to his old truck.

Eureka turned to Cat, cradling the book against her chest. "So the question is—"

"How do we get it translated?" Cat rapped silver fingernails on the dash. "I had a date last week with a classicist-veterinarian double major at UL. He's only a sophomore, but he might know."

"Where'd you meet this Romeo?" Eureka asked. She couldn't help but think of Ander, though nothing Ander had done in Eureka's presence bore the vaguest semblance of romance.

"I have a method." Cat smiled. "I go through my dad's student rosters online, pick out the hotties, and then position myself strategically in the student union after class gets out." Her dark eyes flicked up to Eureka and a rare self-consciousness displayed itself. "You will never tell anyone any of that. Rodney thinks our meeting was pure serendipity." She grinned. "He's got dreads down to here. Wanna see a picture?"

As Cat pulled out her phone and scrolled through her photos, Eureka looked back at the spot where Ander's truck had been. She imagined it was still there, and that Ander had brought Magda back to her, only now the Jeep was painted with snakes and flames and asymmetrical emeralds.

"Cute, huh? Want me to call him? He speaks, like, fifty-seven languages. If your uncle's telling the truth, we really should get it translated."

"Maybe." Eureka was distracted. She slung the book and the thunderstone and her mother's letter into her backpack. "I don't know if I'm up for this today."

"Sure." Cat nodded. "Your call."

"Yeah," Eureka mumbled, fidgeting with her seat belt,

not thinking about her mother's tears. "Would you mind if we don't talk about it right now?"

"Course not." Cat put the car in drive and ambled toward the exit of the parking lot. "Dare I suggest we actually study? That *Moby-Dick* exam and our GPAs' subsequent plunges might take your mind off things."

Eureka looked out the window and watched pale golden buttonwood leaves drift over Ander's empty space. "What do you say we *don't* study—"

"Say no more. I'm your gal. Whatcha got in mind, sister?"

"Well . . ." Was there really any point in lying? With Cat, probably not. Eureka raised her shoulders sheepishly. "A drive-by at Manor's cross-country practice?"

"Why, Miss Boudreaux." Cat's eyes took on their captivating glimmer, usually reserved for older guys. "Whatever took you so long to say so?"

∞

Manor was several times bigger than Evangeline and several times less funded. The only other coed Catholic school in Lafayette, it had long been Evangeline's chief rival. The student body was more diverse, more religious, more competitive. Manor kids seemed cold and aggressive to Eureka. They won district championships in most sports most years, though last year Evangeline went to State for cross-country. Cat was determined to hold on to the title this year.

So it was like crossing enemy lines when Cat pulled into the Manor Panthers' jock lot, which opened onto the bayou.

When Eureka opened her door, Cat frowned down at her own knee-length navy uniform skirt. "We can't go out there dressed like this."

"Who cares?" Eureka got out of the car. "Are you worried they'll think Evangelinos are here to sabotage them?"

"No, but there might be some studs out there working up a sweat, and I look like a total frau in this skirt." She unlocked the trunk, her mobile closet. It was heaped with colorful prints, a lot of Lycra, and more shoes than a department store. "Cover me?"

Eureka shielded Cat and faced the track. She scanned the field for signs of Ander's frame. But the sun was in her eyes and all the cross-country boys looked similarly tall and lanky from here.

"So. You've decided to get yourself a crush." Cat rummaged through her trunk, muttering to herself about a belt she'd left at home.

"I don't know if it's that acute," Eureka said. *Was it?* "He came over a couple nights ago—"

"You didn't tell me that."

Eureka heard a zipper and glimpsed Cat's body shimmying out of something.

"It was nothing, really. I left some stuff in his car and he came by to return it. Brooks was there." She paused, thinking about the moment she'd stood sandwiched between two boys on the brink of a fight. "Things were really tense."

"Was Ander weird with Brooks or was Brooks weird with Ander?" Cat spritzed perfume on her neck. It smelled like honeydew and jasmine. Cat was a microclimate.

"What do you mean?" Eureka asked.

"Just"—Cat was hopping on one foot, fastening a high heel's strap—"you know, Brooks can be rather possessive about you."

"Really? You think so—" Eureka broke off, rising swiftly on her toes as a tall blond boy rounded the curve of the track ahead of them. "I think that's Ander—no." She lowered her heels back to the ground, disappointed.

Cat whistled in amazement. "Wow. You don't think your crush is 'that acute'? Are you kidding me? You were just crestfallen that that dude wasn't him. I have never seen you like this."

Eureka rolled her eyes. She leaned against the car and looked at her watch. "Are you dressed yet? It's almost five; they're probably about to start cooling down." She and Cat didn't have a lot of time.

"No comments on my look?"

When Eureka turned around, Cat was wearing a skintight leopard-print tube dress, black stilettos, and the little lynx beret they'd bought together last summer in New Orleans. She twirled, looking like a taxidermist's centerfold. "I call it the Triple-Cat." She made claws with her hands. *"Rawr."*

"Careful." Eureka nodded at the Manor kids on the field. "Those carnivores might eat you up."

They crossed the parking lot, past the line of yellow buses waiting to take kids home, past the phalanx of orange water coolers and skinny-legged freshman boys doing sit-ups on the bleachers. Cat was getting catcalls.

"Hey, homie," she purred at a black kid checking her out while he jogged past.

Eureka wasn't used to seeing Cat around black kids. She wondered whether these boys saw her best friend as half white, the way white kids at Evangeline saw Cat as half black.

"He smiled!" Cat said. "Should I catch up? I don't think I can run in this dress."

"Cat, we came here to look for Ander, remember?"

"Right. Ander. Supertall. Skinny—not too skinny. Delightful blond curls. Ander."

They stopped at the edge of the track. Even though Eureka had already run six miles that afternoon, when the toe of her shoe touched the pebbly red gravel, she got the urge to sprint.

They watched the team. Boys and girls staggered around the track, running at different speeds. All of them wore the same white polo shirt with the dark yellow collar and yellow running shorts.

"That ain't him," Cat said, her pointer finger following the runners. "And that ain't him—cute, but not him. And that guy *certainly* ain't him." She frowned. "It's weird. I can picture the aura he projects, but it's hard to remember his face clearly. Maybe I just didn't see him up close?"

"He's unusual-looking," Eureka said. "Not in a bad way. Striking."

His eyes are like the ocean, she wanted to say. *His lips are coral-colored. His skin holds the kind of power that makes a compass needle jump.*

She didn't see him anywhere.

"There's Jack." Cat pointed at a dark-haired beanpole with muscles who'd stopped to stretch on the side of the track. "He's the captain. Remember when I played Seven Minutes in Heaven with him last winter? Want me to ask him?"

Eureka nodded, following Cat's saunter toward the boy.

"Say, Jack." Cat slid onto the bleacher above the one Jack's outstretched leg was using. "We're looking for a guy on your team named Ander. What's his last name, Reka?"

Eureka shrugged.

So did Jack. "No Anders on this team."

Cat kicked her legs out, crossed her ankles. "Look, we had that rained-out meet against you guys two days ago, and he was there. Tall lad, blond—help me out, Reka?"

Ocean eyes, she almost blurted out. *Hands that could catch a falling star.*

"Kinda pale?" she managed to say.

"Kinda not on the team." Jack retied his running shoe and straightened up, signaling he was done.

"You're kinda a crap captain if you don't know your teammates' names," Cat called as he walked away.

"Please," Eureka said with an earnestness that made Jack stop and turn around. "We really need to find him."

The boy sighed. He walked back toward the girls, grabbed a black shoulder bag from under the bleachers. He pulled out an iPad, swiped it a few times. When he handed it to Eureka the screen displayed an image of the cross-country team posing on the bleachers. "Yearbook pictures were last week. This is everyone on the team. See your Xander here?"

Eureka pored over the photograph, looking for the boy she'd just seen in the parking lot, the one who'd hit her car, the one she couldn't get out of her mind. Thirty young and hopeful boys smiled out at her, but none of them was Ander.

10

WATER AND POWER

Eureka squeezed a dab of coconut sunblock into her palm and slathered a second coat onto William's white shoulders. It was a warm, sunny Saturday morning, so Brooks had driven Eureka and the twins down to his family's camp on Cypremort Point at the edge of Vermilion Bay.

Everyone who lived along the southern stretch of Bayou Teche wanted a spot at the Point. If your family didn't have a camp along the two-mile corridor of the peninsula near the marina, you made a friend whose family did. Camps were weekend homes, mostly an excuse to have a boat, and they ranged from little more than a trailer parked on a grassy lot to million-dollar mansions raised on cedar stilts, with private slips for boats. Hurricanes were commemorated by black paint markers on the camps' front doors, denoting each point to which the water rose—*Katrina '05, Rita '05, Ike '08.*

The Brookses' camp was a four-bedroom clapboard with a corrugated aluminum roof and petunias potted in faded Folgers cans lining the windowsills. It had a cedar dock out back that looked endless in the afternoon sun. Eureka had known a hundred happy hours out there, eating pecan pralines with Brooks, holding a sugarcane fishing pole, its line painted green with algae.

The plan that day had been to fish for lunch, then pick up some oysters at the Bay View, the only restaurant in town. But the twins were bored with fishing as soon as the worms vanished beneath the murky water, so they'd all ditched their rods and driven up to the narrow stretch of beach looking out on the bay. Some people said the artificial beach was ugly, but when the sunlight glittered on the water, and the golden cordgrass rippled in the wind, and the seagulls cawed as they dipped low to fish, Eureka couldn't imagine why. She slapped a mosquito off her leg and watched the black stillness of the bay at the edge of the horizon.

It was her first time near a big body of water since Diana's death. But, Eureka reminded herself, this was her childhood; there was no reason to be nervous.

William was erecting a sand McMansion, his lips pursed in concentration, while Claire demolished his progress wing by wing. Eureka hovered over them with the bottle of

Hawaiian Tropic, studying their shoulders for the slightest blush of pink.

"You're next, Claire." Her fingers rubbed lotion along the border of William's inflatable orange water wings.

"Uh-uh." Claire rose to her feet, knees caked with wet sand. She eyed the sunscreen and started to run away, but she tripped over the sand McMansion's pool.

"Hurricane Claire strikes again." Brooks hopped up to chase her.

When he came back with Claire in his arms, Eureka went at her with the sunscreen. She writhed, shrieking when Brooks tickled her.

"There." Eureka snapped the lid back on the bottle. "You're protected for another hour."

The kids ran off, sand architecture abandoned, to look for nonexistent seashells at the water's edge. Eureka and Brooks flopped back on the blanket, pushed their toes down into cool sand. Brooks was one of the few people who remembered to always sit on her right side so she could hear him when he talked.

The beach was uncrowded for a Saturday. A family with four young kids sat to the left, everyone angling for shade beneath a blue tarp pitched across two poles. Scattered fishermen roved the shore, their lines slicing into the sand before the water washed them clean. Farther down, a group of middle school kids Eureka recognized from church threw ropes of seaweed at each other. She watched the water lap against the twins' ankles, reminding herself that four miles out, Marsh Island kept the larger Gulf waves at bay.

Brooks passed her a dewy can of Coke from the picnic basket. For a guy, Brooks was strangely good at picnic packing. There was always a variety of junk and healthy food: chips and cookies and apples, turkey sandwiches and cold drinks. Eureka's mouth watered at the sight of a Tupperware of some of his mom Aileen's leftover spicy shrimp étouffée over dirty rice. She took a swig of the soda, leaned back on her elbows, resting the cold can between her bare knees. A sailboat cruised east in the distance, its sails blurring into the low clouds on the water.

"I should take you sailing soon," Brooks said, "before the weather changes." Brooks was a great sailor—unlike Eureka, who could never remember which way to crank the levers. This was the first summer he'd been allowed to take friends out on the boat alone. She'd sailed with him once in May and had planned to do it every weekend after that, but then the accident happened. She was working her way back to being around water. She had these nightmares where she was sinking in the middle of the darkest, wildest ocean, thousands of miles from any land.

"Maybe next weekend?" Brooks said.

She couldn't avoid the ocean forever. It was as much a part of her as running.

"Next time, we can leave the twins at home," she said.

She felt bad about bringing them. Brooks had already gone far out of his way, driving twenty miles north to pick up Eureka in Lafayette, since her car was still in the shop. When he got to her house, guess who begged and pleaded and pitched small fits to come along? Brooks couldn't say no to them. Dad said it was okay and Rhoda was at some meeting. So Eureka spent the next half hour moving car seats from Dad's Continental into the backseat of Brooks's sedan, struggling with twenty different buckles and infuriating straps. Then there were the beach bags, the floaties that needed blowing up, and the snorkel gear William insisted on retrieving from the farthest recesses of the attic. Eureka imagined there were no such obstacles when Brooks spent time with Maya Cayce. She imagined Eiffel Towers and candlelit tables set with platters of poached lobster springing up in fields of thornless red roses whenever Brooks hung out with Maya Cayce.

"Why should they stay home?" Brooks laughed, watching Claire fashion a seaweed mustache on William. "They'd love it. I've got kiddie life jackets."

"Because. They're exhausting."

Brooks reached into the basket for the étouffée. He took a forkful, then passed Eureka the tub. "You'd be more exhausted by guilt if you didn't bring them."

Eureka lay back on the sand and put her straw hat over her face. He was annoyingly right. If Eureka ever let herself add up how exhausted by guilt she already was, she'd probably be bedridden. She felt guilty for how distant she'd grown with Dad, for the unending wave of panic she'd unleashed on the household by swallowing those pills, for the smashed Jeep Rhoda insisted on paying to fix so that she could hold the expense over Eureka's head.

She thought of Ander and felt more guilt at being gullible enough to believe he'd take care of her car. Yesterday afternoon, Eureka had finally worked up the courage to dial the number he'd slipped inside her wallet. A thick-voiced woman named Destiny picked up and told Eureka she'd just hooked up her phone service the day before.

Why drive to her house just to give her a fake number? Why lie about being on Manor's cross-country team? How had he found her at the lawyer's office—and why had he driven away so suddenly?

Why did the possibility of never seeing him again fill Eureka with panic?

A sane person would realize Ander was a creep. That was Cat's conclusion. For all the nonsense Cat put up with from her various boys and men, she didn't tolerate a liar.

Okay, he'd lied. Yes. But Eureka wanted to know *why.*

Brooks lifted a corner of the straw hat to peek at her face. He'd rolled over onto his stomach next to her. He had sand on the side of his tanned cheek. She could smell the sun on his skin.

"What's on my favorite mind?" he asked.

She thought about how trapped she'd felt when Ander had grabbed Brooks by the collar. She thought about how quick Brooks had been to make fun of Ander afterward. "You don't want to know."

"That's why I asked," Brooks said. "Because I do not want to know."

She didn't want to tell Brooks about Ander—and not just because of the hostility between them. Eureka's secrecy had to do with her, with how intensely Ander made her feel. Brooks was one of her best friends, but he didn't know this side of her. *She* didn't know this side of her. It wouldn't go away.

"Eureka." Brooks tapped a thumb on her lower lip. "What's up?"

She touched the center of her chest, where her mother's triangular lapis locket rested. In two days she'd gotten used to its weight around her neck. Brooks reached out and met her fingers on the locket's face. He held the locket up and thumbed the clasp.

"It doesn't open." She tugged it free, not wanting him to break it.

"Sorry." He flinched, then rolled away onto his back. Eureka eyed the line of muscles on his stomach.

"No, I'm sorry." She licked her lips. They tasted salty. "It's just delicate."

"You still haven't told me how it went at the lawyer's," Brooks said. But he wasn't looking at her. He was staring up at the sky, where a gray cloud filtered the sun.

"You want to know if I'm a billionaire?" Eureka asked. Her inheritance had left her bewildered and sad, but it was an easier subject than Ander. "Honestly, I'm not quite sure what Diana left me."

Brooks tugged at some beach grass poking up through the sand. "What do you mean? It looks like a broken locket."

"She also left me a book in a language no one can read. She left me something called a thunderstone—some ball of archaeological gauze I'm not supposed to unwrap. She wrote a letter that says these things *matter*. But I'm not an archaeologist; I'm just her daughter. I have no idea what to do with them, and it makes me feel stupid."

Brooks pivoted on the blanket so that his knees brushed Eureka's side. "We're talking about Diana. She loved you. If the heirlooms have a purpose, it's certainly not to make you feel bad."

William and Claire had visited the tarp down the shore and found a couple of kids to splash around with. Eureka was grateful for a few moments alone with Brooks. She hadn't realized how burdened her inheritance had made her feel, how much of a relief it would be to share the burden. She looked out at the bay and pictured her heirlooms flying away like pelicans, not needing her anymore.

"I wish she'd told me about these things while she was alive," she said. "I didn't think we had secrets."

"Your mom was one of the smartest people who ever lived. If she left you a ball of gauze, maybe it's worth investigating. Think of it as an adventure. That's what she would do." He tossed his drained soda can into the picnic basket and took off his straw fedora. "I'm gonna take a dip."

"Brooks?" She sat up and reached for his hand. When he turned to face her, his hair flopped down over his eyes. She reached to brush it aside. The wound on his forehead was healing; there was just a thin, round scab above his eyes. "Thanks."

He smiled and stood up, straightening his blue bathing suit, which looked good against his tan skin. "No sweat, Cuttlefish."

As Brooks walked to the water, Eureka eyed the twins and their new friends. "I'll wave at you from the breakers," she called to Brooks, like she always did.

There was a legend about a bayou boy who'd drowned in Vermilion Bay on a late summer afternoon, just before sunset. One minute, he was racing with his brothers, sloshing in the shallow far reaches of the bay; the next—maybe on a dare—he swam past the breakers and was swept out to sea. Accordingly, Eureka had never dared to swim near the red-and-white-buoyed breakers as a kid. Now she knew the story was a lie told by parents to keep their kids scared and safe.

Vermilion Bay waves barely qualified as waves. Marsh Island fought the real ones off, like a superhero guarding his home metropolis.

"We're hungry!" Claire shouted, shaking sand from her short blond ponytail.

"Congratulations," Eureka said. "Your prize is a picnic." She swung open the basket's lid and spread out its wares for the kids, who raced over to see what was there.

She popped straws into juice boxes, opened several bags of chips, and pulled all evidence of tomato from William's turkey sandwich. She hadn't thought about Ander in a good five minutes.

"How's the grub?" She chomped a chip.

The twins nodded, mouths full.

"Where's Brooks?" Claire asked between the bites she was taking from William's sandwich, even though she had her own.

"Swimming." Eureka scanned the water. Her eyes were bleary from the sun. She'd said she'd wave to him; he must have been at the breakers by them. The buoys were only a hundred yards from shore.

There weren't many people swimming, just the middle school boys laughing at the futility of their boogie boards on her right. She'd seen Brooks's dark curls bob above water and the long stroke of his tanned arm about halfway to the breakers—but that had been a while ago. She cupped a hand over her eyes to block the sun. She watched the line dividing water from sky. Where was he?

Eureka rose to her feet for a better view of the horizon. There was no lifeguard on this beach, no one keeping watch on distant swimmers. She imagined she could see forever— past Vermilion, south to Weeks Bay, to Marsh Island and beyond to the Gulf, to Veracruz, Mexico, to ice caps near the South Pole. The farther she saw, the darker the world became. Every boat was tattered and abandoned. Sharks and snakes and alligators laced through the waves. And Brooks was out there, swimming freestyle, far away.

There was no reason to panic. He was a strong swimmer. Yet she was panicking. She swallowed hard as her chest tightened, closed.

"Eureka." William fit his hand in hers. "What's wrong?"

"Nothing." Her voice wobbled. She had to calm down. Nerves were distorting her perception. The water looked choppier than it had before. A gale of wind rushed at her, carrying a deep, murky odor of humus and beached gars. The gust flattened Eureka's black caftan across her body and sent the twins' chips scattering across the sand. The sky rumbled. A greenish cloud rolled in from nowhere and snickered from behind the thick banana trees at the western curve of the bay. The dense, queasy sensation of something *bad* brewing spread through her stomach.

Then she saw the whitecap.

The wave skimmed the water's surface, building on itself half a mile past the breakers. It rolled toward them in textured whorls. Eureka's palms began to sweat. She couldn't move. The wave pulled closer toward the shore as if attracted by a powerful magnetic force. It was ugly and ragged, tall and then taller. It swelled to twenty feet, matching the height of the cedar stilts holding up the row of houses on the south side of the bay. Like an uncoiling rope it lashed toward the peninsula of camps, then seemed to change course. At the wave's highest point, the frothy coat angled a pointer toward the center of the beach—toward Eureka and the twins.

The wall of water advanced, deep with myriads of blue. It blazed with diamonds of sun-cut light. Small islands of flotsam roiled across its surface. Vast eddies swirled, as if the wave were trying to devour itself. It stank of rotting fish and—she breathed in—citronella candles?

No, it *didn't* smell like citronella candles. Eureka took another whiff. But the scent was in her mind for some reason, as if she'd conjured it from a memory of another wave, and she didn't know what that meant.

Facing the wave, Eureka saw that it resembled the one that ripped apart the Seven Mile Bridge in Florida and Eureka's entire world. She hadn't remembered what it looked like until now. From the depths of this wave's roar, Eureka thought she heard her mother's last word:

"No!"

Eureka covered her ears, but it was her own voice shouting. When she realized that, determination filled her. She got the buzzing in her feet that meant she was running.

She'd already lost her mother. She would not lose her best friend. "Brooks!" She sprinted into the water—"Brooks!"— splashing in up to her knees. Then she stopped.

The ground shuddered from the force of the bay water retreating. Ocean rushed against her calves. She braced for the undertow. As the wave pulled back toward the Gulf, it stripped away the sand beneath her feet, leaving rank mud and rocky sediment and unrecognizable debris.

Around Eureka, muddy swaths of seaweed lay abandoned by the waves. Fish flopped on exposed earth. Crabs scrambled to catch up with the water in vain. Within seconds, the sea had retreated all the way out to the breakers. Brooks was nowhere to be seen.

The bay was drained, its water gathered up in the wave she knew was on its way back. The boys had dropped their boogie boards and were jogging toward the shore. Fishing poles lay abandoned. Parents grabbed children, which reminded Eureka to do the same. She ran toward Claire and William and tucked a twin under each arm. She ran away from the water, through the fire-ant-thick grass, past the small pavilion, and onto the hot pavement of the parking lot. She held the kids tight. They stopped, forming a line with the other beachgoers. They watched the bay.

Claire whimpered at Eureka's grip around her waist, which grew tighter as the wave peaked in the distance. The crest was frothy, a sickly yellow color.

The wave curled, foamed. Just before it broke, its roar drowned out the crest's terrifying hiss. Birds silenced. Nothing made a sound. Everything watched as the wave threw itself forward and slammed onto the muddy floor of the bay, skewering the sand. Eureka prayed that was the worst of it.

Water rushed forward, flooding the beach. Umbrellas were uprooted, carried like spears. Towels swirled in violent whirlpools, shredded against arsenical rocks. Eureka watched their picnic basket float along the wave's surface and up onto grass. People screamed, running across the parking lot. Eureka was turning to run when she saw the water cross the edge of the parking lot. It flowed over her feet, splashing her legs, and she knew she'd never outrun it—

Then suddenly, swiftly, the wave retreated, out of the parking lot, back down the lawn, washing almost everything on the shore into the bay.

She released the kids onto the wet pavement. The beach was wrecked. Lawn chairs floated out to sea. Umbrellas drifted, flipped inside out. Trash and clothing lay everywhere. And in the center of the garbage and dead-fish-strewn sand—

"Brooks!"

She sprinted toward her friend. He lay facedown in the

sand. In her eagerness to reach him, she stumbled, falling across his soaked body. She turned him on his side.

He was so cold. His lips were blue. A storm of emotion rose in her chest and she came close to letting out a sob—

But then he rolled onto his back. With his eyes closed, he smiled.

"Does he need CPR?" a man asked, pushing past a gathering mass of people around them on the beach.

Brooks coughed, waved off the man's offer. He looked up at the crowd. He stared at each person as though he'd never seen anything like him or her before. Then his eyes fixed on Eureka. She flung her arms around him, buried her face in his shoulder.

"I was so scared."

He patted her back weakly. After a moment, he slid from her embrace to stand. Eureka rose, too, not sure what to do next, sick with relief that he seemed okay.

"You're okay," she said.

"Are you kidding?" He patted her cheek and gave her a charmingly inappropriate grin. Maybe he felt uncomfortable with so many people around. "Did you see me bodysurf that shit?"

There was blood on his chest, on the right side of his torso. "You're hurt!" She circled around and saw four parallel slashes on each side of his back, along the curve of his rib cage. Red blood diluted by seawater trickled down.

Brooks flinched away from her fingers against his side. He shook the water out of his ear and glanced at what he could see of his bloody back. "I scraped a rock. Don't worry about it." He laughed and it didn't sound like him. He tossed his wet hair out of his face and Eureka noticed that the wound on his forehead was blazing red. The wave must have aggravated it.

The onlookers seemed assured that Brooks was going to be all right. The circle around them broke up as people searched for their things along the beach. Bewildered whispers about the wave ran up and down the shore.

Brooks high-fived the twins, who seemed shaky. "You guys should have been out there with me. That wave was epic."

Eureka shoved him. "Are you crazy? That wasn't *epic*. Were you trying to kill yourself? I thought you were just going out to the breakers."

Brooks held up his hands. "That's all I did. I looked for you to wave—ha!—but you seemed preoccupied."

Had she missed him while she was thinking about Ander?

"You were underwater forever." Claire seemed unsure whether to be scared or impressed.

"Forever! What do you think I am? Aquaman?" He lunged toward her exaggeratedly, grabbing long chains of seaweed from the shore and slinging them across his body. He chased the twins up the shore.

"Aquaman!" they shrieked, running away and laughing.

"No one escapes Aquaman! I will take you to my underwater lair! We will battle mermen with our webbed fingers and dine on coral plates of sushi, which in the ocean is just food."

As Brooks twirled one twin in the air and then the other, Eureka watched the sun play off his skin. She watched the blood taper along the muscles in his back. She watched him turn around and wink, mouthing, *Relax. I'm totally fine!*

She looked back at the bay. Her eyes traced the memory of the wave. The sandy ground beneath her disintegrated in another lap of water and she shivered despite the sun.

Everything felt tenuous, as if everything she loved could be washed away.

11

SHIPWRECK

"I never meant to scare you."

Brooks sat on the side of Eureka's bed, his bare feet propped on her windowsill. They were alone at last, partway recovered from the scare that afternoon.

The twins were in bed after hours of Rhoda's concentrated scrutiny. She'd grown hysterical one sentence into the story of their adventure, blaming both Eureka and Brooks that her children had been so close to danger. Dad tried to smooth things over with his cinnamon hot cocoa. But instead of it bringing them together, everyone just took mugs to their own corners of the house.

Eureka sipped hers in the old rocking chair next to her window. She watched Brooks's reflection in her antique *armoire à glace*, a wooden wardrobe with a single door and a mirrored front, which had belonged to Sugar's mother. His lips moved, but her head was resting on her right hand, blocking her good ear. She lifted her head and heard the lyrics of "Sara" by Fleetwood Mac, which Brooks was playing on her iPod.

> *. . . in the sea of love, where everyone would*
> *love to drown.*
> *But now it's gone; they say it doesn't matter*
> *anymore. . . .*

"Did you say something?" she asked him.

"You seemed mad," Brooks said, a little louder. Eureka's bedroom door was open—Dad's rule when she had guests—and Brooks knew as well as Eureka what volume they could speak at to avoid being heard downstairs. "Like you thought the wave was my fault."

He reclined between the wooden posters of her grandparents' old bed. His eyes were the same color as the chestnut-colored throw draped over her white bedspread. He looked like he was up for anything—a velvet-rope party, a cross-country drive, a swim in cold darkness to the edge of the universe.

Eureka was exhausted, as if she'd been the one devoured and spat out by a wave.

"Of course it wasn't your fault." She stared into her mug. She wasn't sure if she'd been mad at Brooks. If she had been, she didn't know why. There was a space between them that wasn't usually there.

"Then what is it?" he asked.

She shrugged. She missed her mother.

"Diana." Brooks said the name as if he were putting the two events together for the first time. Even the best boys could be clueless. "Of course. I should have realized. You're so brave, Eureka. How do you handle it?"

"I don't handle it, that's how."

"Come here."

When she looked up, he was patting the bed. Brooks was trying to understand, but he couldn't, not really. It made her sad to see him try. She shook her head.

Rain pelted the windows, giving them zebra stripes. Rhoda's favorite meteorologist, Cokie Faucheux, had predicted sun the whole weekend, which was the only thing that seemed right—Eureka was content to disagree with Rhoda.

From the corner of her eye, she saw Brooks rise from the bed and walk to her. He extended his arms in a hug. "I know it's hard for you to open up. You thought that wave today was going to—"

"Don't say it."

"I'm still here, Eureka. I'm not going anywhere."

Brooks took her hands and pulled her to him. She let him

hug her. His skin was warm, his body taut and strong. She laid her head against his collarbone and closed her eyes. She hadn't been embraced in a long time. It felt wonderful, but something nagged at her. She had to ask.

When she stepped away, Brooks held her hand for a moment before he let go.

"The way you acted when you stood up after the wave . . . ," she said. "You laughed. I was surprised."

Brooks scratched his chin. "Imagine coming to, coughing up a lung, and seeing twenty strangers looking down at you—one of whom is a dude getting ready to give you mouth-to-mouth. What choice did I have but to play it off?"

"We were worried about you."

"*I* knew I was fine," Brooks said, "but I must have been the only one who knew it. I saw how scared you were. I didn't want you to think I was . . ."

"What?"

"Weak."

Eureka shook her head. "Impossible. You're Powder Keg."

He grinned and tousled her hair, which led to a brief wrestling match. She ducked under his arm to get away, grabbed his T-shirt as he reached around his back to pick her up. Soon she had him in a headlock, backed up against her dresser, but then, in one quick move, he'd tossed her backward onto her bed. She flopped against the pillow, laughing, like she'd done at the end of a thousand other matches with Brooks. But he wasn't laughing. His face was flushed and he stood stiffly at the foot of the bed, looking down at her.

"What?" she asked.

"Nothing." Brooks looked away and the fire in his eyes seemed to dwindle. "What do you say you show me what Diana gave you? The book, that . . . wonder rock?"

"Thunderstone." Eureka slid off the bed and sat at her desk, which she'd had since she was a kid. Its drawers were so full of keepsakes there was no room for homework or books or college applications, so she'd stacked those in piles she'd promised Rhoda she would organize. But what annoyed Rhoda delighted Eureka, so the piles had grown to precarious heights.

From the top drawer, she pulled out the book Diana had left her, then the small blue chest. She laid them both on her bedspread. With her inheritance between them, she and Brooks faced each other cross-legged on the bed.

Brooks reached for the thunderstone first, releasing the faded clasp on the chest, reaching inside to hold up the gauze-covered stone. He examined it from all sides.

Eureka watched his fingers troll the white dressing. "Don't unwrap it."

"Of course not. Not yet."

She squinted at him, grabbed the stone, surprised again by its heaviness. She wanted to know what it looked like inside—and obviously Brooks did, too. "What do you mean, 'not yet'?"

Brooks blinked. "I mean your mom's letter. Didn't she say you would know when the time was right to open it?"

"Oh. Right." She must have told him about that. She rested her elbows on her knees, chin in her palms. "Who knows when that time will be? Might make a good Skee-Ball in the meantime."

Brooks stared at her, then ducked his head and swallowed the way he did when he got embarrassed. "It must be precious if your mother left it to you."

"I was kidding." She eased the thunderstone back into its chest.

He picked up the ancient-looking book with a reverence Eureka wasn't expecting. He turned the pages more delicately than she had, which made her wonder whether she deserved her inheritance.

"I can't read it," he whispered.

"I know," she said. "It looks like it's from the distant future—"

"Of a past never fully realized." Brooks sounded like he was quoting one of the science fiction paperbacks Dad used to read.

Brooks kept turning pages, slowly at first, then faster, stopping at a section Eureka hadn't discovered. Midway through the book, the strange, dense text was interrupted by a section of intricate illustrations.

"Are those woodcuts?" Eureka recognized the method from the xylography class she'd once taken with Diana—though these illustrations were far more intricate than anything Eureka had been able to carve into her stubborn block of beech.

She and Brooks studied an image of two men wrestling. They were dressed in plush, fur-lined robes. Large jeweled necklaces draped across their chests. One man wore a heavy crown. Behind a crowd of onlookers stretched a cityscape, tall spires of unusual buildings framing the sky.

On the opposite page was an image of a woman in an equally luxurious robe. She was on her hands and knees at the edge of a river dotted with tall, blooming jonquils. Hatched shadows of clouds bordered her long hair as she studied her reflection in the water. Her head was down, so Eureka couldn't see her face, but something about her body language was familiar. Eureka knew she was weeping.

"It's all here," Brooks whispered.

"This makes sense to you?"

She turned the parchment page, looking for more illustrations, but instead found the short, jagged edges of several torn-out pages. Then the incomprehensible text resumed. She touched the rough edges near the binding. "Look, it's missing a few pages."

Brooks held the book close to his face, squinting at the place where the missing pages would have been. Eureka noticed there was one more illustration, on the back of the page with the kneeling woman. It was much simpler than the others: three concentric circles centered on the page. It looked like a symbol for something.

On instinct, she reached for Brooks's forehead, pushing his dark hair back. His wound was circular, which wasn't remarkable. But the scab had been so irritated by the rough wave that afternoon that Eureka could see . . . rings inside of it. They bore an uncanny resemblance to the illustration in her book.

"What are you doing?" He brushed her hand away, flattened his hair.

"Nothing."

He closed the book and pressed a hand on its cover. "I doubt you'll be able to get this translated. Trying to will just send you on a painful journey. Do you really think there's going to be someone in Podunk, Louisiana, who can translate something of this magnitude?" His laughter sounded mean.

"I thought you liked Podunk, Louisiana." Eureka's eyes narrowed. Brooks was the one who always defended their hometown when Eureka bashed it. "Uncle Beau said Diana could read this, which means there must be someone who can translate it. I just have to find out who."

"Let me try. I'll take the book with me tonight and save you the heartache. You're not ready to confront Diana's death, and I'm happy to help."

"No. I'm not letting that book out of my sight." She reached for the book, which was still in Brooks's grasp. She had to pry it from his hands. The binding creaked from the strain of being pulled.

"Wow." Brooks let go, held up his hands, and gave her a look intended to convey she was being melodramatic.

She looked away. "I haven't decided what I'm going to do with it yet."

"Okay." His tone softened. He touched her fingers where they encased the book. "But if you do get it translated," he said, "take me with you, okay? It might be hard to digest. You'll want someone there you trust."

Eureka's phone buzzed on her nightstand. She didn't recognize the number. She held the face of the phone up to Brooks with a shrug.

He winced. "That might be Maya."

"Why would Maya Cayce call *me*? How would she get my number?"

Then she remembered: Brooks's broken cell phone. They'd found it in two pieces on the beach after the wave had dropped on it like a piano. Eureka had been absent-minded enough to leave her phone at home that morning, so it was intact.

Maya Cayce had probably called Brooks's house and been given Eureka's number by Aileen, who must have forgotten how nasty high school girls can be.

"Well?" Eureka held out the phone to Brooks. "Talk to her."

"I don't want to talk to her. I want to be with you. I mean—" Brooks rubbed his jaw. The phone stopped buzzing, but its effect did not. "I mean, we're hanging out and I don't want to be distracted when we're finally talking about . . ." He paused, then muttered what Eureka thought was a curse under his breath. She turned her good ear toward him, but he was quiet. When he looked at her, his face was flushed again.

"Is something wrong?" she asked.

He shook his head. He leaned closer to her. The springs beneath them creaked. Eureka dropped the phone and the book, because his eyes looked different—smooth around the edges, bottomless brown—and she knew what was going to happen.

Brooks was going to kiss her.

She didn't move. She didn't know what to do. Their eyes were locked for his entire descent to her lips. His weight came down against her legs. A silent sigh escaped her. His lips were gentle but his hands were firm, pressing into her to wrestle in a new way. They rolled into each other as his mouth closed around hers. Her fingers crept up his shirt, touching his skin, as smooth as stone. His tongue traced the tip of her tongue. It was silky. She arched her back, wanting to be even closer.

"This is—" he said.

She nodded. "So right."

They gasped for air, then went back in for another kiss.

Eureka's history of kisses had been Spin the Bottle pecks, dares, sloppy gropes, and slips of tongue outside school dances. This was galaxies away.

Was this Brooks? It was like she was kissing someone with whom she'd once shared a powerful affair, the kind Eureka had never allowed herself to desire. His hands swept her skin as if she were a voluptuous goddess, not the girl he'd known his whole life. When had Brooks become so muscular, so sexy? Had he been like this for years and she'd missed it? Or could a kiss, done right, metabolize a body, kicking in an instant growth spurt, making them both so suddenly mature?

She pulled away to look at him. She studied his face and his freckles and the cowlicks in his brown hair and she saw that he was someone entirely different. She was scared and exhilarated, knowing there was no going back after anything, especially something like this.

"What took you so long?" Her voice was a hoarse whisper.

"To do what?"

"To kiss me."

"I . . . well . . ." Brooks frowned, pulled away.

"Wait." She tried to pull him back. Her fingers brushed the back of his neck, which felt suddenly stiff. "I didn't mean to kill the mood."

"There are reasons I've waited so long to kiss you."

"Such as?" She wanted to sound sunny, but she was already wondering: Was it Diana? Was Eureka so damaged she'd scared Brooks off?

That moment's hesitation was all it took for Eureka to convince herself that Brooks saw her the way the rest of their school saw her—a freak show, bad luck, the last girl any normal guy should pursue. So she blurted out: "I guess you've been busy with Maya Cayce."

Brooks's face darkened into a scowl. He rose to stand at the foot of her bed, his arms crossed over his chest. His body language was as distant as the memory of the kiss.

"That is so typical," he said to the ceiling.

"What?"

"It couldn't possibly have anything to do with you. It must be someone else's fault."

But Eureka knew it had everything to do with her. The knowledge was so painful she'd tried to cover it up with something else. *Displacement,* any of her last five shrinks would inform her, *a dangerous habit.*

"You're right—" she said.

"Don't patronize me." Brooks didn't look like her best friend *or* the boy she'd kissed. He looked like someone who resented everything about her. "I don't want to be placated by someone who thinks she's better than everyone."

"What?"

"You're right. The rest of the world is wrong. Isn't that the way it is?"

"No."

"You dismiss everything immediately—"

"I do not!" Eureka shouted, realizing she was immedi-

160

ately dismissing his claim. She lowered her voice and closed her bedroom door, not caring about the consequences if Dad walked by. She couldn't let Brooks think these lies. "I don't dismiss you."

"Sure about that?" he asked coldly. "You even dismiss the things your mother left you in her will."

"That's not true." Eureka obsessed over her inheritance night and day—but Brooks wasn't even listening to her. He paced her room, his anger making him seem possessed.

"You keep Cat around because she doesn't notice when you tune her out. You can't stand anyone in your family." He flung his hand in the direction of the den downstairs, where Rhoda and Dad had been watching the news but were now surely tuning in to the argument above. "You're certain every therapist you go to is an idiot. You've pushed away all of Evangeline because there's no way anyone could ever understand what you've been through." He stopped pacing and looked straight at her. "Then there's me."

Eureka's chest ached as if he'd punched her in the heart. "What about you?"

"You use me."

"No."

"I'm not your friend. I'm a sounding board for your anxiety and depression."

"You—you're my best friend," she stammered. "You're the reason I'm still here—"

"Here?" he said bitterly. "The last place on earth you

want to be? I'm just the prelude to your future, your *real* life. Your mom raised you to follow your dreams, and that's all you've ever cared about. You have no idea how much other people care for you because you're too wrapped up in yourself. Who knows? Maybe you're not even suicidal. Maybe you took those pills for attention."

Eureka's breath escaped her chest as if she'd been dropped from an airplane. "I confided in you. I thought you were the only one who didn't judge me."

"Right." Brooks shook his head, disgusted. "You call everyone you know judgmental, but have you ever considered what a total bitch you are to Maya?"

"Of course, let's not forget about Maya."

"At least she cares about other people."

Eureka's lip trembled. Thunder boomed outside. Was she that bad a kisser?

"Well, if you've made up your mind," she shouted, "call her! Be with her. What are you waiting for? Take my phone and make a date." She threw the phone at him. It bounced off the pectoral she couldn't believe she'd just laid her head against.

Brooks eyed the phone as if he were considering the offer. "Maybe I will," he said slowly, under his breath. "Maybe I don't need you as much as I thought I did."

"What are you talking about? Am I being punked or something?"

"The truth hurts, huh?" He knocked her shoulder as he brushed past. He swung open her door, then glanced back at her bed, at the book and the thunderstone in its chest.

"You should go," she said.

"Say that to a couple more people," Brooks said, "and you'll be all alone."

Eureka listened to him thunder down the stairs and she knew what he'd look like, grabbing his keys and shoes off the entry bench. When the door slammed, she imagined him marching toward his car in the rain. She knew the way his hair would splay, the way his car would smell.

Could he imagine her? Would he even want to see her pressed against the window, staring at the storm, gulping with emotion, and holding back her tears?

12

NΣPTUNΣ'S

Εureka picked up the thunderstone and hurled it at the wall, wanting to smash everything that had happened since she and Brooks had stopped kissing. The stone left a dent in the plaster she'd painted with blue polka dots during some happier lifetime. It landed with a thump next to her closet door.

She knelt to assess the damage, her flea-market Persian rug soft beneath her hands. It wasn't as deep a dent as the one from two years ago, when she'd punched the wall next to the stove, arguing with Dad over whether she could miss a week of school to go to Peru with Diana. It wasn't as shocking as the barbell Dad had broken when she was sixteen—screaming at her after she'd bailed on the summer job he'd gotten her at Ruthie's Dry Cleaners. But the dent was bad enough to scandalize Rhoda, who seemed to think drywall could not be repaired.

"Eureka?" Rhoda shouted from the den. "What did you do?"

"Just an exercise Dr. Landry taught me!" she hollered, making a face she wished Rhoda could see. She was furious. If she were a wave, she'd make continents crumble like stale bread.

She wanted to hurt something the way Brooks had hurt her. She grabbed the book he'd been so interested in, gripped its spread pages, and considered ripping it in two.

Find your way out of a foxhole, girl. Diana's voice found her again.

Foxholes were small and tight and camouflaged. You didn't know you were in one until you couldn't breathe and had to break free. They equaled claustrophobia, which, to Eureka, had always been an enemy. But foxes lived in foxholes; they raised families there. Soldiers shot from inside them, shielded from their enemies. Maybe Eureka didn't want to find her way out of this one. Maybe she was a soldier fox. Maybe this foxhole of her fury was where she most belonged.

She exhaled, relaxed her grip on the book. She put it down carefully, as if it were one of the twins' art projects. She walked to the window, stuck her head outside, and looked for stars. Stars grounded her. Their distance offered perspective when she couldn't see beyond her own pain. But the stars weren't out in Eureka's sky tonight. They were hidden behind a cloak of thick gray clouds.

Lightning splintered the darkness. Thunder boomed again. Rain came heavier, thrashing the trees outside. A car on the street sloshed through a pond-sized puddle. Eureka thought of Brooks driving home to New Iberia. The roads were dark and slick, and he'd left in such a hurry—

No. She was mad at Brooks. She shuddered, then shuttered the window, leaned her head against the cold pane.

What if what he said was true?

She didn't think she was better than anyone—but did she come off as if she did? With a handful of barbed comments, Brooks had planted the idea in Eureka that the whole planet was against her. And tonight there weren't even stars, which made everything even murkier.

She picked up her phone, blocked Maya Cayce's number with a scowling press of three buttons, and texted Cat.

Hey.

Weather sucks, her friend answered instantly.

Yeah, Eureka typed slowly. *Do I?*

Not that I've heard. Why? Is Rhoda being Rhoda?

Eureka could imagine Cat snorting a laugh in her candle-lit bedroom, her feet propped on her desk, while she stalked future boyfriends on her laptop. The speed of Cat's response comforted Eureka. She picked the book up again, opened it in her lap, and ran her finger around the circles of the final illustration, the one she'd thought she'd seen mirrored in Brooks's wound.

Brooks isn't being Brooks, she typed back. *Huge fight.*

A moment later, her phone rang.

"You two bicker like old marrieds," Cat said as soon as Eureka picked up.

Eureka looked at the dent in her polka-dot wall. She imagined a similar-sized bruise on Brooks's chest where she'd hit him with the phone.

"This was bad, Cat. He told me I think I'm better than everyone else."

Cat sighed. "That's just because he wants to do you."

"You think everything is about sex." Eureka didn't want to admit they'd kissed. She didn't want to think about that after what Brooks had said. Whatever that kiss meant, it was so far in the past it was a dead language no one knew how to speak anymore, more inaccessible than Diana's book. "This was bigger than that."

"Look," Cat said, chomping on something crunchy, probably Cheetos. "We know Brooks. He'll apologize. I give him until Monday, first period. In the meantime, I have some good news."

"Tell me," Eureka said, though she would rather have pulled the covers over her head until doomsday, or college.

"Rodney wants to meet you."

"Who's Rodney?" she groaned.

"My classicist fling, remember? He wants to see your book. I suggested Neptune's. I know you're over Neptune's, but where else is there to go?"

Eureka thought about Brooks wanting to go with her when she got the book translated. That was before he'd exploded like a levee in a flood.

"Please don't sit around feeling guilty about Brooks." Cat could be surprisingly telepathic. "Put on something cute. Rodney might bring a friend. I'll see you at Tune's in half an hour."

Neptune's was a café in a strip mall on the second story, above Ruthie's Dry Cleaners and a video game store that was slowly going out of business. Eureka put on sneakers and her raincoat. She jogged the mile and a half in the rain to avoid asking Dad or Rhoda if she could borrow one of their cars.

Up the wooden staircase, through the tinted glass door, you knew you would find at least two dozen Evangelinos sprawled out over laptops and doorstop-sized textbooks. The decor was candy apple red and worn, like an aging bachelor's pad. A sinkhole aroma hung like a cloud over its slanted pool table and its flipperless *Creature from the Black Lagoon* pinball machine. Neptune's served food no one ate twice, beer to college kids, and enough coffee, soda, and atmosphere to keep the high school kids hanging out all night.

Eureka used to be a regular. Last year she'd even won the

pool tournament—beginner's luck. But she hadn't been back since the accident. It made no sense that a ridiculous place like Neptune's still existed and Diana had been swept away.

Eureka didn't notice she was dripping wet until she walked in and heavy eyes fell on her. She wrung out her ponytail. She spotted Cat's braids and moved toward the corner table where they always used to sit. The Wurlitzer was playing "Hurdy Gurdy Man" by Donovan as NASCARs circled on TV. Neptune's was the same, but Eureka had changed so much it might as well have been McDonald's—or Gallatoire's in New Orleans.

She passed a table of arduously identical cheerleaders, waved to her friend Luke from Earth Science, who seemed to be under the impression that Neptune's was a good place for a date, and smiled wanly at a table of freshman cross-country girls brave enough to be there. She heard somebody mutter, "Didn't think she was allowed out of the ward," but Eureka was here for business, not to care what some kid thought about her.

Cat wore a cropped purple sweater, ripped jeans, and the lighter-than-average makeup meant to impress college men. Her latest victim sat beside her on the torn red vinyl bench. He had long blond dreads and an angular profile as he slung back a swig of Jax beer. He smelled like maple syrup—the fake, sugary kind Dad didn't use. His hand was on Cat's knee.

"Hey." Eureka slid into the opposite bench. "Rodney?"

He was only a few years older, but he looked so *college* with his nose ring and faded UL sweatshirt, it made Eureka feel like a little kid. He had blond eyelashes and sunken cheeks, nostrils like different-sized kidney beans.

He smiled. "Let's see that crazy book."

Eureka pulled the book from her backpack. She wiped the table with a napkin before she slid it to Rodney, whose mouth stretched into an intrigued, academic frown.

Cat leaned over, her chin on Rodney's shoulder as he turned the pages. "We stared at the thing forever trying to make sense of it. Maybe it's from outer space."

"Inner space is more like it," Rodney said.

Eureka watched him, the way he looked up at Cat and chuckled, the way he seemed to enjoy her every wacky remark. Eureka didn't think Rodney was particularly attractive, so she was surprised by the twinge of jealousy that snuck into her chest.

His flirtation with Cat made what had just passed between her and Brooks feel like a Tower of Babel–scale miscommunication. She looked up at the cars circling the track on TV and imagined she was driving one of them, but instead of her car being covered in advertisements, it was covered in the inscrutable language of the book Rodney was pretending to read across the table.

She should never have kissed Brooks. It was a huge mistake. They knew each other too well to try to know each

other any better. And they'd already broken up once before. If Eureka was ever going to get involved with someone
romantically—which, since the accident, she wouldn't wish
on her worst enemy—it should be someone who didn't know
anything about her, someone who came into the relationship
ignorant of her complexities and flaws. She shouldn't be with
a critic ready to pull away from their first kiss and list everything about her that was wrong. She knew better than anyone
that the list was endless.

She missed Brooks.

But Cat was right. He'd been a jerk. He should apologize.
Eureka checked her phone discreetly. He hadn't texted.

"What do you think?" Cat asked. "Should we do it?"

Eureka's left ear rang. What had she missed?

"Sorry, I . . ." She turned her good ear toward the conversation.

"I know what you're thinking," Rodney said. "You think
I'm sending you to some New Age nut job. But I know clas-
sical and vulgar Latin, three dialects of early Greek, and a bit
of Aramaic. And this writing"—he tapped a page of dense
text—"isn't like anything I've seen."

"Isn't he a genius?" Cat squeaked.

Eureka hurried to catch up. "So you think we should take
the book to . . . ?"

"She's a little eccentric, a self-taught expert in dead languages," Rodney said. "Makes her living telling fortunes. Just

ask her to look at the text. And don't let her rip you off. She'll respect you more. Whatever she asks for, offer half and settle for a quarter less than her original price."

"I'll bring my calculator," Eureka said.

Rodney reached across Cat, pulled a napkin from the dispenser and scribbled:

Madame Yuki Blavatsky, 321 Greer Circle.

"Thanks. We'll go check her out." Eureka slid the book back in her bag and zipped it up. She motioned to Cat, who unpeeled herself from Rodney and mouthed, *Now?*

Eureka rose from the booth. "Let's go make a deal."

13

MADAME BLAVATSKY

Madame Blavatsky's storefront was in the older part of town, not far from St. John's. Eureka had passed the neon-green hand in the window ten thousand times. Cat parked in the potholed parking lot and they stood in the rain before the nondescript glass-panel door, rapping the antique brass knocker shaped like a lion's head.

After a few minutes, the door swung open, sending a clatter of bells ringing from the inside handle. A stout woman with wild, frizzy hair stood in the entry, arms akimbo. From behind her came a red glow that obscured her face in shadows.

"Here for a reading?"

Her voice was rough and raspy. Eureka nodded as she pulled Cat into the dark foyer. It looked like a dentist's waiting room after hours. A single red-bulbed lamp lit two folding chairs and a nearly empty magazine rack.

"I do palms, cards, and leaves," Madame Blavatsky said, "but you must pay separately for the tea." She looked about seventy-five, with painted red lips, a constellation of moles on her chin, and thick, muscular arms.

"Thank you, but we have a special request," Eureka said.

Madame Blavatsky eyed the heavy book tucked under Eureka's arm. "Requests are not special. Presents are special. A vacation—that would be special." The old woman sighed. "Step into my atelier."

Blavatsky's big black dress wafted the stench of a thousand cigarettes as she led the girls through a second door and into a main room.

Her atelier was drafty, with a low ceiling and black-on-black embossed wallpaper. There was a humidifier in the corner, a vintage hot pot on top of a perilously stuffed bookcase, and a hundred old frowning portraits hanging in slanted frames on the wall. A broad desk held a frozen avalanche of books and papers, an old desktop computer, a vase of rotting purple freesias, and two turtles that were either napping or dead. Elegant gold cages hung in each corner of the room, holding so many birds Eureka stopped counting. They were small birds, the size of an open palm, with slender lime-green bodies and red beaks. They chirped resoundingly, melodically, incessantly.

"Abyssinian lovebirds," Madame Blavatsky announced. "Exceptionally intelligent." She slid a finger coated with peanut butter through the bars of one of the cages and giggled like a child as the birds flocked to peck her skin clean. One bird rested on her index finger longer than the others. She leaned close, puckering red lips and making kissing noises at him. He was larger than the others, with a bright red crown and a diamond of gold feathers on his breast. "And the brightest of all, my sweet, sweet Polaris."

At last Madame Blavatsky sat down and motioned for the girls to join her. They sat quietly on a low black velour couch, rearranging the twenty-odd stained and mismatched pillows to make room. Eureka glanced at Cat.

"Yes, yes?" Madame Blavatsky asked, reaching for a long, hand-rolled cigarette. "I can surmise what you want, but you must ask, children. There is great power in words. The universe flows out of them. Use them now, please. The universe awaits."

Cat raised one eyebrow at Eureka, tilted her head in the woman's direction. "Better not piss off the universe."

"My mother left me this book in her will," Eureka said. "She died."

Madame Blavatsky waved her bony hand. "I doubt that very much. There is no death, no life, either. Only congregation and dispersal. But that's for another conversation. What do you *want*, child?"

175

"I want to get her book translated." Eureka's palm pressed into the raised circle on the book's green cover.

"Well, hand it over. I am psychic, but I cannot read a closed book five feet away."

When Eureka held out the book, Madame Blavatsky jerked it from her hand as if she were reclaiming a stolen purse. She flipped through it, pausing here and there to mutter something to herself, shoving her nose into the pages with the woodcut illustrations, giving no indication of whether she could make sense of it or not. She didn't look up until she reached the fused section of pages near the back of the book.

Then she put out her cigarette and popped an orange Tic Tac in her mouth. "When did this happen?" She held up the chunk of stuck pages. "You didn't try to dry it after you spilled— What is this?" She sniffed the book. "Smells like Death in the Afternoon. You're too young to be drinking wormwood, you know."

Eureka had no idea what Madame Blavatsky was talking about.

"It's most unfortunate. I might be able to fix it, but it will require the wood kiln and expensive chemicals."

"It was like that when I got it," Eureka said.

Blavatsky slipped on wire-rimmed glasses, slid them down to the end of her nose. She studied the book's spine, its inside front and back covers. "How long was your mother the proprietor?"

"I don't know. My dad said she found it at a flea market in France."

"So many lies."

"What do you mean?" Cat asked.

Blavatsky looked up over the rims of her glasses. "This is a family tome. Family tomes stay within the family line unless there are tremendously unusual circumstances. Even under such circumstances, it is nearly impossible a book like this would fall into the hands of someone who would sell it at a flea market." She patted the cover. "This is not the stuff of swap meets."

Madame Blavatsky closed her eyes and tilted her head toward the birdcage over her left shoulder, almost as if she were listening to the lovebirds' song. When she opened her eyes, she looked directly into Eureka's. "You say your mother is dead. But what of your desperate love for her? Is there a faster way to immortality?"

Eureka's throat burned. "If this book had been in my family, I would have known about it. My grandparents didn't keep secrets. My mom's sister and brother were both there when I inherited it." She thought about Uncle Beau's story of Diana reading it. "They barely knew anything about it."

"Perhaps it did not come from your mother's parents," Madame Blavatsky said. "Perhaps it found her through a distant cousin, a favorite aunt. Was your mother's name, by chance, Diana?"

"How did you know that?"

Blavatsky closed her eyes, tilted her head to the right, toward another birdcage. Inside, six lovebirds scampered to the side of the cage nearest Blavatsky. They chirped high, intricate staccatos. She chuckled. "Yes, yes," she murmured, not to the girls. Then she coughed and looked at the book, pointing to the bottom corner of the inside back cover. Eureka stared at the symbols written in different shades of fade.

"This is a list of names of the book's previous proprietors. As you can see, there have been many. The most recent one reads *Diana.*" Madame Blavatsky squinted at the symbols preceding Eureka's mother's name. "Your mother inherited this book from someone named Niobe, and Niobe received it from someone named Byblis. Do you know these women?"

While Eureka shook her head, Cat sat up straight. "You can read it."

Blavatsky ignored Cat. "I can inscribe your name at the end of the list, seeing as the tome is now yours. No extra charge."

"Yes," Eureka said softly. "Please. It's—"

"Eureka." Madame Blavatsky smiled, picking up a felt-tipped pen and scrawling a few strange symbols onto the page. Eureka stared at her name in the mystifying language. "How did you—"

"This is similar to the old Magdalenian script," Blavatsky said, "though there are differences. Vowels are absent. The spellings are quite absurd!"

"Magdalenian?" Cat looked at Eureka, who had never heard of it, either.

"*Very* ancient," Blavatsky said. "Found in those prehistoric caves in southern France. This is not a sister to Magdalenian, but perhaps it is a second cousin. Languages have complicated family trees, you know—mixed marriages, stepchildren, even bastards. There are countless scandals in the history of languages, many murders, much incest."

"I'm listening," Cat said.

"It's very rare to find such a text." Madame Blavatsky scratched a thin eyebrow, affecting a weary air. "It will not be easy to translate."

Heat tingled the back of Eureka's neck. She didn't know if she was happy or afraid, only that this woman was the key to something she needed to understand.

"It might be dangerous," Blavatsky continued. "Knowledge is power; power corrupts. Corruption brings shame and ruin. Ignorance may not be bliss, but it is perhaps preferable to a life lived in shame. Do you agree?"

"I'm not sure." Eureka sensed Diana would have liked Madame Blavatsky. She would have trusted this translator. "I think I'd rather know the truth, regardless of the consequences."

"So you shall." Blavatsky offered a mysterious smile.

Cat leaned forward in her chair, clasped the edge of the woman's desk. "We want your best price. No funny business."

"I see you've brought your business manager." Blavatsky

cackled, then inhaled and contemplated Cat's request. "For something of this magnitude and intricacy . . . It's going to be very taxing for an old woman."

Cat held up her hand. Eureka hoped she wouldn't tell Madame Blavatsky to talk to it. "Cut to the chase, lady."

"Ten dollars a page."

"We'll give you five," Eureka said.

"Eight." Blavatsky pinched another cigarette between her bright red lips, clearly enjoying this ritual.

"Seven-fifty"—Cat snapped her fingers—"and you throw in the chemicals to fix that water damage."

"You won't find anyone else who can do what I can do. I could ask for a hundred dollars a page!" Blavatsky dabbed her eyes with a faded handkerchief, measured Eureka. "But you look so very beaten down, even though you have more help than you know. Know that." She paused. "Seven-fifty is a fair price. You have a deal."

"What happens now?" Eureka asked. Her ear was ringing. When she rubbed it, for a moment she thought she heard the chatter of the birds' song coming clearly through her left ear. Impossible. She shook her head and noticed Madame Blavatsky notice.

The woman nodded at the birds. "They tell me he's been watching you for a very long time."

"Who?" Cat looked around the room.

"She knows." Madame Blavatsky smiled at Eureka.

Eureka whispered, "Ander?"

"Shhh," Madame Blavatsky cooed. "My lovebirds' song is brave and auspicious, Eureka. Do not be troubled by the things you cannot yet understand." Suddenly she swiveled in her chair to face her computer. "I will send the translated pages in batches via email, along with a link to my Square account for payment."

"Thanks." Eureka scrawled her email address, slid the paper to Cat to add hers.

"It's funny, isn't it?" Cat handed Madame Blavatsky the paper with their information. "Emailing a translation of something so ancient?"

Madame Blavatsky rolled her watery eyes. "What you think is advanced would embarrass any of the masters of the old. Their capabilities vastly surpassed ours. We are a thousand years behind what they achieved." Blavatsky opened a drawer and pulled out a sack of baby carrots, breaking one in half to split it between the two turtles awakening from their nap on her desk. "There, Gilda," she sang. "There, Brunhilda. My darlings." She leaned toward the girls. "This book will tell of far more exciting innovations than cyberspace." She slid her glasses back up on her nose and gestured at the door. "Well, good night. Don't let the turtles bite you on your way out."

Eureka rose shakily from the couch as Cat gathered their things. Eureka paused, looking at the book on the desk. She thought of what her mother would do. Diana had lived her life trusting her instincts. If Eureka wanted to know what her inheritance meant, she had to trust Madame Blavatsky. She had to leave the book behind. It wasn't easy.

"Eureka?" Madame Blavatsky raised a pointer finger. "You know what they told Creon, of course?"

Eureka shook her head. "Creon?"

" 'Suffering is wisdom's schoolteacher.' Think about it." She drew in her breath. "My, what a path you are on."

"I'm on a path?" Eureka said.

"We look forward to your translation," Cat said in a much steadier voice.

"I may start right away; I may not. But don't hassle me. I work here"—she pointed at her desk—"I live upstairs"— she jerked her thumb toward the ceiling. "And I protect my privacy. Translation requires time and positive vibrations." She looked out the window. "That would be a good tweet. I should tweet that."

"Madame Blavatsky," Eureka said before she stepped through the atelier door. "Does my book have a title?"

Madame Blavatsky seemed far away. Without looking at Eureka, she said very softly, "It is called *The Book of Love.*"

From: savvyblavy@gmail.com
To: reka96runs@gmail.com
Cc: catatoniaestes@gmail.com
Date: Sunday, October 6, 2013, 1:31 a.m.
Subject: first salvo

Dear Eureka,

By dint of many hours of focused concentration, I have translated the following. I have tried not to take liberties with the prose, only to make the content as clear as water for your reading ease. I hope this meets your expectations. . . .

On the vanished isle where I was born, I was called Selene. This is my book of love.

Mine is a tale of catastrophic passion. You may wonder whether it is true, but all true things are questioned. Those who allow themselves to imagine—to believe—may find redemption in my story.

We must start at the beginning, in a place that has long ceased to exist. Where we'll end . . . well, who can know the ending until the last word has been written? Everything might change with the last word.

In the beginning, the island stood beyond the Pillars of Hercules, alone in the Atlantic. I was raised in the mountains, where magic was abided. Daily,

I gazed upon a beautiful palace that sat like a dia-mond in the sun-dappled valley far below. Legends told of a city with an astonishing design, waterfalls ringed with unicorns—and twin princes maturing in-side the castle's ivory walls.

The elder prince and would-be king's name was Atlas. He was known to be gallant, to favor hibiscus milk, to never shy away from a wrestling match. The younger prince was an enigma, rarely seen or heard from. He was called Leander, and from an early age he found his passion in voyaging by sea to the king's many colonies around the world.

I had listened to other mountain girls recount vivid dreams in which Prince Atlas carried them away on a horse of silver, made them his queen. But the prince slept in the shadows of my consciousness when I was a child. Had I known then what I know now, my imagination might have let me love him be-fore our worlds collided. It would have been easier that way.

As a girl, I yearned for naught outside the en-chanted, wooded fringes of our island. Nothing interested me more than my relatives, who were sorceresses, telepathists, changelings, alchemists. I flitted through their workshops, apprentice to all but the gossipwitches—whose powers rarely tran-

scended petty human jealousies, which they never tired of saying were what really made the world go round. I was filled with the stories of my numinous ancestors. My favorite tale was of an uncle who could project his mind across the ocean and inhabit the bodies of Minoan men and women. His escapades sounded delicious. In those days I relished the taste of scandal.

I was sixteen when the rumors wafted from the palace to the mountains. Birds sang that the king had fallen ill with a strange sickness. They sang of the rich bounty Prince Atlas promised anyone who could cure his father.

I had never dreamed of crossing the threshold of the palace, but I had once cured my father's fever with a powerful local herb. And so, under a waning moon, I traveled the twenty-six miles down to the palace, a poultice of artemisia in a pouch hanging from my belt.

Would-be healers formed a line three miles long outside the castle. I took my place at the back. One by one, magicians entered; one by one, they left, indignant or ashamed. When I was just ten deep in the line, the palace doors were closed. Black smoke twisted from the chimneys, signaling that the king was dead.

Wails rose from the city as I made my sad way home. When I was halfway there, alone in a wooded glen, I came across a boy about my age kneeling over a sparkling river. He was knee-deep in a patch of white narcissus, so immersed in his thoughts he seemed in another realm. When I saw that he was crying, I touched his shoulder.

"Are you hurt, sir?"

When he turned to me, the sorrow in his eyes was overwhelming. I understood it like I knew the language of the birds: he had lost the dearest thing he had.

I held out the poultice in my hand. "I wish I could have saved your father."

He fell upon me, weeping. "You can still save me."

The rest is yet to come, Eureka. Stand by.
SWAK

Madame B, Gilda, and Brunhilda

14

THE SHADOW

Tuesday meant another session with Dr. Landry. The therapist's New Iberia office was hardly the first place Eureka wanted to drive to in her newly repaired Jeep, but in the cold standoff at breakfast that morning, Rhoda had ended all discussion with her usual soul-chilling line:

As long as you live in my house, you follow my rules.

She'd given Eureka a list of phone numbers for her three assistants at the university, in case Eureka got into trouble while Rhoda was in a meeting. They weren't taking any more chances, Rhoda said when she handed Eureka back her keys. Dad's wife could probably make *I love you* sound menacing— not that Eureka had ever received that particular threat from Rhoda.

Eureka was nervous about getting back behind the wheel. She'd transformed into a hyperdefensive driver—counting three seconds of space between cars, putting on her blinker half a mile before she turned. Her shoulder muscles were knotted by the time she got to Dr. Landry's office. She sat in Magda under the beech tree, trying to breathe the tension out.

At 3:03 she slumped onto the therapist's couch. She wore her weekly scowl.

Dr. Landry wore another pair of slip-on shoes. She kicked her feet out of the clunky orange flats, which had never been in style.

"Catch me up." Dr. Landry tucked her bare feet under her on the chair. "What's happened since we talked?"

Eureka's uniform itched. She wished she'd peed before the session started. At least there was no issue of having to race back to school for the cross-country meet today. Even Coach would have given up on her by now. She could drive home slowly, on different dirt roads, paths not frequented by phantom boys.

She wouldn't see him, so he couldn't sort of make her cry. Or brush the corner of her eye with his finger. Or smell like an undiscovered ocean she wanted to swim in. Or be the only one around who didn't know a single catastrophic thing about her.

Eureka's cheeks were hot. Landry tilted her head, as if noting each shade of scarlet Eureka turned. No way. Eureka was keeping Ander's appearance—and disappearance—to herself. She reached for one of the hard candies on the coffee table and threw up a screen of noise with the wrapper.

"That wasn't supposed to be a trick question," Landry said.

Everything was a trick. Eureka considered opening her calculus book, struggling through a theorem for the balance of the hour. Maybe she had to *be* here, but she didn't have to cooperate. But that broadcast would travel back to Rhoda, whose pride would lead to some inanity like car revoking, grounding, or some other dark threat that wouldn't sound absurd inside the walls of her house, where Eureka had no allies. None with power, anyway.

"Well." She sucked on the candy. "I did get my inheritance from my mom." This was no-brainer therapy fodder. It had everything: deep symbolic meaning, family history, and the gossipy novelty therapists couldn't resist.

"I assume your father will manage the funds until you are of age?"

"It's nothing like that." Eureka sighed, bored but not surprised by the assumption. "I doubt there's any monetary value to my inheritance. There wasn't any monetary value to my mother's life. Just things she liked." She tugged on the chain around her neck to lift the lapis lazuli locket from under her white blouse.

"That's beautiful." Dr. Landry leaned forward, weakly

feigning appreciation for the weathered piece. "Is there a picture inside?"

Yes, it's a picture of a million billable hours, Eureka thought, imagining an hourglass filled with tiny Dr. Landrys instead of sand slipping through.

"It doesn't open," Eureka said. "But she wore it all the time. There were a couple of other archaeological objects she found interesting. This rock called a thunderstone."

Dr. Landry nodded blankly. "It must make you feel loved, knowing your mother wanted you to have these things."

"Maybe. It's also confusing. She left me an old book written in an ancient language. At least I found someone who can translate it."

Eureka had read Madame Blavatsky's translated email several times. The story was interesting—both she and Cat agreed—but Eureka found it frustrating. It felt so far removed from reality. She didn't understand how it related to Diana.

Landry was frowning, shaking her head.

"What?" Eureka heard her voice rise. This meant she was defensive. She'd made a mistake bringing it up. She'd meant to stay in safe and neutral territory.

"You're never going to know your mother's full intentions, Eureka. That's the reality of death."

There is no death. . . . Eureka heard Madame Blavatsky drowning out the therapist's voice. *Only congregation and dispersal.*

"This desire to translate some old book seems fruitless," Landry said. "To pin your hopes on a new connection with your mother now might be very painful."

Suffering is wisdom's schoolteacher.

Eureka was already on the path. She was going to connect this book to Diana, she just didn't know how yet. She grabbed a fistful of disgusting candy, needing to keep her hands busy. Her therapist sounded like Brooks, who still had not apologized. They had tensely avoided each other in the halls at school for two days.

"Leave the dead to rest," Landry said. "Focus on your living world."

Eureka gazed out the window at a sky whose color was typical of the days after a hurricane: unapologetic blue. "Thank you for that chicken soup for the soul."

She heard Brooks buzzing something nasty in her ear about how Eureka was convinced all her therapists were stupid. This one really was! She'd been considering apologizing to him, just to break the tension. But every time she saw him, he was surrounded by a wall of boys, football jocks she'd never seen him hang out with before this week, guys whose precious machismo used to be the brunt of some of Brooks's best jokes. He'd catch her eye, then make a lewd gesture that cracked the circle of boys up.

He was making Eureka crack up, too, just in a different way.

"Before you jump into a costly translation of this book," Landry said, "at least think about the pros and cons."

There was no question in her mind. Eureka was continuing with the translation of *The Book of Love*. Even if it turned out to be nothing more than a love story, maybe it would help her understand Diana better. Once, Eureka had asked her what it was like when she met Eureka's dad, how she'd known she wanted to be with him.

It felt like being saved, Diana had told her. It reminded Eureka of what the prince in the story said to Selene: *You can still save me.*

"Have you ever heard of Carl Jung's idea of the shadow?" Landry tried.

Eureka shook her head. "Something tells me I'm about to."

"The idea is that we all have a shadow, which comprises denied aspects of the self. My sense is that your extreme aloofness, your emotional unavailability, the guardedness that I must say is palpable in you, comes from a core place."

"Where else would it come from?"

Landry ignored her. "Perhaps you had a childhood in which you were told to repress your emotions. A person who does that for long enough might find that those neglected aspects of the self begin to bubble up elsewhere. Your stifled emotions may very well be sabotaging your life."

"Anything's possible," Eureka said. "I suggest my stifled emotions take a number, though."

"It's very common," Landry said. "We often seek the companionship of others who display aspects we've repressed to the depths of our shadow. Think about your parents'—well, your father and stepmother's—relationship."

"I'd rather not."

Landry sighed. "If you don't confront this aloofness, it will lead you to narcissism and isolation."

"Is that a threat?" Eureka asked.

Landry shrugged. "I've seen it before. It's a type of personality disorder."

This was where therapy inevitably led: the reduction of individuals to types. Eureka wished herself outside these walls. She glanced at the clock. She'd only been here for twenty minutes.

"Does it insult your pride to hear you're not unique?" Landry asked. "Because that is a symptom of narcissism."

The only person who understood Eureka was scattered across the sea.

"Tell me where your mind went just then," Landry said.

"St. Lucia."

"You want to leave?"

"I'll make a deal with you. I never come here again, you bill Rhoda for the time, and no one needs to be the wiser."

Landry's voice hardened. "You will wake up at forty with no husband, no children, and no career if you don't learn to engage with the world."

Eureka rose to her feet, wishing that someone like Madame Blavatsky sat in the chair across from her instead of Dr. Landry. The translator's intriguing remarks had felt more insightful than any board-certified babble ever to emerge from this therapist's lips.

"Your parents have paid for another half hour. Don't walk out that door, Eureka."

"My dad's wife paid for another half hour," she corrected. "My mother is Friday Night Fish Dinner." She gagged on her own horrible words as she walked past Landry.

"You're making a mistake."

"If you think so"—Eureka opened the door—"I'm convinced I'm making the right decision."

15

BLUE NOTE

"Do you think I'm fat?" Cat asked in the lunch line on Wednesday. Eureka still hadn't spoken to Brooks.

It was fried pork chop day, the gastronomical highlight of Cat's week. But on her tray was a brownish mound of shredded iceberg lettuce, a scoop of gummy black-eyed peas, and a healthy squirt of hot sauce.

"Another one bites the dust." Eureka pointed at Cat's food. "Literally." She swiped her card at the register to pay for her pork chop and chocolate milk. Eureka was bored by diet conversations. She would have loved to fill a bathing suit as well as Cat.

"*I* know I'm not fat," Cat said as they navigated through the dizzying maze of tables. "And *you* know, apparently. But does *Rodney* know?"

"He'd better." Eureka avoided the eyes of the sophomore cross-country girls at whom Cat blew a superior air kiss. "Did he say something? And if he did, do you care?"

Eureka wished she hadn't said that. She didn't want to be jealous of Cat. She wanted to be the best friend who was entranced by discussions of dieting and dating and dirt on the other kids in their class. Instead she was bitter and bored. And bruised from being practically deboned by Rhoda the night before over her early exit from Landry's office. Rhoda had been so furious she couldn't even think of a strong enough punishment, which now was pending and keeping Eureka on edge.

"No, it's nothing like that." Cat glanced at the cross-country seniors' table, which was set back from the rest of the cafeteria in the alcove by the window. Theresa Leigh and Mary Monteau had two empty seats next to them on the black metal bench. They waved to Cat, smiled tentatively at Eureka.

Since she'd come back to school this year, Eureka had been eating lunch with Cat outside under the huge pecan tree in the courtyard. The cacophony of so many students eating, joking, arguing, selling crap for whatever church field trip they were trying to raise money for, was too much for Eureka, who'd barely gotten out of the hospital. Cat had never uttered a peep about missing the action inside, but today she winced as Eureka walked toward the back door. It was cold and blustery, and Cat was wearing the plaid skirt option of the Evangeline uniform with no stockings.

"Would you hate staying in today?" Cat nodded toward the empty seats at the cross-country table. "I'll be a Catsicle out there."

"No problem." Though it seemed like a death sentence as Eureka slid onto the bench across from Cat, said hey to Theresa and Mary, and tried to pretend the whole table wasn't staring at her.

"Rodney hasn't said anything overt about my weight." Cat swirled a piece of lettuce around in a puddle of hot sauce. "But he's rail thin, and it makes me jumpy to think I might weigh more than my dude. You know how it is. It's hard not to anticipate the future criticisms of someone you really like. Something about me is going to bug him eventually, the question is—"

"How long is the list going to be?" Eureka stared at her tray. She crossed and uncrossed her legs, thinking about Brooks.

"Take your mystery guy," Cat said.

Eureka tugged the elastic band from her hair, then swept her hair back up in a bun identical to the one she'd just had. She knew her face was red. "Ander."

"You're blushing."

"I am not." Eureka shook Tabasco sauce violently onto food she wasn't hungry for anymore. She just needed to drown something. "I'll never see him again."

"He'll be back. It's what boys do." Cat chewed a bite of lettuce slowly, then reached over to steal a hunk of Eureka's pork chop. Her diets were experiments, and this one, thankfully, had ended. "Fine, then, take Brooks. When you were dating him—"

Eureka motioned for Cat to stop. "There's a reason I quit my therapist. I'm not up for rehashing my fifth-grade romance with Brooks."

"Have you two not kissed and made up yet?"

Eureka nearly gagged on her chocolate milk. She hadn't told Cat about the kiss that seemed to have ended her relationship with her oldest friend. Eureka and Brooks could barely look at each other now.

"We're still fighting, if that's what you mean."

She and Brooks had sat through an entire Latin class, their chairs bumping up against each other in the cramped language lab, without making eye contact. This required focus—Brooks usually mimed at least three jokes at the expense of Mr. Piscidia's silver forest of chest hair.

"What's his problem?" Cat asked. "His dickhead-to-penitent turnaround is usually swifter. It's been three whole days."

"Almost four," Eureka said automatically. She felt the other girls at the table swivel their heads to listen in. She lowered her voice. "Maybe he doesn't have a problem. Maybe it's me." She rested her head in the crook of her elbow on the table and pushed her dirty rice around with her fork. "Selfish, haughty, critical, manipulative, inconsiderate—"

"Eureka."

She slid upright at the deep-voiced sound of her name, as if pulled by puppet strings. Brooks stood at the head of the table, watching her. His hair fell over his forehead, obscuring his eyes. His shirt was too small in the shoulders, which was annoyingly sexy. He'd gone through puberty early and had been taller than the rest of the boys his age, but he'd stopped growing in freshman year. Was he having a second growth spurt? He looked different, and not just taller and brawnier. He didn't seem shy about walking right up to their table, though all twelve of its female inhabitants had stopped their conversations to look at him.

He didn't have this lunch hour. He was supposed be the office aide fourth period, and she didn't see any blue summoning notes in his hand. What was he doing here?

"I'm sorry," he said. "I've been in an avocado."

Cat smacked her forehead. "WTF, Brooks, *that's* your apology?"

Eureka felt the corners of her mouth making a smile. Once, the year before, when Eureka and Brooks were watching TV after school, they'd overheard Dad on the phone saying he was sorry for being incommunicado. The twins misunderstood and Claire came running for Eureka, wondering why Dad had been in an avocado.

"That must be the pits," Brooks had said, and a legend had been born.

Now it was up to Eureka to decide whether to complete the joke and end the silence. All the girls at the table were watching her. Two of them, she knew, had crushes on Brooks. It was going to be embarrassing, but the power of shared history coaxed it from Eureka.

She took a deep breath. "These past few days have been the pits."

Cat groaned. "You two need your own planet."

Brooks grinned and knelt down, planting his chin on the edge of the table.

"Lunch is only thirty-five minutes long, Brooks," Cat said. "That's not enough time for how much you need to apologize for all the baloney you said. I wonder if the human race will last long enough for you to apologize for all the baloney—"

"Cat," Eureka said. "We get it."

"Want to go somewhere and talk?" Brooks said.

She nodded. Rising from her chair, Eureka grabbed her bag and slid her tray across to Cat. "Finish my pork chop, waif."

She followed Brooks through the maze of tables, wondering whether he'd told anyone about their fight, about their kiss. As soon as the path was wide enough to walk side by side, Brooks moved next to her. He put his hand on her back. Eureka wasn't sure what she wanted from Brooks, but his hand on her felt nice. She didn't know what period Maya Cayce had lunch, but she wished it was now so the girl could watch them leave the cafeteria together.

They pushed through the orange double doors and walked down the empty hallway. Their feet echoed in unison on the linoleum floor. They'd shared the same gait since they were kids.

Near the end of the hallway, Brooks stopped and faced her. He probably didn't mean to stop in front of the trophy case, but Eureka couldn't help looking at her reflection. Then, through the glass, she saw the hefty cross-country trophy that her team had won the year before, and next to it, the smaller, second-place trophy from two years earlier, when they'd lost first place to Manor. Eureka didn't want to think about the team she'd quit or their rivals—or the boy who'd lied about being one of them.

"Let's go outside." She jerked her head for Brooks to follow her. "More privacy."

The paved courtyard separated the classrooms from the glass-walled administration center. It was surrounded on three sides by buildings, all built around a huge, moss-slathered pecan tree. The nuts' rotting husks quilted the grass, giving off a fecund odor that reminded Eureka of climbing pecan branches on her grandparents' farm with Brooks as a kid. Hyacinth vines crept along the coulee of the Band Room, behind them. Hummingbirds darted from blossom to blossom, sampling nectar.

A cold front was moving in. The air was brisker than it had been in the morning when she left for school. Eureka drew her green cardigan tight around her shoulders. She and

Brooks leaned their backs against the rough bark of the tree and watched the parking lot as if it were a vast expanse of something pretty.

Brooks didn't say anything. He watched her carefully in the diffused sunlight under the canopy of moss. His gaze was as intense as the one Ander had turned on her in his truck, and when he'd come to her house, and even outside Mr. Fontenot's office. That was the last time she'd seen him—and now Brooks seemed to be doing an impersonation of the boy he hated.

"I was a jerk the other night," Brooks said.

"Yeah, you were."

That made him laugh.

"You were a jerk to say those things—even if you were right." She rolled toward him, her shoulder pressed against the tree trunk. Her eyes found his lower lip and could not move. She couldn't believe she'd kissed him. Not just once, but several times. Thinking about it made her body buzz.

She wanted to kiss him now, but that was where they'd gotten into trouble before. So she dropped her gaze to her feet, stared at the pecan shells scattered across the patchy grass.

"What I said the other night wasn't fair," Brooks said. "It was about me, not you. My anger was a cover."

Eureka knew you were supposed to roll your eyes when boys said that it was them, not you. But she also knew that the statement was true, even if boys didn't know it. So she let Brooks go on.

"I've had feelings for you for a long time." He didn't falter when he said it; he didn't say "uh" or "um" or "like." Once the words were out of his mouth, he didn't look like he wanted to suck them back in. He held her gaze, waited for her response.

A breeze swept across the courtyard, and Eureka thought she might fall. She thought of the Himalayas, which Diana said were so windy she couldn't believe the mountains themselves hadn't blown over. Eureka wanted to be that sturdy.

She was surprised how easily Brooks's words had come. They were usually candid with each other, but they had never talked about this stuff. Attraction. Feelings. For each other. How could he be so calm when he was saying the most intense thing anyone could say?

Eureka imagined saying these words herself, how nervous she would be. Only, when she pictured saying them, something funny happened: the boy standing across from her wasn't Brooks. It was Ander. He was the one she thought about lying in bed at night, the one whose turquoise eyes gave her the sense that she was tumbling through the most serene and breathtaking waterfall.

She and Brooks weren't like that. They'd messed up the other day by trying to pretend they were. Maybe Brooks thought that after kissing her he had to say he liked her, that she'd be upset if he pretended it meant nothing.

Eureka pictured the Himalayas, told herself she wouldn't

fall. "You don't have to say that to make up with me. We can go back to being friends."

"You don't believe me." He exhaled and looked down, muttering something Eureka couldn't understand. "You're right. Maybe it's best to wait. I've been waiting so long already, what's another eternity?"

"Waiting for what?" She shook her head. "Brooks, that kiss—"

"It was a blue note," he said, and she almost knew exactly what he meant.

Technically, a certain sound could be all wrong, out of key. But when you find the blue note—Eureka knew this from the YouTube blues videos she'd watched trying to teach herself guitar—everything felt right in a surprising way.

"You're really going to try to get away with that bad jazz metaphor?" Eureka teased, because—honestly?—the kiss itself hadn't been wrong. One might even use the word "miraculous" to describe that kiss. It was the people doing the kissing that were wrong. It was the line they'd crossed.

"I'm used to you not feeling for me the way I feel for you," Brooks said. "On Saturday, I couldn't believe that you might . . ."

Stop, Eureka wanted to say. If he kept talking, she'd start to believe him, decide they should kiss again, maybe frequently, definitely soon. She couldn't seem to find her voice.

"Then you made that joke about what took me so long, when I had been wanting to kiss you forever. I snapped."

"I screwed it up."

"I shouldn't have lashed out like that," Brooks said. Notes from a saxophone in the Band Room floated into the courtyard. "Did I hurt you?"

"I'll recover. We both will, right?"

"I hope I didn't make you cry."

Eureka squinted at him. The truth was, she'd been close to tears watching him drive away, imagining him heading straight to Maya Cayce's house for comfort.

"Did you?" he asked again. "Cry?"

"Don't flatter yourself." She tried to say it lightly.

"I was worried that I went too far." He paused. "No tears. I'm glad."

She shrugged.

"Eureka." Brooks wrapped her in an unexpected hug. His body was warm against the wind, but she couldn't breathe. "It'd be okay if you broke down. You know that, right?"

"Yes."

"Every member of my family cries at patriotic commercials. You didn't even cry when your mother died."

She pushed him back, palms on his chest. "What does that have to do with us?"

"Vulnerability isn't the worst thing in the world. You have a support system. You can trust me. I'm here if you need a shoulder to lean on, someone to pass the tissues."

"I'm not made out of stone." She grew defensive again. "I cry."

"No you don't."

"I cried last week."

Brooks looked shocked. "Why?"

"Do you *want* me to cry?"

Brooks's eyes had a coldness in them. "Was it when your car got hit? I should have known you wouldn't cry for me."

His gaze pinned her, made her claustrophobic. The urge to kiss him faded. She looked at her watch. "The bell's about to ring."

"Not for ten minutes." He paused. "Are we . . . friends?"

She laughed. "Of course we're friends."

"I mean, are we *just* friends?"

Eureka rubbed her bad ear. She found it difficult to look at him. "I don't know. Look, I've got a presentation on Sonnet Sixty-Four next period. I should look over my notes. 'Time will come and take my love away,' " she said in a British accent intended to make him laugh. It didn't. "We're cool again," she said. "That's all that matters."

"Yeah," he said stiffly.

She didn't know what he wanted her to say. They couldn't lurch from kissing to arguing back to kissing just like that. They were great at being friends. Eureka intended to keep it that way.

"So, I'll see you later?" She walked backward, facing him, as she headed toward the door.

"Wait, Eureka—" Brooks called her name just as the doors swung open and someone plowed into her back.

"Can't you walk?" Maya Cayce asked. She squealed when she saw Brooks. She was the only person Eureka knew who could skip intimidatingly. She was also the only person whose Evangeline slacks fit her body like an obscene glove.

"There you are, baby," Maya cooed at Brooks, but she looked at Eureka, laughing with her eyes.

Eureka tried to ignore her. "Were you going to say something else, Brooks?"

She already knew the answer.

He caught Maya when she flung her body at his in an X-rated hug. His eyes were barely visible over the crown of her black hair. "Never mind."

16

HECKLER

Like every kid at Evangeline, Eureka had taken a dozen field trips to the Lafayette Science Museum on Jefferson Street downtown. When she was a child, it dazzled her. There was nowhere else she knew of where you could see rocks from prehistoric Louisiana. Even though she'd seen the rocks a hundred times, on Thursday morning she boarded the school bus with her Earth Science class to make it a hundred and one.

"This is supposed to be a cool exhibit," her friend Luke said as they descended the bus stairs and gathered in the driveway before entering the museum. He pointed at the banner advertising MESSAGES FROM THE DEEP in wobbly white letters that made the words look like they were underwater. "It's from Turkey."

"I'm sure the curators here will find some way to ruin it," Eureka snapped. Her conversation with Brooks the day before had been so frustrating, she couldn't help taking it out on the entire gender.

Luke had reddish hair and pale, bright skin. They'd played soccer together when they were younger. He was a genuinely nice person who would spend his life in Lafayette, happy as a sand dab. He eyed Eureka for a moment, maybe remembering that she'd been to Turkey with her mother and that her mother was dead now. But he didn't say anything.

Eureka turned inward, staring at the opalescent button on her school blouse as if it were an artifact from another world. She knew *Messages from the Deep* was supposed to be a great exhibit. Dad had taken the twins to see it when it opened two weeks earlier. They were still trying to get her to play "shipwreck" with them using couch cushions and broomsticks in the den.

Eureka couldn't blame William and Claire for their insensitivity. In fact, she appreciated it. There was so much cautious whispering around Eureka that slaps in the face, like a game called "shipwreck," or even Brooks's tirade the other night, were refreshing. They were ropes flung out to a drowning girl, the opposite of Rhoda sighing and Googling "teen post-traumatic stress disorder."

She waited outside the museum with her class, cloaked in humidity, for the bus from the other school to arrive so the docent could start the tour. Her classmates' bodies pressed around her in a suffocating cluster. She smelled Jenn Indest's strawberry-scented shampoo and heard Richard Carp's hay-fever-belabored breathing, and she wished she were eighteen and had a waitressing job in another city.

She would never admit it, but sometimes Eureka thought she was owed a new life somewhere else. Catastrophes were like sick days you should be able to spend any way you wanted. Eureka wanted to raise her hand, announce that she was very, very sick, and disappear forever.

Maya Cayce's voice popped into her head: *There you are, baby.*

She wanted to scream. She wanted to run, to bulldoze any classmates between her and the woods of the New Iberia City Park.

The second bus pulled into the lot. Boys from Ascension High wearing navy blazers with gold buttons filed down the steps and stopped short of the Evangeline kids. They did not mingle. Ascension was wealthy and one of the hardest schools in the parish. Every year there was an article in the paper about its students getting into Vanderbilt or Emory or some other fancy place. They had a reputation for being nerdy and reserved. Eureka had never thought much about Evangeline's reputation—everything about her school seemed so ordinary to her. But as Ascension eyes scampered over her and her classmates, Eureka saw herself being re-

210

duced to whatever stereotype the boys had told themselves Evangelinos fit.

She recognized one or two of the Ascension boys from church. A few kids from her class waved at a few kids from theirs. If Cat were here, she'd whisper dirty comments about them under her breath—how "well-endowed" Ascension was.

"Welcome, scholars," the young museum docent called. She had a light brown bowl cut and wore slouchy tan slacks, one leg of which was rolled up to her ankle. Her bayou twang gave her voice the quality of a clarinet. "I'm Margaret, your guide. Today, you are in for an overwhelming adventure."

They followed Margaret inside, got their hands stamped with an LSU Tigers stamp to show they'd been paid for, and gathered in the lobby. Masking tape marked rows on the carpet for them to stand along. Eureka fell as far back in the crowd as she could.

Construction-paper art projects faded along cinder-block walls. The visible curve of the planetarium reminded Eureka of the Pink Floyd laser-light show she'd seen with Brooks and Cat on the last day of junior year. She'd brought a sack of Dad's dark-chocolate popcorn, Cat had snuck a bottle of bad wine from her parents' stash, and Brooks had brought painted domino masks for them to wear. They'd laughed through the entire show, harder than the stoned college kids behind them. It was such a happy memory that it made Eureka want to die.

"A little background." The docent turned in the direction opposite the planetarium and waved for the students to follow her. They walked through a dimly lit corridor that smelled like glue and Lean Cuisine, then stopped before closed wooden doors. "The artifacts you are about to see come to us from Bodrum, Turkey. Does anyone know where that is?"

Bodrum was a port city in the southwestern corner of the country. Eureka had never been there; it was one of the stops Diana had made after they'd hugged goodbye in the Istanbul airport and Eureka flew home to start school. The postcards Diana had sent from those trips were tinged with a melancholy that made Eureka feel closer to her mother. They were never as happy apart as they were together.

When no one raised a hand, the docent pulled a laminated map from her tote bag and held it over her head. Bodrum was marked with a large red star.

"Thirty years ago," Margaret said, "divers discovered the Uluburun shipwreck six miles off the coast of Bodrum. The remains y'all will see today are thought to be nearly *four thousand* years old." Margaret looked at the students, hoping someone would be impressed.

She opened the wooden doors. Eureka knew the exhibition room wasn't much bigger than a classroom, so they were going to have to cram themselves in. As they entered the blue hush of the exhibit, Belle Pogue fell in line behind Eureka.

"God had barely made the earth six thousand years

ago," Belle muttered. She was president of the Holy Rollers, a Christian roller-skating club. Eureka imagined God roller-skating through oblivion, passing shipwrecks on his way to the Garden of Eden.

The walls of the exhibition room had been draped in blue netting to suggest the ocean. Someone had glued plastic star-fish to form a border near the floor. A boom box played ocean sounds: water burbling, the occasional caw of a seagull.

In the center of the room, a spotlight shone from the ceiling, illuminating the highlight of the exhibition: a reconstructed ship. It resembled some of the rafts people sailed around Cypremort Point. It was built from cedar planks, and its broad hull curved at the bottom, forming a fin-shaped keel. Near the helm, the low protrusion of a galley was capped by a flat, shingled roof. Metal cables held the ship a foot off the floor, so the deck hovered just above Eureka's head.

As students banked left or right to walk around the ship, Eureka chose left, passing a display of tall, narrow terra-cotta vases and three huge stone anchors speckled with verdigris.

Margaret waved her laminated map, beckoning the students to the other side of the ship, where they found a cross-section of the helm. The interior was open, like a dollhouse. The museum had furnished it to suggest how the ship might have looked before it sank. There were three levels. The lowest was storage—copper ingots, crates of blue glass bottles, more of the long-necked terra-cotta vases nestled upright in beds of straw. In the middle was a row of sleeping pallets, along with bins of grain and plastic food and double-handled drinking vessels. The top story was an open deck edged with a few feet of cedar railing.

For some reason, the museum had dressed scarecrows in togas and stationed them at the helm with an ancient-looking telescope. They gazed out as if the museumgoers were whales among waves. When some of Eureka's classmates snickered at the seafaring scarecrows, the docent flicked her laminated map to get their attention.

"Over eighteen thousand artifacts were recovered from the shipwreck, and not all of them are recognizable to the modern eye. Take this one." Margaret held up a color photocopy of a finely carved ram's head that looked like it had been broken off at the neck. "I see you wondering, Where's the rest of this little guy's body?" She paused to eye the students. "In fact, the hollowed neck is intentional. Can anyone guess what his purpose was?"

"A boxing glove," a boy's voice called from the back, eliciting new snickers.

"Quite a pugilistic speculation." Margaret waved her illustration. "In fact, this is a ceremonial wine chalice. Now, doesn't that make you wonder—"

"Not really," the same voice called from the back.

Eureka glanced at her teacher, Ms. Kash, who turned sharply toward the voice, then gave a sniff of relieved indignation when she was sure it hadn't come from one of her students.

"Imagine a future civilization examining some of the artifacts you or I might leave behind," Margaret continued. "What would the people think of us? How might our brightest innovations—our iPads, solar panels, or credit cards—appear to distant generations?"

"Solar panels are Stone Age compared to what's been done before." The same voice from the back rang out again.

Madame Blavatsky had said something similar, minus the obnoxiousness. Eureka rolled her eyes and shifted her weight and didn't turn around. AP Earth Science student from Ascension back there was clearly trying to impress a girl.

Margaret cleared her throat and pretended her rhetorical questions hadn't been heckled. "What will our distant descendants make of our society? Will we appear advanced . . . or provincial? Some of you might be looking at these artifacts, finding them old or outdated. Even, dare I say, boring."

Kids nodded. More snickering. Eureka couldn't help but like the old anchors and terra-cotta vases, but the scarecrows should be drowned.

The docent fumbled her hands into a pair of white gloves, the kind Diana had worn when handling artifacts. Then she reached into a box at her feet and produced an ivory carving. It was an actual-sized duck, very detailed. She tilted the duck toward her audience and used her fingers to part its wings, exposing a cleanly hollowed basin inside. "Ta-da—Bronze Age cosmetics case! Note the craftsmanship. Can anyone deny how finely made he is? This was thousands of years ago!"

"What about these Bronze Age shackles over here?" the same voice jeered from the back of the room. Students jostled to get a look at the persistent heckler. Eureka didn't waste the energy.

"Looks like your fine craftsmen owned slaves," he continued.

The docent stood on her toes and squinted at the dark back of the room. "This is a guided tour, young man. There's an order to things. Does anyone have an actual question back there?"

"Modern tyrants are fine craftsmen, too," the boy continued, amusing himself.

His voice was starting to sound familiar. Eureka turned around. She saw the top of a blond head facing forward while everyone else was looking back. She crept along the edge of the group to get a clearer look.

"That's enough," Ms. Kash scolded, eyeing the Ascension faculty disdainfully, as if amazed none of them had quieted the student.

"Yes, be silent, sir, or leave," Margaret snapped.

Then Eureka saw him. The tall, pale boy in the corner at the edge of the spotlight's beam, the tips of his wavy blond hair illuminated. His tone and smirk were casual, but his eyes flashed something darker.

Ander was wearing the same pressed white shirt and dark jeans. Everyone was looking at him. He was looking at Eureka.

"Silence is what causes most of humanity's problems," he said.

"It's time for you to leave," Margaret said.

"I'm done." Ander spoke so quietly, Eureka barely heard him.

"Good. Now, if you don't mind, I'll explain the purpose of this early sea voyage," Margaret said. "The ancient Egyptians established a trade route, perhaps the first one . . ."

Eureka didn't hear the rest. She heard her heart, which thundered. She waited for the other students to give up hope of another outburst, to swivel their heads back to the docent; then she edged around the group toward Ander.

His lips were closed, and it was hard to imagine them uttering the obnoxious comments that had drawn her over here. He gave her a slight smile, the last thing she expected. Standing close to him again gave Eureka the feeling of being by the ocean—independent of the starfish border, the sailor-crows, and the *Ocean Breeze* CD sloshing from the speakers. The ocean was in Ander, his aura. She'd never thought to use a word like "aura" before. He made uncharacteristic impulses feel as natural to her as breathing.

She stood on his left side, both of them facing the docent, and whispered from the corner of her mouth. "You don't go to Ascension."

"The docent thinks I go to Condescension." She heard the smile in his voice.

"You're not on the Manor track team, either."

"Can't get anything past you."

Eureka's voice wanted to rise. His composure made her angry. Where they stood, a few steps back from the group and just past the edge of the spotlight, the light was dim, but anyone who turned around could see them. The teachers and kids would hear if she didn't keep her whisper steady and low.

It seemed strange that more people weren't staring at Ander. He was so different. He stood out. But they barely noticed him. Apparently everyone assumed Ander went to the school they didn't, so his behavior wasn't interesting. His heckling was a forgotten artifact Margaret was delighted to leave unrecovered.

"I know you don't go to Evangeline," Eureka said through her teeth.

"For neither education nor entertainment."

"So what are you doing here?"

Ander turned and faced her. "I'm looking for you."

Eureka blinked. "You have a very disruptive way of going about it."

Ander scratched his forehead. "I get carried away." He

sounded regretful, but she couldn't be sure. "Can we go somewhere and talk?"

"Not exactly." She gestured toward the tour group. She and Ander were standing five feet behind the other students. They couldn't leave.

What did he want from her? First the car wreck, then showing up at her house, then following her to the lawyer's office, and now this? Every time she'd encountered him, it was an invasion of privacy, a crossing of some boundary.

"Please," he said. "I need to talk to you."

"Yeah, well, I needed to talk to you, too, back when my dad got the quote for my car repair. Remember that? Except when I called the number you gallantly gave me, someone who'd never heard of you picked up—"

"Let me explain. You're going to want to know the things I have to tell you."

She tugged on her collar, which was too tight around her neck. Margaret was saying something about a drowned princess's dowry. The mass of students began to shift toward some glass cases on the right side of the room.

Ander reached for her hand. His firm touch and soft skin made her shiver. "I'm serious. Your life is—"

She jerked her hand away. "I say one word to any teacher in here and you're handcuffed like a stalker."

"Will they use the bronze handcuffs?" he joked.

She looked daggers at him. Ander sighed.

The rest of the tour moved toward a display case. Eureka had no urge to join them. She both yearned and was afraid to stay with Ander. He put both hands on her shoulders.

"Getting rid of me would be a huge mistake." He pointed over his head to a glowing exit sign half covered by blue gauze so that it read only IT. He held out his hand. "Let's go."

17

SKIMMING A SURFACE

Through the door beneath the exit sign, down a short, dark hallway, Ander led Eureka toward another door. They didn't speak. Their bodies were close together. It was easier than she'd expected to hold on to Ander's hand—it fit hers. Some hands just fit other hands. It made her think of her mother.

When Ander reached for the handle of the second door, Eureka stopped him.

She pointed at a red band across the door. "You'll set off the alarm."

"How do you think I got in?" Ander released the door. No alarm sounded. "No one's going to catch us."

"You're pretty sure of yourself."

Ander's jaw tensed. "You don't know me very well."

The door opened to a lawn Eureka had never seen before. It faced a circular pond. Across the pond sat the planetarium, a ring of tinted glass windows just below its dome. The air was gray, windless, a little cold. It smelled like firewood. Eureka stopped at the edge of a short concrete ledge just past the exit. She dragged the toe of her oxford through the grass.

"You wanted to talk?" she said.

Ander glanced at the moss-slicked pond framed by live oaks. The branches curled down like gnarled witches' fingers reaching for the ground. Orange moss hung like spiders dangling from green webs. Like most of the standing water in this part of Louisiana, you could barely see the pond for all the *flottants* of trembling marsh, the moss and lily pads and purple-blossomed water shield carpeting its surface. She knew precisely the way it would smell down there—rich, fetid, dying.

Ander walked toward the water. He didn't motion for her to follow, but she did. When he reached the edge of the pond, he stopped.

"What are these doing here?" He crouched before a patch of creamy white jonquils at the edge of the water. The flowers made Eureka think of the pale gold variety that slipped up under the mailbox of her old house in New Iberia every year around her birthday.

"Jonquils are common here," she said, though it was late in the year for their trumpetlike blossoms to look so sturdy and fresh.

"Not jonquils," Ander said. "Narcissus."

He ran his fingers along one flower's thin stem. He plucked it from the earth and rose to his feet so that the flower was at Eureka's eye level. She noticed the butter-yellow trumpet at its center. The difference from the cream-colored outer petals was so slight you had to look closely to see it. Inside the trumpet, a black-tipped stamen shivered in a sudden breeze. Ander held the flower out, as if he were going to give it to Eureka. She lifted her hand to receive it, remembering another jonquil—another narcissus—she'd seen recently: in the woodcut image of the weeping woman from Diana's book. She thought of a line in the passage Madame Blavatsky had translated, about Selene finding the prince kneeling near the river in a patch of narcissus flowers.

Instead of handing her the flower, Ander crushed the petals inside a tight, shaking fist. He yanked the stem free and flung it to the ground. "She did this."

Eureka took a step back. "Who?"

He looked at her, as if he'd forgotten she was there. The tension in his jaw relaxed. His shoulders rose and sank with resigned melancholy. "No one. Let's sit down."

She pointed to a nearby bench between two oak trees, probably where the museum staff came for lunch on days when it wasn't too humid. Brown nesting pelicans wandered the path leading to the pond. Their feathers were slick with mossy water. Their long necks curved like the handles of umbrellas. They scattered when Eureka and Ander approached.

223

Who was Ander talking about? What was wrong with flowers lining a pond?

As Ander walked past the bench, Eureka asked, "Didn't you want to sit?"

"There's a better spot."

He pointed at a tree she hadn't noticed before. Live oak trees in Louisiana had famously twisted limbs. The tree in front of St. John's was the most photographed tree in the South. This live oak tree in the deserted museum garden was exceptional. It was a massive knot with branches so warped they looked like the world's most complicated jungle gym.

Ander crawled through a web of wide, crooked branches—straddling one, ducking under another, until he seemed to disappear. Eureka realized that beneath the tangled canopy of branches was a second, secret bench. She had a partial view of Ander as he reached it agilely, sat down, and draped his elbows over the back.

Eureka tried to follow his route. She started off okay, but after a few steps, she stalled. It was harder than it looked. Her hair tangled on the knob of a branch. Sharp twigs jabbed her arms. She pushed on, swatting moss from her face. She was less than a foot from the clearing when she reached an impasse. She couldn't see how to go forward—or back.

Sweat formed on her hairline. *Find your way out of a fox-hole, girl.* Why was she even in this foxhole to begin with?

"Here." Ander reached through the tangled branches. "This way."

She took his hand for the second time in five minutes. His grip was firm and warm and still fit hers.

"Step there." He pointed at a pocket of mulchy ground between two curving branches. Her shoe sank into the dank, supple soil. "Then slide your body through here."

"Is this worth it?"

"Yes."

Annoyed, Eureka craned her neck to the side. She swiveled her shoulders, then her hips, took two more careful steps, ducked under a low branch—and was free.

She righted herself to stand inside the oak lagoon. Dark and secluded, it was the size of a small gazebo. It was surprisingly beautiful. A pair of dragonflies appeared between Eureka and Ander. Their slate-blue wings blurred; then the insects came to rest, iridescent, on the bench.

"See?" Ander sat back down.

Eureka stared at the branches forming a dense maze around them. She could barely see the pond on the other side. From underneath, the tree was magical, otherworldly. She wondered if anyone else knew about this spot, or if the bench had gone unnoticed for generations, ever since the tree tucked it away.

Before she sat down, she looked for the quickest way out. It couldn't be the way she'd come in.

Ander pointed to a gap in the branches. "That might be the best exit."

"How'd you know I was—"

"You seem nervous. Are you claustrophobic? Me, I like being cocooned, secluded." He swallowed and his voice dropped. "Invisible."

"I like open spaces." She barely knew Ander, and no one knew where she was.

So why had she come here? Anyone would say it was stupid. Cat would punch her in the face for this. Eureka mentally retraced her steps. She didn't know why she'd taken his hand.

She did like looking at him. She liked the way his hand felt and his voice sounded. She liked the way he walked, by turns cautious and confident. Eureka wasn't a girl who did things because a hot boy said to. But she was here.

The place Ander had pointed out did look to be the largest gap in the branches. She imagined herself bounding through it, running for the woods beyond the pond, running all the way to Avery Island.

Ander swiveled on the bench. His knee dragged against her thigh. He quickly jerked it away. "Sorry."

She glanced down at her thigh, his knee. "Good heavens," she joked.

"No, I'm sorry I snuck up on you here."

She wasn't expecting that. Surprises confused her. Confusion had a track record of making her cruel. "Do you want to add the lawyer's office parking lot? And your very subtle sneak-up at the stop sign?"

"Those, too. You're right. Let's complete the list. The disconnected number. Not being on the track team."

"Where did you get that ridiculous uniform? That was maybe my favorite touch." She wanted to stop being sarcastic. Ander seemed sincere. But she was nervous about being there and it was coming out in ugly ways.

"Garage sale." Ander leaned down and ran his fingers through the grass. "I have an explanation for everything, really." He picked up a round, flat stone and wiped the dirt from its surface. "There's something I need to tell you, but I keep chickening out."

Eureka watched his hands polish the stone. What could he possibly be afraid to tell her? Did he . . . did Ander *like* her? Could he see past her sarcasm, to the mosaic of the broken girl inside? Had he been thinking about her the way she'd been thinking about him?

"Eureka, you're in danger."

The way he said it, a reluctant rush of words, made Eureka pause. His eyes looked wild and worried. He believed what he'd just said.

She drew her knees to her chest. "What do you mean?"

In one smooth motion, Ander wound up and released the stone. It rocketed impressively through the gaps among the branches. Eureka watched the stone skip across the pond. It dodged lily pads, ferns, and slicks of green moss. Somehow, everywhere it skimmed the surface, the water was clear. It was startling. The stone skipped a hundred yards across the pond and landed on the muddy bank on the opposite side.

"How did you do that?"

"It's your friend Brooks."

"He can't skip a stone to save his life." She knew that wasn't what Ander meant.

He leaned close. His breath tickled her neck. "He's dangerous."

"What is the deal with guys?" She understood why Brooks had been wary of Ander. He was her oldest friend, looking out for her, and Ander was a bizarre stranger who'd suddenly appeared at her door. But there was no reason for Ander to be wary of Brooks. Everyone liked Brooks. "Brooks has been my friend since my first breath. I think I can handle him."

"Not anymore."

"So we had a fight the other day. We made up." She paused. "Not that it's any of your business."

"I know you think he's your friend—"

"I think it because it's *true.*" Her voice sounded different under the canopy of branches. She sounded about as old as the twins.

Ander reached down to select another stone. He picked a good one, brushed it off, and handed it to her. "You want to try?"

She took the stone from his hand. She knew how to skip. Dad had taught her. He was good at it, far better than she was. Skipping stones was a way of passing time in the South, a means of marking time's absence. To be good at it, you needed to practice, but you also need to develop the skill to identify the good stones lying on the bank. You had to be strong to do it well, but you also needed grace, a lightness of touch. She'd never seen a fluke like the one Ander just skipped. It annoyed her. She flung the stone toward the water without bothering to aim.

The stone didn't make it past the nearest branch of the oak tree. It ricocheted off a limb and rolled on its side in an arc, stopping near her toe. Ander rose, picked up the stone. His fingers grazed her shoe.

Again he made the stone dance across the pond, picking up speed, sailing absurd lengths between each skip. It landed beside the first stone on the other side of the pond.

A thought occurred to Eureka. "Did Maya Cayce hire you to tell me to back off of Brooks?"

"Who's Maya Cayce?" Ander asked. "The name sounds familiar."

"Maybe I'll introduce you. You could discuss stalking techniques—"

"I'm not stalking you." Ander cut her off, but his tone was unconvincing. "I'm observing you. There's a difference."

"Did you just hear yourself?"

"You need help, Eureka."

Her cheeks reddened. Despite what her mountain of past

therapists suggested, Eureka hadn't needed help from anyone since her parents divorced years ago. "Who do you think you are?"

"Brooks has changed," Ander said. "He's not your friend anymore."

"And when did this metamorphosis occur, pray tell?"

Ander's eyes brimmed with emotion. He looked reluctant to say the words. "Last Saturday when you went to the beach."

Eureka opened her mouth but was speechless. This guy had been spying on her even more than she knew. Goose bumps rose on her arms. She watched an alligator raise its flat green head in the water. She was used to gators, of course, but you never knew when even the laziest-looking one might snap.

"Why do you think you got in a fight that evening? Why do you think he blew up after you kissed? Would the Brooks you know—would your best friend have done that?" Ander's words came out in rushes, as if he knew if he paused she would shut him up.

"That's enough, creep." Eureka stood up. She had to get out of here, somehow.

"Why else wouldn't Brooks apologize for days after your fight? What took him so long? Is that the way a friend behaves?"

At the edge of the canopy of branches, Eureka balled her fists. It gave her a sleazy sensation to imagine what Ander

230

would have had to do in order to know these things. She'd bar her windows, get a restraining order. She wished she could push him through these branches and into that alligator's jaws.

And yet.

What *had* taken Brooks so long to apologize? Why was he still acting strange since they'd made up?

She turned around, still wanting to feed Ander to the alligator. But seeing him now, her mind was at odds with her body. She couldn't deny it. She wanted to run away—and run to him. She wanted to throw him to the ground—and fall on top of him. She wanted to call the police—and for Ander to know more things about her. She wanted never to see him again. If she never saw him again, he couldn't hurt her, and her desire would disappear.

"Eureka," Ander said quietly. Reluctantly she turned her good ear toward him. "Brooks will hurt you. And he isn't the only one."

"Oh yeah? Who else is in on this? His mother, Aileen?"

Aileen was the sweetest woman in New Iberia—and the only woman Eureka knew whose sweetness wasn't saccharine. She wore heels to do dishes but let her hair go naturally gray, which had happened early, raising two boys by herself.

"No, Aileen's not involved," Ander said, as if incapable of recognizing sarcasm. "But she is worried about Brooks. Last night she searched his room for drugs."

Eureka rolled her eyes. "Brooks doesn't do drugs and he

and his mom have a great relationship. Why are you making this up?"

"Actually, the two of them had a screaming fight last night. All the neighbors heard it; you might try asking one of them if you don't trust me. Or ask yourself: Why else would his mother have stayed up all night baking cookies?"

Eureka swallowed. Aileen did bake when she was upset. Eureka had eaten the proof a hundred times when Brooks's older brother had become a teenager. The instinct must have come from the same place as Dad's need to nourish sadness with his cooking.

And just this morning, before first bell, Brooks *had* passed around a Tupperware of peanut butter cookies in the hall, laughing when people called him a mama's boy.

"You don't know what you're talking about." She meant: *How could you know these things?* "Why are you doing this?"

"Because I can stop Brooks. I can help you, if you'll let me."

Eureka shook her head. Enough. She winced as she dove in among the branches and clawed her way through, snapping twigs and tearing at the moss. Ander didn't try to stop her. From the corner of her eye she saw him wind up to skip another stone.

"You were a lot cuter before you started talking to me," she shouted back at him, "when you were just a guy who hit my car."

232

"You think I'm cute?"

"Not anymore!" She was bound up in branches, thrashing hatefully at everything in her path. She stumbled, gashed her knee, pushed on.

"Do you want some help?"

"Leave me alone! Right now and going forward!"

At last she shoved through the final layer of branches and stumbled to a stop. Cool air stroked her cheeks.

A stone whizzed through the gap in the branches her body had created. It skimmed the water three times, like wind rippling silk; then it ricocheted upward, into the air. It sailed higher, higher . . . and smashed into a window of the planetarium, where it left a jagged, gaping hole. Eureka imagined all the artificial stars inside swirling out into the true gray sky.

In the silence that followed, Ander said: "If I leave you alone, you'll die."

18

PALE DARKNESS

"I feel like a narc," Eureka told Cat in the waiting room at the Lafayette police station that evening.

"It's a precaution." Cat held out a short tube of Pringles from the vending machine, but Eureka wasn't hungry. "We'll throw out a description of Ander, see if it sticks. Wouldn't you want to know if they already had a file for him?" She rattled the can to slide out more chips and chewed contemplatively. "He did make a death threat."

"He did not make a death threat."

" 'If I leave you alone, you'll die'? He's not here now and you're alive, right?"

Both girls looked at the opposite window as if it occurred to them simultaneously that Ander might be watching them.

It was Thursday, dinnertime. It had taken less than five minutes after leaving Ander under the oak tree for Eureka to breathlessly share the details of their encounter with Cat over the phone. Now she regretted opening her mouth.

The station was cold and smelled like stale coffee and Styrofoam. Aside from the heavyset black woman staring flatly at them from across a table strewn with *Entertainment Weekly*s from three Brad Pitts ago, Eureka and Cat were the only two civilians there. Beyond the small square lobby, keyboards clicked from within cubicles. There were water stains on the drop panel ceiling; Eureka found dinosaurs and Olympic track stars in their cloudlike shapes.

The sky outside was navy blue with mottled gray clouds. If Eureka stayed out much later, Rhoda would grill her along with the flank steaks she prepared the one night a week Dad worked the dinner shift at Prejean's. Eureka hated these dinners, when Rhoda probed into everything Eureka did not want to talk about—which was everything.

Cat licked her fingers, tossed the Pringles can in the trash. "Bottom line, you have a crush on a psycho."

"That's why you brought me to the police?"

Cat held up a finger like a lawyer. "Let the record reflect that the defendant does not contest the psycho allegation."

"If being weird is a crime, we should both turn ourselves in while we're here."

She didn't know why she was defending Ander. He'd lied

about Brooks, admitted to spying on her, made vague threats about her being in danger. It might be enough to press charges, but it seemed wrong. What Ander had said wasn't what was dangerous about him. What was dangerous about him was the way he made her feel . . . emotionally out of control.

"Please don't chicken out now," Cat said. "I told my new friend Bill we'd make a statement. We met at my pottery workshop last night. He already thinks I'm too artsy—I don't want to flake and prove him right. Then he'll never ask me out."

"I should have known this was a ploy for sex. What happened to Rodney?"

Cat shrugged. "Eh."

"Cat—"

"Look, you just give a basic description, they'll run a search. If nothing turns up, we'll scoot."

"I'm not sure the Lafayette Police possess the most reliable criminal database."

"Don't say that in front of Bill." Cat's eyes grew earnest. "He's new on the force and very idealistic. He wants to make the world a better place."

"By hitting on a seventeen-year-old girl?"

"We're *friends*." Cat grinned. "Besides, you know my birthday's next month. Oh, look—there he is." She jumped to her feet and started waving, laying on the flirt like mayonnaise on a po'boy.

Bill was a tall, lanky young black man with a shaved head, a thin goatee, and a baby face. He was cute, minus the pistol strapped to his waist. He winked at Cat and beckoned the girls to his desk in a front corner of the room. He didn't have his own cubicle yet. Eureka sighed and followed Cat.

"So what's the story, ladies?" He sat down in a dark green swivel chair. There was an empty Cup Noodles container on his desk; three more were in the trash can behind him. "Somebody botherin' you?"

"Not really." Eureka shifted her weight, avoiding the commitment of sitting down on one of the two folding chairs. She didn't like being here. She was getting nauseated from the stench of stale coffee. The cops who'd been around in the days after Diana's accident had worn uniforms that smelled like this. She wanted to leave.

Bill's name tag said MONTROSE. Eureka knew Montroses from New Iberia, but Bill's accent was more Baton Rouge than bayou. Eureka also knew without a doubt that Cat was mentally practicing her *Catherine L. Montrose* signature, like she did with all of them. Eureka didn't even know Ander's last name.

Cat scooted one of the chairs close to Bill's desk and sat down, planting an elbow near his electric pencil sharpener, sliding a pencil seductively in and out. Bill cleared his throat.

"She's being modest," Cat said over the pulse of the machine. "She has a stalker."

Bill shot cop eyes at Eureka. "Cat says a friend of yours has admitted to following you."

Eureka looked at Cat. She didn't want to do this. Cat was nodding encouragement. What if she was right? What if Eureka described him and something terrible flashed on a screen? But if nothing showed up, would she feel any better?

"His name is Ander."

Bill pulled a spiral notepad from a drawer. She watched him scrawl the name in thin blue ink. "Last name?"

"I don't know."

"This a boy from school?"

Eureka blushed despite herself.

The bell attached to the door of the police station chimed. An older couple entered the lobby. They sat down in the seats Eureka and Cat had just been sitting in. The man wore gray slacks and a gray sweater; the woman wore a long gray slip dress with a heavy silver chain. They resembled each other, both slender and pale; they could have been siblings, possibly twins. They folded their hands on their laps in unison and looked straight ahead. Eureka got the sense they could hear her, which made her more self-conscious.

"We don't know his last name." Cat cozied closer to Bill, her bare arms splayed across the desk. "But he's blond, kinda wavy." She mimed Ander's mop of hair with her hand. "Right, Reka?"

Bill said "kinda wavy" and wrote it down, which embarrassed Eureka further. She'd never been more conscious of wasting time.

"He drives an old white pickup truck," Cat added.

Half the parish drove old white pickup trucks.

"Ford or Chevy?" Bill asked.

Eureka remembered the first thing Ander had ever said to her, which she'd relayed to Cat.

"It's a Chevy," Cat said. "And there's one of those air fresheners hanging from the rearview mirror. Silver. Right, Reka?"

Eureka glanced at the people waiting in the lobby. The black woman had her eyes closed, her swollen, sandaled feet up on the coffee table, a can of Fanta in her hand. The woman in gray glanced Eureka's way. Her eyes were pale blue, the rare extreme eye color you could see from a distance. They reminded Eureka of Ander's eyes.

"A white Chevy is a start." Bill smiled fondly at Cat. "Any other details you can remember?"

"He's a genius at skipping stones," Cat said. "Maybe he lives down by the bayou, where he can practice all the time?"

Bill laughed under his breath. "I'm getting jealous of this guy. I kind of hope I never find him."

That makes three of us, Eureka thought.

When Cat said "He has pale skin, blue eyes," Eureka had had enough.

"We're done," she said to Cat. "Let's go."

Bill closed his notepad. "I doubt there's enough information here for me to run a search. Next time you see this kid, give me a call. Take a picture of him on your phone, ask him for his last name."

"Did we waste your time?" Cat folded down her lip in a mini pout.

"Never. I'm here to serve and protect," Bill said, as if he'd just collared the entire Taliban.

"We're going to get banana freezes." Cat stood up, stretching so that her shirt drifted above her skirt, showing off a band of smooth dark skin. "Want to come?"

"Thanks, but I'm on duty. I'm on duty for a good while longer." Bill smiled and Eureka took the hint that was meant for Cat.

They waved goodbye and headed for the door, for Eureka's car, for home, where there waited something known as Rhoda. As they passed, the elderly couple rose from their seats. Eureka suppressed her instinct to jump backward. *Relax.* They were just moving toward Bill's desk.

"Can I help you two?" Eureka heard Bill ask behind her. She stole one last glance at the couple, but saw only the gray backs of their heads.

Cat reached for Eureka's arm. "Bill . . . ," she sang out wistfully as she pressed the metal bar on the front door.

The air was cold and smelled like a trash can fire. Eureka wished she were curled up in her bed with the door closed.

"Bill's nice," Cat said as they crossed the parking lot. "Isn't he nice?"

Eureka unlocked Magda. "He's nice."

Nice enough to humor them—and why should he have taken them seriously? They shouldn't have gone to the police. Ander wasn't an open-and-shut stalking case. She didn't know what he was.

He was standing across the street, watching her.

Eureka froze mid-slide onto the driver's seat and watched him through the window. He leaned against the trunk of a chinaberry tree, arms crossed over his chest. Cat didn't notice. She was teasing her bangs in the sun visor mirror.

From thirty feet away, Ander looked furious. His posture was rigid. His eyes were as cold as they'd been when he grabbed Brooks by the collar. Should she turn around and run back into the station to tell Bill? No, Ander would be gone by the time she stepped through the door. Besides, she was too afraid to move. He knew she'd gone to the cops. What would he do about it?

He stared at her for a moment, then flung his arms down at his sides. He stormed through the brush that edged the Roi de Donuts parking lot across the street.

"Feel like starting the car anytime this year?" Cat asked, smacking glossed lips together.

In the instant Eureka glanced at Cat, Ander vanished. When she looked back at the lot, it was empty except for two cops walking out of the donut shop with to-go bags. Eureka exhaled; started Magda; blasted the heat to fend off the cold, damp air that had settled like a cloud inside her car. She didn't want a banana freeze anymore.

"I've got to get home," she told Cat. "It's Rhoda's night to cook."

"So you all have to suffer." Cat understood, or she thought she did. Eureka didn't want to discuss the fact that Ander knew they'd just tried to turn him in.

In the sun visor mirror, Cat practiced a human highlight reel of the doe-eyed expressions she had just used on Bill. "Don't be discouraged," she said as Eureka turned out of the parking lot and started winding back toward Evangeline, where she'd drop Cat at her car. "I just hope I'm with you the next time you see him. I'll squeeze the truth from him. Milk it right on out."

"Ander is good at changing the subject when the subject is himself," Eureka said, thinking he was even better at disappearing.

"What teenage boy doesn't want to talk about himself? He'll be no match for the Cat." Cat turned up the radio, then changed her mind and turned it all the way down. "I can't believe he told you you were in danger. It's like, 'Hmm, should I go with the tried-and-true *Does Heaven know it's missing an angel?* Nah, I'll scare the crap out of her instead.' "

They passed a few blocks of dilapidated duplexes; drove

by the drive-through daiquiri stand, where a girl stuck her big chest out the window and handed gallon-sized Styrofoam cups to boys in souped-up low-riders. That was flirting. What Ander did this morning, and just now across the street, that was different.

"He isn't hitting on me, Cat."

"Oh, come on," Cat sputtered. "You have always, like since the age of twelve, put off this sexy-broken-girl air that guys find irresistible. You're just the kind of crazy every boy wants to wreck his life."

Now they were out of the city, turning onto the windy road that led to Evangeline. Eureka rolled down the windows. She liked the way this road smelled in the evenings, like rain falling on night-blooming jasmine. Locusts sang old songs in the darkness. She enjoyed the combination of cold air brushing her arms and heat blasting her feet.

"Speaking of which," Cat said. "Brooks interrogated me about your 'emotional state' today."

"Brooks is like my brother," Eureka said. "He's always been protective. Maybe it's a little more intense since Diana and . . . everything else."

Cat propped up her feet on the dashboard. "Yeah, he asked about Diana, only"—she paused—"it was weird."

They passed dirt roads and old railroad tracks, log cabins chinked with mud and moss. White egrets moved through the black trees.

"What?" Eureka said.

"He called it—I remember because he said it twice—'the killing of Diana.'"

"Are you sure?" Eureka and Brooks had talked a million times about what happened, and he'd never used that phrase.

"I reminded him of the rogue wave," Cat said, and Eureka swallowed the bitter taste that came every time she heard those words. "Then he was all, 'Well, that's what it was: she *was killed* by a rogue wave.'" Cat shrugged as Eureka pulled into the school parking lot, stopped next to Cat's car. "It creeped me out. Like when he dressed up as Freddy Krueger three years in a row for Halloween."

Cat got out of the car, then glanced back at Eureka, expecting her to laugh. But things that used to be funny had darkened, and things that used to be sad now seemed absurd, so Eureka hardly ever knew how to react anymore.

Back on the main road, heading home, headlights lit Eureka's rearview mirror. She heard Cat's wimpy honk as her car swerved into the left lane to pass her. Cat would never criticize how cautiously Eureka drove these days—but she also wouldn't get stuck behind her at the wheel. The engine gunned, and Cat's taillights disappeared around a curve.

For a moment, Eureka forgot where she was. She thought about Ander skipping stones, and she wished Diana were still alive so Eureka could tell her about him.

But she was gone. Brooks had put it plainly: a wave had killed her.

Eureka saw the blind curve ahead. She'd driven it a thousand times. But as her thoughts had wandered, her speed had increased, and she took the bend too fast. Her tires bumped over the grooves in the center divider for an instant before she straightened out. She blinked rapidly, as if startled from a sleep. The road was dark; there were no streetlights on the outskirts of Lafayette. But what was . . . ?

She squinted ahead. Something was blocking the road. Was it Cat playing a joke? No, Eureka's headlights revealed a gray Suzuki sedan parked across the middle of the road.

Eureka slammed on the brakes. It wasn't going to be enough. She spun the wheel right, tires screeching. She swerved onto the shoulder, across a shallow ditch. Magda came to a halt with her hood five feet deep in sugarcane.

Eureka's chest heaved. The smell of burnt rubber and gasoline fumes made her want to gag. There was something else in the air—the scent of citronella, strangely familiar. Eureka tried to breathe. She'd almost hit that car. She'd almost been in her third accident in six months. She'd slammed on the brakes ten feet short and probably destroyed her alignment. But she was okay. The other car was okay. She hadn't hit anyone. She might still make it home in time for dinner.

Four people appeared in the shadows on the far side of the road. They passed the Suzuki. They were coming toward Magda. Slowly Eureka recognized the gray couple from the police station. There were two others with them, also dressed in gray, as if the first couple had been multiplied. She could see them so clearly in the darkness—the cut of the dress of the woman from the station; the hairline of the man who was new to the group; the pale, pale eyes of the woman Eureka hadn't seen before.

Or had she? They looked somehow familiar, like family you met for the first time at a reunion. There was something about them, something tangible in the air around them.

Then she realized: They weren't just pale. They were glowing. Light limned the edges of their bodies, blazed outward from their eyes. Their arms were locked like links in a chain. They walked closer, and as they did, it seemed like the whole world closed in on Eureka. The stars in the sky, the branches of the trees, her own trachea. She didn't remember putting her car in park, but there it was. She couldn't remember how to get it back in drive. Her hand shook on the gearshift. The least she could do was roll up the windows.

Then, in the darkness behind Eureka, a truck rumbled around the bend. Its headlights were off, but when the driver punched the gas, the lights came on. It was a white Chevy, driving straight toward them, but at the last moment it swerved to miss Magda—

And plowed into the Suzuki.

The gray car caved around the fender of the truck, then slid backward, as if on ice. It rolled once, nearing Magda, Eureka, and the quartet of glowing people.

Eureka ducked across the center console. Her body shook. She heard the thump of the car landing upside down, the

246

smash of its windshield. She heard the screech of truck tires and then silence. The truck's engine died. A door slammed. Footsteps crunched gravel on the shoulder of the road. Someone pounded on Eureka's window.

It was Ander.

Her hand trembled as she rolled the window down.

He used his fingers to force it down more quickly. "Get out of here."

"What are you doing here? You just hit those people's car!"

"You need to get out of here. I wasn't lying to you earlier." He glanced over his shoulder at the darkened road. The gray people were arguing near the car. They looked up at Ander with glowing eyes.

"Leave us!" the woman from the station shouted.

"Leave *her!*" Ander shouted back coldly. And when the women cackled, Ander reached into the pocket of his jeans. Eureka saw a flash of silver at his hip. At first she thought it was a gun, but then Ander pulled out a silver case about the size of a jewelry box. He thrust it toward the people in gray. "Stay back."

"What's in his hand?" The elder of the two men asked, stepping closer to the car.

Behind him, the other said, "Surely it's not the—"

"You will leave her alone," Ander warned.

Eureka heard Ander's breath coming quickly, the tension straining his voice. As he fumbled with the clasp on the box, a gasp came from the foursome on the road. Eureka realized they knew exactly what the box held—and it terrified them.

"Child," one of the men warned venomously. "Do not abuse what you do not understand."

"Perhaps I do understand." Slowly Ander flipped open the lid. An acid-green glow emanated from within the case, brightening his face and the dark space around him. Eureka tried to discern the box's contents, but the green light inside was nearly blinding. A sharp, untraceable odor stung her nostrils, dissuading her from peering any deeper.

The four people who had been advancing now took several quick steps away. They stared at the case and the shining green light with sick trepidation.

"You can't have her if we're dead," a woman's voice called. "You know that."

"Who are these people?" Eureka said to Ander. "What is in that box?"

With his free hand, he grabbed Eureka's arm. "I'm begging you. Get out of here. You have to survive." He reached into the car, where her hand was stiff and cold on the gearshift. He pressed down on her fingers and slid the lever to reverse. "Hit the gas."

She nodded, terrified, then reversed hard, wheeling back the way she'd come. She drove into the darkness and didn't dare look back at the green light pulsing in her rearview mirror.

From: savvyblavy@gmail.com
To: reka96runs@gmail.com
Cc: catatoniaestes@gmail.com
Date: Friday, October 11, 2013, 12:40 a.m.
Subject: second salvo

Dear Eureka,

Voilà! I am cooking with gas now and should have additional passages for you by tomorrow. I'm beginning to wonder if this is an ancient bodice-ripper. What do you think?

The prince became the king. Tearfully, he pushed his father's blazing funeral pyre into the sea. Then his tears dried and he begged me to remain.

With a bow, I shook my head. "I must return to my mountains, resume my place among my family. It is where I belong."

"No," Atlas said simply. "You belong here now. You will stay."

Uneasy as I was, I could not refuse my king's demand. As the smoke from the sacrificial mourning fires cleared, word spread throughout the kingdom: the young King Atlas would take a bride.

So it was: I learned I would be queen via a rumor. It occurred to me that the gossipwitches might have spoken the truth.

Had true love entered into the story, I would gladly have exchanged my mountain life for it. Or, had I ever dreamed of power, perhaps I could have overlooked the absence of love. I had lavish chambers in the palace, where my every wish was granted. King Atlas was handsome—distant but not unkind. But when he became king, he spoke to me less, and the possibility of ever loving him began to flicker like a mirage.

The wedding date was set. Atlas still had not proposed to me. I was confined to my chambers, a splendid prison whose iron bars were velvet-covered. Alone in my dressing room one dusk, I put on my wedding gown and the lustrous orichalcum crown I would wear when I was presented to the kingdom. Twin tears welled in my eyes.

"Tears suit you even less than a vulgar crown," a voice said from behind me.

I turned to find a figure sitting in shadows. "I thought no one could enter."

"You'll grow accustomed to being wrong," the shadowed figure said. "Do you love him?"

"Who are you?" I demanded. "Step into the light, where I can see you."

The figure rose from the chair. Candlelight caressed his features. He looked familiar, as if he were a fragment of a dream.

"Do you love him?" he repeated.

It was as if someone had stolen the breath from my lungs. The stranger's eyes entranced me. They were the color of the cove where I swam in the morning as a girl. I could not help wanting to dive in.

"Love?" I whispered.

"Yes. Love. That which makes a life worth living. That which arrives to carry us where we need to go."

I shook my head, though I knew it was treason to the king, punishable by death. I began to regret everything. The boy before me smiled.

"Then there's hope."

Once I had crossed the blue boundary of his eyes, I never wanted to find my way back. But I soon realized I was trespassing in a dangerous realm.

"You are Prince Leander," I whispered, placing his fine features.

He nodded stiffly. "Back from five years' traveling in the name of the Crown—though my own brother would have had the kingdom think that I was lost at sea." He smiled a smile I was sure I'd seen before. "Then you, Selene, had to go and discover me."

"Welcome home."

He stepped from the shadows, pulled me to him, and kissed me with matchless abandon. Until that moment, I had not known bliss. I would have stayed locked in his kiss forever, but a memory returned to me. I pulled away, remembering a piece of the gossipwitches' timeworn chatter.

"I thought you loved—"

"I never loved until I found you." He spoke sincerely from a soul I knew I could never doubt. From that moment into infinity, nothing would matter to us but each other.

Only one thing stood between us and a universe of love . . .

SWAK

Madame B, Gilda, and Brunhilda

19

STORM CLOUDS

On Friday morning, before the bell, Brooks was waiting at Eureka's locker. "You weren't at Latin Club."

His hands were stuffed in his pockets and he looked like he'd been waiting there awhile. He was blocking the locker next to Eureka's, which belonged to Sarah Picou, a girl so terribly shy she'd never tell Brooks to move even if it meant going to class without her books.

Rhoda had insisted it would rain, and though the drive to school had been clear and bright, Eureka had her heather-gray slicker on. She liked hiding under its hood. She'd hardly slept and didn't want to be at school. She didn't want to talk to anyone.

"Eureka"—Brooks watched her twirl the dial on her combination lock—"I was worried."

"I'm fine," she said. "And late."

Brooks's green sweater was too snug. He wore shiny new loafers. The hallway was choked with shouting kids, and the seed of a headache was splitting open and sprouting a razor-wire beanstalk in Eureka's brain.

Five minutes separated them from the bell, and her English class was two flights up and at the other end of the building. She opened her locker and threw in some binders. Brooks hovered over her like a hall monitor from an eighties teen movie.

"Claire was sick last night," she said, "and William threw up this morning. Rhoda was gone, so I had to . . ." She waved her hand, as if he should understand the scope of her responsibilities without being told.

The twins were not sick. Eureka was the one who'd had a cramp across her entire being, the kind she used to get before cross-country meets when she was a freshman. She couldn't stop reliving the encounter with Ander and his truck, the four pedestrians from hell glowing in the darkness—and the mysterious green light Ander had turned on them like a weapon. She'd picked up her phone three times the night before to call Cat. She'd wanted to set the story free, to unburden herself.

But she couldn't tell anyone. After she drove home, Eureka had spent ten minutes pulling sugarcane from Magda's grille. Then she ran up to her room, shouting down to Rhoda that she was too swamped with homework to eat. "Swamped in the swamp" was a joke she had with Brooks, but nothing seemed funny anymore. She'd stared out the window, imagining every headlight was a pale psychopath searching for her.

When she heard Rhoda's footsteps on the stairs, Eureka had grabbed her Earth Science book and opened it just in time before Rhoda carried in a plate of flank steak and mashed potatoes.

"You'd better not be messing around in here," Rhoda said. "You're still on thin ice after that Dr. Landry stunt."

Eureka flashed her textbook. "It's called homework. They say it's highly addictive, but I think I can handle it if I only try it at parties."

She hadn't been able to eat. At midnight she'd surprised Squat with the kind of meal a dog on death row might request. At two, she heard Dad come home. She got as far as her door before she stopped herself from rushing into his arms. There was nothing he could do about her troubles, and he didn't need another weight to drag him down. That was when she checked her email and found the second translation from Madame Blavatsky.

This time, when Eureka read from *The Book of Love,* she forgot to wonder how its story might apply to Diana. She found too much strange symmetry between Selene's predicament and her own. She knew what it was like to have a boy burst into your life out of nowhere, leaving you haunted and wanting more. The two boys even had similar names. But unlike the boy in the story, the boy on Eureka's mind didn't sweep her off her feet and kiss her. He slammed into her car, followed her around, and said she was in danger.

As sun rays tentatively fingered her window that morning, Eureka had realized that the only person she could turn to about all of her questions was Ander. And it wasn't up to her when she saw him.

Brooks leaned casually into Eureka's locker. "Did it freak you out?"

"What?"

"The twins' being sick."

Eureka stared at him. His eyes wouldn't hold hers for more than a moment. They'd made up—but had they really? It was like they'd slipped into an eternal war, one you could retreat from but never actually end, a war where you did your best not to see the whites of your opponent's eyes. It was like they'd become strangers.

Eureka ducked behind her locker door, separating herself from Brooks. Why were lockers always gray? Wasn't school already enough like a prison without the trimmings?

Brooks pushed the locker door flush against Sarah Picou's locker. There was no barrier between them. "I know you saw Ander."

"And now you're mad that I possess eyesight?"

"This isn't funny."

Eureka was amazed he hadn't chuckled. They couldn't even joke now?

"You know, if you miss two more Latin Club meetings," Brooks said, "they won't put your name in the yearbook on the club page, and then you won't be able to put it on your college applications."

Eureka shook her head as if she'd misheard him. "Uhhh . . . what?"

"Sorry." He sighed, and his face relaxed, and for a moment nothing was weird. "Who cares about Latin Club, right?" Then a glimmer came into his eye, a smugness that was new. He unzipped his backpack and pulled out a Ziploc bag of cookies. "My mom is on a mad baking spree recently. Want one?" He opened the bag and held it out to her. The smell of oatmeal and butter made her stomach turn. She wondered what had kept Aileen up baking the night before.

"I'm not hungry." Eureka glanced at her watch. Four minutes until the bell. When she reached into her locker for her English book, an orange flyer fluttered to the ground. Someone must have slipped it through the slats.

SHOW YOUR FACE.
TREJEAN'S FIFTH ANNUAL MAZE DAZE.
FRIDAY, OCTOBER 11, AT 7 P.M.
DRESS TO SCARE THE CROWS.

Brad Trejean had been the most popular senior at Evangeline the year before. He was loud and wild, redheaded, flirtatious. Most girls, including Eureka, had crushed on him at some point. It was like a job they worked in shifts, though Eureka had quit the first time Brad, who knew about LSU football and nothing else, actually spoke to her.

Every October, Brad's parents went to California and he threw the best party of the year. His friends constructed a maze out of haystacks and spray-painted poster board and set it up in the Trejeans' sprawling backyard on the bayou. People swam and, as the party went on, skinny-dipped. Brad mixed his signature drink, the Trejean Colada, which was horrible and strong enough to guarantee an epic party. Late in the night, there was always a seniors-only game of Never-Ever, exaggerated details of which were slowly leaked to the rest of the school.

Eureka realized Brad's younger sister Laura was carrying on the tradition. She was a sophomore, less notorious than Brad. But she was nice and not a label-whore, unlike most of the other sophomores. She started on the volleyball team, so she and Eureka used to see each other in the locker room after school.

For the past three years, Eureka had heard about this party on Facebook a month in advance. She and Cat would go shopping for their outfits the weekend before. She hadn't logged in to Facebook in forever, and now that she thought about it, she remembered a text from Cat that proposed shopping last Sunday after church. Eureka had been too preoccupied with her fight with Brooks to consider fashion.

She held up the flyer and tried a smile. Last year she and Brooks had had one of their most fun nights at that party. He'd brought black sheets from home, and they'd turned invisible to haunt what was known as the Maze. They'd terrified some seniors in some compromising positions.

"I'm the ghost of your father's eyesight," Brooks had warbled heavily to a girl in a half-unbuttoned blouse. "Tomorrow you're off to the convent."

"Not cool!" her companion had shouted, but he'd sounded scared. It was a miracle no one ever figured out who was behind the Maze haunting.

"Shall the spiritus interruptus return again this year?" Eureka waved the flyer.

He took it from her hand. He didn't look at it. It was like being slapped.

"You're too cavalier," he said. "That psycho wants to hurt you."

Eureka groaned, then inhaled a whiff of patchouli, which only meant one thing:

Maya Cayce was approaching. Her hair was woven in a long, intricate fishtail that draped down her side, and her eyes were lined with heavy kohl. She'd pierced her nasal septum since the last time Eureka saw her. A tiny black ring looped through her nose.

"Is that the psycho you're talking about?" Eureka asked Brooks. "Why don't you protect me? Go kick her ass."

Maya stopped at the door to the bathroom. She flicked her braid to the other side and looked over her shoulder at them. She made the bathroom look like the sexiest spot on earth. "Did you get my message, B?"

"Yeah." Brooks nodded, but he didn't seem interested. His gaze kept moving toward Eureka. Did he want to make Eureka jealous? It wasn't working. Not really.

Maya blinked heavily, and when her eyes opened, they were on Eureka. She stared for a moment, sniffed, then slipped inside the bathroom. Eureka was watching her disappear when she heard a tearing sound.

Brooks had ripped the flyer. "You're not going to this party."

"Don't be such a drama queen." Eureka slammed her locker door and spun away—right toward Cat, who'd rounded the corner, hair wild and makeup smudged, like she'd just been interrupted in the Maze. But knowing Cat, she might have spent an hour perfecting that look this morning.

Brooks grabbed Eureka's wrist. She twisted to glare at him ferociously, and it was nothing like wrestling when they were kids. Her eyes were exclamation points of anger. Neither of them spoke.

Slowly he let go of her wrist, but as she walked away he called, "Eureka, trust me. Don't go to that party."

Across the hall, Cat extended her elbow to Eureka, who slipped her arm through. "What's he yapping about? Hopefully something lame, because the bell rings in two and I

260

would much rather gossip about Madame Blavatsky's latest email. *Hot.*" She fanned herself and dragged Eureka into the bathroom.

"Cat, wait." Eureka looked around the bathroom. She didn't have to kneel down and search to know Maya Cayce was in one of the stalls. Patchouli was pungent.

Cat plopped her purse on the sink and pulled out a tube of lipstick. "I just hope there's a real sex scene in the next email. I hate books that are all foreplay. I mean, I love foreplay, but at some point, it's, like, let's *play.*" She glanced over at Eureka in the mirror. "What? You're paying good money for this. Madame B needs to deliver the goods."

Eureka was not going to talk about *The Book of Love* in front of Maya Cayce. "I didn't . . . I couldn't really read it."

Cat squinted. "Dude, you're missing out."

A toilet flushed. A door lock clicked. Maya Cayce exited a stall, pushing between Eureka and Cat to stand before the mirror and touch up her long, dark hair.

"Do you want to borrow some of my bitch gloss, Maya?" Cat said, rummaging through her purse. "Oh, I forgot. You bought every tube of it in the world."

Maya kept smoothing her braid.

"Don't forget to wash your hands," Cat chirped.

Maya turned on the tap and reached over Cat to get some soap. As she lathered her hands, she watched Eureka in the mirror. "*I'm* going to the party with him, not you."

Eureka nearly choked. Was that why Brooks had told her

not to go? "I have other plans anyway." She was living in a bruise where everything hurt all the time, one pain exacerbating another.

Maya turned off the faucet, flicked her wet hands in Eureka's direction, and left the bathroom like a dictator leaving a podium.

"What was that about?" Cat laughed when Maya Cayce was gone. "We are going to that party. I've already checked in on Foursquare."

"Did you tell Brooks I saw Ander yesterday?"

Cat blinked. "No. I've barely talked to him."

Eureka stared at Cat, who widened her eyes and shrugged. Cat stammered when she lied; Eureka knew that from years of them getting caught by their parents. But how else would Brooks have known she'd seen Ander?

"More importantly," Cat said, "I will not let Maya Cayce psych you out of the best party of the year. I need my wing girl. Are we clear?" The bell rang and Cat moved toward the door, calling over her shoulder, "You have no say in the matter. We shall dress to attract the crows."

"We're supposed to *scare* the crows, Cat."

Cat grinned. "So you *can* read."

20

NƐVƐR-ƐVƐR

The Trejeans lived on a restored plantation in the wealthy district south of town. Cotton fields flanked the small historic neighborhood. Houses were columned, two-storied, snug in blankets of pink azaleas, and shaded by antebellum oaks. The bayou bent around the Trejeans' backyard like an elbow, providing a double waterfront view.

The entire senior class and the well-connected underclassmen had been invited to the Maze Daze. It was customary to catch a boat ride and pull up bayou-side to the party. The year before, Eureka and Cat had made the journey in the rickety motorboat with a creaking tiller that Brooks's older brother, Seth, left behind when he went to LSU. The freezing half-hour ride up the bayou from New Iberia had been almost as fun as the party.

Tonight, since Brooks was not an option, Cat had put out feelers for other rides. As she was getting dressed, Eureka couldn't help imagining Maya Cayce sitting next to Brooks on the boat, plugging her metal-heavy iPod into the portable speakers, caressing Brooks's bicep. She imagined Maya's hair streaming behind her like the tentacles of a black octopus as the boat skimmed across the water.

In the end, Cat scored a ride from Julien Marsh, whose friend Tim had a mint-green 1960s party barge with empty seats. At eight o'clock, when Julien's truck pulled up outside Eureka's house, Dad was standing at the window, drinking cold leftover coffee from the maroon mug that used to say *I love Mom,* before the dishwasher sanded down the paint.

Eureka zipped her raincoat to cover the low sequined neckline of a dress Cat had just spent five minutes on Face-time convincing her was not trampy. She'd borrowed the satin shift from Cat's closet that afternoon, even though she looked terrible in brown. Cat was debuting a similar dress in orange. They were going as fall leaves. Cat said she liked the vivid, sensual colors; Eureka didn't voice her perverse enjoyment at dressing as an object with a second life when it was dead.

Dad raised one of the blinds to look at Julien's Ford. "Who's the truck?"

"You know Cat, what she likes."

He sighed, exhausted, just off his shift at the restaurant. He smelled like crawfish. As Eureka slid through the doorway, he said, "You know you want better than those kinds of boys, right?"

"That truck doesn't have anything to do with me. It's a ride to a party, that's all."

"If someone does have something to do with you," Dad said, "you'll bring him inside? I'll meet him?" His eyes turned down, a look the twins got when they were about to cry, like a swollen cloud rolling in from the Gulf. She'd never realized they inherited that meteorological event from him. "Your mom only ever wanted the best for you."

"I know, Dad." The coldness with which Eureka grabbed her purse made her glimpse the depths of the anger and confusion rooted inside her. "I've got to go."

"Back by midnight," Dad said as she walked out the door.

The party barge was nearly full when Eureka, Cat, and Julien arrived at Tim's family's dock. Tim was blond and skinny, with an eyebrow ring, big hands, and a smile as constant as the Eternal Flame. Eureka had never had a class with him, but they were friends from back when Eureka went to parties. His costume was an LSU football jersey. He held out a hand to steady her as she stepped onto the party barge.

"Good to see you out, Boudreaux. Saved y'all three seats."

They wedged in next to some cheerleaders, some theater kids, and a boy from the cross-country team named Martin. The rest of them had taken the party barge last weekend, Eureka realized from the jokes they cracked. This was the first time all year she'd been out with anyone besides Cat or Brooks.

She found the back corner of a bench where she'd be the least claustrophobic. She remembered what Ander had said under the tree about enjoying being cocooned. She couldn't relate. The entire world was too tight a space for Eureka.

She reached down to touch the bayou, taking comfort in its fragile timelessness. There was little chance a wave bigger than a boat's wake would come coursing through. Still, her hand shook against the surface of the water, which felt colder than she knew it was.

Cat sat next to her, on Julien's lap. As she penciled a few leaves on Eureka's face with gold eyeliner, she made up a Maze Daze song to the tune of "Love Stinks," accompanied by shimmying against Julien's chest.

"Maze Daze, yeah, yeah!"

A six-pack appeared while Tim filled the tank. Tops popped around the boat like fireworks. The air smelled like gasoline and dead water beetles and the mushrooms rising from the soil along the bank. A slick-furred nutria cut a tiny wake as it swam past them on the bayou.

As the party barge slowly left the dock, a bitter breeze slapped Eureka's face and she hugged her arms to her chest. Kids around her huddled together and laughed, not because anything funny had happened, but because they were together and eager about the night ahead.

By the time they got to the party, they were either buzzed or pretending they were. Eureka accepted Tim's help off the barge. His hand around hers was dry and big. It gave her a twinge of longing, because it was nothing like Ander's hand. Nausea spread through her stomach as she remembered sugarcane and skin as white as sea foam and ghastly green light in Ander's panicked eyes the night before.

"Come along, my brittle little leaf." Cat swung an arm around Eureka. "Let us tumble through this fete bringing all glad men to grief."

They entered the party. Laura Trejean had classed up her brother's tradition. Tiki torches lit the pebbled allée from the dock to the iron gate that led to the backyard. Tin lanterns twinkled in the giant weeping willows. Up on the balcony, overlooking the moonlit pool, everyone's favorite local band, the Faith Healers, tuned their instruments. Laura's clique mingled across the lawn, passing tin trays of Cajun hors d'oeuvres.

"Amazing what a lady's touch will do," Eureka said to Cat, who snatched a mini fried oyster po'boy from a passing platter.

"That's what he said," Cat mumbled through a mouthful of bread and lettuce.

You didn't have to tell Catholic school kids twice to dress up for a party. Everyone came decked out in costume. Maze Daze was explicitly not a Halloween party; it was a harvest celebration. Among the many LSU jerseys, Eureka spotted some more inventive attempts. There were several scarecrows and a smattering of tipsy jack-o'-lanterns. One junior boy had duct-taped sugarcane stalks to his T-shirt in honor of the harvest later that month.

Cat and Eureka passed a tribe of Pilgrim-costumed freshmen gathered around a fire pit in the center of the lawn, their faces lit orange and yellow by the flames. When they passed the Maze and heard laughter inside, Eureka tried not to think of Brooks.

Cat steered her up the stairs to the back patio, past a big black cauldron of crawfish surrounded by kids snapping off the tails and sucking fat from the heads. Shucking crawfish was one of a bayou child's earliest rites of passage, so its savagery felt natural everywhere, even in costume, even drunk in front of your crush.

When they got in line for punch, Eureka heard a loud male voice in the distance call out, "Make like a tree and leave."

"I think we're the hottest leaves here," Cat said as the band began to play from the patio above. She pushed Eureka through underclassmen to the front of the drinks line. "Now we can relax and enjoy ourselves."

The idea of a relaxed Cat made Eureka smirk. She looked out at the party. The Faith Healers were playing "Four Walls" and they sounded good, giving the party a soul. She'd been waiting for this moment, to experience joy without a wave of guilt immediately following. Eureka knew Diana wouldn't want her moping in her room. Diana would want her to be at the Maze Daze in a short brown dress, drinking punch with her best friend, having fun. Diana would picture Brooks there, too. Losing his friendship would be like mourning another death, but Eureka didn't want to think about that now.

Cat slipped a plastic cup of punch into Eureka's hand. It was not the lethal purple poison of the Trejean colada of years past. It was an appetizing shade of red. It actually smelled fruity. Eureka was about to take a sip when she heard a familiar voice behind her say, "It's bad luck to drink without a toast."

Without turning around, Eureka took a gulp of punch. "Hey, Brooks."

He stepped before her. She couldn't make sense of his costume—a thin gray long-sleeved shirt with a hint of silver shimmer, paired with what looked like matching pajama pants. His hair was wild from the boat ride she'd imagined he took with Maya. His blank eyes held none of their usual mischief. He was alone.

Cat pointed at his outfit and hooted. "Tin Man?"

Brooks turned on her icily. "It's a precise replica of ancient harvesting attire. Precise and practical."

"Where?" Cat said. "On Mars?"

Brooks studied the low cut of Eureka's dress. "I thought we were better friends than this. I asked you not to come."

Eureka leaned in to Cat. "Could you give us a minute?"

"You two have a blast." Cat backed away, finding Julien on the edge of the balcony. He was wearing a horned Viking cap, which Cat lifted off his head and placed on hers. An instant later they were cracking up, arms entwined.

Eureka compared Brook's odd costume with last year's elaborate Spanish moss suit. She'd helped him staple a hundred shreds of it to a vest he'd cut from a paper bag.

"I asked you not to come for your own safety," he said.

"I'm doing fine making my own rules."

His hands rose like he was going to grab her shoulders, but he grabbed air. "Do you think you're the only one affected by Diana's death? Do you think you can swallow a bottle of pills and not gut the people who love you? That's why I look out for you, because you quit looking out for yourself."

Eureka swallowed, speechless a moment too long.

"There you are." Maya Cayce's deep voice made Eureka's skin crawl. She wore black roller skates, a tiny black dress showing nine of her ten tattoos, and shoulder-grazing raven feather earrings. She skated toward Brooks from across the porch. "I lost you."

"For my safety?" Eureka muttered quickly. "Did you think I'd die of shock seeing you here with her?"

Maya rolled into Brooks, scooping his arm to drape it around her neck. She was half a foot taller than him in her roller skates. She looked amazing. Brooks's hand dangled where Maya had placed it near her chest. It drove Eureka crazier than she would ever admit. He had kissed *her* less than a week ago.

If Cat were in Eureka's shoes, she'd compete with Maya Cayce's oppressive sensuality. She'd contort her body into a pose that made male circuitry go haywire. She'd have her body entwined with Brooks's before Maya could bat her fake lashes. Eureka didn't know how to play games like those, especially not with her best friend. All she had was honesty.

"Brooks." She looked straight at him. "Would you mind if I talked to you alone?"

The official Olympics timekeepers couldn't have clocked how quickly Brooks's arm was off Maya. An instant later, he and Eureka were trotting down the patio stairs, toward the shelter of a chinaberry tree, almost like the friends they were. They left Maya making crazy eights on the porch.

Eureka leaned against the tree. She wasn't sure where to begin. The air was sweet and the ground was soft with mulching leaves. The party noise was distant, an elegant sound track for a private conversation. Tin lanterns in the branches cast a shimmer on Brooks's face. He'd relaxed.

"I'm sorry I was so crazy," he said. Wind blew some of the small yellow drupes from the tree's branches. The fruits brushed Eureka's bare shoulders on their way to the earth. "I've been worried about you since you met that guy."

"Let's not talk about him," Eureka said, because an

embarrassing gush of emotion might pour out of her if they spoke about Ander. Brooks seemed to take her dismissal of the subject another way. It seemed to make him happy.

He touched her cheek. "I never want bad things to happen to you."

Eureka tilted her cheek into his hand. "Maybe the worst is over."

He smiled, the old Brooks. He left his hand against her face. After a moment he looked over his shoulder at the party. The mark on his forehead from last week's wound was now a very light pink scar. "Maybe the best is yet to come."

"You didn't happen to bring any sheets?" Eureka nodded at the Maze.

The mischief returned to his eyes. Mischief made Brooks look like Brooks. "I think we'll be too busy for that tonight."

She thought about his lips on hers, how the heat of his body and the strength of his arms had overwhelmed her when they kissed. A kiss so sweet should not have been tainted by an aftermath so bitter. Did Brooks want to try it again? Did she?

When they'd made up the other day, Eureka hadn't felt capable of clarifying where on the friends/more-than-friends continuum they stood. Now every exchange had the potential to confuse. Was he flirting? Or was she reading into something innocent?

She blushed. He noticed.

"I mean Never-Ever. We're seniors, remember?"

Eureka hadn't considered playing that stupid game, regardless of her status as senior and its status as tradition. Haunting the Maze sounded like more fun. "My secrets are none of the whole school's business."

"You only share what you want to share, and I'll be right there next to you. Besides"—Brooks's sly grin told Eureka he had something up his sleeve—"you might learn something interesting."

The rules of Never-Ever were simple: You sat in a circle and the game moved clockwise. When it was your turn, you began with "Never have I ever . . . ," and you confessed something you'd never done before, the more salacious the better.

NEVER HAVE I EVER . . .
- *lied at Confession,*
- *made out with my friend's sister,*
- *blackmailed a teacher,*
- *smoked a joint,*
- *lost my virginity.*

They way they played it at Evangeline, people who had done what you had not done had to tell their story and pass you their drink to gulp. The purer your past, the faster you got drunk. It was a corruption of the innocent, a confession in reverse. No one knew how the tradition got started. People said Evangeline seniors had played it for the past thirty years, though nobody's parents would admit it.

At ten o'clock, Eureka and Brooks joined the line of seniors holding plastic cups filled with punch. They followed the garbage-bag path taped to the carpet, filing into one of the guest bedrooms. It was cold and vast—a king-sized bed with a massive carved headboard at one end, severe black velour curtains lining the wall of windows on the other.

Eureka entered the circle on the floor and sat cross-legged next to Brooks. She watched the room fill up with sexy pumpkins, Goth scarecrows, Black Crows band members, gay kids dressed as farmers, and half the LSU football hall of fame. People sprawled on the bed, on the love seat near the dresser. Cat and Julien came in carrying folding chairs from the garage.

Forty-two seniors out of a class of fifty-four had shown up to play the game. Eureka envied whoever was sick, grounded, teetotaling, or otherwise absent. They'd be left out for the rest of the year. Being left out was a kind of freedom, Eureka had learned.

The room was crammed with dumb costumes and exposed flesh. Her least favorite Faith Healers song meandered endlessly outside. She nodded toward the velour curtains to her right and murmured to Brooks, "Any urge to jump through that window with me? Maybe we'll land in the pool."

He laughed under his breath. "You promised."

Julien had finished taking a head count and was about to close the door when Maya Cayce skated in. A boy dressed like a crowbar and his friend, a bad attempt at gladiator Russell Crowe, separated to let her pass. Maya rolled up to Eureka and Brooks and tried to wedge her way between them. But Brooks moved closer to Eureka, creating a tiny space on his other side. Eureka couldn't help admiring the way Maya took what she could get, snuggling next to Brooks as she removed her roller skates.

When the door was shut and the room buzzed with nervous laughter, Julien walked to the center of the circle. Eureka glanced at Cat, who was trying to mask her pride that her secret date for the night was the secret leader of this most secret class event.

"We all know the rules," Julien said. "We all have our punch." Some kids whooped and raised their glasses. "Let the Never-Ever game of 2013 begin. And may its legend never, ever end—or leave this room."

More cheers, more toasting, more whole- and halfhearted laughter. When Julien spun and pointed randomly at a shy Puerto Rican girl named Naomi, you could have heard an alligator blink.

"Me?" Naomi's voice wavered. Eureka wished Julien had chosen someone more extroverted to start the game. Everyone stared at Naomi, waiting. "Okay," she said. "Never have I ever . . . played Never-Ever."

Over embarrassed snickers, Julien admitted his mistake. "Okay, let's try this again. Justin?"

Justin Babineaux, hair spiked skyward as if he were in mid-fall, could be described in three words: rich soccer player. He grinned. "Never have I ever had a job."

"You jerk." Justin's best friend, Freddy Abair, laughed, and passed Justin his cup to swig. "That's the last time you're getting free burgers during my shift at Hardee's." Most of the rest of the class rolled their eyes as they passed their cups around the circle toward a chugging Justin.

Next it was a cheerleader's turn. Then the boy who was first-chair saxophone in the band. There were popular plays—"Never have I ever kissed three boys in the same night"—and unpopular plays—"Never have I ever popped a zit." There were plays intended to single out another senior—"Never have I ever made out with Mr. Richman after eighth-period science in the supply closet"—and plays intended purely for showing off—"Never have I ever been turned down for a date." Eureka sipped her punch independent of her class-mates' divulgences, which she found painfully mundane. This was not the game she'd imagined it being all these years.

Never, she thought, had reality ever compared with what might have been if any of her classmates dared to dream be-yond their ordinary worlds.

The only bearable aspect of the game was Brooks's mut-tered commentary about each classmate taking a turn: "Never has she ever considered wearing pants that didn't show her thong. . . . Never has he ever not judged others for doing things he does daily. . . . Never has she ever left the house without a pound of makeup."

By the time the game got around to Julien and Cat, most peoples' punch cups had been taken, drained, returned, and refilled a few times. Eureka didn't expect much out of Julien—he was so jocky, so cocky. But when it was his turn, he said to Cat, "Never have I ever kissed a girl I actually like— but I'm hoping to change that tonight."

The boys booed and the girls whooped and Cat fanned herself dramatically, loving it. Eureka was impressed. Someone had finally figured out that ultimately this game wasn't about divulging shameful secrets. They were supposed to use Never-Ever to get to know each other better.

Cat raised her cup, took a breath, and looked at Julien. "Never have I ever told a cute guy that"—she hesitated— "I got a 2390 on my SATs."

The room was riveted. No one could make her drink for that. Julien grabbed her and kissed her. The game got better after that.

Soon it was Maya Cayce's turn. She waited until the room was quiet, until all eyes were moving over her. "Never have I ever"—her black-lacquered fingernail traced the border of her cup—"been in a car accident."

Three nearby seniors shrugged and handed Maya their

drinks, bringing up tales of run red lights and drunken off-roading. Eureka's grip tightened on her cup. Her body stiffened as Maya looked at her. "Eureka, you're supposed to pass me your drink."

Her face was hot. She glanced around the room, noticing everyone's eyes on her. They were waiting for her. She imagined throwing her drink in Maya Cayce's face, the red punch dripping in bloodlike rivulets along her pale neck, down her cleavage.

"Did I do something to offend you, Maya?" she asked.

"All the time," Maya said. "Right now, for example, you're cheating."

Eureka thrust out her cup, hoping Maya choked.

Brooks laid a hand on her knee and murmured, "Don't let her get to you, Reka. Let it go." The old Brooks. His touch was medicinal. She tried to let it take effect. It was his turn.

"Never have I ever . . ." Brooks watched Eureka. He narrowed his eyes and lifted his chin and something shifted. New Brooks. Dark, unpredictable Brooks. Suddenly Eureka braced herself. "Attempted suicide."

The entire room gasped, because everyone knew.

"You bastard," she said.

"Play the game, Eureka," he said.

"No."

Brooks grabbed her drink and chugged the rest, wiping his mouth with his hand like a redneck. "It's your turn."

She refused to have a nervous breakdown in front of the majority of the senior class. But when she inhaled, her chest was electric with something it wanted to release, a scream or an inappropriate laugh or . . . tears.

That was it.

"Never have I ever broken down and sobbed."

For a moment no one said anything. Her classmates didn't know whether to believe her, to judge her, or to take it as a joke. No one moved to pass Eureka their drink, though over twelve years of school together she realized she'd seen most of them cry. The pressure built in her chest until she couldn't take it anymore.

"Screw all of y'all." Eureka stood up. No one followed her as she left the dumbstruck game and ran toward the nearest bathroom.

∞

Later, on the frozen boat ride home, Cat leaned close to Eureka. "Is what you said true? You've never cried?"

It was just Julien, Tim, Cat, and Eureka cruising up the bayou. After the game Cat had rescued Eureka from the bathroom where she'd been staring numbly into a toilet. Cat insisted the boys take them home immediately. Eureka hadn't seen Brooks on the way out. She never wanted to see him again.

The bayou hummed with locusts. It was ten minutes to midnight, nudging dangerously against her curfew, and so unworthy of the trouble she'd be in if she was one minute late. The wind was biting. Cat rubbed Eureka's hands.

"I said I haven't sobbed." Eureka shrugged, thinking all the clothes in the world couldn't counter the sensation of utter nakedness pulsing through her. "You know I've teared up before."

"Right. Of course." Cat looked at the shore as it glided by, as if she was trying to recall bygone tears on her friend's cheeks.

Eureka had chosen the word "sobbed" because shedding that single tear in front of Ander had felt like a betrayal of her promise to Diana years ago. Her mother had slapped her when she was weeping uncontrollably. That was what she'd never done again, the vow she would never break, not even on a night like tonight.

21

LIFE PRESERVER

One moment Eureka thought she was flying. The next—a violent crash into cold blue water. Her body split the surface. She clenched her eyes shut as the sea swallowed her. A wave canceled the sound of something—someone screaming above water—as the hush of ocean flowed in. Eureka heard only the crackle of fish feeding on coral, the gurgle her underwater gasp produced, and the quiet before the next colossal thrash of tide.

Her body was caught in something constricting. Her probing fingers found a nylon strap. She was too stunned to move, to wrestle free, to remember where she was. She let the ocean entomb her. Was she drowning yet? Her lungs knew no difference between being in water and being in the open air.

The surface danced above, an impossible dream, an effort she couldn't see how to make.

She felt one thing above all else: unbearable loss. But what had she lost? What did she long for so viscerally that her heart pulled like an anchor?

Diana.

The accident. The wave. She remembered.

Eureka was there again—inside the car, in the waters beneath Seven Mile Bridge. She'd been given a second chance to save her mother.

She saw everything so clearly. The clock on the dashboard read 8:09. Her cell phone drifted across the flooded front seat. Yellow-green seaweed fringed the center console. An angelfish flitted through the open window as if it were hitch-hiking to the bottom. Next to her, a flowing curtain of red hair masked Diana's face.

Eureka thrashed for the clasp of her seat belt. It dissolved into bits of debris in her hands, as if it were long-decayed. She lunged toward her mother. As soon as she reached Diana, her heart swelled with love. But her mother's body was limp.

"Mom!"

Eureka's heart seized. She brushed the hair from Diana's face, longing to see her. Then Eureka stifled a scream. Where her mother's regal features should have been, there was a black void. She couldn't tear her eyes away.

Bright rays of something like sunlight suddenly rained

down around her. Hands gripped her body. Fingers squeezed her shoulders. She was being pulled from Diana against her will. She writhed, screaming. Her savior neither heard nor cared.

She never surrendered, lashing at the hands that separated her from Diana. She would have preferred to drown. She wanted to stay in the ocean with her mother. For some reason, when she glared up at the owner of the hands, she expected to see another black and voided face.

But the boy was bathed in such bright light she could barely see him. Blond hair waved in the water. One hand reached for something above him—a long black cord stretching vertically through the sea. He grasped it hard and pulled. As Eureka soared upward through the cold glaze of sea, she realized the boy was holding on to an anchor's thick metal chain, a lifeline to the surface.

Light suffused the ocean around him. His eyes met hers. He smiled, but it looked like he was crying.

Ander opened his mouth—and began to sing. The song was strange and otherworldly, in a language Eureka could almost understand. It was bright and high-pitched, replete with baffling scales. It sounded so familiar . . . almost like the chirping of a lovebird.

Her eyes opened in the solitary darkness of her bedroom. She gulped air and wiped her sweat-dampened brow. The dream song rang though her mind, a haunting sound track in the night's stillness. She massaged her left ear, but the sound didn't go away. It grew louder.

She rolled over to read a glowing 5:00 a.m. on her phone's display. She realized the sound was just the song of morning birds that had infiltrated her dream and woken her. The culprits were likely speckled starlings, which migrated to Louisiana this time every fall. She wedged a pillow over her head to block out their chirping, not ready to rise and recall how thoroughly Brooks had betrayed her at the party the night before.

Tap. Tap. Tap.

Eureka shot up in bed. The sound came from her window.

Tap. Tap. Tap.

She threw off her blankets and hovered near the wall. The palest thread of predawn light brushed her gauzy white curtains, but she saw no shadow darkening them to indicate a person outside. She was dizzy from the dream, from how close she'd been to Diana and to Ander. She was delirious. There was no one outside her window.

Tap. Tap. Tap.

In a single motion Eureka threw back the curtains. A small lime-green bird waited calmly outside on the white windowsill. He had a diamond of golden feathers on his breast and a bright red crown. His beak tapped three times on the glass.

"Polaris." Eureka recognized Madame Blavatsky's bird.

She slid the window up and opened the wooden shutters wider. She'd cut the screen out years ago. Icy air billowed in. She held out her hand.

Polaris hopped onto her index finger and resumed singing vibrantly. This time, Eureka was certain she heard the bird in stereo. Somehow his song came through the left ear that had heard nothing but muffled ringing for months. She realized he was trying to tell her something.

His green wings flapped against the quiet sky, propelling his body inches above her finger. He swooped closer, chirped at Eureka, then turned his body toward the street. He flapped his wings again. At last he perched on her finger to chirp a final crescendo.

"Shhh." Eureka glanced over her shoulder at the wall her room shared with the twins'. She watched Polaris repeat the same pattern: hovering above her hand, turning toward the street, and chirping another—quieter—crescendo as he landed back on her finger.

"It's Madame Blavatsky," Eureka said. "She wants me to follow you."

His chirp sounded like a *yes*.

Minutes later, Eureka slipped out her front door wearing leggings, her running shoes, and a navy Windbreaker from the Salvation Army over the Sorbonne T-shirt she'd slept in. She smelled dew on the petunias and the oak branches. The sky was muddy gray.

A choir of frogs croaked under Dad's rosemary bushes. Polaris, who'd been roosting on one of the feathery boughs, fluttered to Eureka as she closed the screen door behind her. He settled on her shoulder, momentarily nuzzled her neck. He seemed to understand that she was nervous, and embarrassed by what she was about to do.

"Let's go."

His flight was swift and elegant. Eureka's body loosened, warming, as she jogged down the street to keep up. The only person she passed was a groggy newspaper-delivery kid in a red low-rider pickup, who took no notice of the girl following the bird.

When Polaris reached the end of Shady Circle, he cut behind the Guillots' lawn and flew toward an unfenced entrance to the bayou. Eureka banked east just as he did, moving against the bayou's current, hearing it rustle as it flowed on her right side, feeling worlds away from the sleepy row of fenced-in houses on her left.

She had never run this path of narrow, uneven terrain. In the dark hours before the day, it possessed a strange, elusive luster. She liked the way the still gloom of the night held on, trying to eclipse mist-slathered morning. She liked the way Polaris shone like a green candle in the cloud-colored sky. Even if her mission turned out to be senseless, even if she'd invented the bird's summons at her window, Eureka convinced herself that running was better for her than lying in bed, furious with Brooks and pitying herself.

She hurdled wild ferns and camellia vines and the purple

wisteria shoots that crept down from landscaped yards like tributaries trying to reach the bayou. Her shoes slapped the damp earth and her fingers tingled with cold. She lost Polaris around a hard bend in the bayou and sprinted to catch up. Her lungs burned and she panicked, and then, in the distance, through the wispy branches of a willow tree, she saw him perch on the shoulder of an old woman wearing a vast patchwork cloak.

Madame Blavatsky reclined against the willow's trunk, her mane of auburn hair haloed in humidity. She faced the bayou, smoking a long, hand-rolled cigarette. Her red lips puckered at the bird. "Bravo, Polaris."

Reaching the willow, Eureka slowed her pace and dipped under the tree's canopy. The shadow of its swaying branches enveloped her like an unexpected embrace. She wasn't prepared for the joy that rose in her heart at the sight of Madame Blavatsky's silhouette. She felt an uncharacteristic urge to rush the woman with a hug.

She hadn't hallucinated this summons. Madame Blavatsky wanted to see her—and, Eureka realized, she wanted to see Madame Blavatsky.

She thought of Diana, how close to life her mother had seemed in the dream. This old woman was the key to the only door Eureka had left to Diana. She wanted Blavatsky to make an impossible wish come true—but what did the woman want from her?

"Our situation has changed." Madame Blavatsky patted the ground beside her, where she'd laid out an acorn-brown quilt. Buttercups and bluebonnets rose from the soil bordering the blanket. "Please sit."

Eureka sat cross-legged next to Madame Blavatsky. She didn't know whether to face her or the water. For a moment they watched a white crane swoop up from a sandbar and glide over the bayou.

"Is it the book?" Eureka asked.

"It is not the physical book so much as it is the chronicle it contains. It has become"—Blavatsky took a slow drag on her cigarette—"too perilous to share via email. No one must know of our discovery, understand? Not some slipshod Internet hacker, not that friend of yours. No one."

Eureka thought of Brooks, who was not her friend now, but who had been when he'd expressed interest in helping her translate the book. "You mean Brooks?"

Madame Blavatsky glanced at Polaris, who had settled on the patchwork cloak covering her knees. He chirped.

"The girl, the one you brought to my office," Madame Blavatsky said.

Cat.

"But Cat would never—"

"The last thing we expect others to do is the last thing they do before we learn we cannot trust them. If you desire to glean knowledge from these pages," Blavatsky said, "you must swear its secrets will remain between you and me. And the birds, of course."

Another chirp from Polaris made Eureka massage her left ear again. She wasn't sure what to make of her new selective hearing. "I swear."

"Of course you do." Madame Blavatsky reached into a leather knapsack for an ancient-looking black-bound journal with thick, rough-cut pages. As the old woman flipped through the pages, Eureka saw they were splattered with wildly varying handwriting in a plethora of colored inks. "This is my working copy. When my task is complete, I will return *The Book of Love* to you, along with a duplicate of my translation. Now"—she used a finger to hold open a page— "are you ready?"

"Yes."

Blavatsky dabbed her eyes with a gingham handkerchief and frown-smiled. "Why should I believe you? Do you even believe yourself? Are you truly ready for what you are about to hear?"

Eureka straightened, attempting to look more prepared. She closed her eyes and thought about Diana. There was nothing anyone could tell her that could change the love she had for her mother, and that was the most important thing.

"I'm ready."

Blavatsky stamped her cigarette out in the grass and withdrew a small, round tin container from a pocket of her cloak.

She placed the blackened butt inside, next to a dozen others. "Tell me, then, where we left off."

Eureka recalled the story of Selene finding love in Leander's arms. She said: "Only one thing stood between them."

"That's right," Madame Blavatsky said. "Between them and a universe of love."

"The king," Eureka guessed. "Selene was supposed to marry Atlas."

"One would think that would indeed be an obstacle. However"—Blavatsky buried her nose in her book—"there appears to be a plot twist." She straightened her shoulders, tapped her throat, and began to read Selene's tale:

"*Her name was Delphine. She loved Leander with all her being.*

"*I knew Delphine well. She was born in a lightning storm to a departed mother and had been nursed by rain. When she learned to crawl, she climbed down from her solitary cave and came to live among us in the mountains. My family welcomed her into our home. As she grew older, she embraced some of our traditions, rejected others. She was a part of us, yet apart. She frightened me.*

"*Years earlier, I had stumbled accidentally upon Delphine embracing a lover in the moonlight, pressed against a tree. Though I never saw the boy's face, the gossipwitches used to titter rumors that she had the mysterious younger prince in her thrall.*

"Leander. My prince. My heart.

"'I saw you in the moonlight,' he later confessed to me. 'I had seen you before many times. Delphine had me spellbound, but I swear I never loved her. I fled the kingdom to be free of her enchantment; I came home hoping to find you.'

"As our love deepened, we feared the wrath of Delphine more than anything King Atlas could do. I had seen her destroy life in the forest, turn kind animals to beasts; I did not want her magic touching me.

"On the eve of my wedding to the king, Leander spirited me from the castle through a series of secret tunnels he had run through as a boy. As we hurried to his waiting ship under the glow of the midnight moon, I pleaded:

"'Delphine must never know.'

"We boarded his boat, buoyant with the freedom promised by the waves. We knew not where we were going; we only knew we would be together. As Leander pulled up the anchor, I looked back to bid farewell to my mountains. I will always wish that I had not.

"For there I saw a fearsome sight: a hundred gossipwitches—my aunts and cousins—had gathered in the crags of the cliff to watch me go. The moon lit their craggy faces. They were old enough to lose their minds but not their power.

"'Flee, cursed lovers,' one of the elder witches called. 'You cannot outrun your destiny. Doom decorates your hearts, and will forevermore.'

"I remember Leander's startled face. He was unaccustomed to the witches' way of speaking, though it was as natural to me as loving him.

"'What darkness could corrupt a love as bright as this?' he asked.

"'Fear her heartbreak,' the witches hissed.

"Leander wrapped his arm around me. 'I will never break her heart.'

"Laughter echoed from the scarp.

"'Fear the heartbreak in maiden tears that bring oceans crashing into earths!' one of my aunts cried.

"'Fear the tears that seal worlds off from space and time,' another added.

"'Fear the dimension made of water known as Woe, where the lost world will wait until the Rising Time,' a third one sang.

"'Then fear its return,' they sang in unison. 'All because of tears.'

"I turned to Leander, deciphering their curse. 'Delphine.'

"'I will go to her and make amends before we sail,' Leander said. 'We must live unhaunted.'

"'No,' I said. 'She must not know. Let her think that you have drowned. My betrayal will break her heart more deeply.' I kissed him as if I were unafraid, though I knew there was no stopping the gossipwitches from spreading our story through the hills.

"Leander watched the witches hunching in their scarp. 'It is *the only way I will feel free to love you like I want to. As soon as I say goodbye, I will return.'*

"With that, my love was gone and I was left alone with the gossipwitches. They eyed me from the shore. I was now an outcast. I could not yet glimpse the shape of my apocalypse, but I knew it lay just beyond the horizon. I will not forget their whispered words before they disappeared into the night. . . ."

Madame Blavatsky looked up from the journal and dotted her handkerchief along her pale brow. Her fingers trembled as she closed her book.

Eureka had sat motionless, breathless, the whole time Madame Blavatsky read. The text was captivating. But now that the chapter was over, the book closed, it was just a story. How could it be so dangerous? As a hazy orange sun crept up over the bayou, she studied the erratic pattern of Madame Blavatsky's breathing.

"You think this is real?" Eureka asked.

"Nothing is real. There is only what we believe in and what we reject."

"And you believe in this?"

"I believe I have an understanding of the origins of this text," Blavatsky said. "This book was written by an Atlantean sorceress, a woman born of the lost island of Atlantis thousands of years ago."

"Atlantis." Eureka took in the word. "You mean the

underwater island with mermaids and sunken treasures and guys like Triton?"

"You are thinking of a bad cartoon," Madame Blavatsky said. "All anyone really knows of Atlantis comes to us from Plato's dialogues."

"And why do you think this story is about Atlantis?" Eureka asked.

"Not simply *about* but *from.* I believe Selene was an inhabitant of the island. Remember her manner of description in the beginning—her island stood 'beyond the Pillars of Hercules, alone in the Atlantic'? That is just as Plato describes it."

"But it's fiction, right? Atlantis wasn't really—"

"According to Plato's *Critias* and *Timeaus,* Atlantis was an ideal civilization in the ancient world. Until—"

"Some girl got her heart broken and cried the whole island into the sea?" Eureka raised an eyebrow. "See? Fiction?"

"And they say there are no new ideas," Blavatsky said softly. "This is very dangerous information to possess. My judgment tells me not to carry on—"

"You have to carry on!" Eureka said, startling a water moccasin coiled in a low branch of the willow. She watched as it slithered into the brown bayou. She didn't necessarily believe Selene had lived on Atlantis—but she now believed that Madame Blavatsky believed it. "I need to know what happened."

"Why? Because you enjoy a good story?" Madame Blavatsky asked. "A simple library card might satisfy your need and put us both at less risk."

"No." There was more to it, but Eureka wasn't sure how to say it. "This story matters. I don't know why, but it has something to do with my mother, or . . ."

She trailed off for fear that Madame Blavatsky would give her the same disapproving look Dr. Landry had when Eureka had spoken of the book.

"Or it has something to do with you," Blavatsky said.

"Me?"

Sure, at first she'd related to how fast Selene had fallen for a boy she shouldn't fall for—but Eureka hadn't even seen Ander since that night on the road. She didn't see what her accident had to do with a mythical sunken continent.

Blavatsky stayed quiet, as if waiting for Eureka to connect some dots. Was there something else? Something about Delphine the abandoned lover, whose tears were said to have sunk the island? Eureka had nothing in common with Delphine. She didn't even cry. After last night, her whole class knew about that—more reason to think she was a freak. So what did Blavastky mean?

"Curiosity is a cunning paramour," the woman said. "He has me seduced as well."

Eureka touched Diana's lapis locket. "Do you think my mother knew this story?"

"I believe she did."

295

"Why didn't she tell me? If it was so important, why didn't she explain it?"

Madame Blavatsky stroked Polaris's crown. "All you can do now is absorb the tale. And remember our narrator's advice: Everything might change with the last word."

In the pocket of her Windbreaker, Eureka's phone buzzed. She pulled it out, hoping Rhoda hadn't discovered her empty bed and concluded she'd snuck out after curfew.

It was Brooks. The blue screen lit up with one big block of text, then another, then another, then another, as Brooks sent a rapid succession of texts. After six of them came through, the final text stayed illuminated on her phone:

Can't sleep. Sick with guilt. Let me make it up to you—next weekend, you and me, sailing trip.

"Hell no." Eureka stuffed her phone in her pocket without reading his other texts.

Madame Blavatsky lit another cigarette, blew the smoke in a long, thin draft across the bayou. "You must accept his invitation."

"What? I'm not going anywhere with— Wait, how did you know?"

Polaris fluttered from Madame Blavatsky's knee onto Eureka's left shoulder. He chirped softly in her ear, which tickled, and she understood. "The birds tell you."

Blavatsky puckered her lips in a kiss at Polaris. "My pets have their fascinations."

"And they think I should go out on a boat with a boy who betrayed me, who made a fool out of me, who suddenly behaves like my nemesis instead of my oldest friend?"

"We believe it is your destiny to go," Madame Blavatsky said. "What happens once you do is up to you."

22

HYPOTHESIS

On Monday morning Eureka put on her uniform, packed her bag, gnawed miserably on a Pop-Tart, and started Magda before she accepted that she could not possibly go to school.

It was more than the humiliation of the Never-Ever game. It was the translation of *The Book of Love*—which she'd sworn she'd discuss with no one, not even Cat. It was her sunken-car dream, in which Diana's and Ander's roles had seemed so clear. It was Brooks, whom she was used to turning to for support—but since they'd kissed, their friendship had gone from stable to critically wounded. Perhaps most hauntingly, it was the vision of the glowing foursome surrounding her car on the dark road, like antibodies fighting a disease. Whenever she closed her eyes she saw green light illuminating Ander's face, suggesting something powerful and dangerous. Even if there were someone left to turn to, Eureka would never find words to make that scene sound true.

So how was she supposed to sit through Latin class and pretend she had herself together? She had no outlets, only blockades. There was just one kind of therapy that might soothe her.

She reached the turnoff for Evangeline and kept driving, heading east toward the green allure of nearby Breaux Bridge's loamy pastures. She drove twenty miles east and several more south. She didn't stop until she no longer knew where she was. It was rural and quiet and no one would recognize her, and that was all she needed. She parked under an oak tree sheltering a family of doves. She changed in the car into the spare running clothes she always kept in the backseat.

She wasn't warmed up when she slipped into the hushed woods behind the road. She zipped her sweatshirt and started jogging lightly. At first, her legs felt like they were running through swamp water. Without the motivation of the team, Eureka's only competition was her imagination. So she pictured a cargo plane as big as Noah's Ark landing right behind her, its house-sized engines sucking trees and tractors into whirring blades, while she alone raced past every piece of backward-zooming matter in the world.

She'd always disliked weather forecasts, preferred finding spontaneity in the atmosphere. The early morning had been bright, with dregs of former clouds sticking to the sky. Now those high clouds turned gold in the thinning light, and hair-like wisps of fog filtered through the oaks, giving the forest a dim incandescence. Eureka loved fog in the woods, the way the wind made the ferns along the oak branches reach for mist. The ferns were greedy for moisture that, if it turned to rain, would change their fronds from tawny red to emerald.

Diana was the only person Eureka had ever known who would also rather run in rain than in shine. Years of jogging with her mother had taught Eureka to appreciate how "bad" weather enchanted an ordinary run: rain pattering on leaves, storm scrubbing tree bark clean, tiny rainbows cast on crooked boughs. If that was bad weather, Diana and Eureka had agreed, they didn't want to know good. So as the mist rolled over her shoulders, Eureka thought of it as the kind of shroud Diana would have liked to wear if she'd had her choice of funeral.

Before long, Eureka reached a white wooden marker some other runner must have nailed to an oak tree to mark his or her progress. She slapped the wood the way a runner does when she hits her halfway mark. She kept going.

Her feet pounded the worn path. Her arms pumped harder. The woods darkened as rain began to fall. Eureka ran on. She didn't think about the classes she was missing, the whispers whirling around her empty seat in calculus or English. She was in the forest. There was no place she'd rather be.

Her clearing mind was like an ocean. Diana's hair flowed

weightlessly across it. Ander drifted by, reaching for that strange chain that seemed to have no beginning and no end. She wanted to ask why he'd saved her the other night—and what exactly he'd saved her from. She wanted to know more about the silver box and the green light it contained.

Life had become so convoluted. Eureka had always thought she loved to run because it was an escape. Now she realized that every time she went into the woods, she sought to find something, someone. Today she was chasing after nothing and no one because she didn't have anyone left.

An old blues song she used to play on her radio show streamed into her mind:

> *Motherless children have a hard time when their*
> *mother's dead.*

She'd been running for miles when her calves began to burn and she realized she was desperate for water. It was raining harder, so she slowed her pace and opened her mouth to the sky. The world above was rich, dewy green.

"Your time is improving."

The voice came from behind her. Eureka spun around.

Ander wore faded gray jeans, an Oxford shirt, and a navy vest that somehow looked spectacular. He gazed at her with a brazen confidence quickly belied by his fingers running nervously through his hair.

He had a peculiar talent for blending into the background

until he wanted to be seen. She must have sprinted past him, even though she prided herself on her alertness while running. Her heart had already been racing from the workout—now it sprinted because she was alone again with Ander. Wind rustled the leaves in the trees, sending a spray of raindrops to the ground. It carried the softest whiff of ocean. Ander's scent.

"Your timing is becoming absurd." Eureka stepped backward. He was either a psychopath or a savior, and there was no way of getting a straight answer out of him. She remembered the last thing he'd said to her: *You have to survive*—as if her literal survival were in question.

Her gaze swept the forest, seeking signs of those strange people, signs of that green light or any other danger—or signs of someone who might help her if it turned out Ander was the danger. They were alone.

She reached for her phone, envisioned dialing 911 if anything got weird. Then she thought of Bill and the other cops she knew and realized it was useless. Besides, Ander was just standing there.

The sight of his face made her want to run away and straight to him, to see how intense those blue eyes could get.

"Don't call your friend at the police station," Ander said. "I'm just here to talk to you. But, for the record, I don't have one."

"One what?"

"Record. Criminal file."

"Records are meant to be broken."

Ander stepped closer. Eureka stepped back. Rain studded her sweatshirt, sending a deep chill through her body.

"And before you ask, I wasn't spying on you when you went to the cops. But those people you saw in the lobby, then later on the road—"

"Who were they?" Eureka asked. "And what was in that silver box?"

Ander pulled a tan rain hat from his pocket. He tugged it low over his eyes, over hair that, Eureka noticed, didn't seem wet. The hat made him look like a detective from an old film noir. "Those are my problems," he said, "not yours."

"That's not how you made it seem the other night."

"How about this?" He stepped closer again, until he was only inches away and she could hear him breathing. "I'm on your side."

"What side am I on?" A surge in the rain made Eureka retreat a step, under the canopy of leaves.

Ander frowned. "You're so nervous."

"I am not."

He pointed at her elbows, jutting from the pockets into which she'd stuffed her fists. She was shaking.

"If I'm nervous, your sudden pop-ups aren't helping."

"How can I convince you that I'm not going to hurt you, that I'm trying to help?"

"I never asked for help."

"If you can't see that I'm one of the good guys, you're never going to believe—"

"Believe *what*?" She crossed her hands tightly over her chest to compress her shaking elbows. Mist hung in the air around them, making everything a little blurry.

Very gently, Ander put his hand on her forearm. His touch was warm. His skin was dry. It made the hairs on her damp skin rise. "The rest of the story."

The word "story" made Eureka think of *The Book of Love*. Some ancient tale about Atlantis had nothing to do with what Ander was talking about, but she still heard Madame Blavatsky's translation run through her head: *Everything might change with the last word.* "Is there a happy ending?" she asked.

Ander smiled sadly. "You're good at science, right?"

"No." To look at Eureka's last report card, you'd think she wasn't good at anything. But then she saw Diana's face in her memory—the way anytime Eureka joined her on one of the location digs, her mother bragged to her friends about embarrassing things like Eureka's analytical mind and advanced reading level. If Diana were here, she'd speak up about how irrefutably good Eureka was at science. "I guess I'm all right."

"What if I assigned you an experiment?" Ander said.

Eureka thought about the classes she'd missed today,

about the trouble she'd be in. She wasn't sure she needed to add another assignment.

"What if it was something that sounded impossible to prove?" he added.

"What if you just tell me what this is all about?"

"If you *could* prove this impossible hypothesis," he said, "would you trust me then?"

"What's the hypothesis?"

"The stone your mother left you when she died—"

Her eyes whipped up, finding his. Against the verdant forest, Ander's turquoise irises were edged with green. "How did you know about that?"

"Try getting it wet."

"Wet?"

Ander nodded. "My hypothesis is you won't be able to."

"Everything can get wet," she said, even as she wondered about his dry skin when he'd reached for her moments ago.

"Not that stone," he said. "If it turns out I'm right, will you promise to trust me?"

"I don't see why my mother would leave me a water-repellent stone."

"Look, I'll throw in an incentive—if I'm wrong about the stone, if it's just a regular old rock, I'll disappear and you'll never hear from me again." He tilted his head, watching her reaction without any of the playfulness she expected. "I promise."

Eureka wasn't ready to never see him again, even if the stone didn't get wet. But his gaze pressed on her like the sand-bags tamping the batture along the bayou. His eyes wouldn't let her break free. "Fine. I'll give it a try."

"Do it"—Ander paused—"by yourself. No one else can know what you have. Not your friends. Not your family. Especially not Brooks."

"You know, you and Brooks should get together," Eureka said. "You seem to be all the other thinks about."

"You can't trust him. I hope you can see that now."

Eureka wanted to shove Ander. He didn't get to bring up Brooks like he knew something she didn't. But she was afraid that if she shoved him, it wouldn't be a shove. It would be an embrace, and she would lose herself. She wouldn't know how to break free.

She bounced on her heels in the mud. She could think only of fleeing. She wanted to be home, to be in a safe place, though she didn't know how or where to find either of those things. They had eluded her for months.

The rain intensified. Eureka looked back the way she'd come, deep into the green oblivion, trying to see Magda miles away. The lines of the forest dissolved in her vision into pure shape and color.

"I can't trust anyone, it seems." She started to run back through the driving rain, wanting, with every step away from Ander, to turn around and run back to him. Her body warred over her instincts until she wanted to scream. She ran faster.

"Soon you'll see how wrong you are!" Ander shouted, standing still where she had left him. She'd thought he might follow her, but he didn't.

She stopped. His words had left her out of breath. Slowly, she turned around. But when she looked through the rain and mist and wind and leaves, Ander had already disappeared.

23

THE THUNDERSTONE

"As soon as your homework is finished," Rhoda said from across the dinner table that night, "you're going to email an apology to Dr. Landry, cc'ing me. And tell her you'll see her next week."

Eureka shook Tabasco sauce violently onto her étouffée. Rhoda's orders didn't even merit a glare.

"Your dad and I brainstormed with Dr. Landry," she continued. "We don't think you'll take therapy seriously unless you're held accountable. Which is why you're going to pay for the sessions." Rhoda sipped her rosé. "Out of your pocket. Seventy-five dollars a week."

Eureka clenched her jaw to keep her mouth from dropping open. So they'd finally settled on a punishment for last week's outrage.

"But I don't have a job," she said.

"The dry cleaners will give you back your old job," Rhoda said, "assuming you can prove you've become more responsible since you were fired."

Eureka hadn't become more responsible. She'd become suicidally depressed. She looked to Dad for help.

"I talked to Ruthie," he said, glancing down as if he were talking to his étouffée instead of his daughter. "You can manage two shifts a week, can't you?" He picked up his fork. "Now eat up, food's getting cold."

Eureka couldn't eat. She considered the many sentences forming in her mind: *You two sure know how to handle a suicide attempt. Could you possibly make a bad situation any worse? The secretary from Evangeline called to see why I wasn't in class today, but I already deleted the voice mail. Did I mention I also quit cross-country and don't plan on returning to school? I'm leaving and I'm never coming back.*

But Rhoda's ears were deaf to uncomfortable honesty. And Dad? Eureka scarcely recognized him. He seemed to have crafted a new identity out of not contradicting his wife. Maybe because he'd never been able to pull that off when he was married to Diana.

Nothing Eureka could say would change the cruel rules of this house, which only ever applied to her. Her mind was on fire, but her eyes stayed downturned. She had better things to do than fight with the monsters across the table.

Fantasies of plans were gathering at the limits of her mind.

Maybe she would get a job on a fishing skiff that sailed near where *The Book of Love* said Atlantis had been. Madame Blavatsky seemed to think the island had really existed. Maybe the old woman would even want to join Eureka. They could save money, buy an old boat, and sail into the brutal ocean that held everything she loved. They could find the Pillars of Hercules and keep going. Maybe then she'd feel at home— not like the alien she was at this dinner table. She moved some peas around with her fork. She stuck a knife in her étouffée to see if it would stand on its own.

"If you're going to disrespect the food we put on this table," Rhoda said, "I think you're excused."

Dad added, in a softer voice, "Have you had enough to eat?"

It took all Eureka's strength not to roll her eyes. She stood, pushed in her chair, and tried to imagine how different this scene would look if it were just Eureka and Dad, if she still respected him, if he'd never married Rhoda.

As soon as the thought formed in Eureka's mind, her eyes found her siblings and she regretted her wish. The twins wore profound frowns. They were silent, as if bracing for Eureka to throw a screaming fit. Their faces, their little hunched shoulders, made her want to swoop them up and take them with her to wherever she escaped. She kissed the tops of their heads before climbing the stairs to her room.

She closed her door and fell onto her bed. She'd showered after her run, and her wet hair had dampened the collar of the flannel pajamas she liked to wear when it was raining. She lay still and tried to translate the code of the rain on the roof.

Hold on, it was saying. *Just hold on.*

She wondered what Ander was doing, and in what kind of room he might be lying in bed, staring up at the ceiling. She knew he thought about her at least occasionally; it required some foresight to wait for someone in the woods and all the other places he had waited for her. But *what* did he think about her?

What did she really think about him? She was afraid of him, drawn to him, provoked by him, surprised by him. Thoughts of him lifted her from her depression—and threatened to send her more deeply into it. There was an energy about him that distracted her from grief.

She thought of the thunderstone and Ander's hypothesis. It was stupid. Trust wasn't something born from an experiment. She thought of her friendship with Cat. They had earned each other's trust over time, strengthened it slowly like a muscle, until it contained a power all its own. But sometimes trust struck the intuition like a thunderbolt, fast and deep, the way it had happened between Eureka and Madame Blavatsky. One thing was certain: Trust was mutual, and that was the problem with her and Ander. He held all the cards. Eureka's role in the relationship seemed to be merely being alarmed.

But . . . she didn't have to trust Ander to learn more about the thunderstone.

She opened her desk drawer and set the small blue chest in the center of her bed. She was embarrassed to be considering testing his hypothesis, even alone in her room with the door and the shutters closed.

Downstairs, plates and forks clanked on their way to the sink. It was her night to do the dishes, but no one came to nag her about it. It was like she already wasn't there.

Footsteps on the stairs sent Eureka lunging for her schoolbag. If Dad came in, she'd need to affect an air of study. She had hours of calculus homework, a Latin test on Friday, and untold amounts of makeup work from the classes she'd missed today. She filled her bed with textbooks and binders, covering the thunderstone chest. She slid her calculus book onto her knees just before he knocked on the door.

"Yeah?"

Dad leaned his head in. He had a dish towel slung over his shoulder and his hands were red from hot water. Eureka glowered at the random page in her calculus book and hoped its abstractness would distract her from the guilt of leaving him to do her chores.

He used to stand over her bed offering smart, surprising tips on her homework. Now he wouldn't even step into her room.

He nodded toward her book. "The uncertainty principle? Tough one. The more you know about how one variable changes, the less you know about the other. And everything is changing all the time."

Eureka looked at the ceiling. "I don't know the difference between variables and constants anymore."

"We're only trying to do what's best for you, Reka."

She didn't answer. She had nothing to say to that, to him.

When he closed the door, she read the paragraph introducing the uncertainty principle. The chapter's title page featured a large triangle, the Greek symbol for change, delta. It was the same shape as the gauze-wrapped thunderstone.

She pushed aside her book and opened the box. The thunderstone, still wrapped in its odd white gauze, looked small and unassuming. She picked it up, remembering how delicately Brooks had handled it. She tried to achieve the same level of reverence. She thought about Ander's warning that she must test the stone alone, that Brooks was not to know what she had. What *did* she have? She'd never even seen what the stone looked like. She thought of Diana's postscript:

Don't unwrap the gauze until you need to. You'll know when the time comes.

Eureka's life was in chaos. She was on the brink of being kicked out of the house she hated living in. She hadn't been going to school. She was alienated from all her friends and

313

was following birds through the predawn bayou to meet elderly psychics. How was she supposed to know if *now* was Diana's mystical *when*?

As she reached for the glass on her nightstand, she kept the stone in its gauze. She placed it on top of her Latin binder. Very carefully, she poured a small stream of last night's water directly over the stone. She watched the wet spot seeping through gauze. It was just a rock.

She put the stone down and kicked her legs out across the bed. The dreamer in her was disappointed.

Then, in her peripheral vision, she saw the smallest movement. The stone's gauze had lifted in one corner, as if loosened by the water. *You'll know when.* She heard Diana's voice as if she were lying next to Eureka. It made her shiver.

She peeled back more of the corner of the gauze. This sent the stone spinning, shedding layer after layer of white wrapping. Eureka's fingers sifted through the loosening fabric as the triangular shape of the stone shrank and sharpened in her hands.

At last the final layer of gauze fell away. She held in her hands an isosceles-sided stone about the size of the lapis lazuli locket, but several times heavier. She studied its surface—smooth, with some crags and imperfections, like any other rock. It was shot through here and there with grainy blue-gray crystals. It would have made a good skipping stone for Ander.

Eureka's phone buzzed on her nightstand. She lunged for

314

it, inexplicably certain it would be him. But it was coquettish, half-dressed Cat's photo on her phone's display. Eureka let it go to voice mail. Cat had been texting and calling every few hours since first period that morning. Eureka didn't know what to tell her. They knew each other too well for her to lie and say nothing was going on.

When her phone faded to black and her bedroom was dim again, Eureka became aware of a faint blue light emanating from the stone. Tiny blue-gray veins glowed along the surface of the rock. She stared at them until they began to resemble the abstractions of a language. She turned the stone over and watched a familiar shape form on the back. The veins were making circles. Her ears rang. Goose bumps blanketed her skin. The image on the thunderstone looked precisely like the scar on Brooks's forehead.

A faint crack of thunder sounded in the sky. It was only a coincidence, but it startled her. The stone slipped from her fingers and slid into a recess of her comforter. She reached for the glass again and poured its contents onto the bare thunderstone like she was putting out a fire, like she was extinguishing her friendship with Brooks.

Water splashed back from the stone and hit her in the face.

She spat and wiped her brow. She gazed down at the stone. Her bedspread was wet, her notes and textbooks, too. She blotted them with a pillow and moved them aside. She picked up the stone. It was as dry as a cow's skull on a juke-joint wall.

"No way," she muttered.

She slid off the bed, carrying the stone, and cracked open her door. The TV downstairs was tuned to local news. The twins' night-light cast feeble rays through the open door of the room they shared. She tiptoed to the bathroom, shut and locked the door. She stood with her back against the wall and looked at herself holding the stone in the mirror.

Her pajamas were splattered with water. The edges of the hair framing her face were wet. She held the stone under the faucet and turned the water on all the way.

When the stream hit the stone, it was instantly repelled. No, that wasn't it—Eureka looked closer and saw that the water never even hit the stone. It was repelled in the air above and around it.

She turned off the tap. She sat on the lip of the copper baignoire tub, which was crammed with the twins' bath toys. The sink, the mirror, the rug—all were soaking wet. The thunderstone was absolutely dry.

"Mom," she murmured, "what have you gotten me into?"

She held the stone close to her face and examined it, turning it over in her hands. A small hole had been made at the top of the triangle's widest angle, large enough for a chain to slip through. The thunderstone could be worn as a necklace.

Then why keep it wrapped in gauze? Maybe the gauze

protected whatever sealant had been added to repel water. Eureka looked out the bathroom window at the rain falling on darkened branches. She got an idea.

She dragged a towel across the sink and floor, trying to mop up as much water as she could. She slipped the thunderstone into her pajama pocket and crept down the hall. At the head of the stairs she looked down and saw Dad asleep on the couch, his body lit up by the glow of the TV. A bowl of popcorn was balanced on his chest. She heard frantic typing coming from the kitchen that could only be Rhoda torturing her laptop.

Eureka stole down the stairs and gently opened the back door. The only one who saw her was Squat, who came trotting out with her because he loved to get muddy in the rain. Eureka scratched his head and let him jump up to kiss her face, a habit Rhoda had been working on breaking him of for years. He followed Eureka as she moved down the porch stairs and headed for the back gate to the bayou.

Another crack of thunder forced Eureka to remind herself that it had been raining all evening, that she'd just heard Cokie Faucheux say something on TV about a storm. She raised the latch on the gate and stepped onto the dock where their neighbors slipped their fishing pirogue into the water. She sat down at the edge, rolled up her pajama legs, and sank her feet into the bayou. It was so cold her body stiffened. But she left her icy feet there, even as they started to burn.

With her left hand, she pulled the stone from her pocket and watched thin raindrops ricochet off its surface. They drew Squat's bewildered attention as he sniffed the stone and got water up his nose.

She made a fist around the thunderstone and plunged it into bayou, leaning over and straightening her arm in the water, inhaling sharply from the cold. The water shuddered; then its level rose, and Eureka saw that a large bubble of air had formed around the thunderstone and her arm. The bubble ended just below the surface of the water, where her elbow was.

With her right hand, Eureka explored the underwater bubble, expecting it to pop. It didn't. It was malleable and strong, like an indestructible balloon. When she pulled her wet right hand from the water, she could feel a difference. Her left hand, still underwater, encased by the pocket of air, wasn't wet at all. Finally, she pulled the thunderstone out of the water and saw that it, too, had remained absolutely dry.

"Okay, Ander," she said. "You win."

24

THE DISAPPEARANCE

Tap. Tap. Tap.

When Polaris arrived at her window before sunrise Tuesday morning, Eureka was out of bed by the third tap on the glass. She parted her curtains and slid the cold pane up to greet the lime-green bird.

The bird meant Blavatsky, and Blavatsky meant answers. Translating *The Book of Love* had become Eureka's most compelling mission since Diana died. Somehow, as the tale grew wilder and more fanciful, Eureka's connection to it cemented. She felt a childlike curiosity to know the details of the gossipwitches' prophecy, as if it bore some relevance to her own life. She could hardly wait to meet the old woman down at the willow tree.

She'd slept with the thunderstone on the same chain as the lapis lazuli locket. She couldn't bear to wrap it up and stow it away again. It was heavy around her neck, warm from lying against her chest all night. She decided to ask Madame Blavatsky's opinion on it. It meant welcoming the old woman deeper into her private life, but Eureka trusted her own instincts. Maybe Blavatsky would know something that would help Eureka better understand the stone—maybe she could even explain Ander's interest in it.

Eureka held out her hand to Polaris, but the bird flew past her. He swooped inside her room, flew in an agitated circle near the ceiling, then darted back out the window into the charcoal sky. He flapped his wings, sending a draft of pine-scented air Eureka's way, exposing the variegated feathers where his inner wings met his breastbone. His beak widened skyward in a shrill squawk.

"Now you're a rooster?" she said.

Polaris squawked again. The sound was wretched, nothing like the melodic notes she'd heard him trill before.

"I'm coming." Eureka looked at her pajamas and bare feet. It was cold outside, the air moist and the sun a long way off. She grabbed the first thing her hands found in her closet: the faded green Evangeline tracksuit she used to wear to cross-country away meets. The nylon suit was warm and she could run in it, and there was no reason to be sentimental about the team she'd had to beg to quit. She brushed her teeth and whipped her hair into a braid. She met Polaris by the rosemary bush at the edge of the front porch.

The morning was wet, filled with the gossip of crickets and the clean whisper of rosemary swaying in the wind. This time, Polaris didn't wait for Eureka to tie her running shoes. He flew in the same direction she'd followed him the other day, but faster. Eureka started to jog. Her eyes were somewhere between groggy and alert. Her calves burned from yesterday's run.

The bird's squawk was persistent, abrasive against the dormant street at five in the morning. Eureka wished she knew how to quiet him. Something was different about his mood today, but she didn't speak his language. All she could do was keep up.

She was sprinting when she passed the paperboy's red truck at the end of Shady Circle. She waved as if she were friendly, then turned right to cut through the Guillots' lawn. She reached the bayou, with its army-green morning glow. She'd lost sight of Polaris, but she knew the way to the willow tree.

She could have run it with her eyes closed, and it almost seemed as if she did. Days had passed since Eureka had slept well. Her tank was nearly empty. She watched the moon's reflection shimmering on the surface of the water and imagined it had spawned a dozen baby moons. The infant crescents swam upstream, leaping like flying fish, trying to outpace

Eureka. Her legs pumped faster, wanting to win, until she stumbled over the woody roots of a fern and tumbled into the mud. She landed on her bad wrist. She winced as she regained her footing and her pace.

Squawk!

Polaris swooped over her shoulder as she ran the last twenty yards to the willow tree. The bird held back, still making the strangled squawks that hurt both of Eureka's ears. It wasn't until she reached the tree that she realized the reason for his noise. She leaned against the smooth white tree trunk and rested her hands on her knees to catch her breath. Madame Blavatsky was not there.

There was now an angry undertone to Polaris's chirping. He moved in wide circles over the tree. Eureka looked up at him, bewildered, exhausted—and then she understood. "You didn't want me to come here in the first place."

Squawk!

"Well, how am I supposed to know where she is?"

Squawk!

He flew in the direction Eureka had just come from, turning back once in what was clearly, if absurdly, a glare. Chest heaving, stamina fading, Eureka followed.

<hr />

The sky was still dark when she parked Magda in the pot-holed parking lot outside Blavatsky's office. Wind scattered shadowed oak leaves across the uneven pavement. A street-light lit the intersection but left the strip mall eerily dark.

Eureka had scribbled a note saying she was going to school early for science lab and left it on the counter in the kitchen. She knew it must have looked absurd when she opened the car door for Polaris to fly in, but so did most of Eureka's actions recently. The bird was a great navigator once Eureka realized that two hops to one side or the other on the dashboard indicated which way she was supposed to turn. Heat on, windows and sunroof rolled down, they'd sped toward the translator's storefront on the other side of Lafayette.

Only one other car was in the lot. It looked like it had been parked in front of the tanning salon next door for a decade, which made Eureka wonder about Madame Blavatsky, how the old lady got around.

Polaris soared out the open window and up the exterior flight of stairs before Eureka had turned off the car. When she caught up to him, her hand hovered anxiously over the antique lion's-head knocker.

"She said not to bother her at home," Eureka told Polaris. "You were there, remember?"

The pitch of Polaris's squawk made her jump. It didn't feel right to knock so early, so instead Eureka gave the door a light shove with her hip. It swung open to Blavatsky's low-ceilinged foyer. Eureka and Polaris moved inside. The entry was quiet and humid and smelled like spoiled milk. The two folding chairs were still there, as were the red lamp and the empty magazine rack. But something felt different. The door to Madame Blavatsky's atelier was ajar.

Eureka looked at Polaris. He was silent, wings close to his body, as he flew through the doorway. After a moment, Eureka followed.

Every inch of Madame Blavatsky's office had been ransacked; everything breakable had been broken. All four birdcages were mangled by wire cutters. One cage hung misshapen from the ceiling; the rest had been tossed to the floor. A few birds chattered nervously on the sill of the open window. The rest must have flown away—or worse. Green feathers were everywhere.

The frowning portraits lay smashed on the muddied Persian rug. The pillows on the couch had been slashed. Stuffing spilled from them like pus from a wound. The humidifier near the back wall was burbling, which Eureka knew from nursing the twins' allergies meant it was almost out of water. A bookcase lay in splinters on the floor. One of the turtles explored the jagged mountain range of texts.

Eureka paced the room, stepping carefully over the books and shattered picture frames. She noticed a little butter dish brimming with bejeweled rings. The scene did not look typical of a robbery.

Where was Blavatsky? And where was Eureka's book?

She started to sift through some crumpled papers on the desk, but she didn't want to go through Madame Blavatsky's private things, even if someone else already had. Behind the desk, she noticed the ashtray where the translator put out her cigarettes. Four cigarette butts were kissed with Blavatsky's unmistakable red lipstick. Two were as pale as the paper.

Eureka touched the pendants around her neck, hardly realizing she was developing a habit of calling on them for help. She closed her eyes and lowered herself onto Blavatsky's desk chair. The black walls and ceiling felt like they were closing in.

Pale cigarettes made her think of pale faces, calm enough to smoke before . . . or after, or during, the destruction of Blavatsky's office. What had the intruders been looking for?

Where was her book?

She knew she was biased, but she couldn't picture any culprits other than the ghostly people from the dark road. The idea of their pale fingers holding Diana's book made Eureka shoot to her feet.

At the back of the office, near the open window, she discovered a tiny alcove she hadn't seen on her first visit. The doorway was strung with a purple beaded curtain that rattled when she passed through. The alcove held a little galley kitchen with a small sink, an overgrown planter of dill, a three-legged wooden stool, and, behind the micro-fridge, a surprising flight of stairs.

Madame Blavatsky's apartment was on the floor above her

office. Eureka took the stairs three at a time. Polaris chirped approvingly, as if this was the direction he'd wanted her to take all along.

The stairs were dark, so she used her phone to light the way. At the top stood a closed door with six enormous deadbolts. Each of the locks was unique and antique—and looked utterly impregnable. Eureka was relieved, thinking that at least whoever had ransacked the downstairs atelier wouldn't have been able to break into Madame Blavatsky's apartment.

Polaris squawked angrily, as if he'd expected Eureka to have a key. He swooped down and pecked the ragged carpet at the foot of the door like a chicken desperate for feed. Eureka shined her phone's light down to see what he was doing.

She wished she hadn't.

A pool of blood had seeped through the crack between the door and the landing. It had soaked most of the top step and was now spreading downward. In the silent darkness of the stairwell, Eureka heard a droplet fall from the top step onto the one where she was standing. She inched away, repulsed and afraid.

Dizziness gripped her. She leaned forward, intending to rest her hand on the door for a moment to regain her balance—but she flailed backward as the door gave way under the slightest pressure of her touch. It tumbled, like a felled tree, into the apartment. The door's weighty thud was accompanied by a damp slap on the carpet, which Eureka realized had to do with the blood pooled behind the door. The impact sent red splatters sloshing up onto the smoke-stained walls.

Whoever had been here had taken the door cleanly off its hinges and, before leaving, had propped it up so that it still looked bolted from the outside.

She should leave. She should turn around right now, rush down the stairs, and get out of here before she saw something she did not want to see. Her mouth filled with a sickly taste. She should call the police. She should get out and not come back.

But she couldn't. Something had happened to a person she cared about. As loudly as her instincts screamed *Run!* Eureka could not turn her back on Madame Blavatsky.

She stepped over the bloody landing, onto the fallen door, and followed Polaris into the apartment. It smelled like blood and sweat and cigarettes. Dozens of nearly extinguished candles flickered along a mantel. They were the only source of light in the room. Outside the single small window, an electric bug-killer zapped in a steady beat. In the center of the room, sprawled across the blue industrial carpet, in the first place Eureka suspected and the last place she allowed herself to look, was Madame Blavatsky, dead as Diana.

Eureka's hand went to her throat to choke off a gasp. Over her shoulder, the stairwell to the exit looked endless, like she'd never make it without fainting. On instinct, she felt in her pocket for her phone. She dialed 911, but she could not bring herself to press the call button. She had no voice, no way to communicate to a stranger on the other end of a line that the woman who'd become the closest thing Eureka had to a mother was dead.

The phone fell back inside her pocket. She moved closer to Madame Blavatsky but was careful to stay beyond the spread of blood.

Clumps of auburn hair lay on the floor, surrounding the old woman's head like a crown. There were bald patches of pink skin where the hair had been ripped from her scalp. Her eyes were open. One stared vacantly at the ceiling. The other had been torn completely from its socket. It dangled near her temple, hanging on by a thin pink artery. Her cheeks were lacerated, as if sharp nails had dragged across them. Her legs and arms were sprawled at her sides, making her look like a kind of mangled snow angel. One hand grasped a rosary. Her patchwork cloak was slick with blood. She had been beaten, shredded, stabbed repeatedly in the chest by something that left much larger slashes than a knife. She'd been left to bleed out on the floor.

Eureka staggered against the wall. She wondered what Madame Blavatsky's last thought had been. She tried to imagine the kind of prayers the woman might have said on her way out of the world, but her mind was blank with shock. She sank to her knees. Diana always said that everything in the world was connected. Why hadn't Eureka stopped to consider what *The Book of Love* had to do with the thunderstone Ander knew so much about—or the people he'd protected her from on the road? If they were the ones who'd done this to Madame Blavatsky, she felt certain they'd come in search of *The Book of Love.* They had murdered someone over it.

And if that was true, Madame Blavatsky's death had been her fault. Her mind went to the Confession booth, where she'd go on Saturday afternon with Dad. She had no idea how many Hail Marys and Our Fathers she'd have to say to clear that sin.

She should never have insisted they carry on with the translation. Madame Blavatsky had warned her of the risks. Eureka should have connected the old woman's hesitation to the danger Ander said Eureka was in. But she hadn't. Maybe she hadn't wanted to. Maybe she wanted one thing sweet and magical in her life. Now that sweet and magical thing was dead.

She thought she was going to gag, but she didn't. She thought she might scream, but she didn't. Instead she knelt closer to Madame Blavatsky's chest and resisted the urge to touch her. For months she had longed for the impossible opportunity to cradle Diana after her death. Now Eureka wanted to reach for Madame Blavatsky, but the open wounds held her back. Not because Eureka was disgusted—though the woman was in gruesome shape—but because she knew better than to implicate herself in this murder. She held back, knowing that no matter how much she cared, there was nothing she could do for Blavatsky.

She imagined others coming upon this sight: the gray pallor Rhoda's skin would take on, the way it did when she was nauseated, making her orange lipstick look clownish; the prayers that would stream from the lips of Eureka's most pious classmate, Belle Pogue; the disbelieving curses Cat would spew. Eureka imagined she could see herself from outside herself. She looked as lifeless and immobile as a boulder that had been lodged in the apartment for millennia. She looked stoic and unreachable.

Diana's death had killed death's mysteries for Eureka. She knew death was waiting for her, like it had been for Madame Blavatsky, like it was for everyone she loved and didn't love. She knew that human beings were born to die. She remembered the last line of a Dylan Thomas poem she'd once read on an online grief forum. It was the only thing that made sense to her when she was in the hospital:

After the first death, there is no other.

Diana was Eureka's first death. It meant that Madame Blavatsky's death was *no other*. Even Eureka's own death would be *no other*.

Her grief was powerful; it just looked different from what people were used to.

She was afraid, but not of the dead body before her—

she'd seen worse in too many nightmares. She was afraid of what Madame Blavatsky's death meant for the other people close to her, dwindling as their numbers were. She couldn't help feeling robbed of something, knowing that she would never understand the rest of *The Book of Love.*

Had the murderers taken her book? The thought of someone else possessing it, knowing more of it than she did, enraged her. She rose and moved toward Blavatsky's breakfast bar, then her nightstand, searching for any sign of the book, being as careful as possible not to alter what she knew would be a crime scene.

She found nothing, only heartache. She was so miserable she could hardly see. Polaris squawked and pecked the edges of Madame Blavatsky's cloak.

Everything might change with the last word, Eureka thought. But *this* couldn't be Madame Blavatsky's last word. She deserved so much more than this.

Again Eureka lowered herself to the floor. Her fingers found their way across her chest intuitively, making the sign of the cross. She pressed her hands together and bowed her head in a silent prayer to Saint Francis, asking for serenity on the old woman's behalf. She kept her head bowed and her eyes closed until she sensed that her prayer had left the room and was on its way into the atmosphere. She hoped it made it to its destination.

What would become of Madame Blavatsky? Eureka had

no way of knowing who would find the woman next, whether she had friends or family nearby. As her mind reeled around the simplest possibilities of getting Madame Blavatsky help, she imagined terrifying conversations with the sheriff. Her chest tightened. It wouldn't bring the old woman back to life if Eureka embroiled herself in a criminal investigation. Still, she had to find some way to let the police know.

She gazed around the room, despondent—and then she had an idea.

Back on the landing she had passed a commercial fire alarm, probably installed before the building became a residence. Eureka stood and stepped around the pool of blood, sliding a little bit as she crossed the door. She regained her balance and tugged the sleeve of her tracksuit over her hand to avoid leaving fingerprints. She reached for the red hatch and pulled the metal handle down.

The alarm was instantaneous, earsplitting, almost comically loud. Eureka buried her head between her shoulders and started toward the exit. Before she left, she gazed into the room once more at Madame Blavatsky. She wanted to say she was sorry.

Polaris was perched on the woman's shredded chest, pecking lightly where her heart had once beat. He seemed phosphorescent in the candlelight. When he noticed Eureka watching, he raised his head. His black eyes gleamed demonically. He hissed at her, then squawked once, so shrilly it pierced the sound of the fire alarm.

Eureka jumped, then spun around. She ran the rest of the way down the stairs. She didn't stop until she'd passed through Madame Blavatsky's atelier, through the red-lit foyer, until she stood gasping in the parking lot, where a golden sun was just beginning to burn into the sky.

25

LOST AT SEA

Early Saturday morning, the twins bounded into Eureka's room.

"Wake up!" Claire bounced onto the bed. "We're spending the day with you!"

"That's great." Eureka rubbed her eyes and checked her phone for the time. Her browser was still open to the Google search "Yuki Blavatsky," which she'd been refreshing continually, hoping for a story on the murder.

Nothing had come up. All Eureka got was an old yellow pages listing for Blavatsky's business, which she alone seemed to know was out of business. She had driven by the strip mall on Tuesday after an unbearably long day at school, but at the turn into the empty parking lot, she'd lost her nerve and sped up, until the unlit neon palm sign was no long visible in her rearview mirror.

Haunted by the lack of obvious police presence, by thoughts of Madame Blavatsky decaying alone in the studio, Eureka had driven to the university. Setting off the fire alarm clearly had not been enough, so she sat down at one of the free student union computers and filled out an anonymous crime report form online. It was safer to do it there, in the middle of the bustling student union, than to have the police Web page on her laptop's browser history at home.

She kept her report simple, providing the name and address of the deceased woman. She left blank the fields asking for information on suspects, though Eureka was inexplicably certain she could pick Madame Blavatsky's murderer out of a lineup.

When she'd driven by Blavatsky's storefront again on Wednesday, yellow crime-scene tape barred the front door and cop cars crammed the lot. The shock and grief she'd refused to feel in the presence of Madame Blavatsky's body had washed over Eureka, a rogue wave of crippling guilt. It had been three days since then, and she'd heard nothing on the radio or TV news, online, or in the paper. The silence was driving her crazy.

She'd suppressed the urge to confide in Ander, because she couldn't share what had happened with anyone, and even if she could, she wouldn't know how to find him. Eureka was on her own.

"Why are you wearing water wings?" She squeezed William's inflatable orange muscle as he wiggled under her covers.

"Mom said you'd take us to the pool!"

Wait. Today was the day Eureka had agreed to sail with Brooks.

It is your destiny, Madame Blavatsky had said, piquing Eureka's curiosity. She wasn't eager to spend time with Brooks, but she was at least ready to face him. She wanted to do what little she could to honor the old woman's memory.

"We'll go to the pool another day." Eureka scooted William aside so she could climb out of bed. "I forgot I have to—"

"Don't tell me you forgot you were watching the twins?" Rhoda appeared in the doorway wearing a red crepe dress. She worked a bobby pin into her tightly coiffed hair. "Your dad's at work and I'm delivering the keynote at the dean's luncheon."

"I made plans with Brooks."

"Rearrange them." Rhoda tilted her head and frowned. "We were doing so well."

She meant that Eureka had been going to school, had suffered through her hour of hell with Dr. Landry Tuesday afternoon. Eureka had forked over the last three twenties she owned, then dumped out onto Landry's coffee table a battered sack of nickels, dimes, and pennies amounting to the extra fifteen dollars she needed to pay for the session. She had no idea how she would afford to suffer again next week, but at the rate the past few days had crawled, Tuesday was an eternity away.

"Fine. I'll watch the twins."

She didn't have to tell Rhoda what they'd be doing while she watched them. She texted Brooks, the first communication she'd initiated since Never-Ever: *Okay if I bring the twins?*

Absolutely! His response was immediate. *Was going to suggest that myself.*

"Eureka," Rhoda said. "The sheriff called this morning. Do you know a woman named Mrs. Blavatsky?"

"What?" Eureka's voice died in her throat. "Why?"

She imagined her fingerprints on the papers on Madame Blavatsky's desk. Her shoes unknowingly dipping into the woman's blood, screaming out proof of her visit.

"Evidently she's . . . missing." Rhoda lied badly. The police would have told her Madame Blavatsky was dead. Rhoda must not have thought Eureka could handle hearing about another death. She didn't know one percent of what Eureka was handling. "For some reason, the police think you know each other."

There was no indictment in Rhoda's voice, which meant the cops weren't treating Eureka as a suspect—yet.

"Cat and I went to her storefront once." Eureka tried not to say anything that was a lie. "She's a fortune-teller."

"That junk is a waste of money, you know that. The sheriff is going to call back later. I said you'd answer some questions." Rhoda leaned over the bed and kissed the twins. "I'm almost late. Don't take any chances today, Eureka."

Eureka nodded as her phone buzzed in her palm with a text from Cat. *The freaking sheriff called my house about Blavatsky. WHAT HAPPENED?*

No clue, Eureka responded, feeling dizzy. *They called here, too.*

What about your book? Cat typed back, but Eureka didn't have an answer, only a heavy weight in her chest.

∞

Sunlight glittered on the water as Eureka and the twins walked the long cedar planks to the edge of Brooks's Cypremort Point dock. His lean silhouette bent forward, checking the halyards that would raise the sails once the boat was in the bay.

The family sloop was christened *Ariel.* It was a long-seasoned, weather-stained, beautiful forty-foot sailboat with a deep hull and a square stern. It had been in the family for decades. Today its bare mast stood up stiffly, cutting the dome of the sky like a knife. A pelican sat on the line that tethered the boat to the dock.

Brooks was barefoot, in cutoffs and a green Tulane sweatshirt. He wore his father's old army baseball cap. For a moment Eureka forgot she was mourning Madame Blavatsky.

338

She even forgot she was mad at Brooks. As she and the twins approached the boat, she enjoyed his simple movements—how familiar he was with every inch of the boat, the strength he displayed tightening the sheets. Then she heard his voice.

He was shouting as he moved from the cockpit to the main deck. He leaned down the stairs, head level with the galley below. "You don't know me and you never will, so stop trying."

Eureka stopped short on the dock, holding the twins' stiff hands. They were used to Eureka shouting at home, but they'd never seen Brooks like this.

He looked up and saw her. His posture loosened. His face lit up.

"Eureka." He grinned. "You look terrific."

She squinted toward the galley, wondering whom Brooks had been yelling at. "Is everything okay?"

"Never better. Top of the morning, Harrington-Boudreauxs!" Brooks lifted his cap at the twins. "Are you ready to be my double first mates?"

The twins jumped into Brooks's arms, forgetting how scary he'd just been. Eureka heard someone climbing from the galley to the deck. The silver crown of Brooks's mother's head appeared. Eureka was stunned that he would say what he'd said to Aileen. She stood on the gangway and held out a hand to help Aileen up the steep, slightly rocking steps.

Aileen offered Eureka a weary smile and held out her

arms for a hug. Her eyes were wet. "I loaded up the galley with lunch." She straightened the collar of her striped jersey dress. "There are plenty of brownies, baked fresh last night."

Eureka imagined Aileen wearing a flour-dusted apron at three in the morning, baking her anxiety into sweet-smelling steam that carried the secret of the change in Brooks. He wasn't just wearing Eureka down. His mother seemed like a smaller, faded version of herself.

Aileen slipped off her kitten heels and held them in her hands. She turned her deep brown eyes on Eureka; they were the same color as her son's. She lowered her voice. "Have you noticed anything strange about him recently?"

If only Eureka could open up to Aileen, hear what she'd been going through, too. But Brooks came and stood between them, putting an arm around each of them. "My two favorite ladies," he said. And then, before Eureka could register Aileen's reaction, Brooks removed his arms and walked to the helm. "You ready to do this, Cuttlefish?"

I haven't forgiven you, she wanted to say, though she had read all sixteen groveling text messages he'd sent this week, and the two letters he'd left in her locker. She was here because of Madame Blavatsky, because something told her that destiny mattered. Eureka was trying to replace her final image of Blavatsky dead in her studio with the memory of the woman at peace under the willow tree by the bayou, the one who'd seemed convinced there was good reason for Eureka to sail with Brooks today.

What you do once you're there is up to you.

But then Eureka thought about Ander, who insisted Brooks was dangerous. The scar on Brooks's forehead was half hidden under the shadow of his baseball cap. It looked like an ordinary scar, not some ancient hieroglyph—and for a moment Eureka felt crazy for thinking that the scar might be evidence of something sinister. She looked down at the thunderstone, flipping it over. The rings were barely visible in the sun. She'd been acting like a conspiracy theorist who'd spent too many days cooped up with only the Internet to talk to. She needed to relax and get some sun.

"Thanks for lunch," Eureka said to Aileen, who'd been chatting with the twins from the gangplank. She stepped closer and lowered her voice so that Aileen alone could hear. "About Brooks." She shrugged, attempting lightness. "Just boys, you know. I'm sure William will grow up to terrorize Rhoda someday." She tousled her brother's hair. "Means he loves you."

Aileen looked out at the water again. "Children grow up so fast. I guess sometimes they forget to forgive us. Well"— she looked back at Eureka, forced a smile—"you kids have fun. And if there's any weather, turn back right away."

Brooks held out his arms and looked up at the sky, which was blue and immense and cloudless but for an innocent cotton puff in the east just underneath the sun. "What could possibly go wrong?"

The breeze rustling Eureka's ponytail became bracing as Brooks started *Ariel*'s engine and steered away from the dock. The twins squealed, looking cute in their life jackets. They balled their hands into excited fists at the first jolt of the boat. The tide was soft and steady, the air perfectly briny. The shore was lined with cypress trees and family camps.

When Eureka rose from her bench to see if Brooks needed help, he waved for her to sit down. "Everything's under control. You just relax."

Though anyone else would say that Brooks was trying to make amends and that the bay today was serene—a sun-blasted sky making the waves glisten, the smallest shimmer of pale fog lazing on the distant horizon—Eureka was uneasy. She saw the sea and Brooks as capable of the same dark surprise: out of nowhere they could morph into knives and stab you in the heart.

She thought she'd hit the bottom at the Trejean party the other night, but since then Eureka had lost both *The Book of Love* and the only person who could help her understand it. Worse, she believed that the people who killed Madame Blavatsky were the same ones hunting her. She really could have used a friend—and yet she found it nearly impossible to smile at Brooks across the deck.

The deck was made of treated cedar, dimpled by a million dents from cocktail-partiers' stilettos. Diana used to go to Aileen's parties on this boat. Any of these marks could have been made by the single pair of high heels she'd owned. Eureka imagined using her mother's dents to clone her back to life, to put her on the deck right now, dancing to no music in daylight. She imagined that the surface of her own heart probably looked like this deck. Love was a dance floor, where everyone you lost left a mark behind.

Bare feet slapped the deck as the twins ran around, shouting "Goodbye!" or "We're sailing!" to every camp they passed. The sun warmed Eureka's shoulders and reminded her to show her siblings a beautiful time. She wished Dad were here to see their faces. With her phone, she snapped a picture and texted it to him. Brooks grinned at her. She nodded back.

They glided past two men in mesh baseball caps fishing from an aluminum canoe. Brooks greeted each of them by name. They watched a crabbing boat coast by. The water was rich blue opal. It smelled like Eureka's childhood, much of which had been spent on this boat with Brooks's uncle Jack at the helm. Now Brooks was steering the ship with easy confidence. His brother, Seth, always said that Brooks was born to sail, that he wouldn't be surprised if Brooks became an admiral in the navy or a tour guide in the Galápagos. Whatever kept Brooks on the water was likely what Brooks would do.

It wasn't long before *Ariel* left behind the camp houses

and trailers, rounding a bend to face broad, shallow Vermilion Bay.

Eureka gripped the whitewashed bench beneath her at the sight of the small man-made beach. She hadn't been back since the day Brooks had almost drowned here—the day they had kissed. She felt a mix of nerves and embarrassment, and she couldn't look at him. He was busy anyway, cutting the engine and hoisting the mainsail from the cockpit; then he raised the jib up the forestay.

He handed William and Claire the jib and asked them to tug the corners, making them feel they were helping to bring the sails aloft. They squealed when the crisp white sail slid up the mast, locked into place, and filled with wind.

The sails billowed, then grew taut with the strong eastern breeze. They started on a close haul course, at forty-five degrees to the wind, and then Brooks maneuvered the boat into a comfortable broad reach, easing the sails appropriately. *Ariel* was majestic with the wind at its back. Water split across its bow, sending smothers of foam splashing softly onto the deck. Black frigate birds swooped in grand circles overhead, keeping pace with the leeward glide of the sails. Flying fish soared above waves like shooting stars. Brooks let the kids stand with him at the helm as the boat clipped west past the bay.

Eureka brought juice boxes and two of Aileen's sandwiches up from the galley for the twins. The kids chewed quietly, sharing a lounge chair in the shady corner of the deck. Eureka stood next to Brooks. The sun bore down on her shoulders and she squinted ahead at a long, flat stretch of low-lying land overgrown with pale green reeds in the distance.

"Still mad at me?" he asked.

She didn't want to talk about it. She didn't want to talk about anything that might scratch her brittle surface and expose every secret she held inside.

"Is that Marsh Island?" She knew it was. The barrier island kept the heavier waves from breaking in the bay. "We should stay to the north of it. Right?"

Brooks patted the broad wooden wheel. "You don't think *Ariel* can handle the open seas?" His voice was playful, but his eyes had narrowed. "Or is it me you're worried about?"

Eureka breathed in a gust of briny air, certain she could see whitecaps beyond the island. "It's rough out there. It might be too much for the twins."

"We want to go out *far*!" Claire shouted between gulps of grape juice.

"I do this all the time." Brooks moved the wheel slightly east so they'd be able to slide around the edge of the approaching island.

"We didn't go out that far in May." It was the last time they'd sailed together. She remembered because she'd counted the four circles they'd made around the bay.

"Sure we did." Brooks stared past her at the water. "You've got to admit your memory has become disorganized since—"

"Don't do that," Eureka snapped. She looked back in the direction they'd come. Gray clouds had joined the softer pink clouds near the horizon. She watched the sun slip behind one, its rays frisking the cloud's dark coat. She wanted to turn back. "I don't want to go out there, Brooks. This shouldn't be a fight."

The boat swayed and they stepped on each other's feet. She closed her eyes and let the rocking slow her breathing.

"Let's take it easy," he said. "This is an important day."

Her eyes flashed open. "Why?"

"Because I can't have you mad at me. I messed up. I let your sadness scare me and I lashed out when I should have supported you. It doesn't change how I feel. I'm here for you. Even if more bad things happen, even if you get sadder."

Eureka shrugged his hands away. "Rhoda doesn't know I brought the twins. If anything happens . . ."

She heard Rhoda's voice: *Don't take any chances, Eureka.*

Brooks rubbed his jaw, clearly annoyed. He cranked one of the levers on the mainsail. He was going past Marsh Island. "Don't be paranoid," he said harshly. "Life is one long surprise."

"Some surprises can be avoided."

"Everybody's mother dies, Eureka."

"That's very supportive, thank you."

"Look, maybe you're special. Maybe nothing bad will ever happen to you or anyone you love again," he said, which made Eureka laugh bitterly. "All I meant was I'm sorry. I broke your trust last week. I'm here to earn it back."

He was waiting for her forgiveness, but she turned and gazed at the waves, which were the color of another pair of eyes. She thought about Ander asking her to trust him. She still didn't know if she did. Could a dry thunderstone open a portal to trust as quickly as Brooks had closed one? Did it even matter? She hadn't seen or heard from Ander since that rainy night's experiment. She didn't even know how to look for him.

"Eureka, please," Brooks whispered. "Say you trust me."

"You're my oldest friend." Her voice was rough. She didn't look at him. "I trust that we'll get over this."

"Good." She heard a smile in his voice.

The sky dimmed. The sun had gone behind a cloud shaped strangely like an eye. A beam of light shot through its center, illuminating a circle of sea in front of the boat. Somber clouds rolled toward them like smoke.

They had sailed past Marsh Island. The waves were rolling in quick succession. One rocked the boat so violently that Eureka stumbled. The kids rolled around on the deck, shrieking with laughter, not scared at all.

Glancing at the sky, Brooks helped Eureka up. "You were right. I guess we should turn back."

She hadn't expected that, but she agreed.

"Take the wheel?" He crossed the deck to tack the sails to turn the boat around. The blue sky had succumbed to advancing dark clouds. The wind grew fierce and the temperature dropped.

When Brooks returned to the wheel, Eureka covered the twins with beach towels. "Let's go down to the galley."

"We want to stay up here and watch the big waves," Claire said.

"Eureka, I need you to hold the wheel again." Brooks handled the sails, trying to get the bow of the boat to face the waves head on, which would be safer, but the swells slammed the starboard side.

Eureka made William and Claire stand next to her so she could keep an arm around them. They'd stopped laughing. The waves had grown too rough.

A powerful surge crested before the boat as if it had been rising from the bottom of the sea for eternity. *Ariel* rode up the face of the wave, higher and higher, until it slammed down and struck the surface of the water with a boom that shuddered hard up to the deck. It knocked Eureka away from the twins, against the mast.

She'd hit her head, but she struggled to her feet. She shielded her face from the bursts of white water flung across the deck. She was five feet from the kids, but she could barely move for the ship's rocking. Suddenly the boat turned against the force of another wave, which crested over the deck and swamped it with water.

Eureka heard a scream. Her body froze as she saw William and Claire swept up in the flow of water and carried toward the stern. Eureka couldn't reach them. Everything was rocking too hard.

The wind shifted. A gust slam-jibed the boat, causing the mainsail to violently switch sides. The boom slid starboard with a creak. Eureka watched it swing toward where the twins were struggling to stand on a bench in the cockpit, away from the swirling water.

"Look out!" Eureka screamed too late. The side of the boom hit Claire and William in their chests. In one horrifically simple motion, it flung their bodies overboard, as if they were weightless as feathers.

She threw herself against the rail of the ship and searched for the twins among the waves. It only took a second, but it felt like an eternity: orange lifejackets bobbed to the surface and tiny arms flailed in the air.

"William! Claire!" she shouted, but before she could jump in, Brooks's arm shot across her chest to hold her back. He held one of the life preservers in his other hand, its rope looped over his wrist.

"Stay here!" he shouted.

He dove into the water. He tossed the life ring toward the twins as his strong strokes brought him to them. Brooks would save them. Of course he would.

Another wave crested over their heads—and Eureka didn't see them anymore. She shouted. She ran up and down the deck. She waited three, maybe four seconds, certain they'd reappear at any moment. The sea was black and churning. There was no sign of the twins or Brooks.

She struggled onto the bench and dove into the roiling sea, saying the shortest prayer she knew as her body tumbled down.

Hail Mary, full of grace . . .

In midair she remembered: she should have dropped the anchor before she left the boat.

As her body broke the surface, Eureka braced for the shock—but she didn't feel anything. Not wet, not cold, not even that she was underwater. She opened her eyes. She was holding on to her necklace, the locket and the thunderstone.

The thunderstone.

Just as it had done in the bayou behind her house, the mysterious stone had cast some sort of impenetrable water-resistant balloon—this time around Eureka's entire body. She tested its boundaries. They were pliant. She could stretch without feeling cramped. It was like a kind of wetsuit, shielding her from the elements. It was a bubble-shaped thunderstone shield.

Free from gravity, she levitated inside the shield. She could breathe. She could move by making normal swimming strokes. She could see the sea around her as well as if she were wearing a scuba mask.

Under any other circumstances, Eureka would not have believed this was happening. But she didn't have time to not believe. Her faith would be the twins' salvation. And so she surrendered to her new, dreamlike reality. She searched the undulating ocean for her siblings and for Brooks.

When she saw the kick of a little leg fifty feet in front of her, she whimpered with relief. She swam harder than she'd ever done anything, propelling her arms and her legs forward in a desperate crawl. As she grew closer, she could see that it was William. He was kicking violently—and his hand was clasping Claire's.

Eureka strained with the strange effort of swimming inside her shield. She reached out—she was so close—but her hand wouldn't break the surface of the bubble.

She jabbed at William senselessly, but he couldn't see her. The twins' heads kept ducking underwater. A dark shadow behind them might have been Brooks—but the shape never came into focus.

William's kicks grew weaker. Eureka was screaming with futility when suddenly Claire's hand swooped down and accidentally penetrated the shield. It didn't matter how Claire did it. Eureka grabbed her sister hard and pulled her in.

The drenched little girl gasped for air when her face broke through. Eureka prayed that William's hand would stay in Claire's so she could pull him into the shield, too. His grip seemed to be loosening. From lack of oxygen? For fear of what his sister was being drawn into?

"William, *hold on!*" Eureka shouted as loudly as she could, not knowing whether he could hear. She only heard the slosh of water against the surface of the shield.

His tiny fist broke through the barrier. Eureka pulled the rest of him in with a single heave, the way she'd once seen a calf being born. The twins gagged and coughed—and levitated with Eureka in the shield.

She swept both of them into a hug. Her chest shuddered and she almost lost control of her emotions. But she couldn't, not yet.

"Where's Brooks?" She looked beyond the shield. She didn't see him.

"Where are we?" Claire asked.

"This is scary," William said.

Eureka sensed the waves crashing above them, but they were now fifteen feet below the surface, where the water was much calmer. She steered the shield in a circle, searching the surface for signs of Brooks or the boat. The twins wailed, terrified.

She had no idea how long the shield would last. If it burst or sank or disappeared, they'd be dead. Brooks would be able to make it back to the boat on his own, to sail it back to camp. She had to believe he would. If she didn't believe, she could never allow herself to focus on getting the twins to safety. And she had to get the twins to safety.

She couldn't see above water to determine which way to go, so she stayed still and watched the currents. There was an infamous chaotic riptide just south of Marsh Island. She would have to avoid that.

When the current pulled her in one direction, she knew to swim against it. Cautiously, she began to paddle. She would swim until the tides changed on the bay side of Marsh Island. From there, she hoped, the waves would move with her, carrying the three of them to shore in a smother of foam.

The twins didn't ask any more questions. Maybe they knew she couldn't answer them. After a few minutes of watching her strokes, they began to swim with her. They helped the shield move faster.

They swam through the gloom beneath the surface of the sea—past strange, bloated black fish, past rocks shaped like ribs, slick with moss and sludge. They found a rhythm—the twins paddled, then rested, while Eureka swam steadily on.

After what seemed like an hour, Eureka saw the submerged sandbar of Marsh Island, and she almost collapsed with relief. It meant they were going the right way. But they weren't there yet. They had three miles to go. Swimming inside the shield was less taxing than swimming in open water, but three miles was a long way to travel with half-drowned four-year-old twins in tow.

After another hour of paddling, the bottom of the shield struck something. Sand. The ocean floor. The water was getting shallower. They had almost made it ashore. Eureka swam forward with renewed strength. At last they reached an up-hill slope of sand. The water was shallow enough that a wave broke below the top of the shield.

When that happened, the shield popped like a soap bubble. It left no trace behind. Eureka and the twins shuddered back to gravity, touching the earth again. She was knee-deep in the water, hoisting them up as she stumbled through reeds and mud to the deserted Vermilion shore.

The sky was awash with thunderclouds. Lightning danced above the trees. The only signs of civilization were a sand-caked LSU T-shirt and a faded Coors Light can wedged into the mud.

She set the twins down on the edge of the beach. She fell onto the sand. William and Claire curled into balls on either side of her. They shivered. She covered them with her arms and rubbed their goose-bumped skin.

"Eureka?" William's voice shook.

She could barely nod.

"Brooks is gone, isn't he?"

When Eureka didn't answer, William began to cry, and then Claire began to cry, and Eureka couldn't think of anything to say to make them feel better. She was supposed to be strong for them, but she wasn't strong. She was broken. She writhed on the sand, feeling a strange nausea enter her body. Her vision blurred, and an unfamiliar sensation coiled around her heart. She opened her mouth and struggled to breathe. For a moment, she thought she might cry.

That was when it started raining.

26

SHELTER

The clouds thickened as rain swept across the bay. The air smelled like salt and storm and rotting seaweed. Eureka sensed the gale strengthening over the entire region as if it were an extension of her emotions. She imagined her throbbing heart accentuating the rain, slamming sheets of icy water up and down Bayou Teche as she lay paralyzed by sorrow, feverish in a rank pool of Vermilion Bay mud.

Raindrops flew off the thunderstone, making soft zinging sounds as they smacked her chest and chin. The tide rolled in. She let it slap her sides, the contours of her face. She wanted to flow back into the ocean and find her mother and her friend. She wanted the ocean to become an arm, a perfect rogue wave that would carry her out to sea like Zeus carried Europa.

Tenderly, William shook Eureka into an awareness that she needed to rise. She needed to take care of him and Claire, seek help. The rain had increased to a torrential downpour, like a hurricane had appeared without warning. The steely sky was frightening. It made Eureka wish absurdly that a priest would appear on the beach in the rain, offering absolution just in case.

She dragged herself to her knees. She forced herself to stand and take her siblings' hands. The raindrops were gigantic, and so fierce in their velocity they bruised her shoulders. She tried to cover the twins' bodies as they walked through mud and grass and along jagged, rocky paths. She scanned the beach for shelter.

About a mile up the dirt road, they came across an Airstream. Painted sky blue and strung with Christmas lights, it stood alone. Its salt-cracked windows were lined with pipe tape. As soon as the thin door swung open, Eureka pushed the twins inside.

She knew apologies and explanations were expected by the startled middle-aged couple who'd answered the door in matching slippers, but Eureka couldn't spare the breath. She fell despairingly onto a stool by the door, shivering in her rain-glazed clothes.

"B-borrow your phone?" she managed to stutter as thunder shook the trailer.

The phone was old, attached to the wall with a pale green

cord. Eureka dialed Dad at the restaurant. She had the number memorized from before she'd had a cell phone. She didn't know what else to do.

"Trenton Boudreaux," she rushed out his name to the hostess who shouted a memorized greeting over the background din. "It's his daughter."

The lunch-rush roar silenced when Eureka was put on hold. She waited for centuries, listening to the waves of rain come in and go out, like radio reception on a road trip. Finally someone shouted to Dad to pick up the phone in the kitchen.

"Eureka?" She imagined him cradling the phone under a tucked chin, his hands slick with marinade for shrimp.

His voice made everything better and everything worse. Suddenly she couldn't speak, could barely breathe. She gripped the phone. *Daddy* rose in the back of her throat, but she couldn't get it out.

"What happened?" he shouted. "Are you okay?"

"I'm at the Point," she said. "With the twins. We lost Brooks. Dad . . . I need you."

"Stay where you are," he shouted. "I'm coming."

Eureka dropped the phone into the hand of the confused man who owned the trailer. Distantly, over the shrill ringing in her ear, she heard him describe the Airstream's location near the shore.

They waited silently, for what might have been forever, as the rain and wind wailed against the roof. Eureka imagined the same rain lashing Brooks's body, the same wind tossing him in a realm beyond her reach, and she buried her face in her hands.

The streets were flooded by the time Dad's pale blue Lincoln pulled up outside the trailer. Through the tiny Airstream window she saw him run from his car toward the half-submerged wooden steps. He waded through muddy water flowing like a wild river along new ruts in the terrain. Debris swirled around him. She flung open the door of the trailer, the twins at her sides. She shook when his arms embraced her.

"Thank God," Dad whispered. "Thank God."

He called Rhoda on the slow drive home. Eureka heard her hysterical voice through the speaker, shouting *What were they doing at the Point?* Eureka cupped her good ear and tried to tune their conversation out. She squeezed her eyes shut each time the Lincoln hydroplaned in high water. She knew without looking that they were the only ones on the road.

She couldn't stop shaking. It occurred to her that she might never stop, that she'd live her life in a mental institution on an avoided floor, a legendary recluse covered in tatty old blankets.

The sight of her front porch opened a deeper chamber of shivers. Whenever Brooks left her house, they always spent twenty more minutes on that porch before they actually said goodbye. She hadn't told him goodbye today. He'd shouted "Stay here!" before he dove off the boat.

She'd stayed; she was still here. Where was Brooks?

She remembered the anchor she should have thought to drop. It only took pressing a button. She was such an idiot.

Dad put the car in park and waded around to open the passenger-side door. He helped her and the twins get out. The temperature was dropping. The air smelled singed, as if lightning had struck nearby. The streets were white-capped rivers. Eureka staggered out of the car, slipping on the pavement submerged under a foot of water.

Dad squeezed her shoulder as they walked up the stairs. He had Claire, asleep, in his arms. Eureka was holding William. "We're home now, Reka."

It was little comfort. She was horrified to be home without knowing where Brooks was. She watched the street, wanting to slip into its current and flow back to the bay, a one-girl floating search party.

"Rhoda's been on the phone with Aileen," Dad said. "Let's see what they know."

Rhoda swung the porch door open wide. She leapt for the twins, holding them so tightly her fists turned white. She wept softly, and Eureka couldn't believe how simple it looked when Rhoda cried, like a character in a movie, relatable, almost pretty.

She looked past Rhoda and was stunned to see several

silhouettes moving through the foyer. She hadn't noticed the cars parked on the street outside her house until now. There was a flutter of limbs down the porch stairs, and then Cat threw her arms around Eureka's neck. Julien stood behind Cat. He looked supportive, his hand on her back. Cat's parents were there, too, inching closer with Cat's little brother, Barney. Bill stood on the porch with two cops Eureka didn't recognize. He seemed to have forgotten Cat's advances; he was watching Eureka instead.

She felt as stiff as a corpse as Cat held her elbows. Her friend seemed aggressively worried, eyes roaming Eureka's face. Everyone was looking at Eureka with expressions similar to the ones people wore after she'd swallowed the pills.

Rhoda cleared her throat. She hoisted a twin in each arm. "I'm so glad you're all right, Eureka. *Are* you all right?"

"No." Eureka needed to lie down. She pressed past Rhoda, felt Cat's arm link with hers, felt Julien's presence on her other side.

Cat led her to the small bathroom off the foyer, flipped on the light, and closed the door. Wordlessly, she helped Eureka out of her clothes. Eureka drooped like a sodden rag doll as Cat peeled the drenched sweatshirt over her head. She tugged down Eureka's soaking-wet cutoffs, which felt like they'd been surgically attached. She helped Eureka out of her bra and underwear, pretending they weren't both thinking they hadn't seen each other completely naked since middle school. Cat glanced at Eureka's necklace, but she didn't say anything about the thunderstone. She folded Eureka's body into a plush white terry cloth robe she took from the hook near the door. With her fingers, Cat combed Eureka's hair and secured it with an elastic band from her wrist.

Eventually she opened the door and led Eureka to the couch. Cat's mom covered Eureka with a blanket and rubbed her shoulder.

Eureka turned her face into the pillow as voices flickered around her like candlelight.

"If there's anything she can tell us about when she last saw Noah Brooks . . ." The policeman's voice seemed to fade as someone led him out of the room.

Eventually she slept.

When she awoke on the couch, she didn't know how much time had passed. The storm was still brutal, the sky dark outside the wet windowpanes. She was cold but sweating. The twins were on their stomachs on the rug, watching a movie on the iPad, eating macaroni and cheese in their pajamas. The others must have gone home.

The TV was muted, showing a reporter huddled under an umbrella in the deluge. When the camera cut to a dry newscaster behind a desk, the white space next to his head filled with a block of text headed *Derecho*. The word was defined inside a red box: *A straight swath of driving rain and wild wind usually occurring in the Plains states during the summer months.* The newscaster shuffled papers on his desk, shook his head in disbelief as the broadcast cut to a commercial about a marina that sheltered boats during the winter.

On the coffee table in front of Eureka, a mug of lukewarm tea sat next to a stack of three business cards left by the police. She closed her eyes and tugged the blanket higher around her neck. Sooner or later, she would have to talk to them. But if Brooks stayed missing, it seemed impossible Eureka would ever speak again. Just the thought caused her chest to cave in.

Why hadn't she let down the anchor? She'd heard the rule from Brooks's family her whole life: the last person to leave the boat was always supposed to drop the anchor. She hadn't done it. If Brooks had tried to board the boat again, it would have been an arduous task with those waves and those winds. She had the sudden sick urge to say aloud that Brooks was dead because of her.

She thought of Ander holding the chain of the anchor underwater in her dream and she didn't know what it meant.

The phone rang. Rhoda answered it in the kitchen. She spoke in low tones for a few minutes, then carried the cordless to Eureka on the couch. "It's Aileen."

Eureka shook her head, but Rhoda pressed the phone into her hand. She tilted her head to tuck it under her ear.

"Eureka? What happened? Is he . . . is he . . . ?"

Brooks's mother didn't finish, and Eureka couldn't say a word. She opened her mouth. She wanted to make Aileen feel better, but all that came out was a moan. Rhoda retrieved the phone with a sigh and walked away.

"I'm sorry, Aileen," she said. "She's been in shock since she got home."

Eureka held her pendants clasped inside her palm. She opened her fingers and eyed the stone and the locket. The thunderstone had not gotten wet, just as Ander had promised. What did it mean?

What did any of it mean? She'd lost Diana's book and any answers it could have offered. When Madame Blavatsky died, Eureka had also lost the last person whose advice felt reasonable and true. She needed to talk to Ander. She needed to know everything he knew.

She had no way of reaching him.

A glance at the TV sent Eureka groping for the remote. She pressed the button to unmute the sound just in time to see the camera pan the soggy courtyard in the center of her high school. She sat up straight on the couch. The twins looked up from their movie. Rhoda poked her head into the den.

"We're live at Evangeline Catholic High School in South Lafayette, where a missing local teenager has inspired a very special reaction," a female newscaster said.

A plastic tarp had been pitched like a tent below the giant pecan tree where Eureka and Cat ate lunch, where she'd made up with Brooks the week before. Now the camera panned a group of students in raincoats standing around a balloon- and flower-strewn vigil.

And there it was: the white poster board with a blown-up photo of Brooks's face—the picture Eureka had taken on the boat in May, the image on her phone whenever he called. Now he was calling from the center of a glowing ring of candles. It was all her fault.

She saw Theresa Leigh and Mary Monteau from the cross-country team, Luke from Earth Science, Laura Trejean, who'd thrown the Fall Sprawl. Half the school was there. How had they put together a vigil so quickly?

The reporter pushed a microphone into the face of a girl with long, rain-lashed black hair. A tattoo of an angel wing was visible just above the low V-neck of her shirt.

"He was the love of my life." Maya Cayce sniffed, looking straight into the camera. Her eyes welled up with tiny tears that flowed cleanly down either side of her nose. She dabbed her eyes with the corner of a black lace handkerchief.

Eureka squeezed her disgust into the couch cushion. She watched Maya Cayce perform. The beautiful girl clutched a hand to her breast and said passionately, "My heart's been broken into a million little pieces. I'll never forget him. Never."

"Shut up!" Eureka cried. She wanted to hurl the mug of tea at the television, at Maya Cayce's face, but she was too shattered even to move.

Then Dad was lifting her from the couch. "Let's get you to bed."

She wanted to writhe against his grip but lacked the strength. She let him carry her upstairs. She heard the news return to the weather. The governor had declared a state of emergency in Louisiana. Two small levees had already crevassed, unleashing the bayou onto the alluvial plain. According to the news, similar things were happening in Mississippi and Alabama as the storm spread across the Gulf.

At the top of the stairs, Dad carried her down the hallway to her bedroom, which looked like it belonged to someone else—the white four-poster bed, the desk made for a child, the rocking chair where her father used to read her stories back when she believed in happy endings.

"The police had lots of questions," he said as he laid Eureka on her bed.

She rolled onto her side so that her back was to him. She didn't have a response.

"Is there anything you can tell me that would help them with their search?"

"We went out in the sloop past Marsh Island. The weather got bad and—"

"Brooks fell over?"

Eureka curled into a ball. She couldn't tell Dad that Brooks had not fallen but jumped over, that he'd jumped to rescue the twins.

"How did you get the boat ashore yourself?" he asked.

"We swam," she whispered.

"You *swam*?"

"I don't remember what happened," she lied, wondering

whether Dad thought it sounded familiar. She'd said the same thing after Diana died, only then it had been true.

He stroked the back of her head. "Can you sleep?"

"No."

"What can I do?"

"I don't know."

He stood there for several minutes, through three bolts of lightning and a long shattering of thunder. She heard him scratch his jaw, the way he did during arguments with Rhoda. She heard the sound of his feet against the carpet, then his hand turning the doorknob.

"Dad?" She looked over her shoulder.

He hovered in the doorway.

"Is it a hurricane?"

"They haven't called it that yet. But it looks clear as day to me. Call if you need anything. Get some rest." He closed the door.

Lightning split the sky outside and a blast of wind loosened the lock on the shutters. They creaked aside. The pane was already raised. Eureka leapt up to shut it.

But she didn't leap fast enough. A shadow fell across her body. The dark shape of a man moved across the bough of the oak tree by her window. A black boot stepped into her room.

27

THE VISITOR

Eureka did not scream for help.

As the man climbed through her window, she felt as ready for death as she had when she'd swallowed the bottle of pills. She'd lost Brooks. Her mother was gone. Madame Blavatsky had been murdered. Eureka was the hapless thread connecting all of them.

When the black boot came through her window, she waited to see the rest of the person who might finally put her and those around her out of the misery she produced.

The black boots were connected to black jeans, which were connected to a black leather jacket, which was connected to a face she recognized.

Rain spat through the window, but Ander had stayed dry.

He looked paler than ever, as if the storm had washed the pigment from his skin. He seemed to glow as he stood against the window, towering over her. His measuring eyes made her bedroom smaller.

He closed the window, slid the bolt into place, and closed the shutters as if he lived there. He took off his jacket and draped it over her rocking chair. The definition of his chest was clear through his T-shirt. She wanted to touch him.

"You're not wet," she said.

Ander combed his fingers through his hair. "I tried to call you." His tone sounded like arms reaching out.

"I lost my phone."

"I know." He nodded and she understood that somehow he really *did* know what had happened today. He took a long stride toward Eureka, so quickly she couldn't see what was coming—and then she was in his arms. Her breath stuck in her throat. A hug was the last thing she'd expected. Even more surprising: it felt wonderful.

Ander's hold on her had the kind of depth she'd felt with only a few people before. Diana, Dad, Brooks, Cat—Eureka could count them. It was a depth that suggested profound affection, a depth that bordered on love. She expected to want to pull away, but she leaned closer.

His open hands came to rest against her back. His shoulders spanned hers like a protective shield, which made her think of the thunderstone. He tilted his head to cradle hers against his chest. Through his T-shirt, she could hear his heart throbbing. She loved the sound it made.

She closed her eyes and knew that Ander's eyes were closed, too. Their closed eyes cast a heavy silence on the room. Eureka suddenly felt she was in the safest place on earth and she knew she had been wrong about him.

She remembered what Cat always said about it feeling "easy" with some guys. Eureka had never understood that—her time with most boys had been halting, nervous, embarrassing—until now. Holding on to Ander was so easy that not holding on to him felt unthinkable.

The only thing awkward was her arms, pinned to her sides by his embrace. During their next inhalation, she drew them up and threaded them around Ander's waist with a grace and a naturalness that surprised her. *There.*

He drew her in tighter, making every hug Eureka had ever witnessed in the hallways at Evangeline, every hug between Dad and Rhoda, seem a sad imitation.

"I'm so relieved you're alive," he said.

His earnestness made Eureka shudder. She remembered the first time he'd touched her, his fingertip dotting the damp corner of her eye. *No more tears,* he'd said.

Ander lifted her chin so that she was looking up at him. He gazed at the corners of her eyes, as if surprised to find them dry. He looked unbearably conflicted. "I brought you something."

370

He reached behind him, pulling out a plastic-sheathed object that had been tucked inside the waist of his jeans. Eureka recognized it instantly. Her fingers latched onto *The Book of Love* in its sturdy waterproof pouch.

"How did you get this?"

"A little bird showed me where to find it," he said with a complete lack of humor.

"Polaris," Eureka said. "How did you—"

"It isn't easy to explain."

"I know."

"Your translator's insight was impressive. She had the sense to bury your book and her notebook under a willow tree by the bayou the night before she was—" Ander paused, his eyes downcast. "I'm sorry."

"You know what happened to her?" Eureka whispered.

"Enough to be vengeful," he muttered. His tone convinced Eureka that the gray people on the road had been the killers. "Take the books. Clearly, she wanted them returned to you."

Eureka put both books on her bed. Her fingers ran over the worn green cover of *The Book of Love,* traced the three ridges on its spine. She touched the peculiar raised circle on the cover and wished she knew what it had looked like when the book was newly bound.

She felt the rough-cut pages of Madame Blavatsky's old black journal. She didn't want to violate the dead woman's privacy. But any notes inside this book held all that Eureka might know of the legacy Diana had left her. Eureka needed answers.

Diana, Brooks, and Madame Blavatsky had each found *The Book of Love* fascinating. Eureka didn't feel worthy of having it all to herself. She was afraid to open it, afraid it would make her more alone.

She thought of Diana, who believed Eureka to be tough and smart enough to find her way out of any foxhole. She thought of Madame Blavatsky, who hadn't blinked when asking if she could inscribe Eureka's name as the rightful owner of the text. She thought of Brooks, who said that her mother was one of the smartest people who'd ever lived—and if Diana thought there was something special about this book, Eureka owed it to her to understand its complexities.

She opened Blavatsky's translation journal. She leafed through it slowly. Just before a block of blank pages was a single sheet scribbled in violet ink, titled *The Book of Love, Fourth Salvo.*

She glanced at Ander. "Have you read this?"

He tossed his head. "I know what it says. I grew up with a version of the story."

Eureka read aloud:

"Sometime, somewhere, in the future's remote nook, a girl will come into being and meet the conditions to commence the Rising Time. Only then will Atlantis return."

Atlantis. So Blavatsky had been right. But did it mean the story was real?

"The girl must be born on a day that does not exist, as we Atlanteans ceased to exist when the maiden tear was shed."

"How can a day not exist?" Eureka asked. "What does that mean?"

Ander watched her closely but didn't say anything. He waited. Eureka considered her own birthday. It was February 29. Leap day. Three years out of four, it didn't exist.

"Go on," Ander coaxed, smoothing the page of Blavatsky's translation.

"She must be a childless mother and a motherless child."

Immediately, Eureka thought of Diana's body in the ocean. "Motherless child" defined the shadowy identity she'd inhabited for months. She thought of the twins, for whom she'd risked everything that afternoon. She'd do it again tomorrow. Was she a childless mother, too?

"Finally, her emotions must be tempered, must brew like a storm too high in the atmosphere to be felt on earth. She must never cry until the moment her grief surpasses what any mortal being can bear. Then she will weep—and open up the fissure to our world."

Eureka looked up at the painting of Saint Catherine of Siena hanging on her wall. She studied the saint's single, picturesque tear. Was there a relationship between that tear and the fires from which the saint offered protection? Was there a relationship between Eureka's tears and this book?

She thought of how lovely Maya Cayce looked when she cried, how naturally Rhoda wept at the sight of her kids.

Eureka envied these direct displays of emotion. They felt antithetical to everything she was. The night Diana slapped her was the only time she remembered sobbing.

Never, ever cry again.

And the most recent tear she'd cried? Ander's fingerprints had absorbed it.

There, now. No more tears.

Outside, the storm raged furiously. Inside, Eureka tempered her emotions, just as she'd been doing for years. Because she'd been told to. Because it was all she knew how to do.

Ander pointed at the page where, after a few lines of blank space, the violet ink resumed. "There's one last part."

Eureka took a deep breath and read the final words of Madame Blavatsky's translation:

"One night into our voyage, a violent storm split our ship. I washed up upon a nearby shore. I never saw my prince again. I do not know if he survived. The witches' prophecy is the only lasting remnant of our love."

Diana knew this story contained in *The Book of Love*, but had she believed it? Eureka closed her eyes and knew that, yes, Diana had. She'd believed it so fervently she'd never breathed a word of it to her daughter. She'd meant to save it for a moment when Eureka might be able to believe it for herself. The moment had to be now.

Could Eureka go there? Allow herself to consider that *The*

Book of Love had something to do with her? She expected to want to dismiss it as a fairy tale, something lovely based on what might have once been based on something true, but was now mere make-believe. . . .

But her inheritance, the thunderstone, the accidents and deaths and ghostly people, the way this storm's rage felt too in tune with the storm inside of her . . .

It wasn't a hurricane. It was Eureka.

Ander stood quietly at the edge of her bed, giving her time and space. His eyes revealed a desperation to hold her again. She wanted to hold him, too.

"Ander?"

"Eureka."

She pointed to the last page of the translation, which laid out the conditions of the prophecy. "Is this me?"

His hesitation caused Eureka's eyes to sting. He noticed and inhaled sharply, as if in pain. "You can't cry, Eureka. Not now."

He moved toward her swiftly and lowered his lips to her eyes. Her eyelids fluttered closed. He kissed her right eyelid, then her left. Then there was a quiet moment when Eureka could not move, could not open her eyes because it might interrupt the feeling that Ander was closer to her than anyone had ever been before.

When he pressed his lips to hers, she was not surprised. It happened the way the sun rose, the way a flower blossomed, the way rain fell from the sky, the way the dead stopped breathing. Naturally. Inevitably. His lips were firm, slightly salty. They made her body flush with heat.

Their noses touched and Eureka opened her mouth to take in more of his kiss. She touched his hair, her fingers tracing the path his fingers followed when he was nervous. He didn't seem nervous now. He was kissing her as if he'd been wanting to for a very long time, as if he'd been born to do it. His hands caressed her back, pressed her against his chest. His mouth folded hungrily on hers. The heat of his tongue made her dizzy.

Then she remembered Brooks was gone. This was the most insensitive moment to cash in on a crush. Only it didn't feel like a crush. It felt life-altering and unstoppable.

She was out of breath but didn't want to interrupt the kiss. Then she felt Ander's breath inside her mouth. Her eyes shot open. She pulled away.

First kisses were about discovery, transformation, wonder.

Then why did his breath in her mouth feel familiar?

Somehow, Eureka remembered. After Diana's accident, after the car was swept to the bottom of the Gulf and Eureka washed ashore, miraculous, alive—never before had she evoked this memory—someone had given her mouth-to-mouth resuscitation.

She closed her eyes and saw the halo of blond hair above her, blocking out the moon, and felt the life-giving air entering her lungs, the arms that carried her there.

Ander.

"I thought it was a dream," she whispered.

Ander sighed heavily, as if he knew exactly what she meant. He took her hand. "It happened."

"You pulled me out of the car. You swam me ashore. You saved me."

"Yes."

"But why? How would you even know I was there?"

"I was in the right place at the right time."

It seemed as impossible as all the other things Eureka knew were real. She stumbled to her bed and sat down. Her mind was spinning.

"You saved me and let her die."

Ander closed his eyes as if in pain. "If I could have saved you both, I would have. I had to choose. I chose you. If you can't forgive me, I understand." His hands were shaking when he ran them through his hair. "Eureka, I am so sorry."

He had said those same words, just like that, on the first day they met. The sincerity of his apology had surprised her then. It had seemed inappropriate to apologize so passion- ately for something so slight, but now Eureka understood. She felt Ander's grief about Diana. Regret filled the space around him like his own thunderstone shield.

Eureka had long resented the fact that she'd lived and Diana hadn't. Now here was the person responsible. Ander had made that decision. She could hate him for it. She could blame him for her crazy sorrow and attempted suicide.

377

He seemed to know it. He hovered over her, waiting to see which direction she'd take. She buried her face in her hands.

"I miss her so much."

He fell to his knees before her, his elbows on her thighs. "I know."

Eureka's hand closed around her necklace. She opened her fist to expose the thunderstone, the lapis lazuli locket.

"You were right," she said. "About the thunderstone and water. It does more than not get wet. It's the only reason the twins and I are alive. It saved us, and I would never have known how to use it if you hadn't told me."

"The thunderstone is very powerful. It belongs to you, Eureka. Always remember that. You must protect it."

"I wish Brooks . . . ," she started to say, but her chest felt like it was being crushed. "I was so afraid. I couldn't think. I should have saved him, too."

"That would have been impossible." Ander's voice was cold.

"You mean the way you saving both me and Diana would have been impossible?" she asked.

"No, I don't mean that. Whatever happened to Brooks— you wouldn't have been able to find him in that storm."

"I don't understand."

Ander looked away. He didn't elaborate.

"You know where Brooks is?" Eureka asked.

"No," he said quickly. "It's complicated. I've been trying to tell you, he's not who you think he is anymore—"

"Please, don't say anything bad about him." Eureka waved Ander off. "We don't even know if he's alive."

Ander nodded, but he seemed tense.

"After Diana died," Eureka said, "it never occurred to me that I could lose anyone else."

"Why do you call your mother Diana?" Ander seemed eager to steer the subject away from Brooks.

No one except Rhoda had asked Eureka that question, so she'd never had to voice a real answer. "When she was alive I called her Mom, like most kids do. But death turned Diana into someone else. She isn't my mother anymore. She's more than that"—Eureka clutched the locket—"and less."

Slowly Ander's hand cupped her hand cupping the two pendants. He squinted at the locket. His thumb rolled over the clasp.

"It doesn't open," she said. Her fingers curled around his to still them. "Diana said it was rusted shut when she bought it. She liked the design so much she didn't care. She wore it every day."

Ander rose on his knees. His fingers crept around the back of Eureka's neck. She leaned into his addictive touch. "May I?"

When she nodded, he unclasped the chain, kissed her softly on the lips, then sat next to her on the bed. He touched the gold-flecked blue of the stone. He flipped the locket over and touched the raised intersecting rings on the underside. He examined the locket's profile on either side, fingered the hinges, then the clasp.

"The oxidation is cosmetic. That shouldn't prevent the locket from opening."

"Then why doesn't it open?" Eureka asked.

"Because Diana had it sealed." Ander slid the locket off the chain, handed the chain and thunderstone back to Eureka. He held the locket with both hands. "I think I can unseal it. In fact, I know I can."

28

SELENE'S TEARLINE

A thunderclap shook the foundation of the house. Eureka scooted closer to Ander. "Why would my mother have sealed her own locket?"

"Maybe it contains something she didn't want anyone to see." He slipped an arm around her waist. It felt like an instinctive motion, but once his arm was there, Ander seemed nervous about it. The tops of his ears were flushed. He kept looking at his hand as it rested on her hip.

Eureka laid her hand over his to reassure him that she wanted it there, that she savored each new lesson on his body: the smoothness of his fingers, the heat inside his palm, the way his skin smelled like summer up close.

"I used to tell Diana everything," Eureka said. "When she died, I learned how many secrets she kept from me."

"Your mother knew the power of these heirlooms. She would have been afraid of having them fall into the wrong hands."

"They fell into my hands, and I don't understand."

"Her faith in you survives her," Ander said. "She left you these because she trusted you to discover their significance. She was right about the book—you got to the heart of its story. She was right about the thunderstone—today you learned how powerful it can be."

"And the locket?" Eureka touched it.

"Let's see if she was right about that, too." Ander stood in the center of the room, holding the locket in his right hand. He turned it over. He touched its back with the tip of his left ring finger. He closed his eyes, pursed his lips as if he were going to whistle, and let out a long exhale.

Slowly his finger moved over its surface, tracking the six interlocking circles Eureka's fingers had traced many times. Only, when Ander did it, he made music, as if sweeping the rim of a crystal goblet.

The sound made Eureka leap to her feet. She clutched her left ear, which was not used to hearing but somehow heard these strange notes as clearly as she'd heard Polaris's song. The locket's rings glowed briefly—gold, then blue—responding to Ander's touch.

As his finger moved in figure eights, mazelike swirls, and roseate patterns around the circles, the sound it produced shifted and spun. A soft hum deepened into a rich and haunting chord, then rose into what sounded almost like a harmony of woodwinds.

He held that note for several seconds, his finger tranquil in the center of the locket's back. The sound was reedy and unfamiliar, like a flute from a far-away, future realm. Ander's finger pulsed three times, creating church-organ-like chords that flowed in waves over Eureka. He opened his eyes, lifted his finger, and the extraordinary concert was over. He gasped for air.

The locket creaked open without another touch.

"How did you do that?" Eureka approached him in a trance. She leaned over his hands to examine the locket's interior. The right side was inlaid with a tiny mirror. Its reflection was clean and clear and slightly magnified. Eureka saw one of Ander's eyes in the mirror and was startled by its turquoise clarity. The left side held what looked like a piece of yellowed paper wedged into the frame near the hinge.

She used her pinky to pry it free. She lifted a corner, feeling how thin the paper was, sliding it carefully out. Beneath the paper she found a small photograph. It had been trimmed to fit the triangular locket, but the image was clear:

Diana, holding baby Eureka in her arms. She couldn't have been more than six months old. Eureka had never seen this picture before, but she recognized her mother's Coke-bottle glasses, the layered shag of her hair, the blue flannel shirt she'd worn in the nineties.

Baby Eureka gazed straight at the camera, wearing a white pinafore Sugar must have sewn. Diana looked away from the camera, but you could see the bright green of her eyes. She looked sad—an expression Eureka didn't associate with her mother. Why had she never shown this picture to Eureka? Why had she gone all these years wearing the locket around her neck, saying it didn't open?

Eureka felt angry with her mother for leaving so many mysteries behind. Everything in Eureka's life had been unstable since Diana died. She wanted clarity, constancy, someone she could trust.

Ander bent down and picked up the little yellowed slip of paper, which Eureka must have dropped. It looked like expensive stationery from centuries ago. He turned it over. A single word was scrawled across it in black ink.

Marais.

"Does this mean anything to you?" he asked.

"That's my mother's handwriting." She took the paper and stared at every loop in the word, the sharply dotted *i*.

"It's Cajun—French—for 'marsh,' but I don't know why she would write it here."

Ander stared at the window, where shutters blocked the view of the rain but not its steady sound. "There must be someone who can help."

"Madame Blavatsky would have been able to help." Eureka stared grimly at the locket, at the cryptic piece of paper.

"That's exactly why they killed her." The words slipped from Ander's mouth before he realized it.

"You know who did it." Eureka's eyes widened. "It was them, those people you ran off the road, wasn't it?"

Ander slipped the locket from her hand and placed it on her bed. He tilted her chin up with his thumb. "I wish I could tell you what you want to hear."

"She didn't deserve to die."

"I know."

Eureka rested her hands on his chest. Her fingers curled around the cloth of his T-shirt, wanting to squeeze her pain into it.

"Why aren't you wet?" she asked. "Do you have a thunderstone?"

"No." He laughed softly. "I suppose I have another kind of shield. Though it's far less impressive than yours."

Eureka ran her hands over his dry shoulders, slid her arms around his dry waist. "I'm impressed," she said quietly as her hands slipped under the back of his shirt to touch his smooth, dry skin. He kissed her again, emboldening her. She felt nervous but alive, bewildered and buzzing with new energy she didn't want to question.

She loved the feel of his arms around her waist. She pulled closer, lifting her head to kiss him again, but then she stopped.

Her fingers froze over what felt like a gash on Ander's back. She pulled away and moved around his side, lifting up the back of his shirt. Four red slashes marked the skin just below his rib cage.

"You're cut," she said. It was the same wound she'd seen on Brooks the day of the freak Vermilion Bay wave. Ander only had one set of gashes, where Brooks's back had borne two.

"They aren't cuts."

Eureka looked up at him. "Tell me what they are."

Ander sat down on the edge of her bed. She sat next to him, feeling warmth emanate from his skin. She wanted to see the marks again, wanted to run her hand over them to see if they were as deep as they looked. He put his hand on her leg. It made her insides buzz. He looked like he was about to say something difficult, something that might be impossible to believe.

"Gills."

Eureka blinked. "Gills. Like a fish?"

"For breathing underwater, yes. Brooks has them now as well."

Eureka moved his hand from her leg. "What do you mean, Brooks *has gills now as well*? What do you mean, *you* have gills?"

The room was suddenly tiny and too hot. Was Ander messing with her?

He reached behind him and held up the green leather-bound book. "Do you believe what you read in this?"

She didn't know him well enough to gauge his tone of voice. It sounded desperate—but what else? Did it also betray anger? Fear?

"I don't know," she said. "It seems too . . ."

"Much like fantasy?"

"Yes. And yet . . . I want to know the rest. Only part of it's been translated and there are all these strange coincidences, things that feel like they have something to do with me."

"They do," Ander said.

"How do you know?"

"Did I lie to you about the thunderstone?"

She shook her head.

"Then give me the chance you're giving this book." Ander pressed a hand to his heart. "The difference between you and me is that from the moment I was born I have been raised with the story you found on these pages."

"How? Who are your parents? Are you in a cult?"

"I don't exactly have parents. I was raised by my aunts and my uncles. I am a Seedbearer."

"A what?"

He sighed. "My people come from the lost continent of Atlantis."

"You're *from* Atlantis?" she asked. "Madame Blavatsky said . . . But I didn't believe . . ."

"I know. How could you have believed? But it is true. My line was among the few who escaped before the island sank. Since then, our mission has been to carry forward the seed of Atlantis's knowledge, so that its lessons will never be forgotten, its atrocities never be repeated. For thousands of years, this story has stayed among the Seedbearers."

"But it's also in this book."

Ander nodded. "We knew your mother possessed some knowledge of Atlantis, but my family still has no idea how much. The person who murdered your translator was my uncle. The people you encountered at the police station, and on the road that night—those people raised me. Those are the faces I saw at the dinner table every night."

"Where exactly is that dinner table?" For weeks, Eureka had been wondering where Ander lived.

"No place interesting." He paused. "I haven't been home in weeks. My family and I had a disagreement."

"You said they wanted to hurt me."

"They *do,*" Ander said miserably.

"Why?"

"Because you are also a descendant of Atlantis. And the women in your lineage carry something very unusual. It is called the *selena-klamata-desmos.* That means, more or less, Selene's Tearline."

"Selene," Eureka said. "The woman engaged to the king. She ran off with his brother."

Ander nodded. "She is your matriarch, many generations back. Just as Leander, her lover, is my patriarch."

"They were shipwrecked, separated at sea," Eureka said, remembering. "They never found each other again."

Ander nodded. "It is said that they searched for each other until their dying day, and even, some say, after death."

Eureka looked deeply into Ander's eyes and the story resonated with her in a new way. She found it unbearably sad—and achingly romantic. Could these thwarted lovers explain the connection Eureka had felt to the boy sitting next to her—the connection she'd felt from the moment she first saw him?

"One of Selene's descendants carries the power to raise Atlantis again," Ander continued. "This is what you just read in the book. This is the Tearline. The Seedbearers' reason for existing hinges on the belief that raising Atlantis would be a catastrophe—an apocalypse. The legends of Atlantis are ugly and violent, filled with corruption, slavery, and worse."

"I didn't read anything about that in here." Eureka pointed at *The Book of Love.*

"Of course not," Ander said darkly. "You've been reading a love story. Unfortunately, there was more to that world than Selene's version. The Seedbearers' goal is to prevent the return of Atlantis from ever happening by—"

"Killing the girl with the Tearline," Eureka said numbly. "And they think I carry it."

"They're fairly certain."

"Certain that if I were to weep, like it says in the book, that—"

Ander nodded. "The world would flood and Atlantis would return to power."

"How often does one of these Tearline girls come along?" Eureka asked, thinking that if Ander was telling the truth, many of her family members might have been hunted or killed by the Seedbearers.

"It hasn't happened in nearly a century, since the thirties," Ander said, "but that was a very bad situation. When a girl begins to show signs of the Tearline, she becomes a kind of vortex. She piques the interest of more than just the Seedbearers."

"Who else?" Eureka wasn't sure she wanted to know.

Ander swallowed. "The Atlanteans themselves."

Now she was even more confused.

"They are evil," Ander continued. "The last possessor of the Tearline lived in Germany. Her name was Byblis—"

"I've heard of Byblis. She was one of the owners of the book. She gave it to someone named Niobe, who gave it to Diana."

"Byblis was your mother's great-aunt."

"You know more about my family than I do."

Ander looked uncomfortable. "I have had to study."

"So the Seedbearers killed my great-aunt when she showed signs of the Tearline?"

"Yes, but not before a great deal of damage was done. While the Seedbearers try to eliminate a Tearline, the Atlanteans try to activate it. They do this by occupying the body of someone dear to the Tearline carrier, someone who can make her cry. By the time the Seedbearers succeeded in murdering Byblis, the Atlantean who had occupied the body of her closest friend was already invested in that world. He stayed in the body even after Byblis's death."

Eureka felt an urge to laugh. What Ander was saying was insane. She hadn't heard anything this crazy during her weeks in the psychiatric ward.

And yet it made Eureka think of something she'd read recently in one of Madame Blavatsky's emails. She picked up the translated pages and thumbed through them. "Look at this part, right here. It describes a sorcerer who could send his mind across the ocean and occupy the body of a man in a place called Minoa."

"Exactly," Ander said. "It's the same magic. We don't know how Atlas learned to channel this sorcerer's power—he's not a sorcerer himself—but somehow he has managed it."

"Where is he? Where are the Atlanteans?"

"In Atlantis."

"And where is that?"

"It's been underwater for thousands of years. We can't access them, and they can't access us. From the moment Atlantis sank, mind channeling has been their only portal to our world." Ander looked away. "Though Atlas is hoping to change that."

"So the Atlanteans' minds are powerful and evil"—Eureka hoped no one was listening at her door—"but the Seedbearers don't seem much better, killing innocent girls."

Ander didn't respond. His silence answered her next question.

"Except Seedbearers don't think we're innocent," she realized. "You were raised to believe that I might do something terrible"—she massaged her ear and couldn't believe what she was about to say—"like flood the world with my tears?"

"I know it's hard to swallow," Ander said. "You were right to call the Seedbearers a cult. My family is skilled at making murder look like an accident. Byblis drowned in a 'flood.' Your mother's car hit by a 'rogue wave.' All in the name of saving the world from evil."

"Wait." Eureka flinched. "Did my mother have the Tearline?"

"No, but she knew you did. Her entire life's work centered on preparing you for your destiny. She must have told you something about it?"

Eureka's chest tightened. "Once she told me never to cry."

"It's true we don't know what would happen if you really cried. My family doesn't want to take the chance of finding out. The wave on the bridge that day was meant for you, not

Diana." He looked down, resting his chin against his chest. "I was supposed to ensure that you drowned. But I couldn't. My family will never forgive me."

"Why did you save me?" she whispered.

"You don't know? I thought it was so obvious."

Eureka lifted her shoulders, shook her head.

"Eureka, from the moment I was conscious, I have been trained to know everything about you—your weaknesses, your strengths, your fears, and your desires—all so that I could destroy you. One Seedbearer power is a kind of natural camouflage. We live among mortals, but they don't really see us. We blend, we blur. No one remembers our faces unless we want them to. Can you imagine being invisible to everyone but your family?"

Eureka shook her head, though she'd often wished for invisibility.

"That's why you never knew about me. I have watched you since you were born, but you never saw me until I wanted you to—the day I hit your car. I've been with you every day for the past seventeen years. I watched you learn to walk, to tie your shoes, to play the guitar"—he swallowed—"to kiss. I watched you get your ears pierced, fail your driver's test, and win your first cross-country race." Ander reached for her, held her close to him. "By the time Diana died, I was so desperately in love with you, I couldn't handle it anymore. I drove into your car at that stop sign. I needed you to see me, finally. Every moment of your life, I have fallen more deeply in love with you."

Eureka flushed. What could she say to that? "I . . . well . . . uh—"

"You don't have to respond," Ander said. "Just know that even as I have begun to distrust everything I was raised to believe, there is one thing I am certain of." He fit his hand in hers. "My devotion to you. It will never fade, Eureka. I swear it."

Eureka was stunned. Her suspicious mind had been wrong about Ander—but her body's instincts had been right. Her fingers reached around his neck, pulled his lips to hers. She tried to transmit the words she couldn't find with a kiss.

"God." Ander's lip brushed hers. "It felt so good to say that aloud. For my whole life, I have felt alone."

"You're with me now." She wanted to reassure him, but worry crept into her mind. "Are you still a Seedbearer? You turned against your family to protect me, but—"

"You could say I ran away," he said. "But my family isn't going to give up. They want you dead very badly. If you cry and Atlantis returns, they think it will mean the death of millions, the enslavement of humanity. The end of the world as we know it. They think it will be the demise of this world and the birth of a terrible new one. They think killing you is the only way to stop it."

"And what do you think?"

"It might be true that you could raise Atlantis," he said slowly, "but no one knows what that would mean."

"The ending isn't written yet," Eureka said. *And every-thing might change with the last word.* She reached for the book to show Ander something that had been bothering her since the reading of Diana's will. "What if the end has been written? These pages are missing from the text. Diana wouldn't have torn them out. She wouldn't even dog-ear a library book."

Ander scratched his jaw. "There is one person who might help us. I've never met him. He was born a Seedbearer, but he defected from the family after Byblis was murdered. My family says he never got over her death." He paused. "They say he was in love with her. His name is Solon."

"How do we find him?"

"None of the Seedbearers have spoken to him in years. The last I heard, he was in Turkey." He spun to face Eureka, eyes suddenly bright. "We could go there and track him down."

Eureka laughed. "I doubt my Dad is going to let me up and go to Turkey."

"They'll have to come with us," Ander said quickly. "All of your loved ones will. Otherwise my family would use your family to drag you back."

Eureka stiffened. "You mean—"

He nodded. "They can justify killing a few in order to save many."

"What about Brooks? If he comes back—"

"He isn't coming back," Ander said, "not in any way

395

you'd want to see him. We need to focus on getting you and your family to safety as soon as possible. Somewhere far from here."

Eureka shook her head. "Dad and Rhoda would commit me again before they'd agree to leave town."

"This isn't a choice, Eureka. It's the only way you'll survive. And you have to survive." Then he kissed her hard, holding her face in his hands, pressing his lips deeply into hers until she was breathless.

"Why do I have to survive?" Her eyes ached with exhaustion she could no longer deny. Ander noticed. He guided her to the bed, pulled back the covers, then laid her down and draped the blankets over her.

He knelt at her side and murmured into her good ear: "You have to survive because I won't live in a world without you."

29

EVACUATION

When Eureka awoke the next morning, dim, silvery light shone through her window. Rain drummed against the trees. She yearned to let the storm lull her back to sleep, but her left ear was ringing, reminding her of the strange melody Ander had conjured when he unsealed Diana's locket. *The Book of Love* was cradled in her arms, spelling out the prophecy of her tears. She knew she had to get up, to face the things she'd learned the night before, but an ache in her heart held her head against her pillow.

Brooks was gone. According to Ander, who seemed to have been right about so much else, Eureka's oldest friend wasn't coming back.

A weight on the other side of her bed surprised her. It was Ander.

"Have you been here all night?" she asked.

"I'm not leaving you."

She crawled across the bed toward him. She was still in her bathrobe. He wore his clothes from the night before. They couldn't help smiling as their faces drew near each other. He kissed her forehead, then her lips.

She wanted to pull him down onto the bed, to hold and kiss him horizontally, to feel the weight of his body on hers, but after a few soft pecks, Ander rose and stood at the window. His arms were crossed behind his back. Eureka could picture the way he would have stood there all night, scanning the street for a Seedbearer silhouette.

What would he have done if one of them had come to her house? She remembered the silver case he'd pulled from his pocket that night. It had terrified his family.

"Ander—" She meant to ask what had been inside that box.

"It's time to go," he said.

Eureka groped for her phone to check the time. When she remembered it was lost, she imagined it ringing somewhere in the rain-swept Gulf, amid a silver school of fish, being answered by a mermaid. She rummaged through her nightstand for her plastic polka-dot Swatch watch. "It's six in the morning. My family will still be asleep."

"Wake them up."

"And tell them what?"

"I'll tell everyone the plan as soon as we're together," Ander said, still facing the window. "It's better if there aren't too many questions. We'll need to move quickly."

"If I'm going to do this," Eureka said, "I need to know where we're going." She'd slid from the bed. Her hand rested on his sleeve. His bicep flexed against her touch.

He faced her and ran his fingers through her hair, drawing his nails softly along her scalp, the nape of her neck. She'd thought it was sexy when he ran his fingers through his own hair. This was even better.

"We are going to find Solon," he said. "The lost Seed-bearer."

"I thought you said he was in Turkey."

For a moment, Ander almost smiled, then his face went strangely blank. "Luckily I salvaged a boat yesterday. We sail as soon your family is ready."

Eureka watched him carefully. There was something in his gaze—satisfaction suppressed by . . . guilt. Her mouth felt dry as her mind made a dark connection. She didn't know how she knew.

"Ariel?" she whispered. Brooks's boat. "How did you do that?"

"Don't worry. It's done."

"I'm worried about Brooks, not his boat. Did you see him? Did you even look for him?"

Ander's face tensed. His eyes flicked to the side. After a

moment, they returned to Eureka's, released of their hostility. "There will come a time when you will know the entirety of Brooks's true fate. For everyone's sake, I hope that is a long way off. In the meantime, you must try to move on."

Her eyes clouded over; she barely saw him standing before her. In that moment, she wanted more than anything to hear Brooks call her Cuttlefish.

"Eureka?" Ander touched her cheek. "Eureka?"

"No," Eureka murmured. She was talking to herself. She stepped away from Ander. Her balance was off. She stumbled into her nightstand and back against the wall. She felt as cold and stiff as if she'd spent the night on an icecap in the middle of the Arctic Circle.

Eureka couldn't deny the change in Brooks the past few weeks, the shockingly cruel and disloyal behavior she didn't recognize. She tallied the number of conversations in which Brooks had probed for information about her emotions, her lack of crying. She thought of Ander's immense and inexplicable hostility toward him from their first encounter—then she thought about the story of Byblis and the man she'd once been close to, the man whose body became possessed by the Atlantean king.

Ander didn't want to say it, but the signs were all pointing toward yet another impossible reality.

"Atlas," she whispered. "The whole time, he wasn't Brooks. He was Atlas."

Ander frowned but said nothing.

"Brooks isn't dead."

"No." Ander sighed. "He isn't dead."

"He was possessed." Eureka could barely get the words out.

"I know you cared for him. I would not wish Brooks's fate on anyone. But it happened, and there's nothing we can do. Atlas is too powerful. What is done is done."

She hated the way Ander spoke in the past tense about Brooks. There had to be a way to save him. Now that she knew what had happened—that it had happened because of her—Eureka owed it to Brooks to get him back. She didn't know how, only that she had to try.

"If I could just find him . . ." Her voice faltered.

"No." Ander's sharpness stole Eureka's breath. He glared into her eyes, searching them for signs of tears. When he didn't find them, he seemed vastly relieved. He slipped the chain with the thunderstone and locket over Eureka's head. "You are in danger, Eureka. Your family is in danger. If you trust me, I can protect you. That's all we can afford to focus on right now. Do you understand?"

"Yes," she said, halfheartedly, because there had to be a way.

"Good," Ander said. "Now it's time to tell your family."

Eureka wore jeans, her running shoes, and a pale blue flannel shirt as she walked down the stairs holding Ander's hand. Her purple school bag was draped over her shoulder, *The Book of Love* and Madame Blavatsky's translation tucked inside. The den was dark. The clock on the cable box blinked 1:43. The storm must have made the power go out in the night.

As Eureka felt her way around the furniture, she heard the click of a door opening. Dad appeared in a sliver of lamplight in his bedroom doorway. His hair was wet, his shirt wrinkled and untucked. Eureka could smell his Irish Spring soap. He noticed the two dark forms in the shadows.

"Who's there?" He moved quickly to turn on the light. "Eureka?"

"Dad—"

He stared at Ander. "Who is this? What's he doing in our house?"

Ander's cheeks had more color than Eureka ever seen in them. He straightened his shoulders and ran his hands through his wavy hair twice. "Mr. Boudreaux, my name is Ander. I'm a . . . friend of Eureka's." He flashed her a small smile, as if, despite everything, he liked saying that.

She wanted to jump into his arms.

"Not at six in the morning you're not," Dad said. "Get out or I'm calling the police."

"Dad, wait." Eureka grabbed his arm the way she used to when she was little. "Don't call the police. Please come and sit down. There's something I have to tell you."

He looked at Eureka's hand on his arm, then at Ander, then back at Eureka.

"Please," she whispered.

"Fine. But first we're making coffee."

They moved to the kitchen, where Dad lit the gas burner and put on a kettle of water. He spooned black coffee into an old French press. Eureka and Ander sat at the table, arguing with their eyes over who should speak first.

Dad kept glancing at Ander. A disturbed expression fixed on his face. "You look familiar, kid."

Ander shifted. "We've never met."

While the water heated, Dad stepped closer to the table. He tilted his head, narrowed his eyes at Ander. His voice sounded distant when he said, "How did you say you knew this boy, Reka?"

"He's my friend."

"You go to school together?"

"We just . . . met." She gave Ander a nervous shrug.

"Your mother said—" Dad's hands began to shake. He set them firmly on the table to quiet them. "She said some-day . . ."

"What?"

"Nothing."

The kettle whistled, so Eureka stood to turn off the burner. She poured water into the French press and gathered three mugs from the cupboard. "I think you should sit down, Dad. What we're about to say might sound strange."

A soft knock at the front door made all three of them jump. Eureka and Ander shared a glance, then she pushed back her chair and moved toward the door. Ander was right behind her.

"Don't open the door," he warned.

"I know who it is." Eureka recognized the shape of the figure through the frosted glass. She yanked on the stuck doorknob, then unlocked the screen door.

Cat's eyebrows arched at the sight of Ander standing over Eureka's shoulder. "Would have gotten here earlier if I'd known there was going to be a sleepover."

Behind Cat, wild wind shook the huge mossy bough of an oak tree as if it were a twig. A rough blast of water splattered the porch.

Eureka motioned Cat inside and offered to help her out of her raincoat. "We're making coffee."

"I can't stay." Cat wiped her feet on the mat. "We're evacuating. My dad's packing the car right now. We're driving to stay with Mom's cousins in Hot Springs. Are you evacuating, too?"

Eureka looked at Ander. "We're not . . . We don't . . . Maybe."

"It's not mandatory yet," Cat explained, "but the TV said if the rain kept up, evacs might be required later on, and you know my parents—they always have to beat the traffic. Freaking storm came out of nowhere."

Eureka swallowed a lump in her throat. "I know."

"Anyway," Cat said, "I saw your light on and wanted to drop this off before we left." She held out the kind of wicker basket her mom was always packing for different fund-raisers and charity organizations. It was stuffed with rainbow confetti, the colors bleeding from the rain. "It's my soul-mending kit: magazines, my mom's meringues, and"—she lowered her voice and flashed a slender brown bottle at the bottom of the basket—"Maker's Mark."

Eureka took the basket, but what she really wanted to hold was Cat. She placed the soul-mending kit at their feet and wrapped her arms around her friend. "Thank you."

She couldn't bear to think how long it might be before she saw Cat again. Ander hadn't mentioned when they'd be coming back.

"Stay for a cup of coffee?"

Eureka fixed Cat's coffee the way she liked it, using most of Rhoda's bottle of Irish Cream Coffee-mate. She poured a mug for herself and one for Dad and sprinkled cinnamon on top of both. Then she realized she didn't know how Ander took his coffee, and it made her feel reckless, as if they'd run off and gotten engaged without knowing each other's last name. She still didn't know his last name.

"Black," he said before she had to ask.

For a moment, they sipped quietly and Eureka knew that soon she had to do it: shatter this peace. Say goodbye to her best friend. Convince Dad of absurd, fantastic truths. Evacuate. She would take this small sip of false normalcy before things fell further apart.

Dad hadn't said a word, hadn't even looked up to say hello to Cat. His face was ashen. He pushed back his chair and stood up. "Can I talk to you, Eureka?"

She followed him to the back of the kitchen. They stood in the doorway that elbowed off into the dining room, out of earshot of Ander and Cat. From the side of the stove hung the backyard landscapes the twins had painted in watercolor at their preschool. William's was realistic: four green oak trees, a weathered swing set, the bayou twisting in the background. Claire's was abstract, wholly purple, a glorious rendering of what their yard looked like when it stormed. Eureka could hardly look at the paintings, knowing that, in the best-case scenario, she had to rip the twins and their parents from the life they knew because she had put everyone in danger.

She didn't want to tell Dad. She really didn't want to tell him. But if she didn't tell him, something worse might happen. "The thing is, Dad—" she started to say.

"Your mother said that someday something might happen," Dad interrupted.

Eureka blinked. *"She warned you."* She took his hand, which was cold and clammy, not strong and reassuring the

406

way she was used to it feeling. She tried to stay as calm as possible. Maybe this would be easier than she'd thought. Maybe Dad already had some sense of what to expect. "Tell me *exactly* what she said."

He closed his eyes. His lids were creased and damp and he looked so frail it scared her. "Your mother was prone to delirium. She'd be out with you at the park or some store buying clothes. This was back when you were little, always when the two of you were alone. It never seemed to happen when I was there to see it. She'd come home and insist that impossible things had occurred."

Eureka inched closer to him, attempting to inch closer to Diana. "Like what?"

"It was like she would fall into a fever. She'd repeat the same thing over and over. I thought she was ill, maybe schizophrenic. I've never forgotten what she said." He looked at Eureka and shook his head. She knew he didn't want to tell her.

"What did she say?"

That she came from a long line of Atlanteans? That she possessed a book prophesying a lost island's second coming? That a cult of fanatics might someday seek to kill their daughter for her tears?

Dad wiped his eyes with the heel of his hand. "She said: 'Today I saw the boy who's going to break Eureka's heart.'"

A chill ran down Eureka's spine. "What?"

"You were four years old. It was absurd. But she wouldn't let it go. Finally, the third time it happened, I made her draw me a picture."

"Mom was a good artist," Eureka murmured.

"I kept that picture in my closet," Dad said. "I don't know why. She'd drawn this sweet-looking kid, six or seven years old, nothing disturbing in the face, but in all the years we lived in town, I never saw the boy. Until . . ." His lip trembled and he took Eureka's hands again. He glanced over his shoulder in the direction of the breakfast table. "The likeness is unmistakable."

Tension twisted through Eureka's chest, crippling her breath like a bad cold. "Ander," she whispered.

Dad nodded. "He's the same as he was in the drawing, just grown up."

Eureka shook her head, as if that would shake the sensation of nausea. She told herself an old drawing didn't matter. Diana couldn't have read this future. She couldn't have known Eureka and Ander might someday truly care for one another. She thought of his lips, his hands, the unique protectiveness that came through everything Ander did. It made her skin tingle with pleasure. She had to trust in that instinct. Instinct was all she had left.

Maybe Ander had been raised to be her enemy, but he was different now. Everything was different now.

"I trust him," she said. "We're in danger, Dad. You and

me, Rhoda, the twins. We need to get out of here today, now, and Ander is the only one who can help us."

Dad gazed at Eureka with profound pity and she knew it was the same look he must have given to Diana when she said things that sounded crazy. He tweaked her chin. He sighed. "You've had a real hard time of it, kid. All you need to do today is relax. Let me make you something for breakfast."

"No, Dad. Please—"

"Trenton?" Rhoda appeared in the kitchen wearing a red silk robe. Her loose hair flowed down her back—a style Eureka wasn't used to seeing on her. Her face was bare of makeup. Rhoda looked pretty. And frantic. "Where are the children?"

"They're not in their room?" Eureka and Dad asked simultaneously.

Rhoda shook her head. "Their beds are made. The window was wide open."

A terrific clap of thunder gave way to a faint rapping on the back door that Eureka almost didn't hear. Rhoda and Dad sprinted to open it, but Ander got there first.

The door blew back with a sharp gust of wind. Rhoda, Dad, and Eureka halted at the sight of the Seedbearer standing in the doorway.

Eureka had seen him before at the police station and on the side of the road later that night. He looked sixty, with pale skin, slickly parted gray hair, and a pale gray tailored suit that gave him the appearance of a door-to-door salesman. His eyes glowed the same bright turquoise as Ander's.

The resemblance between them was undeniable—and alarming.

"Who are you?" Dad demanded.

"If you're looking for your children," the Seedbearer said as a strong odor of citronella wafted in from the backyard, "step outside. We'd be happy to arrange an exchange."

30

THE SEEDBEARERS

Rhoda shoved past the Seedbearer, who glanced bitterly at Eureka, then spun around to cross the porch.

"William!" Rhoda shouted. "Claire!"

Ander rushed through the door after Rhoda. By the time Eureka, Dad, and Cat made it to the covered patio outside, the Seedbearer was at the bottom of the porch stairs. At the top, Ander had tackled Rhoda. He had her pinned against one of the colonettes of the balustrade. Her arms writhed at her sides. She kicked, but Ander held her body still as easily as if she were a child.

"Let go of my wife," Dad snarled, and lunged toward Ander.

With a single hand Ander held him back, too. "*You* can't

save them. That isn't how this works. All you'll do is get your-self hurt."

"My children!" Rhoda wailed, keeling over in Ander's arms.

The odor of citronella was overpowering. Eureka's eyes traveled past the porch to the lawn. Standing among acid-green ferns and the mottled trunks of live oaks were the same four Seedbearers she'd encountered on the road. They formed a line facing the porch, steely gazes eyeing the scene Eureka and her family were making. The Seedbearer who had knocked on their door had rejoined his group. He stood half a foot ahead of the others, hands crossed over his chest, tur-quoise eyes challenging Eureka to do something.

And behind the Seedbearers— Eureka's body seized and a wave of red spots swam before her eyes. Suddenly she knew why Ander was holding Rhoda back.

The twins were hog-tied to the swing set. One metal chain from each swing bound the wrists of each twin. Their arms stretched above their heads, linked by the knotted chain that had been looped over the long horizontal top bar of the swing set. The other two chains had been used to bind the twins' ankles. Those chains were then secured in knots on the sides of the swing set's A-frame bars. William and Claire hung at a slant.

The worst part was that the swings' splintery wooden seats had been wedged into the twins' mouths. Duct tape held the seats in as gags. Tears streamed down the children's faces. Their eyes bulged in pain and fear. Their bodies shook with whimpers the gags prevented Eureka from hearing.

How long had they been tied up like that? Had the Seedbearers broken into the twins' bedroom in the night, while Ander was guarding Eureka? She felt sick with rage, consumed by guilt. She had to do something.

"I'm going out there," Dad said.

"Stay here if you want your kids returned alive." Ander's command was quiet but authoritative. It stopped Dad at the top step of the porch. "This has to be handled exactly right—or we're going to be very sorry."

"What kind of sick jerks would do that to a couple of kids?" Cat whispered.

"They call themselves Seedbearers," Ander said, "and they raised me. I know their sickness well."

"I'll kill them," Eureka muttered.

Ander relaxed his grip on Rhoda, let her fall into her husband's arms. He turned to Eureka, his expression overwhelmingly sad. "Promise me that will be a very last resort."

Eureka squinted at Ander. She *wanted* to kill the Seedbearers, but she was unarmed, outnumbered, and had never punched anything more animate than a wall. But Ander looked so concerned that she was serious, she felt the need to reassure him it wasn't a fully cooked plan. "Okay"—she felt ridiculous—"I promise."

Dad and Rhoda took each other's arms. Cat's gaze was welded to the swing set. Eureka forced herself to look where she did not want to look. The twins' bodies were still and taut. Their terrified eyes were their only moving parts.

"This isn't fair," she told Ander. "It's me the Seedbearers want. I'm the one who should go out there."

"You will need to face them"—Ander took her hand—"but you must not be a martyr. If something should happen to the twins, to anyone else you care about, you have to understand that it is more important *you* survive."

"I can't think about that," she said.

Ander stared at her. "You have to."

"I think this pep talk has gone on long enough," the Seedbearer in the gray suit called from the lawn. He motioned for Ander to wrap it up.

"And I think you four have been here long enough," Eureka called back at the Seedbearers. "What will it take for you to leave?" She strode forward, approaching the stairs, trying to look calm even as her heart thundered in her chest. She had no idea what she was doing.

She realized there was something else disconcerting about the scene beyond the porch: the rain had stopped.

No. Eureka heard the downpour against trees nearby. She smelled the salty electricity of the storm right under her nose. She felt the humidity like a pelt over her skin. She saw the brown current at the edge of the lawn—the bayou, flooded

414

and rough and nearly overflowing its banks the way it did during a hurricane.

The bad weather hadn't blown over, but somehow the twins, and the Seedbearers, and the lawn they stood on, weren't getting wet. The wind was still, the temperature cooler than it should have been.

Eureka hovered at the edge of the covered porch. Her eyes rose skyward and she squinted into the atmosphere. The storm roiled overhead. Lightning surged. She *saw* the torrent of raindrops falling. But something happened to the rain along its path from the turbulent black clouds to Eureka's backyard.

It disappeared.

There was a foreign dimness to the yard that made Eureka claustrophobic, as if the sky were caving in.

"You're wondering about the rain." Ander extended an open palm beyond the limit of the porch. "In their immediate vicinity, Seedbearers have power over wind. One of the more common ways it's used is to create atmospheric buffers. The buffers are called 'cordons.' They can be any shape and many magnitudes."

"That's why you weren't wet when you came through my window last night," Eureka guessed.

Ander nodded. "And that's why no rain falls in this yard. Seedbearers don't like to get wet if they can help it, and they can almost always help it."

"What else do I need to know about them?"

Ander leaned in to her right ear. "Critias," he whispered in a voice that was nearly inaudible. She followed his gaze to the male Seedbearer on the far left and realized Ander was giving her a primer. "We used to be close." The man was younger than the other Seedbearers, with wild cowlicks in his thick silver hair. He wore a white shirt and gray suspenders. "He used to be almost human."

Critias watched Eureka and Ander with such inscrutable interest Eureka felt naked.

"Starling." Ander moved on to the ancient-looking woman wearing slacks and a gray cashmere sweater who stood to Critias's right. She seemed barely able to hold herself up on her own, but her chin was lifted assertively. Her blue eyes beamed a frightening smile. "She feeds on vulnerability. Show none."

Eureka nodded.

"Albion." The next Seedbearer in line was the man who had knocked on Eureka's back door. "The leader," Ander said. "No matter what happens, do not take his hand."

"And the last one?" Eureka glanced at the frail, grand-motherly woman in the gray floral sundress. Her long silver braid draped over her shoulder, ending at her waist.

"Chora," Ander said. "Don't be fooled by her appearance. Every scar on my body comes from her"—he swallowed, and added under his breath—"almost. She crafted the wave that killed your mother."

Eureka's hands balled into fists. She wanted to scream,

416

but that was a kind of vulnerability she refused to show. *Be stoic,* she coached herself. *Be strong.* She stood on the dry grass and faced the Seedbearers.

"Eureka," Dad said. "Come back here. What are you doing—"

"Let them go." She called to the Seedbearers, nodding in the twins' direction.

"Of course, child." Albion extended his pale palm. "Simply place your hand in mine and the twins will be unbound."

"They're innocent!" Rhoda moaned. "My children!"

"We understand," Albion said. "And they'll be free to go as soon as Eureka—"

"First unbind the twins," Ander said. "This has nothing to do with them."

"And nothing to do with you." Albion turned to Ander. "You were released from this operation weeks ago."

"I've reenlisted." Ander glanced at each Seedbearer, as if to ensure they all understood which side he was on now.

Chora scowled. Eureka wanted to lunge at her, to yank every long strand of silver hair from her head, to yank out her heart until it stopped beating, like Diana's had.

"You've forgotten what you are, Ander," Chora said, "It is not our job to be happy, to be in love. We exist to make happiness and love possible for others. We protect this world from the dark encroachment this one wants to enable." She pointed a hooked finger at Eureka.

"Wrong," Ander said. "You live a negative existence with

417

negative goals. None of you know for sure what would happen if Atlantis were to rise."

Starling, the eldest Seedbearer, gave a disgusted cough. "We raised you to be smarter than this. Did you not memorize the Chronicles? Do thousands years of history mean nothing to you? Have you forgotten the dark, hovering spirit of Atlas, who has made no secret of his aim to annihilate this world? Love has blinded you to your heritage. Do something about him, Albion."

Albion thought for a moment. Then he spun toward the swing set and used a fist to belt William and Claire across their stomachs.

Both twins heaved, making retching motions as they gagged on the wooden planks stuffed in their mouths. Eureka heaved in empathy. She couldn't stand it anymore. She looked at her hand, then at Albion's extended hand. What could happen if she touched him? If the twins were freed, then perhaps it would be worth whatever—

A blur of red registered in the corner of Eureka's eye. Rhoda was running for the swing set, for her children. Ander cursed under his breath and raced after her.

"Someone please stop her," Albion said, sounding bored. "We'd really rather not— Oh, well. Too late now."

"Rhoda!" Eureka's shout echoed across the lawn.

As Rhoda was passing Albion, the Seedbearer reached out and grabbed her hand. Instantly she froze, her arm as stiff as a plaster cast. Ander stopped short and hung his head, seeming to know what was coming.

Beneath Rhoda's feet a cone of volcano-shaped earth bloomed from the ground. At first it looked like a sand boil, a bayou phenomenon whereby a dome-shaped mound rises from nothing into a powerful geyser along a flooded alluvial plain. Sand boils were dangerous because of the torrent of water they spewed from the core of their swiftly formed craters.

This sand boil spewed wind.

Albion's hand released Rhoda's, but a connection between them remained. He seemed to hold her by an invisible leash. Her body rose on a sprocket of inexplicable wind that shot her fifty feet into the air.

Her limbs flailed. Her red robe twirled in the air like ribbons on a kite. She soared higher, her body completely out of her control. There was a burst of sound—not thunder, more like a pulse of electricity. Eureka realized Rhoda's body had broken through the cordon over the yard.

When she entered the storm unsheltered, Rhoda screamed. Rain siphoned through the slender gap created by her body. Wind wailed in like a hurricane. Rhoda's red silhouette grew smaller in the sky until she looked like one of Claire's dolls.

The bolt of lightning crackled slowly. It huddled in the clouds, lighting up pockets of dark, twisting atmosphere.

When it broke through cloud and tasted bare sky, Rhoda was the closest target.

Eureka braced herself as lightning struck Rhoda's chest with a single awesome jolt. Rhoda started to scream, but the distant sound cut off in an ugly static sizzle.

When she began to tumble downward, the flailing of her body was different. It was lifeless. Gravity danced with her. Clouds parted sadly as she passed. She crossed the boundary of the Seedbearers' cordon, which resealed itself somehow over the yard. She thudded powerfully to the ground and left an indentation of her crumpled body a foot deep in the earth.

Eureka fell to her knees. Her hands clasped her heart as she took in Rhoda's blackened chest; her hair, which had sizzled into nonexistence; her bare arms and legs, webbed with veiny blue lightning scars. Rhoda's mouth hung open. Her tongue looked singed. Her fingers had frozen into stiff claws, extended toward her children, even in death.

Death. Rhoda was dead because she'd done the only thing any mother would have done: she had tried to stop her children's suffering. But if it weren't for Eureka, the twins wouldn't be in danger and Rhoda wouldn't have had to save them. She wouldn't be burnt up, lying dead on the lawn. Eureka couldn't look at the twins. She couldn't bear to see them as destroyed as she'd been ever since she lost Diana.

An animalistic yelp came from behind Eureka on the porch. Dad was on his knees. Cat's hands hung on his shoul-

420

ders. She looked pale and uncertain, as if she might be sick. When Dad rose to his feet, he staggered shakily down the stairs. He was a foot away from Rhoda's body when Albion's voice stopped him cold.

"You look like a hero, Dad. Wonder what you're going to do."

Before Dad could respond, Ander reached into the pocket of his jeans. Eureka gasped when he pulled out a small silver gun. "Shut up, Uncle."

"'Uncle,' is it?" Albion's smile showed grayish teeth. "Giving up?" He chuckled. "What's he got, a toy gun?"

The other Seedbearers laughed.

"Funny, isn't it?" Ander pulled back the slide to load the gun's chamber. A strange green light emanated from it, forming an aura around the gun. It was the same light Eureka had seen the night Ander brandished the silver case. All four Seedbearers startled at the sight of it. They grew silent, as if their laughter had been sliced off.

"What is that, Ander?" Eureka asked.

"This gun fires bullets made of artemisia," Ander explained. "It is an ancient herb, the kiss of death for Seedbearers."

"Where did you get those bullets?" Starling stumbled a few steps back.

"Doesn't matter," Critias said quickly. "He'll never shoot us."

"You're wrong," Ander said. "You don't know what I'd do for her."

"Charming," Albion said. "Why don't you tell your girl-friend what would happen if you were to kill one of us?"

"Maybe I'm past worrying about that." The gun clicked as Ander cocked it. But then, instead of pointing the gun at Albion, Ander turned it on himself. He held its barrel to his chest. He closed his eyes.

"What are you doing?" Eureka shouted.

Ander turned to face her, the gun still at his chest. In that moment he looked more suicidal than she knew she had ever been. "Seedbearer breath is controlled by a single higher wind. It is called the Zephyr, and each of us is bound by it. If one of us is killed, all of us die." He glanced at the twins and swallowed hard. "But maybe it's better that way."

31

TEARDROP

Eureka didn't think. She charged Ander and knocked the gun from his hand. It spun in the air and slid across the grass, which had been dampened by Rhoda's pocket of open rain. The other Seedbearers lunged for the gun, but Eureka wanted it more. She snatched it, fumbled its slippery grip in her hands. She nearly dropped it. Somehow she managed to hold on.

Her heart thundered. She had never held a gun before, had never wanted to. Her finger found its way around the trigger. She pointed it at the Seedbearers to keep them back.

"You're too in love," Starling taunted. "It's wonderful. You wouldn't dare shoot us and lose your boyfriend."

She looked at Ander. Was it true?

"Yes, I will die if you kill any of them," he said slowly. "But it's more important that you live, that nothing about you be compromised."

"Why?" Her breath came in short gasps.

"Because Atlas will find a way to raise Atlantis," Ander said. "And when he does, this world will need you—"

"This world needs her dead," Chora interrupted. "She is a monster of the apocalypse. She has blinded you to your responsibility to humanity."

Eureka looked around the yard—at her father, who was weeping over Rhoda's body. She looked at Cat, who sat huddled, shaking, on the porch steps, unable to raise her head. She looked at the twins, bound and bruised and made half orphans before their own eyes. Tears streamed down their faces. Blood dripped from their wrists. Finally, she looked at Ander. A single tear slid down the bridge of his nose.

This group comprised the only people Eureka had left to love in the world. All of them were inconsolable. It was all because of her. How much *more* damage was she capable of causing?

"Don't listen to them," Ander said. "They want to make you hate yourself. They want you to give up." He paused. "When you shoot, aim for the lungs."

Eureka weighed the gun in her hands. When Ander said none of them knew for sure what would happen if Atlantis were to rise, it had sent the Seedbearers into a fervor, a total rejection of the idea that what they believed might not be true.

The Seedbearers had to be dogmatic about what they thought Atlantis meant, Eureka realized, because they didn't really *know*.

Then what did they know about the Tearline?

She couldn't cry. Diana had told her so. *The Book of Love* spelled out how formidable Eureka's emotions might be, how they might raise another world. There was a reason Ander had stolen that tear from her eye and made it disappear in his.

Eureka didn't want to cause a flood or raise a continent. And yet: Madame Blavatsky had translated joy and beauty in portions of *The Book of Love*—even the title suggested potential. Love had to be part of Atlantis. At this point, she realized, Brooks was part of Atlantis, too.

She had vowed to find him. But how?

"What is she doing?" Critias asked. "This is taking too long."

"Stay away from me." Eureka wielded the gun from one Seedbearer to the next.

"It's too bad about your stepmother," Albion said. He glanced over his shoulder at the twins writhing on the swing set. "Now give me your hand or let's see who's next."

"Follow your instincts, Eureka," Ander said. "You know what to do."

What could she do? They were trapped. If she shot a Seedbearer, Ander would die. If she didn't, they would hurt or kill her family.

If she lost one more person she loved, Eureka knew she would fall apart and she wasn't allowed to fall apart.

Never, ever cry again.

She imagined Ander kissing her eyelids. She imagined tears welling up against his lips, his kisses skating down the slide of her tears buoyant as sea foam. She imagined great, beautiful, massive teardrops, rare and coveted as jewels.

Since Diana's death Eureka's life had followed the shape of a huge black spiral—the hospitals and broken bones, the swallowed pills and bad therapy, the humiliating bleak depression, losing Madame Blavatsky, watching Rhoda die . . .

And Brooks.

He had no place along the downward spiral. He was the one who'd always lifted Eureka up. She pictured the two of them, eight years old and up in Sugar's soaring pecan tree, the late summer air golden-hued and sweet. She heard his laughter in her mind: the soft glee of their childhood echoing off mossy branches. They climbed higher together than either of them ever would alone. Eureka used to think it was because they were competitive. It struck her now that it was trust in each other that led the two of them almost to the sky. She never thought of falling when she was next to Brooks.

How had she missed all the signs that something was happening to him? How had she ever gotten mad at him? When she thought of what Brooks must have gone through—what he might be going through right now—it was too much. It overwhelmed her.

It started in her throat, a painful lump she couldn't swallow. Her limbs grew leaden and her chest crumpled forward. Her face twisted, as if pinched by pliers. Her eyes squeezed shut. Her mouth stretched opened so wide its corners ached. Her jaw began to shudder.

"She isn't . . . ?" Albion whispered.

"It cannot be," Chora said.

"Stop her!" Critias gasped.

"It's too late." Ander sounded almost thrilled.

The wail that surfaced on her lips came from the deepest reaches of Eureka's soul. She dropped to her knees, the gun at her side. Tears cut trails down her cheeks. Their heat alarmed her. They ran along her nose, slipped into the sides of her mouth like a fifth ocean. Her arms went slack at her sides, surrendering to the sobs that came in waves and racked her body.

What relief! Her heart ached with a strange, new, gorgeous sensation. She lowered her chin to her chest. A tear fell on the surface of the thunderstone around her neck. She expected it to bounce back. Instead, a tiny flash of azure light lit up the stone's center in the shape of the tear. It lasted for an instant and then the stone was dry again, as if the light was evidence of its absorption.

Thunder cracked across the sky. Eureka's head shot up. A splinter of lightning stretched through the trees in the east.

The ominous clouds, which had been shielded by the Seed-bearers' cordon, suddenly dropped. Wind slammed in, an invisible stampede that knocked Eureka to the ground. The clouds were close enough to brush her shoulders.

"Impossible," Eureka heard someone warble. Everyone in the yard was now obscured in fog. "Only we can collapse our cordons."

Sheets of rain lashed Eureka's face, cold drops against hot tears, proof that the cordon was gone. Had she broken it?

Water poured from the sky. It wasn't rain anymore; it was more like a tidal wave, as if an ocean had been turned on its side and ran from the heavens to the shores of Earth. Eureka looked up but she couldn't even see it. There was no sky from which to distinguish water. There was only the flood. It was warm and tasted salty.

Within seconds, the yard had flooded up to Eureka's ankles. She sensed a blurry body moving and knew that it was Dad. He carried Rhoda. He was moving toward the twins. He slipped and fell, and while he tried to right himself, the water rose to Eureka's knees.

"Where is she?" one of the Seedbearers shouted.

She glimpsed gray figures wading toward her. She splashed backward, unsure where to go. She was still weeping. She didn't know if she would ever stop.

The fence at the edge of the yard creaked as the surging bayou tore it down. More water swirled into the yard like a whirlpool, making everything brackish and muddy brown. The water uprooted centuries-old live oak trees, which gave way with long, painful creaks. As it swept under the swing set, its force broke the twins' chains free.

Eureka couldn't see William's or Claire's face, but she knew the twins would be frightened. Water soaked her waist as she leapt to catch them, propelled by adrenaline and love. Somehow, through the deluge, her arms found theirs. Her grip tightened into a stranglehold. She would not let them go. It was the last thing she thought before her feet were swept off the ground and she was treading chest-deep in her own tears.

She pumped her legs. She tried to stay afloat, above the surface. She raised the twins as high as she could. She ripped the duct tape from their faces and tossed the swing seats violently aside. She ached at the sight of the tender red skin along their cheeks.

"Breathe!" she commanded, not knowing how long the chance would last. She tilted her face toward the sky. Beyond the flood, she sensed that the atmosphere was black with the kind of storm no one had ever seen before. What did she do with the twins now? Salty water filled her throat, then air, then more salty water. She thought she was still crying, but the flood made it hard to tell. She kicked twice as hard to make up for the paddling her arms weren't doing. She gagged and choked and tried to breathe, tried to keep the twins' mouths up.

She nearly slipped below with the effort of bracing them

against her body. She felt her necklace floating along the surface, pulling on the back of her neck. The lapis lazuli locket was keeping the thunderstone above the sloshing waves.

She knew what to do.

"Deep breath," she ordered the twins. She clutched the pendants and plunged underwater with the twins. Instantly a pocket of air erupted from the thunderstone. The shield bloomed around all three of them. It filled the space beyond her body and theirs, sealing out the flood like a miniature submarine.

They gasped. They could breathe again. They were levitating just as they had been the day before. She unbound the ropes from their wrists and ankles.

As soon as Eureka was sure the twins were okay, she pressed against the edge of the shield and began to paddle bewildered strokes through the flood of her backyard.

The current was nothing like the steady ocean. Her tears were sculpting a wild and whirling tempest with no discernable shape. The flood had already crested the flight of stairs leading from the lawn to her back porch. She and the twins were floating in a new sea, level with the first story of her house. Water battered the kitchen windows like a burglar. She pictured the flood lashing inside the den, through carpeted hallways, washing away lamps and chairs and memories like an angry river, leaving only glittery silt behind.

The vast trunk of one of the uprooted oak trees swirled

by with chilling force. Eureka braced herself, her body sheltering the twins, as a giant branch thrashed into the side of the shield. The twins screamed as the impact reverberated through them, but the shield did not puncture, did not break. The tree moved on for other targets.

"Dad!" Eureka shouted from inside the shield where no one would hear her. "Ander! Cat!" She paddled furiously, not knowing how to find them.

Then, in the dark chaos of the water, a hand reached toward the boundary of the shield. Eureka knew instantly whose it was. She fell to her knees with relief. Ander had found her.

Behind him, holding his other hand, was her father. Dad was holding on to Cat. Eureka wept anew, this time with relief, and reached her hand toward Ander's.

The barrier of the shield stopped them. Her hand bounced off one side. Ander's bounced off the other. They tried again, pushing harder. It made no difference. Ander looked at her as if she should know how to let him in. She banged on the shield with her fists, but it was useless.

"Daddy?" William called tearfully.

Eureka didn't want to live if they were going to drown. She shouldn't have invoked the shield until she'd found them. She screamed in futility. Cat and Dad were trying to writhe toward the surface, toward air. Ander's hand wouldn't let them go, but his eyes had filled with fear.

Then Eureka remembered: Claire.

For some reason, her sister had been able to penetrate the boundary when they were in the Gulf. Eureka reached for the girl and practically shoved her against the border of the shield. Claire's hand met Ander's and something in the barrier became porous. Ander's hand broke through. Together Eureka and the twins yanked the three soaking bodies inside the shield. It swelled and resealed into a snug space for six as Cat and Dad sank to their hands and knees, gasping to regain their breath.

After a stunned moment, Dad grabbed Eureka in a hug. He was weeping. She was weeping. He gathered the twins in his arms as well. The four of them rolled in a wounded embrace, levitating inside the shield.

"I'm sorry." Eureka sniffed. She'd lost sight of Rhoda after the flood began. She had no idea how to console him or the twins for the loss.

"We're okay." Dad's voice was more uncertain than she'd ever heard. He stroked the twins' hair as if his life depended on it. "We're going to be okay."

Cat tapped Eureka's shoulder. Her braids were beaded with water. Her eyes were red and swollen. "Is this real?" she asked. "Am I dreaming?"

"Oh, Cat." Eureka didn't have to words to explain or apologize to her friend, who should have been with her own family right now.

"It's real." Ander stood at the edge of the shield with his back toward the others. "Eureka has opened a new reality."

He didn't sound angry. He sounded amazed. But she couldn't be certain until she saw his eyes. Were they lit up with turquoise luminescence, or as dark as a storm-covered ocean? She reached for his shoulder, tried to turn him around.

He surprised her with a kiss. It was heavy and passionate, and his lips conveyed everything. "You did it."

"I didn't know this was going to happen. I didn't know it would be like this."

"No one knew," he said. "But your tears were always inevitable, no matter what my family thought. You were on a path." It was the same word Madame Blavatsky had used the first night Eureka and Cat went to her atelier. "And now we are all on that path with you."

Eureka looked around the floating shield as it pitched through the deluged yard. The world beyond was eerie and dim, unrecognizable. She couldn't believe it was her home. She couldn't believe her tears had done this. She had done this. She felt sick with strange empowerment.

An arm of the swing set somersaulted over their heads. Everyone ducked, but they didn't need to. The shield was impenetrable. As Cat and Dad gasped in relief, Eureka realized she hadn't felt less alone in months.

"I owe you my life," Ander said to her. "Everyone here does."

"I already owed you mine." She wiped her eyes. She'd seen these motions made countless times before in movies, and by other people, but the experience was entirely fresh to her, as if she'd suddenly discovered a sixth sense. "I thought you might be mad at me."

Ander tilted his head, surprised. "I don't think I could ever be mad at you."

Another tear spilled down Eureka's cheek. She watched Ander fight the urge to abscond with it to his own eye. Unexpectedly, the phrase *I love you* sprinted to the tip of her tongue. She swallowed hard to keep it back. It was the trauma talking, not real emotion. She hardly knew him. But the urge to voice those words wouldn't go away. She remembered what Dad had mentioned earlier about her mother's drawing, about the things Diana had said.

Ander wouldn't break her heart. She trusted him.

"What is it?" He reached for her hand.

I love you.

"What happens now?" she asked.

Ander looked around the shield. Everyone's eyes were on him. Cat and Dad didn't even seem to begin to know what kinds of questions to ask.

"There is a passage near the end of the Seedbearer Chronicles that my family refused to talk about." Ander gestured at the flood beyond the shield. "They never wanted to anticipate this happening."

"What does it say?" Eureka asked.

434

"It says the one who opens the fissure to Atlantis is the only one who can close it—the only one who can face the Atlantean king." He eyed Eureka, gauging her reaction.

"Atlas?" she whispered, thinking: *Brooks.*

Ander nodded. "If you have done what they predicted you would do, I'm not the only one who needs you. The whole world does."

He turned in what Eureka thought was the direction of the bayou. Slowly he started to swim, a crawl stroke like she and the twins had used to get to shore the day before. His strokes increased as the shield moved toward the bayou. Without a word, the twins began swimming with him, just as they'd swum with her.

Eureka tried to grasp the concept of the whole world needing her. She couldn't. The suggestion overpowered the strongest muscle she possessed: her imagination.

She began a crawl stroke of her own, noticing Dad and Cat slowly do the same. With six of them paddling, the wild currents were just barely manageable. They floated over the flooded wrought-iron gate at the edge of the yard. They pivoted into the swollen bayou. Eureka had no idea how much water had fallen, or when, if ever, it would stop. The shield stayed several feet below the surface. Reeds and mud flanked their path. The bayou Eureka had spent so much of her life on was alien underwater.

They swam past broken, waterlogged boats and busted piers, recalling a dozen hurricanes past. They crossed schools

435

of silver trout. Slick black gars darted before them like rays of midnight.

"Will we still look for the lost Seedbearer?" she asked.

"Solon." Ander nodded. "Yes. When you face Atlas, you're going to need to be prepared. I believe Solon can help you."

Facing Atlas. Ander could call him by that name, but to Eureka what mattered was the body he possessed. Brooks. As they swam toward a new and unknowable sea, Eureka made a vow.

Brooks's body might be controlled by the darkest magic, but inside he was still her oldest friend. He needed her. No matter what the future held, she would find a way to get him back.

EPILOGUE

BROOKS

Brooks ran headfirst into the tree at full speed. He felt the impact above his eyebrow, the deep slice into his skin. His nose was already broken, his lips split and shoulders bruised. And it wasn't over yet.

He had fought himself for nearly an hour, ever since he'd lumbered ashore on the western fringe of Cypremort Point. He didn't recognize the land around him. It looked nothing like home. Rain fell in colossal sheets. The beach was cold, deserted, at a higher tide than he had ever seen. Submerged camps lay all around him, their occupants evacuated—or drowned. He might drown if he stayed out here, but seeking shelter from the storm was the last thing on his mind.

He was being dragged along the wet sand where he'd

slid into a heap. He felt the tree bark in his skin. Every time Brooks verged on losing consciousness, the body he could not control resumed its battle with itself.

He called it the Plague. It had gripped him for fourteen days, though Brooks had sensed an illness coming on earlier than that. First it was faintness, a shortness of breath, a bit of heat across the wound on his forehead.

Now Brooks would have traded anything for those early symptoms. His mind, caged within a body he could not control, was unraveling.

The change had come on the afternoon he'd spent with Eureka at Vermilion Bay. He had been himself until the wave took him out to sea. He'd washed ashore as something else completely.

What *was* he now?

Blood spilled down his cheekbone, ran into his eye, but Brooks could not lift his hand to wipe the blood away. Something else controlled his destiny; his muscles were useless to him, as if he were paralyzed.

Painful movement was the Plague's domain. Brooks had never experienced pain like this, and it was the least of his problems.

He knew what was happening within him. He also knew it was impossible. Even if he'd had control over the words he spoke, no one would believe this story.

He was possessed. Something ghastly had overtaken him,

entering through a set of slashes on his back that wouldn't heal. The Plague had pushed aside Brooks's soul and was living in its place. Something else was inside of him—something loathsome and old and built of a bitterness as deep as the ocean.

There was no way to talk with the monster that was now a part of Brooks. They shared no language. But Brooks knew what it wanted.

Eureka.

The Plague forced him to turn an icy coldness on her. The body that looked like Brooks was making every effort to hurt his best friend, and it was getting worse. An hour earlier, Brooks had watched his hands trying to drown Eureka's siblings when they fell from his boat. *His own hands.* Brooks hated the Plague for that more than anything.

Now, as his fist slammed into his left eye, he realized: he was being punished for failing to finish off the twins.

He wished he could take credit for their wriggling free. But Eureka had saved them, had somehow pulled them from his reach. He didn't know how she had done it or where they had gone. The Plague didn't, either, or Brooks would be stalking her now. As that thought crossed his mind, Brooks punched himself again. Harder.

Maybe if the Plague continued, Brooks's body would become as unrecognizable as what was inside of him. Since the Plague had overtaken him, his clothes didn't fit right. He caught glimpses of his body in reflections and was startled by his gait. He walked differently, lurching. A change had come into his eyes. A hardness had entered. It clouded his vision.

Fourteen days of enslavement had taught Brooks that the Plague needed him for his memories. He hated to surrender them, but he didn't know how to turn them off. Reveries were the only place Brooks felt at peace. The Plague became a patron at a movie theater, watching the show, learning more about Eureka.

Brooks understood more than ever that she was the star of his life.

They used to climb this pecan tree in her grandmother's backyard. She was always several branches above him. He was always racing to catch her—sometimes envious, always awed. Her laughter lifted him like helium. It was the purest sound Brooks would ever know. It still pulled him toward her when he heard it in a hallway or across a room. He had to know what was worth her laughter. He had not heard that sound since her mother died.

What would happen if he heard it now? Would her laughter's music expel the Plague? Would it give his soul the strength to resume its rightful place?

Brooks writhed on the sand, his mind on fire, his body at war. He clawed at his skin. He cried out in anguish. He yearned for a moment's peace.

It would take a special memory to accomplish that—

Kissing her.

His body stilled, soothed by the thought of Eureka's lips on his. He indulged in the entire event: the heat of her, the unexpected sweetness of her mouth.

Brooks would not have kissed her on his own. He cursed the Plague for that. But for a moment—a long, glorious moment—every future ounce of sorrow had been worth having Eureka's mouth on his.

Brooks's mind jolted back to the beach, back to his bloody situation. Lightning struck the sand nearby. He was drenched and shivering, up to his calves in the ocean. He started to devise a plan, stopped when he remembered it was useless. The Plague would know, would prevent Brooks from doing anything that contradicted its desires.

Eureka was the answer, the goal that Brooks and his possessor had in common. Her sadness was unfathomable. Brooks could take a little self-inflicted pain.

She was worth anything, because she was worth everything.

TURN THE PAGE FOR A Q & A
WITH LAUREN KATE

A Q & A with Lauren Kate

What inspired you to write Eureka's story?

When I lived in rural Northern California, the nearby lake was a flooded valley that had once been the site of a small village. Imagined ghosts of this underwater town haunted me, leading to an obsession with flood narratives, from Noah's Ark to Plato's Atlantis to the Epic of Gilgamesh.

I was especially drawn to the legend of Atlantis: a glorious and advanced ancient civilization that disappeared so completely under the ocean it slipped into the realm of myth. For several years I knew I wanted to write about Atlantis, but I didn't know whose voice would tell this story—and isn't that always the most important question?

Inspiration struck one day when I was crying. My husband was listening to my sob story, never mind what it was about. He couldn't reach me; I was trapped under the flood of my emotions, as tear shedders often are. But then he extended his hand, touched the corner of my eye with his finger, and captured the tear welling up. I watched as he brought my tear to his face, as he blinked it into his own eye. Suddenly we were bound by this tear. Suddenly I wasn't alone. And suddenly I had the first scene between my hero and the boy she loved.

That tear unlocked this story. Instead of an angry god generating the deluge, a single tear incites *Teardrop*'s apocalypse.

And in the tale I wanted to tell, I knew that a tear capable of flooding the world could only be shed over a mighty heart broken.

FALLEN fans are a very passionate and vocal bunch. Did you write *Teardrop* anticipating what they'd want, and if so, do you think they'll be pleased?

Fallen fans are so phenomenal it would be impossible for me to write a new book without them in mind. When I first started studying writing and taking workshops, the general consensus among my teachers and classmates seemed to be that it was wrong to write for anyone but yourself. I believe in the idea that writers must only write the stories they want to tell (as opposed to, maybe, the stories they feel they should tell), but I also believe that knowing and considering your audience can make your writing stronger. My readers push me to be a better, more detailed and conscientious writer all the time. Their questions inspire me and allow me to take risks. Because I have been lucky enough to interact with so many of my readers, they stay with me when I write. I'll finish a scene and hope the girl in Memphis, the boy in Sydney, or the book club in Bogotá will like it.

Where do you do your best thinking?

There's a secret trail behind my neighborhood that is almost always empty. I've always taken my dog—and now, my daughter—up for a hike in the hills every morning before I write. It requires some trespassing, but that's half the fun, and on a clear day, you can see snow in the mountains to the east and a shimmering ocean to the west. It's L.A. at its finest. The setting is stunning, but equally important is the intention of this simple ritual. Thinking through story is just as important as writing story. Staring into space is as important as typing words, as long as the staring leads to typing.

My goal each morning is to compose the first paragraph of that day's chapter before I get to the top of the hill. The first paragraph has to do the hard work of establishing the emotional pitch of the chapter. Usually I know what my characters have to do in that day's scene, but I don't know how they feel about it—and emotion determines everything about the way the story is told. So I ask myself questions like . . . how much sleep Eureka got the night before, why she's chosen the clothes she's wearing and whether she feels comfortable in them, what her biggest fear is on that particular day, and what she'd rather be doing than what I'm going to subject her to. By the time I come down the hill and return to my computer, my mind is deep in the emotional world of the story, and—on a good day, anyway—the rest of the chapter flows out of the first paragraph.

Opening *Teardrop* from Ander's point of view gives the reader a unique perspective when approaching the rest of the narrative. Was this always where you wanted to start the book—if so, why? If not, can you share an alternate beginning?
I really value the space a prologue opens between its pages and the first chapter, the way it comments on something essential that can't be said directly in the body of the novel. At

first I thought I'd open *Teardrop* with the flashback scene of Eureka crying as a young child, being warned by her mother to never cry again (which ultimately became chapter 3). That scene feels like the answer to so much—even though it gives very little away.

But when I started writing, I was having trouble finding Eureka's voice. I had been writing in Luce-person for a couple thousand pages, and the shift was difficult. But I remembered one of the ways I used to unlock Luce's voice when I felt distant from her: I would write the same scene from Daniel's point of view. Daniel's love for Luce often let him see things about her that I couldn't see at first. If I could get inside Daniel's mind, I could access Luce. So I tried something similar with *Teardrop*. I wrote Ander's voice to find Eureka's. I fell in love with Eureka through his eyes.

Adult women don't fare very well in *Teardrop*! Is this intentional? Should we read anything into this?
I hope not! I like writing about teens because they take the kinds of risks that allow me to write exciting narratives. What's interesting about the women in *Teardrop* is that they perish taking what I think are big, admirable risks: Rhoda dies defending her children. Blavatsky dies standing by her promise to Eureka. Diana lived her life as a risk taker. The difference, I suppose, is that the adults in the story are not invincible in the same way the teen characters are allowed to be. Eureka, Cat, Brooks, and Ander take as many risks as the adults, and somehow they manage to scrape by. This invincibility is born

out of fearlessness, something I think adults lose more and more of every day. I imagine there's something subconscious going on regarding the ill-fated ladies in *Teardrop*. I might be grappling with my own mortality.

Eureka is faced with some incredible choices as her story develops. Is there a decision you've made in your life that you'd change? How hard is it for you to make choices?

I make a lot of decisions based on instinct. About five years ago, I traded in my career in publishing and a life that I loved in New York for a spot at a graduate writers' workshop in Yolo County, California. My friends and family thought I was crazy for leaving everything behind to move somewhere I'd never been before on a whim—but I had been writing for ten years and was tired of having nothing to show for myself but two mediocre attempts at novels and enough rejection letters to furnish a minor ticker-tape parade. I needed to explode everything and devote myself to writing. So I left New York and drove across the country—terrified, elated, terrified.

A few weeks later, I met the guy I would eventually marry. A few months later, I took the literature course about the Bible that inspired me to write *Fallen*. By the end of my graduate program, I had a book contract with my publisher. I'm writing this paragraph holding my daughter, looking at my bookshelf full of *Fallen* editions from around the world, remembering the moment I drove through the Lincoln Tunnel on my way out of New York thinking *I am making the biggest mistake of my life.*

What's on your must-read list at the moment?

Son by Lois Lowry

Passenger by Andrew Smith

The Girl Who Fell Beneath Fairyland and Led the Revels There by Cathrynne M. Valente

Paper Valentine by Brenna Yovanoff

The film rights for Fallen have been acquired—how does it feel knowing that your books will one day hit the big screen? Does the thought of *Teardrop* becoming a major motion picture influence the decisions you make as a content creator?

When I was writing *Fallen* I was too close to the story to really let in anyone else's conception of the world. I remember seeing the book cover for the first time—which is perfectly mysterious—and thinking, *That's what they think Luce's arm looks like? That's not what her arm looks like!* I certainly wasn't prepared to conceive of a movie that would pin down the characters to a single look and feel for all time. But then a few things happened: I finished the books and got some perspective. I also met so many readers who shared their views and opinions on the characters and the story—and I found beauty in how different their conceptions could be from my own. My readers opened the door to allow me to welcome the *Fallen* film. At this point, I'm excited and can't wait to see what the director does with the series.

As for how I approached writing *Teardrop,* books and film are such different genres that I wouldn't know how to think about a potential film while I was writing a first draft of a novel. That comes later. Writing goes inside characters' minds; film can only show us what they do.

There are two worlds in *Teardrop*: the present-day high school world that Eureka operates in, and the watery, imagery-soaked world of Atlantis that Ander is part of. As we move deeper into the series, how do you see these worlds blending, and is one more interesting to write than the other?
The Atlantean world parallels Eureka's contemporary world, and each of the characters in the series will have his or her own mirroring counterpart in the other world. At first glance, they have little in common—even the language I use to tell the Atlantean sections of the story is different from the language of Eureka's world. In *Teardrop,* the two worlds are discrete, with no means of accessing one another (except for the strange story Eureka finds in *The Book of Love*). But later in the series, the separation between worlds gets hazy. I can't wait to write the scenes where the worlds collide.

What's the best advice you can give to aspiring writers?
Read—but you already know that.

Never push ideas away. Give them space and time to grow up into stories. Live curiously, ask questions, understand that writers can find even boredom fascinating. Hold on to your mystery. Make writing friends. Keep the good ones. Finish your stories. Finish your stories. Finish your stories.

Look for Lauren Kate's next novel about Eureka in 2014, and stay

on top of the latest *Teardrop* news, read extracts,

watch videos and more at **laurenkatebooks.co.uk**

LAUREN KATE is the internationally bestselling author of the FALLEN novels: *Fallen, Torment, Passion, Rapture,* and *Fallen in Love,* as well as *The Betrayal of Natalie Hargrove.* Her books have been translated into more than thirty languages. She lives in Los Angeles. Visit her at laurenkatebooks.net

LOVE NEVER DIES

FALLEN

THE #1 *NEW YORK TIMES* BESTSELLER BY
LAUREN KATE

TORMENT

A FALLEN NOVEL

THE #1 *NEW YORK TIMES* BESTSELLER BY
LAUREN KATE

PASSION

A FALLEN NOVEL

BY THE #1 *NEW YORK TIMES* BESTSELLING AUTHOR
LAUREN KATE

RAPTURE

A FALLEN NOVEL

BY THE #1 *NEW YORK TIMES* BESTSELLING AUTHOR
LAUREN KATE

FALLEN
IN
LOVE

A FALLEN NOVEL IN STORIES

BY THE #1 *NEW YORK TIMES* BESTSELLING AUTHOR
LAUREN KATE

THE FALLEN NOVELS

FROM THE #1 *NEW YORK TIMES* BESTSELLING AUTHOR

LAUREN KATE